To siblings everywhere

I0663904

MIA EVERS

AND THE CHILD OF LIGHT

ANGELA GUAJARDO

Gila Monster Press

Mia Evers and the Child of Light

Cover by Bukovero

Published in the United States by Gila Monster Press.

ISBN: 978-1-961815-05-6

Chapter 1

I sat in a conference room full of angry people. It was me, my family, Nurse Kor, Ms. Weever, Mr. Redd, and the angriest people of them all: the five school board members. Mom clung to Dad's arm while he glared at the ring of adults sitting behind a semicircular wooden desk big enough to fit all of them with room to spare. Bela, my four-year-old sister, sat quietly beside Mom, clinging to the hem of her white summer dress. I sat on Bela's other side.

Each school board member had a speaking stone held up by vines so they hung in front of their mouths. The stone made their voices fill up the high-ceiling room. Next to the speaking stones hovered glowing glass orbs, lighting each school board member's face from below the chin, casting severe shadows and making their faces appear even angrier.

Mrs. Volaire, mother of Gwen, the one girl in

Toolena Mesa that hated me the most, sat in the middle of the semicircle. Her horn-rimmed glasses sat on the end of her nose as she read through reports. Mrs. Volaire had the same tawny hair as her daughter, pulled back in a twist and held in place with a lick of flame made of metal. She wore lipstick that made her mouth look like she'd kissed a pool of blood, and her black business suit neatly contained her wide frame, the shoulders padded and giving her an air of strength. Between the lipstick and severe shadows, she looked ready to breathe fire. Word had it she was aligned with Fire, like her daughter.

Mrs. Volaire picked up a particular piece of parchment, her eyes shadowed as she kept her head up while she read. "Mr. Redd, it shows here that you were fully aware that Miss Mia Evers was aligned with Dark when you allowed her to enroll at Toolena Mesa. You do remember the tragic incident from nearly four years ago, do you not?"

Mr. Redd, principal of Toolena Mesa Middle School and probably the shortest adult I'd ever seen, rose to his feet in the first row, making himself mere inches taller than he was sitting down. He smoothed down the front of his gray suit and cleared his throat. "I will never forget it." He bowed his head slightly, his words sounding rehearsed.

"And yet you saw it fit to accept the child." Mrs. Volaire put the paper down and removed her glasses. "Why?"

"Mrs. Volaire, with all due respect, we're required by law to accept anyone who applies."

"You could've helped place the student elsewhere. You could've encouraged the parents to seek a school better equipped to handle such things."

"I did. I made note of it in Miss Evers' records. I spoke at length with her parents." He glanced at my mom and dad in the row behind him, his face as red as his hair, minus the gray sideburns. Whether it was anger or embarrassment, his straight face offered no clues. "We even discussed the incident and I warned them of how their daughter's presence might be received."

Mom stood, tears in her mismatched eyes. She and I both had heterochromia, meaning we had one brown and one blue eye, and the same long, straight black hair. "We can't afford those schools," she said in a shaky voice. "Our daughter means no harm. She was only trying to save—"

"Mrs. Evers," Mrs. Volaire said in a firm voice that filled the whole room.

My stomach clenched and my throat tightened. The lack of empathy combined with the sound enhancement from the speaking stone filled me with dread. If I moved, she'd bring down her fiery wrath on me.

She put her glasses back on. "I understand your distress, but you will wait your turn to speak, or you will be removed from the meeting until you calm down. Do you understand?"

Mom puffed up her chest and stiffened her arms, but caved when Bela clutched Mom's fist. "Yes, ma'am," she said in a subdued voice and sat down. Dad gave her hand a reassuring squeeze.

Mrs. Volaire studied Mom over the rim of her glasses. The way the light reflected in her eyes gave them a flash of a fiery sheen. Or was that her Fire alignment? I didn't know if it was possible for a Fire to make their eyes light up like that, but I wouldn't put it past Gwen's mom. The sheen faded and she glanced at the parchment again. "Regardless of Miss Evers' intentions, the State will be watching our school district closely. We've had two students die under similar circumstances. This cannot keep happening."

Mr. Redd said, "I assure you, on my integrity, that Miss Evers is not to blame."

"We would like to agree with you, but coincidences cannot be ignored."

"The District has had Darks in the past without incident. I believe her timing was unfortunate. Carlo was sick before her enrollment."

Mrs. Volaire paused. "Do we have documentation of this?"

Mr. Redd gestured to the darkened figure sitting at the end of the front row. A woman wearing scrubs stood. Nurse Kor. I hadn't seen her since Carlo's funeral, the day I'd forced the demon to cross over. That demon, Vergo, was now a black spirit cat with one white toe, curled up under my chair, napping.

No one but me could see him. At least no one else seemed to notice him. He followed me everywhere and not by choice. Whatever the Light had done with him, he had to stay near me while he figured out how to atone for his past sins.

Nurse Kor held up a medical file tied with a leather string. "We do." Mrs. Volaire waved her over. Nurse Kor approached and opened up the file. "Here is where he was sent home the first time, two weeks before Mia arrived." She handed it over and Mrs. Volaire pushed up her glasses. The board members on either side of her, two older men with gray hair, leaned in and read over her arms. One of them gave the file a thoughtful nod.

Mrs. Volaire passed the file to the other board members, who all took turns reading it before finally handing it back to the nurse. "Thank you for this information."

Nurse Kor tied the file back up. "You're welcome. I…"

"It doesn't explain his passing. Stomach bugs do not suddenly turn into a terminal illness."

"I know, but…"

"Please sit down," Mrs. Volaire said in a tone that said the conversation was over.

My heart reached out to Nurse Kor as she returned to her seat with the file hugged to her chest, head bowed. I silently willed her to look at me. Her head rose. A shadow passed over her, like someone had walked in front of a light, and it felt like my chair dropped ten feet. I clutched the edges, half expecting the ground to open up and swallow us all. Nurse Kor turned around as the shadow lifted. She sat back down and the pressure righted itself.

Vergo popped out from under the chair. "What was that?" He stretched his front legs, spreading his little toes as he arched his back. He hopped onto the chair beside me. He looked at Nurse Kor, and then at me when I didn't answer. "Oh, that's right. Don't want to be seen talking to yourself. Did you feel that sudden pressure drop?"

I nodded ever so slightly.

Vergo looked around the room. "Well, whatever it was, it's gone now." He curled up on the chair and tucked his nose under his tail. "Wake me when this farce is over."

I almost asked what a farce was, but Mrs. Volaire

spoke.

"We will deliberate on the information later." She looked down at Mr. Redd. "In the interim, you won't enroll any more Darks, should any approach Toolena Mesa. I'm sure the State would understand." She sounded confident. Maybe State people were afraid of her, too.

"Yes, ma'am." Mr. Redd gave her a slight bow.

"Now, all that aside, there are other damages to consider. They're nothing compared to the loss of a child, but they can't be ignored. Mrs. Lyra Weever."

Ms. Weever, leaning against the wall in the back of the room, unfolded her arms and walked up the aisle created by the two sections of fold-up chairs. Her heels clacked on the wood floor and her skirts swished behind her. She wore a corset, knee-length boots, and overlapping skirts that fell to her knees in the front and heels in the back. Golden curls spilled in waves over the back of her dark green blouse. She stopped in line with the front row of chairs, settling her weight on one foot as she placed her hands on her hips. She stood with her head held high, an air of challenge in her icy blue eyes.

Mrs. Volaire frowned. "We're very disappointed in you."

"If you wish to reprimand me, then I suggest we do this in private," Ms. Weever said tersely. "I will not stand here and be defamed until you run out of insults."

"You will mind your tongue. We *are* your employers."

"And you will mind yours. I trust we can both be civil in the presence of others."

Mom leaned over to me and whispered, "Is that

your tutor?"

I nodded, sinking lower in my chair. Oh, why did my tutor have to talk like that to Mrs. Volaire? At this rate, Mom would want to pull me from the school to keep me away from someone who didn't go out of their way to be polite.

"I like her."

She…what? How?

Vergo laughed. "Yes, we Weevers are not so easily intimidated. That red-lipped beast deserves it. She's probably used to everyone bowing to her and her name."

"That we can," Mrs. Volaire said, annoyed. "I'd like to point out that the future of your career hangs in the balance."

"Then maybe I should save you the trouble and let the State deal with you after I file a grievance. I'm sure they'd love to know why a demon has been haunting this campus for years, yet no one deemed it prudent to do anything about it. I'm sure they'd be thrilled to learn that it claimed two lives before a mere child and a Light priest finally got rid of it."

The entire school board stiffened, even Mrs. Volaire. She visibly paled, but then her eyes narrowed and her face reddened as she stood, making herself tower over Ms. Weever. The desk and chairs sat atop a dais elevated a solid foot above the rest of the room. Gwen's mom looked like a giant, and Ms. Weever a child standing before her, yet my tutor remained tall and proud. "That'll be rich, coming from a Dark. I'd love to see how they handle it, knowing you're a Dark who got fired."

"Quite seriously with a Light priest from the Order

of Leo backing my grievance. Now, do we want to find out firsthand, or do we want to learn from our mistakes and make this school a better place? Every last child deserves as much."

Mrs. Volaire's cheeks calmed to their normal coloring. She even gave me a closed-lipped smile and nodded in my tutor's direction. "Well played. No one's had the gall to stand up to me in a long time. I must be getting rusty." Tucking her skirt against her legs, Mrs. Volaire took her seat. "You are correct, our students deserve the best school we can offer, and we'll give it to them. Now, let's set some very clear expectations. She pushed aside something, opened a notebook and wielded a pen like a wand. "Miss Evers, please come here."

Breakfast made its way up to the back of my throat. Facing a demon was one thing. Facing Mrs. Volaire was another. I couldn't banish her or make her go away. I had to face her on her terms.

Vergo hopped off the chair and trotted to the edge of the row of seats. When I didn't move, he turned around. "Well, come on. Let's face the beast. You won't be alone in this and you have your beloved tutor to protect you. I'll even try biting her, should you ask it of me."

Watching Mrs. Volaire react to getting bit on the foot by a spirit cat would've been funny.

Mom said, "Be polite and respectful." She gave me an encouraging push on the small of my back. Ever since I'd banished the demon, Mom had been more comfortable with physical contact. At least that amount of good had come of it.

I slid off my chair and joined Ms. Weever, Vergo at

my feet. My tutor, brows furrowed, looked in Vergo's direction. "What on…?" she said under her breath.

Vergo looked up and his little blue eyes widened. "Oh, um, greetings, madame."

Ms. Weever's body stiffened as she stared at Vergo a moment longer. Her gaze darted around the room full of people oblivious to the spirit cat. She straightened up, faced the school board, but her attention pressed on me and my cat like the desert sun heating the side of my face.

"Thank you, Ms. Weever. You may return to your seat." Mrs. Volaire dismissed her with a small wave.

With one last peek at Vergo, Ms. Weever headed to the back of the room, her heels thumping on the wood. While her expression was neutral, her eyes radiated annoyance.

"Miss Evers."

I flinched. Sitting down, hiding near my family was one thing. Standing up in the front of the room, alone minus a cat only I and now Ms. Weever could see, was another. I had nowhere to hide, couldn't run. I had no choice but to face the angry people before me. I swallowed the lump in my throat. "Y-yes, ma'am?"

Mrs. Volaire studied me, her sharp eyes ringed by shadows. "What are we to do with you, girl?"

I blinked. Instead of some angry tirade or even her yelling at me like my dad would, my mind blanked out save for one thought. "I'd like to stay." My voice was so tiny that I barely heard myself.

"Louder," Vergo said impatiently.

Mrs. Volaire said, "This is a very sensitive situation. If you were anything but a Dark, you would've been disciplined and sent back to class. But

9

now the District has scared and angry parents to deal with." She nudged some papers around with her fingertips, picked the stack up, and tapped them on the desk several times, straightening them out. "They want someone to blame for this mess. However, despite your alignment, you're still a child."

"She saved a boy's life," Mom said, exasperated.

Mrs. Volaire's eyes glinted in the light under her chin. "And she nearly killed my daughter," she yelled so loud that her sound stone screeched.

I grimaced as the lie kindled anger in my chest, a little bud of fire. What story had Gwen told her mom? I pinned my arms to my sides. "She was picking on me and Deren." I so had not nearly killed her. She was sick, but a long ways off from dying.

Mrs. Volaire's glare rounded on me. "Oh, and that's reason enough to do what you did?"

The fire in my chest went out and my heart sank to my feet. As cruel as Gwen had been, as good as it had felt to stand up to her, giving her the sickness had been wrong. "I took it back. I'm sorry."

"Don't apologize for what you did," Vergo said. "The beast's child deserved that and more."

"I will speak with my daughter, but you will never lay hands on her again."

The memory of Deren's horrified expression made me grimace. I lowered my chin, my hair covering my face. "I won't. I'm sorry."

Mrs. Volaire weighed me with a measuring gaze, the corner of her red mouth curved into a smug smile.

There was the contempt for Darks I knew all too well. Toolena Mesa was already turning into the other schools, where everyone felt a mix of hate and fear of me. It sounded like legal stuff stopped them from getting rid of me outright. They'd find other ways to force me to get an education elsewhere. The other three schools had.

I hated school. Forget what I'd said a minute ago about wanting to stay. If both my parents didn't care, I'd never go back, not even for Deren. Why return to a place full of people that hated me for what I was?

Mrs. Volaire pushed the papers aside and they made a light hiss against the wood desk. "Miss Evers, tell us what happened the other day, along with the events leading up to it. Tell us every detail you can so we can better decide how to move forward."

"With the demon?" The question came out before I could stop myself. Part of my thoughts were stuck on the exchange between me and Gwen that day, but I didn't think that's what she meant.

Mrs. Volaire winced ever so slightly, flashing teeth. Did she just show fear? "Yes. What dangers is this school facing?"

I looked at Vergo.

"Tell her the truth, Little One: the big bad demon has been slain." His chest rose and fell with a huff, and he flicked his tail. "Fair warning, she probably doesn't care what the truth is. She's probably observing formalities should anyone look at the paper trail. Tell her the truth and wash your hands of this."

As much as I knew to expect nothing good from Gwen's mom, the truth still hurt. I was a monster everywhere I went. I took a deep breath and held my chin up, exposing my face to this hateful world. I straightened my shoulders as well. Ms. Weever was watching. At least she would be proud if I did the right thing. As for my parents? Maybe they'd be proud, too.

"Sanctus Bylan and I banished the demon to the Light. He can no longer hurt anyone."

"And what about your ability to make others sick?"

"That was the demon's power. It's gone, too." A tiny part of me would miss it because of how it'd made me feel to put Gwen in her place for once, but the rest of me was relieved it was gone. I'd have to find a better way to handle things for as long as I stayed at Toolena Mesa.

Mrs. Volaire nodded slowly. "Tell us how you encountered the…demon." Her pause was barely perceptible and her tone level, but she probably didn't like this topic one bit. "Start from the beginning. Tell us what happened that led up to recent events."

"Be careful of what you say," Vergo said. "She's hunting for enough reason to get rid of you. Tell her only enough and no more."

I took another calming breath and thought back to the first day I'd encountered the demon in Miss Wren's classroom, to Orton Totes's ghost flying at me out of a picture. "He was the same demon from years ago. The demon was responsible for Orton Totes's death, but he and Carlo are at peace now that the demon's gone." I described how the demon toyed with me, my failed attempt at banishing it, and how Ms. Weever saved me from the demon realm and helped me find the information I needed to get rid of the demon. I left out the parts about how the demon had been influencing Ms. Weever, and that she and Vergo were related. My tutor still didn't know.

When I finished my story, the room went quiet. Something about it was worse than Mrs. Volaire's red-lipped stare. The severe shadows made her look angry, yet the modest light showed she wore no frown. I waited for Vergo to speak, to make some sarcastic remark or anything, but he only watched. Maybe I should go back to my seat. I turned around and Mrs. Volaire's voice filled the room.

"Thank you, Miss Evers. Give us a moment." She pushed aside her speaking stone and leaned to the board member on her right, some broad-shouldered old man I didn't know. His full head of steely gray hair and lines in his cheeks made him look like a frowning frog. They spoke too softly for me to hear, and they exchanged nods and a few head shakes.

Mrs. Volaire then leaned towards the woman on her left, a tiny gray-haired lady with short hair that curved under her ears. The frog man leaned to a lanky man on the end and they whispered to each other as well. The five of them quietly conversed for what felt like years before Mrs. Volaire finally sat up straight. They all looked at me, shadowed gazes unreadable. She took a sip of water from a glass. It reflected a band of light that rose and fell with her movements. She set the glass down with a thud that might as well have been the bang of a gavel.

I swallowed the lump in my throat.

"Your teachers speak well of you, as do the nurse and principal. So you are hereby suspended while we deliberate on a final decision for you. You will be sent song stones with recordings of lessons, along with your classwork and homework. You will hand in your work the following day, each day. You will also speak of these events to no one, even if you return. Do I make myself clear?"

Chapter 2

I barely squeaked out a hoarse "Yes, ma'am" as the room spun. Suspended? I'd never been suspended before. I couldn't bring myself to turn around, much less move. My feet rooted themselves to the wood floor and my arms clamped to my sides. Shapes rose and shuffled around in front of me, but they were mere blurs as the truth sank in.

I was suspended. Dad had to be furious. Mom had to be super upset. This was a new level of trouble for me. What would they do when we got home? When we got in the car? When I turned around? The longer I stayed still, the longer I wouldn't have to find out.

"Mia, let's go," Mom said in a hard voice.

I did a full-body flinch. Oh, no. She wasn't just upset with me. She was as furious as Dad. She rarely used that tone of voice. Usually, she got real sad or scared. She wasn't good at being angry.

"Let's go, Little One," Vergo said, annoyed. He trotted past my legs and towards the back of the room.

I turned in place. Dad towered over Mom, holding Bela in his muscular arms, a knee in front of his stomach. Her dark hair fell past her shoulders, looking so much like mine and Mom's, but she had Dad's pale eyes. Dad glared at one corner of the room, as if watching some ghost or demon I couldn't see. His angular jaw clenched and unclenched. Bela put a hand on his chest. He shook his head and blinked, then looked at Bela and kissed her on the cheek. Without glancing at me, he made his way for the four doors leading out into the district office.

Mrs. Volaire disappeared through a side door in the front of the room, the rest of the school board hurrying after her.

Mom shook her head at the door and her eyes fell on me. Her gaze softened. Actually softened. "I'm going to give that woman a piece of my mind one day." She held out a hand.

Mom had held out her hand to me many times before, but once my alignment manifested, I'd learned to step closer but ignore the hand. I made my way over to Mom, my heart dragging behind me. I flinched when her hand briefly touched my shoulder. She gave me brief eye contact before leading me to Dad, who waited beside Ms. Weever.

Mom wasn't mad at me? The question lodged in my throat, fear keeping my mouth clamped shut. What if she was pretending to be mad at Mrs. Volaire?

"It's a pleasure to see you again, Mr. Evers," Ms. Weever said, her tone all business and no pleasure. "I wish it had been under better circumstances. Your daughter has done nothing to deserve this."

Dad nodded curtly and mumbled thanks, his hard gaze on the doors. "Babe, I'm gonna go start the car." Bela waved to my tutor and wore her adorable smile as they exited.

Ms. Weever's stern face softened with motherly love, and she inclined her head. Bela was too cute for her own good if she could make my tutor smile.

That smile shifted to suspicion when Vergo sat at my feet. Ms. Weever put her fists on her hips and looked up. "Brecca. Good to see you again as well."

"And you. I didn't realize how brave you are."

"What do you mean?"

"With that board member. She's so arrogant and conceited."

Ms. Weever's brows rose with understanding. "Ah. That. Brave. Foolish. Call it what you will. There will always be people in this world whose life's greatest pleasure is stomping on others. You can either get fed up with it or accept it. I chose the former and the consequences that come with it."

Mom nodded sagely.

"Brecca, I don't mean to be rude, but may I have a moment alone with your daughter? We won't be long."

Mom blinked and looked between the two of us. "Oh, um, certainly." She placed a tentative hand on my shoulder. "We'll be in the car." She headed off as if carried away by a breeze, disappearing through the front office doors. Part of me wished she'd planted a kiss on the top of my head. The rest of me wished I'd stop wishing for such contact. It was never going to happen.

"Follow me." Ms. Weever led us deeper inside the

building.

We were the only two people in the area. Nurse Kor and the principal had followed my mom out, and the school board had stayed in that side room. We slipped into a conference room with a large oval table and six chairs. It had no windows. The walls were all white and decorated with students' paintings. Some were well done, as if a high schooler had painted them. Others looked like a kindergartener threw a bunch of paint on the floor and dropped the canvas on top.

Ms. Weever's high heels clacked to a stop. She faced Vergo. "All right, spill it. Who are you and why are you haunting my student?"

"I am not haunting. I'm accompanying, and unwillingly, I might add." He held his furry little chin high.

"Is that right?" She grabbed a pinch of herbs from a hip pouch and dashed them on the cat. Little flecks of shades of green and purple landed on his head and all around him. He sniffed the air and sneezed.

"A delightful bouquet of scents that would have sent me running not long ago, madame, but I'm no longer a demon."

"Who are you?" Mrs. Weever said angrily.

"He's Vergo," I said. "I'm stuck with him until the Light says he can go."

Her sharp features softened into confusion. "Explain."

"The Demon King rejected me and I was sent to the Light the other day by our mutual companion," Vergo said. "But I have been judged unworthy and now must seek atonement if I'm ever to free myself of this limbo. In order to do that, I must aid this child until further notice."

"Aid her how?"

"In every way I can," he said, as if reciting words spoken to him, "be it my knowledge from ages past, to protecting her from evil forces, to being an unflinchingly loyal companion. A truly humbling pursuit considering my former status."

"You better atone. I owe you a lot of pain for all your lies and deception, *Allosyr*."

His lips curled, showing fangs. It looked more like a grimace. "And your every blow would be justice."

"You manipulated me with promises of bringing my baby boy back."

Vergo looked away. "I won't waste your time begging for forgiveness I'll never get."

"Get out of my sight before I lose my temper," she said in a low voice, opening the door.

Vergo opened his mouth to speak, but clamped it shut and trotted through the gap large enough for a cat. Mrs. Weever shut the door.

I said, "I'm sorry. I didn't think anyone else could see him."

"Why did you even bring him to the meeting?"

"I didn't. He followed me." It was like we had an invisible rope that tied us together. If I wandered too far, this horrible pressure filled my body and stilled my feet. And it would trigger again if he tried to wander off as well.

"His spirit is bound to you, then." She took a calming breath. "I don't know what to make of this. It's Light territory. But I can tell you this: the Light chose to bind him to you for a reason. Whether this bodes good or ill in your future is yet to be seen."

"What do you mean?"

She looked squarely at me. "It means you better study hard, learn quickly, and be a model Dark student so you are ready to face any challenges that cross your path."

A model Dark student? "Wait, do you think they'll allow me back?" As much as I hated school, it would be better for me and my family if we didn't have to move again.

"There's always a possibility they won't. That woman likes getting her way. We'll see how she handles my threat to file a grievance."

That reminded me. "How long had Allosyr been here before I got here?"

Ms. Weever glanced at the door. "I'm not sure. He could've followed me while I was mourning the loss of my son and then anchored himself on campus, or he could've been here long before, drawn to another unstable soul before targeting me as well. You'd have to ask *him*."

I would later. "So then why did the school board do nothing about him?"

She raised an eyebrow. "And make it publicly known that Toolena Mesa had a demon wreaking havoc? No. It's better to let that Dark student take the blame and brush the real problem under the proverbial rug. In all honesty, their ignorance of demonology probably led them to believe the demon left with the expelled student."

I would've thought the same thing before crossing paths with Allosyr.

"By the way," Ms. Weever said. "Did you sense that shadow pass over Nurse Kor?"

Memory of that shadow and the sense of my chair dropping ten stories replayed in my mind. "What was that?"

"Good. Your awareness is developing nicely." Ms. Weever took a deep breath and slowly let it out through her nose. "In all honesty, I don't know, but something's wrong. She doesn't look well. Keep an eye on her."

I nodded.

"Do you, by any chance, remember where she was when you performed the crossover ritual? Sanctus Bylan told me she helped you."

I thought a moment. The memory was hazy. I'd been so sick and weak. I remembered walking around with Nurse Kor's help, getting stuff from Sanctus Bylan's fancy car, and then leaving her outside…

I gasped. "She waited for me outside Miss Wren's room."

Yet you have come with a gift for me. I will let you have this one in exchange for another. The Demon King's words sent a shiver up my spine and icy dread filled me. I hadn't understood them at the time, hadn't even given them a single thought. I'd been so focused on banishing Allosyr.

Ms. Weever sucked in a breath. "Oh, no."

"I think the Demon King did something to her." I recited his words to my tutor and her face grew pale.

"Not good. Not good at all."

Chapter 3

The rest of the day went by in a heart-pounding blur. I felt like an invisible barrier rose between me and my dad on the ride home. The fifteen-minute ride was quiet, save for Bela reading haltingly through her numbers book. She was blissfully oblivious to the horrors unfolding around us all. I listened to her cheerful little voice, trying to find comfort in it, but my thoughts kept returning to the last things Mrs. Volaire had said to me.

You are hereby suspended while we deliberate on a final decision for you.

Dad's reaction didn't surprise me, but Mom's did. She was unsure of touching me, but my saving Deren's life had rekindled something in her. It was easier to feel her motherly love for me. While I welcomed it, I wasn't sure what to do with it, or how long it'd last. How long until she got sad and shut me off again?

The board meeting had been held after dinner. It was Bela's bedtime by the time we got home. Mom and Dad put her to bed as they spoke to each other in hushed voices. I scurried off to my room before the temptation to eavesdrop became irresistible.

I threw the blankets over my legs and propped up my latest Yuna book on my thighs. Yuna was a fairy princess and my favorite hero. In the last book, she saved a unicorn forest from a Wild Fire bad guy. As soon as she'd had a moment to celebrate her victory with the unicorns, a satyr crashed the party, begging for her help to save his people from crystal serpents. In this book, Yuna and the satyr hadn't gotten far before problems in the form of Earth elementals, creatures made of chunks of rock bound together and made sentient by magic, tried to stop Yuna from reaching the rest of the satyrs.

Those elementals might as well have been Mrs. Volaire trying to stop me from staying at Toolena Mesa.

I'd barely read two sentences when Mom popped her head into my room, hair swishing. She entered and sat on the edge of my bed.

"How are you feeling?" she said.

"Upset." It was the truth. I'd tried to do the right thing and banish the demon, which had gotten me into trouble.

"You have every right to be. You saved Deren's life and worked with a Light priest to get rid of the monster causing problems. And then they thank you by suspending you. I'm just as upset."

My chest tightened. So she knew exactly what I was thinking. Even though she understood me, hearing those words hurt. I'd tried to do the right thing and people didn't care. I was a Dark. That's all that mattered to them.

"It's not fair. I wish the world was kinder to people with your alignment."

Guilt burned in my chest like a tumbleweed on fire. My family's life would be so much easier, happier, if it wasn't for me. My mother's face blurred into a patchwork of tanned skin and dark hair. "I'm sorry."

Silence followed. A hand rested on my blanket-covered foot. I wiped my eyes and sniffed loudly as more tears fell. I gritted my teeth as hot tears trickled down my cheeks. Another stifled sob shook me.

"Oh, Mia."

My body was wrapped in a vice. I froze. Wait, those were arms around me. Mom's arms. Book falling aside, I leaned into her hug and closed my eyes. And, of course, I cried harder. Stupid tears. It'd been so long since Mom had hugged me like this. She still loved me even after all I'd put everyone through. My hand found her thigh. I put her soft pant leg in a death grip. My other arm hung dead at my side.

I sobbed and sobbed and sobbed. Not once did Mom ever let me go. She sniffed a few times and adjusted her hold to rub her eyes. The dead weight in my chest cracked and fell away, leaving behind a light nothingness, as if whatever had been there before had weighed me down all this time. I could breathe deeper. I gulped in breath after breath. The tears receded and my mom and bedroom came into watery focus.

Mom's hair and shoulder filled my vision. She smelled like sweet pea, a scent that brought back fond memories. Sweet pea was her favorite scent. She always wore it. Between tending the gardens, cleaning the house, making dinner, and playing with toys, that scent was always there. It was the smell of childhood. I'd forgotten after going so long without a real hug. I felt like I should cry again, but my chest was so light and empty that all I could do was breathe.

My mom rubbed my back a moment before sitting up, her long hair framing a puffy yet beautiful face. She'd cried with me. The dark makeup lining her eyes was smudged and outlined tear tracks. She tucked her hair behind her ears and handed me the box of tissues from my desk, which was a slab of wood propped up on four stacks of books.

A figure in the doorway caught my eye as I plucked a tissue free. Dad. His tall, muscular frame filled the doorway. His large arms and broad chest barely fit inside his t-shirt. He wore jeans and had his brown work boots on. His chest rose and fell with a deep breath. Bowing his head, he left, his boots thudding along the wood floor, growing fainter with every step. He'd looked upset, Whether it was at me or for me, I had no clue. I didn't know what to think. I was too tired to think. Crying sucked up all my energy.

Mom fluffed up my pillows and I sat up against them. "Feel better?" she said.

Yes and no. I shrugged and wiped my face. I felt lighter, but our lives weren't fixed, weren't better because I'd cried.

"I'll take that as a yes. Sometimes we all need a good cry to feel better." She gently squeezed my foot. "Anyway, why did you apologize?"

I fidgeted with the tissues. In the first Yuna book, when she was learning her powers and how to be a hero and stuff, she'd cried because her father, the Fairy King, had found out she was training to be a warrior and was very angry with her for doing that. Yuna thought she was doing her duty as princess to protect her people by learning to fight and use her innate powers in battle. But no. Her dad got so mad that he cast her out, leaving her with no idea where to go or what to do with her life. She'd left the city and cried in the nearby forest, only to have her mother find her and give her some gifts and words that filled Yuna with resolve to be a warrior, to embrace the hero she wanted to be.

Here I was with my mom, trying to use my alignment to do good, only to cause so much pain for being what I was. It wasn't fair. Part of me wanted to keep my thoughts to myself, but I feared she'd get angry if I stayed quiet.

"Everything's my fault," I said in a tiny, hoarse voice.

"What on Aardra do you think is your fault?" Her tone was gentle, patient. She wasn't angry. Thank the Light.

"Everything," I said. "Having to move all the time, having to change schools, Dad losing his job, him always being angry and you sad. Everything. My alignment causes so many problems."

"Oh, Mia. That's not true." She hugged me again, briefly. "None of it." She took a deep breath as one thought tumbled over another in her mismatched eyes. "As I'm sure you've already figured out, the world isn't always a nice place. It isn't always fair. We've had to move and whatnot because of the cruelty and unfairness, not because of you."

"Then why is Dad always mad at me?" A stray hiccup of a sob shook me.

Mom tucked stray strands of my hair behind my ear. "I'm so sorry you feel that way. He's not. He's upset with himself."

I believed her, but I didn't know how to believe her words. He was so short-tempered all the time, and ignored me while giving Bela attention. If I wasn't the reason he was so upset, then… "Why?"

She gave me a measuring gaze. "It's adult stuff you're too young to understand."

"I want to understand. A lot of adults have told me I'm wise beyond my years." Ms. Weever and Nurse Kor had said as much, and even Miss Wren. They all believed it had something to do with how hard my life had been already. I had to be old enough to understand Dad.

Mom glanced at the empty doorway. "Fine. But don't tell your dad I told you." She leaned closer and lowered her voice. "He's upset because he's not providing the life he wants us to have. He had a really good job before you were born. He's been struggling ever since you started school. He feels like a failure as a father and husband, no matter how many times I tell him he's not. He loves you, Mia. He doesn't know how to show it right now. Keep loving him back. He needs it."

"I do," I said. "He's my dad. I love him." Despite the confusion and fear I felt around him, I couldn't help but love him. He'd been a part of my life since before I started forming memories. He was my dad, my blood. Nothing could change that. I didn't know how to not love him. He had hugged and kissed and loved me, and brought me gifts of books and treats, and whatnot. I wanted things to go back to the way they used to be, not avoid him for the rest of my life.

"I'm glad. I love him, and I love you, too. I hope everything turns out all right. I hope we get to stay out here, away from the city's noise."

"Me, too."

"Now, get some rest." She kissed my forehead and stood. "We'll figure this out." Her strained smile didn't match her words. "Good night, Mia." She disappeared into the darkness.

Vergo, who'd been curled up at the foot of the bed the entire time, sat up and fixed me with his blue-eyed stare. Mom's soft footsteps padded off into silence.

I broke away from Vergo's stare, my gaze settling on his toes, all but one of them black. The one white patch made it look like he was missing a toe. "What?" I said.

"After all that happened during my lifetime centuries ago, things haven't changed a bit, even for children." He shook his head. "We started the Necromancers War in hopes of making the world a safer, happier place for Darks. We had good intentions, but things went so, so wrong."

"You were a demon back then?" The Necromancers War took place hundreds of years ago. It was the reason society hated and feared Darks, and the reason everyone loved Lights. Lights had saved humanity from Darks and their demons.

"No. I was alive. And I was brainwashed into believing that the rest of the world was the enemy. I did many terrible things that only now do I feel the capacity to regret. This is not the world I'd hoped to help create for fellow Darks."

Despite his confessions, my brain tried to wrap

around his life as a human. "Why did they start hating Darks before the war?"

He shrugged. "Our predecessors could've done it to themselves. A greedy few with an agenda could've swayed Darks to make bad decisions. Who knows? The whole truth has been lost to time. I know the decisions I and my comrades made didn't make things better." He fixed me with his cerulean gaze again and it felt like he saw my soul. "Learn this from me, Little One. The world is full of liars and deceivers, and if anyone should urge you to join the Sable Order, stay far away from them and that Order."

"What's the Sable Order?"

Vergo opened his mouth to respond, pearly fangs framing a pink tongue. He tilted his head. "Did you feel that?"

I didn't. I furrowed my brows.

"Your sister." He hopped off the bed and stopped in the doorway, looking back at me. "Something's happening to her."

The heaviness in my eyes lifted. I threw the blankets aside and silently followed Vergo across the house. It was dark save for the moonlight squeezing through gaps in the curtains, casting the walls and sparse furniture in silver. Despite my experience with Vergo as Allosyr, the dark of night didn't scare me. There was a peace and stillness to this house and the surrounding property. Occasionally, dark shapes of tormented souls were drawn to me, but I made them go away. Shadow figures had bothered me ever since my alignment manifested. I'd quickly learned how to shoo them away with a thought.

The only shadow tonight was Vergo's small body

slinking alongside the couch. He paused at the end, tail in the air. Bela's bedroom lay beyond the other side of the couch, the door sitting wide open. I crouched behind him and peered inside. Her nightlight filled her room with a gentle orange glow, and her song stone clinked out a slow lullaby. Two shapes, one tall and one short, stood over the bed. Mom and Dad.

Vergo said, "You really don't feel that?"

There was nothing in the air but the orange light and the smell of cotton from the couch. I shook my head.

"How old is your sister?"

I held up four fingers. She was four and a half, and would start Kindergarten this coming fall. Her alignment would manifest sometime within the next year. Some developed it sooner, and others later, all within months of their fifth birthday. Mine had manifested within days.

Dad whispered, "What if she turns out to be a Dark? I don't think I could handle it."

"Maybe she won't," Mom whispered back.

"Your family has a history of producing Darks. Her blood works against her."

"We don't know that. The odds of having two children with *that* same alignment are incredibly rare. We're going to have to wait and see."

Dad wrapped an arm around Mom and studied Bela. "You've seen how the world treats Mia, treats us. I don't wish that on her, too. She's too young to understand now, but in a couple of years?" He shook his head. "Do you want to see that happen all over again?"

Mom leaned against him. "No. I don't know what

to do."

Dad picked up a large stuffed animal and squeezed its torso. The bear's four stumpy limbs hung lifeless below it. "What if..." He gave it another squeeze. "...all she ever knew was happiness? She never got to know pain."

"Are you suggesting...?"

"Yes," he said unhappily as if he didn't like his idea.

"What a cowardly piece of work," Vergo said.

Mom seized Dad's arm with both hands and gave him a shake. "Jay. No." His torso swayed, his gaze rooted on Bela, who stirred.

"I don't like it either," he said numbly.

"Then don't do it. That's our daughter."

"I know. I don't like any of this."

I risked sneaking into the doorway when Bela whimpered.

Bela sat up, frowning. "Mommy, I'm scared."

Dad said, "Don't be, baby girl." He tossed the bear aside and reached for her.

Bela's head tilted back, mouth agape, and her body stiffened. Dad stood and backed away.

Mom gasped. "She's..."

"She is," Dad said in open wonder.

"So she is," Vergo said mildly.

Bela's small arms raised, palms facing skyward. She folded her legs under her and slowly stood, making her no taller than Dad's stomach. An otherworldly breeze sent her hair dancing, fanning it out behind her. A white glow outlined her entire body, hair and all, and slowly grew brighter until I had to squint. The room became as bright as day, and then the white light collapsed on a point in front of Bela's forehead. The magical breeze filled the entire room, making even my pajama dress sway. The light morphed into a shape I recognized: a south-facing crescent moon with a white circle inside its mouth, and five elongated diamonds stretching from the crescent, the Light symbol. Bela passed out and whatever magic brought her to her feet gently set her back on the bed.

Both my parents gasped, perfectly mirroring my shock.

"By Shinjan's love," Mom said, calling the god of Light by name, "she's a Light."

Chapter 4

The five of us sat in a huge reception area inside the Order of Leo's headquarters, the Order that Sanctus Bylan worked for. The glass ceiling arced three stories over our heads, desert sunlight pouring in and casting little rainbows all over the place. Everything was white, silver, or made of glass. It gave the building an otherworldly feel, like someplace set in the clouds.

I wore my white All Souls Day dress, as did Bela. Mom wore a simple silver dress and a white shawl over her shoulders to preserve her modesty, Mom had explained. Dad wore a white dress shirt, but his blue jeans stuck out, the only object with color besides the palm ferns spread along the windows. Vergo hid in my backpack. Since he'd been sent to me by Light forces, we'd both agreed it would be best if he stayed hidden.

The people bustling around paid us no mind. I'd never seen so many Light priests in one place before.

All the men and women wore white robes, a tabard with the Light symbol on the front, and the Order of Leo's symbol on the back, a sunburst in the shape of a lion's head. People entered and exited the building with a sense of purpose hurrying their movements. One of those busy people marched up to us, hands hidden in his voluminous sleeves. Sanctus Bylan. The four of us stood.

I let out the breath I didn't know I'd been holding. Despite my positive experiences with Sanctus Bylan, being surrounded by my opposite alignment set me on edge, like I was trespassing in Mr. Redd's office again. I didn't belong here. If anyone but him found out about my alignment, we'd be chased out of here by spirit warriors wielding flaming swords.

Sanctus Bylan gave me a fond smile and inclined his head to us. "Greetings, my children."

"Greetings, Sanctus Bylan," the three of us murmured, me and Dad softly, Mom passionately.

"It's a pleasure to see you all again. I was only told that the Evers family specifically called for me. By what stroke of good fortune do I have the pleasure of seeing you today?"

"It's our youngest daughter, Bela," Mom said, standing Bela on a chair. Bela waved, staring at him in awe.

Bylan reached for her. "Has something happened to her?"

"She's a Light," Dad said, awed. None of us got much sleep last night, except Bela. Mom and Dad fell asleep on the floor in Bela's room. They hadn't let her out of their sight. We'd all stared at her during breakfast. She didn't seem to mind the extra attention one bit. She seemed to be able to sense Vergo's presence, too. Her eyes had followed his movements. She probably wasn't strong enough to see him yet. Just like ghosts and demons had been nothing but shadows for me at first, Vergo must be the same for her.

Gasping, Sanctus Bylan's hand stopped halfway between him and Bela, his aged expression locked in surprise. He glanced between me and Bela. "Truly?"

"It happened last night," Mom said. "She glowed and everything. The Light symbol flashed over her forehead before she passed out. I still can't believe it."

"You came to the right place." Sanctus Bylan lifted Bela into his arms and she sat above his hip, beaming. "And what's your name, sweet child?"

"Bela."

"Hello, Bela. I'm Sanctus Bylan. I hear you're a very special girl. We have lots to discuss. Come. Let's talk in my office." He led us deeper inside, his robes swishing along the tiled floor with a whisper.

I tensed every time we passed a priest, but they merely greeted Sanctus Bylan and nodded to my parents and me before focusing on wherever they were going. They didn't give me a second thought. Even though I knew of no way to sense another person's alignment, I still feared all these Lights would somehow sense mine, their opposite, their opposition.

Sanctus Bylan led us to a black metal platform surrounded by vines on three sides. We stepped on and it swayed under our feet, like a swing getting nudged by a lazy breeze. Sanctus Bylan pulled a matching metal lever and a gated door closed off our only exit. The gate was made of metal that created a diamond pattern. In the middle sat a cutout of the Light symbol. Sanctus

Bylan touched a hanging glass globe the size of an orange. It pulsed with a green glow and the vines shivered. I grabbed Mom's arm as the world around me spun.

"You're all right," Mom said patiently, putting a steadying hand on my backpack strap. "It's just a lift."

I squeezed my eyes shut as vines slithered up and down all around us. I'd been in lifts charmed by Metalminds to rise and fall on command, but not one done by a Florakin. Thankfully, the weightless sensation came and went quickly, and the vines stilled. The gate opened out onto a short glass bridge. Sanctus Bylan led the way with Bela in his arms, who took in everything with open wonder. Three sets of shoes clattered off like a six-legged horse. I stepped onto the bridge and one look down stopped me in my tracks.

It was...

"Gorgeous," Mom said, her voice echoing.

Our first look at the ground floor showed nothing more than a tiled floor cut into odd shapes. From above, it all coalesced into a circle of multicolored bands that swirled towards the center of the building. The chairs, desks, and plants all perfectly fit within the shapes without interruption. All those shapes formed the lion-head-shaped starburst in varying shades of white, the eyes the darkest, mane a soft grayish white, and the roaring face almost pure white. The walls were solid columns of various stones that rose from the ground to a rounded glass and metal dome.

"It was a labor of love when this basilica was built." Sanctus Bylan stopped at the edge of the bridge and faced them. "The architects designed it so it could be best admired from above, so that Shinjan might look upon it and weep with joy."

Vergo let out a muffled snort. I hiked up my backpack when Sanctus Bylan looked at me. Hopefully, giving Vergo a good shake would serve as a reminder to stay quiet.

The Light priest gave me an almost imperceptible shrug. "Look your fill, and then we'll get settled in my office."

My family and I took in the majestic view a moment longer before following a carpeted hallway into an office half as big as our house. The wall opposite the door was all tinted glass, revealing the desert surrounding the edge of the capital city of Marohu. Toolena Mesa lay miles and miles west of Marohu, far enough that the city reminded us it existed only at night with its distant glow.

Marohu wasn't tall so much as it was wide. It was laid out in a tidy grid formation with groups of tall buildings bunched here and there. The desert surrounded it in earthy shades of reds and browns with mountains in the distance. The mountains looked like the fabled edge of the world with nothing but pale blue sky beyond.

Sanctus Bylan handed Bela back to Mom, and we sat opposite him and his sprawling white marble desk. Books and bound parchments sat in tidy stacks, and a basket of scrolls sat in one corner. The wall nearest his desk was covered with books top to bottom, door to window. They were organized by cover color and height, everyone last one of them perfectly placed to stand upright and in line with its neighbors. Various rocks and crystals were clustered in choice corners of the bookshelf.

Sanctus Bylan propped his elbows on the shiny desk and interlaced his fingers. "So, Mia, *who* is in your backpack?"

My stomach felt like I was back on the lift. My parents stiffened.

Bela stuck a finger in her mouth. "What's wrong, Mommy?"

"Nothing at all," the Light priest said calmly. "That spirit is of the Light, not the Dark. We're in no danger. Go ahead," he added when I hesitated.

My hands moved as I paid attention to my family from my peripheral vision. Despite Sanctus Bylan's words, they sat with every muscle tense, eyes full of anxiety. Bela leaned against Mom's chest, finger in her mouth, curious.

Vergo's furry head popped out and he shook it. He took in our company, climbed out, and hopped onto the desk. Mom and Dad stared at my backpack like it was about to grow teeth and start attacking everyone. Bela's gaze followed the cat.

"Greetings, Sanctus," Vergo said stiffly to the books.

Smiling, Sanctus Bylan rose and his robes swished as he crossed his office to a massive open cabinet sitting opposite his small library.

The cabinet was stocked with silver bowls of herbs, roots, and other ingredients Lights used to guide lost souls and whatever else they did. I recognized a couple from when I'd stolen them from his fancy car. Hopefully he'd never noticed. Wooden boxes and leather pouches of unnamed stuff sat among the bowls, all in front of mirrors. Sanctus Bylan picked up a brass bowl and mallet, and ran the mallet along the bowl's rim. A rich tone, a cross between a deep bell and a wolf's howl, filled the room. A wave of calm passed through me. I released the death grip on my backpack and set it on the marble floor. The tone lingered in the air. Sanctus Bylan set the bowl down and picked up a small cloth pouch and a piece of black chalk.

Vergo pricked up his ears and tilted his head at the pouch. "Ah, I see," he said when he spotted the chalk. He stationed himself at the edge of the desk.

Sanctus Bylan drew a power circle on his desk.

"Are you sure you want to let them see me? The parents are very...delicate when it comes to things like me."

"It's time they learn not to fear you," Sanctus Bylan said without looking up. He put the finishing touches on a simple circle accented by a few runes and straightened up. "Please, step in the circle. It won't trap you. You're a benevolent spirit."

Vergo gave him a suffering look before reluctantly stepping into the empty center. Sanctus Bylan dusted him with a pinch of powder and muttered a few words. The circle flashed white.

Nothing about Vergo looked different, but my parents shifted their attention from my backpack to the cat on Sanctus Bylan's desk. Their eyes widened.

"Kitty," Bela said, reaching for Vergo.

Mom held Bela pinned to her chest, but her grip grew slack. "It's..."

"A spirit cat sent by the Light. It's attached to Mia for some reason."

"To atone for my past transgressions," Vergo said wearily.

"But why this child?"

Vergo glanced at me, and then explained the whole thing, from his fall from demonhood to being sent back by the Light to help me for as long as the Light deemed fit.

"The Light forgives, but does not forget," Sanctus Bylan said.

"Lucky me," Vergo said sarcastically.

Bela slid off Mom's lap and stood before Vergo. She held out a hand.

He sniffed it. "Yes, you are most certainly a child of Light. Hello, Little One."

Bela petted his forehead and Vergo closed his eyes. She switched to scratching him under the chin. Purring filled the room as the cat leaned into it. The purring was as calming as the note the brass bowl had sounded.

Vergo's eyes opened and he backed away. He let out a sound that was half hiss, half exasperated sigh. "Curse the Light for giving me this form. I'm not a pet."

"You seemed to like that," Sanctus Bylan said.

"Spirit I may be, but I've been forced to share many traits with the living version, including grooming and purring."

"And enjoying chin scratches," Sanctus Bylan said mildly.

"You finally understand the degree of my condition. This is most certainly penance by humiliation."

Bela giggled. "He's pretty."

"I am not." Vergo rolled his eyes. "Why am I trying to argue with a child?"

Bela scooped him off the desk and carried him over to Mom. Vergo hung with his forelegs stuck out in front of him, his back legs stretched out, and his toes separated as he counterbalanced the awkward position. He was almost half Bela's size.

He gave my mom a suffering look. "My humiliation truly knows no bounds, madame."

Mom tried to hold back a laugh. It came out as a snort.

***

Vergo hid in my backpack for the rest of the meeting. Sanctus Bylan had given him a small copper vial filled with salt and rosemary, and marked with a squiggly rune that was the power word for concealment. Vergo wore it on a hemp cord around his neck. It would hide him from being detected by Lights and Darks, the only two alignments that could sense him in the first place. However, the charm failed to work for me. I could see Vergo whether or not he wore it.

Bela sat in a chair in the middle of a vaulted room buried as far away from the building's entrance as possible. Light funneled down on my sister and our parents standing behind her. I stood beside Sanctus Bylan at the shadowed edge of the octagonal room. The moment felt similar to when I'd stood before Mrs. Volaire at the board meeting, except no one paid attention to me this time. Instead, Bela was under the scrutiny of a bunch of old robed men and women.

Ten Light priests sat at a semicircular marble desk that stretched to fit all of them. Stained glass windows lined four of the room's eight sides, letting little light pour in. The room had a subdued, underwater feel, nothing like what I'd expected from a bunch of Light priests. Despite the white walls and floors, this room didn't fit with the rest of the building. My family looked like they were on trial.

"Why is this room so different?" I whispered to Sanctus Bylan. We stood on the far opposite side of the priests, well out of hearing range.

"It's symbolic," he whispered back. "The darkness before the dawn."

I didn't understand, but I went with it. At least he had an explanation.

An elderly woman stood, adjusting the vine holding up a speaking stone so it hung below her chin. "Welcome to the Order of Leo, Evers family," the lady said formally. "I am Grand Sanctus Meria Kroone." Straight hair that was white or pale yellow, depending on the light angle, fell to her chin. Her tanned skin, spotted with age, hung loosely along her jaw. It wiggled with every syllable. "Sanctus Bylan informed us of your situation and the blessed alignment bestowed upon your youngest." She inclined her head. "Congratulations. You're very lucky."

Mom and Dad replied with awed thanks. Even though it had taken all day to get this meeting, we were still absorbing Bela's alignment.

"Fewer and fewer Lights are being born every year. Some consider this worrisome, but the wisest know that this is a sign of the Light shining brightly upon Aardra. The world seeks balance. A force we do not entirely comprehend sees that our alignments are evenly bestowed upon us. Your daughter being a Light means she has important work ahead to keep the Light shining strong. This will require special care and education."

"Her alignment manifested early. She's only four and a half," Mom said.

"That's fine," one of the elderly men to Kroone's right said in a whispery voice. "She can wait until her fifth birthday to begin her education, or later if she needs more time to mature, but not too long after. A Light's training and education are of paramount importance."

Hands hidden in his sleeves, Sanctus Bylan tilted his head towards me and whispered, "I started when I was five. My parents put me in a private Light academy."

"We understand," Mom said.

"Very good," Kroone said. She took in the elderly robed people on either side of her before addressing my parents again. "Considering the rarity of Lights these days, we urge you to enroll Bela at Little Leos Light Academy. It's right here in Manipool. The Order will help with moving expenses, should you need it."

Mom and Dad exchanged shocked looks. Mom said, "That's wonderful. What about our eldest daughter?"

"What's her alignment?"

Mom fumbled for words and mumbled the truth, but Kroone held an arthritic hand to her ear. "She's a Dark," Mom said.

Every last priest straightened up and Kroone blanched. Whispering filled the vaulted space. The old woman on her left tapped Kroone's arm. They exchanged a few quiet words. Kroone squared her shoulders and held her wobbly chin high. "We don't care. She's not our concern."

Sanctus Bylan muttered something under his breath.

"How could you say something like that?" Mom

said, exasperated.

Sanctus Bylan threw an arm around my shoulders, backpack and all, and guided me to stand beside my parents and Bela. "This child has done nothing wrong to any of you."

"You dare defend a Dark?" Kroone said. "Do you not understand what she'll become?"

"She's not like they were. She'll become a good woman with a big heart. Darks are part of the balance, too."

Kroone crinkled her nose. "Yes, and that role is to unbalance things. Have you forgotten this world's history? Its origins? The one who opposes Shinjan in an eternal struggle for dominance?"

"Don't patronize me, Grand Sanctus. Has it never occurred to you that maybe not all Darks are what you think they are?"

Kroone's eyes narrowed, her chin quivering. She lowered her voice and it carried through the space sharpened with icy tones. "You speak blasphemy and are undermining my authority. You and I will discuss this in private later. You are dismissed."

Sanctus Bylan stood there, matching Kroone glare for glare, his equally soft jaw muscles clenching and unclenching. His face reddened and nostrils flared, but he did an about-face that sent his robes swirling, hitting my legs. Heavy thunks of his shoes chased him into the shadows and out of the room. The door gently swung closed behind him. The heavy granite moaned an echoing boom. That had to be what sounded like a distant dragon roar. I fully understood how Yuna felt when a mudslide trapped her in a cave with a dragon. There was no way out but forward, through the ten robed beasts ready to tear me up and take my sister away.

Kroone took a deep breath and the venom sharpening her features softened into a sweet, grandmotherly face. "Now...I apologize for all that. Sanctus Bylan is a good man, but an odd one. Don't let that exchange worry you. Your daughter will get the best of care at Little Leos."

Mom and Dad exchanged looks, having one of the wordless conversations parents often had. Mom said, "And what kind of education would she get?" She sounded uncertain.

"The same foundation of reading, writing, mathematics, history, and so on, just like at any other school. However, she will also receive extensive training in her alignment, be exposed to all the specialty fields, and then dedicate her training to the one she most excels at. Once she chooses a specific path, she will be enrolled in the appropriate boarding school."

"Boarding school?" Mom said, taken aback.

"Yes. Time has shown that Lights trained in a highly controlled environment produce the best results. You don't want external stimuli tainting or distracting your daughter's training and education, do you?"

"I..." Mom took in all the people in front of us and her eyes glistened. That was her unhappy face, the one she made before she started crying. I wanted to leave the room. I always retreated to my bedroom when she got that face. It made me want to cry, too.

Dad wrapped his arms around Mom and spoke to Kroone. "We need time to think about it. It's a lot to take in all at once."

"It is," Kroone said with a nod. "And you have

time. Remember: the forces of chaos never rest. Your daughter has been called upon to keep them at bay. She's a very special person. You owe it to her to give her the best education and training."

"Thank you for your time," Dad said as he scooped Bela into one arm and held Mom's hand. Mom grabbed mine. Together, the four of us walked out, ten pairs of eyes on our backs. It felt like walking away from a dragon deciding whether or not to chase us out with a breath of fire. However, no heat, no flames licked at us as the door swung closed, separating us from the priests.

Sanctus Bylan waited in the hallway that wrapped around the meeting room. He wore a pensive frown. "What happened? I didn't create trouble for you, did I?"

"Goodness, no," Mom said, reassuringly touching his sleeve. "It's just…I don't know."

Dad shook his head. "Something about them doesn't sit right with me. I thought Light Orders were different than this."

"More kind and loving toward everyone?" Sanctus Bylan said.

"Where did you go to get trained?" Mom said.

"On the other side of the country, in a private academy. I made a pilgrimage in early adulthood and eventually settled here in the desert."

"Were you sent to a boarding school as well?"

"It's a common approach for training Lights. I wouldn't let that part bother you."

"Those people bother me," Dad said, pointing behind him with a thumb.

Sanctus Bylan started to say something, but pressed his mouth in a thin line. He shook his head.

"We've never had an unpleasant exchange before. I've never seen that side of Grand Sanctus Kroone, either. My education was a bit different back east. We were taught to be cautious around Darks, but we were also taught to love everyone no matter their alignment." His pale eyes looked between me and Bela. "I don't want to influence your decision. I'll have to ponder on this."

"Maybe you could teach her," Mom said.

Sanctus Bylan gave them a wan smile. "Would that I could. Your daughters are delightful, but I have a job at the hospital. I cannot abandon my post."

"Oh, goodness, no. I'm sorry for suggesting such a thing."

"Your heart's in the right place, Brecca. I'm flattered you did."

The door behind us opened. A young robed man with a tidy head of brown hair stuck his head in the hallway. "Sanctus Bylan, they've requested your audience immediately."

Chapter 5

The following week dragged by with agonizing slowness. Homework came and went daily via a trip to the main office and back. Mom drove Bela and me in awkward silence, Bela the only one with anything to say. However, even she spoke little. Her alignment left her watching things none of us could see, my only clue being her little brows knotting together and a seriousness coming over her expression. She looked mom-like in those moments, instead of the four-year-old she was. She had the same long black hair and face shape, but unlike us, she had matching brown eyes.

Vergo, wearing his charm that left his presence undetectable to everyone but me, accompanied me everywhere in silence.

Dad was gone during the day, as usual, but he always made it home by dinnertime, something he hadn't done regularly in at least a year. He studied Bela in awed silence while we ate as a family, and gave Mom occasional kisses on the cheek or mouth.

Tail tip touching my arm, Vergo stared longingly at our meal of green chili enchiladas and cheesy refried beans. I must've given him a curious look.

"I miss food," he said. "Even as a demon—"

"Kitty?" Bela ducked her head under the table, a spoon propped up on the edge like she held a spear dripping mashed beans.

Vergo pricked his ears forward. "I guess this charm only masks my presence, not my voice."

"Mia, where's your kitty?" She slid off her chair.

"Bela, eat your dinner," Mom said patiently.

"But I wanna see the kitty." Dumping her spoon, Bela disappeared under the table.

"After you finish eating."

"I'm all done." She had half a plate of enchiladas chopped up into little bites.

Mom retrieved Bela from under the table, plunked her back in her chair, and put the spoon back in my sister's hand for good measure. Bela tried sliding off her chair, but Mom hoisted her back upright.

"I'm all done."

"Bela," Dad said in a warning tone and Bela froze. "Listen to Mommy and eat your dinner."

"But—"

"Eat your dinner." He scooped a bite from his plate and looked pointedly at my sister.

Bela contemplated whatever a four-year-old contemplated when being told to do something she didn't want to, and then she pouted and shoved a spoonful of food in her mouth. Mom and Dad gave me an annoyed look, like it was my fault for distracting

Bela. I lowered my gaze to my plate, my chin inches from the edge. It might as well be my fault. I was the one who'd banished Vergo and got him attached to me in the first place.

I ate, but tasted nothing.

***

One week later, we were all back in the board meeting room, minus Nurse Kor. Ms. Weever stood in the back of the dimly lit room, arms folded in front of her corset. Surrounding my family and me sat a bunch of parents, taking up the rows of seats as far away from us as possible. Despite the abundance of chairs, many stood along the back of the room. The empty chairs might as well have been a moat cast in shadow, full of deadly creatures waiting for us to break the water's surface. Vergo sat under my chair, wearing the charm.

One of those "deadly creatures," an older man wearing overalls strapped over hunched shoulders, leaned towards my tutor and spoke loudly. "You hoping they expel her, too?"

"I'm hoping to see justice meted out," Ms. Weever said coolly. She shifted her weight to her foot farthest from the man.

"I can't believe they allowed one of them Darks at our school," he said plenty loud enough for me to hear. He jutted his bearded chin towards me. "They're nothing but trouble and bad luck."

Ms. Weever's pale blue eyes narrowed ever so slightly as she held her chin high. "Have you ever met one before?"

"Don't have to. This is the second time a student's died with one of them here."

"My heart aches for the parents who lost their

children."

"Same here," the man said, oblivious to my tutor's fuming. "That's why we've got to get rid of the problem."

She slowly faced the man and sized him up. "That we do."

A bell rang in the front of the room and everyone quieted. Mrs. Volaire wore another business suit and skirt, more bright red lipstick, and had her hair pulled back in a tight bun. She idly flipped a few pages in the notebook in front of her. "This meeting will be short. We, the school board, have reached a decision. Miss Evers, you will no longer be attending Toolena Mesa Middle School. It's too much of a risk to have a Dark in our district." She flipped the notebook closed.

My jaw dropped as silence pressed down all around me. The world fell into slow motion. Mrs. Volaire reached for her speaking stone with slow, practiced grace. The other school board members slowly rose like the dust cloud of a distant sandstorm.

I was expelled. Again. I'd tried to do the right thing by getting rid of the demon, but no one cared. I was a Dark and that's all that mattered to anyone. My parents would have to dump me in a boarding school after all. Maybe they'd be happier without all the trouble I caused.

Mom surged to her feet, arms pinned to her sides. "How could you do such a thing?" Her voice was a thunderclap. I flinched and the world sped back up to real time. "Our daughter saved a boy's life and got rid of that thing harming her classmates, and this is how you thank her? You people are disgusting."

Dad stood, his unreadable gaze fixed on Mrs.

Volaire. He looked ready to say something, but only held Bela in his arms, who watched Mrs. Volaire intently.

Mrs. Volaire looked over the rim of her glasses at my mom, who said nothing. She picked up her notebook and tucked it in a cloth bag.

Hateful voices filled the room, all their negativity aimed at me. The bearded man who'd spoken to my tutor shook a fist and yelled at me to get out, using inappropriate words for children.

Vergo hopped onto the chair next to me, placing his front paws atop the chair back. "How delightful," he said sarcastically. "Society's hate for Darks is as fresh as ever. If I were alive, they wouldn't get away with spewing such venom to a mere child. Remember this day, Little One. Never forget their hate."

The moment was already burning itself into memory, a permanent reminder of who and what I was. The anger and hate had left me confused and hurt as a little kid, but now that I was old enough to understand, it left me with memories I would never forget.

Ms. Weever placed a hand on Mom's shoulder. "Your anger is completely justified," she said calmly.

Mom's eyes glistened. "Our daughter did nothing wrong."

"I know. They know, too, but they have other priorities." She raised her voice. "Sometimes it's better to acknowledge when you're not wanted and move on."

"You'd figure I'd be used to this by now." Mom sniffed.

"It never gets easier, which is why it's best to become stronger." Ms. Weever took Mom's hand and held out her other to me. "Come. I'll get you safely out of the Light-forsaken place."

Not sure what else to do, I took my tutor's hand. Her fingers were as cold as her expression. I reflexively tried to let go. Her grip tightened, guiding me towards the doors.

Those doors swung open. At first, I thought the hateful parents were making it easier for us to leave, but they shied away and bowed their heads. Silence spread like a ripple.

Framed in the doorway stood Sanctus Bylan, wide-sleeved arms held out. His white robes seemed to absorb what little light the room hand, and then return it tenfold, glowing. He stood tall and imposing despite his age. He had broad shoulders and a rounded belly, but there was a power to his presence that commanded attention and respect.

"What is the meaning of this?" His aged voice carried across the room.

I clenched my teeth. That was a voice of power. I bowed my head like everyone else, but couldn't take my eyes off him.

He marched inside, robes swishing behind him, and stopped before Mrs. Volaire. He gave her a measuring glare that pushed her back in her chair. The other board members followed suit. He studied Mrs. Volaire a moment longer before rounding on the rest of the room. "There's so much hate and negativity in this room that you are all asking the Demon King to turn his attention to the lot of you. Your behavior is not what the Light teaches. The Light loves every last soul."

The bearded man took a tentative step forward, wringing his gnarly hands. "But Sanctus, that girl's a Dark." He pointed to me. "She's a bringer of

Darkness."

Sanctus Bylan took one deliberate step after another, until mere inches of air separated the two men. Sanctus Bylan stood half a head taller. He brought his hands together, hiding them in the depths of his sleeves. "Did you hear me stutter?" Even though he spoke at normal volume, the anger in his voice filled the whole room.

The man shrank away. "N-no, Sanctus, but—"

"Every last soul, even yours and hers." Sanctus Bylan scanned the room. Everyone remained silent, even Mrs. Volaire, who had gone quite pale. He returned to the front of the room and addressed the parents. "I didn't come here to give a sermon, although I'm sorely tempted. No, I, Sanctus Alexander Bylan, Light Priest of the…" His shoulders drooped ever so slightly before standing tall and proud again. "Order of Leo, came here for the sake of this family and their child you would all so eagerly hate without even knowing her name." He fell silent, his hard gaze sweeping the room.

The silence weighed on the room as if the ceiling was pushing down on us all. The shadowed faces looked cowed and ashamed, gazes downcast, and even a few covered their faces. The weight of justice, of judgment. Sanctus Bylan had rightfully put all these people in their place. A smile stretched my stiff cheeks and I stood taller as well.

"Grandma?" The voice was small, uncertain, hopeful. Bela. She faced Sanctus Bylan, but she stared at something or someone beside him I couldn't see.

Sanctus Bylan looked at the same spot and his face softened with a smile. "I thought I saw a resemblance."

He approached Bela and held out his arms. "May I?" Mom wordlessly handed my sister over, who absently wrapped one arm around Sanctus Bylan's shoulder, and his glow encased her. Bela sucked on a fingertip. "So, Bela, who's this lovely lady?"

"Iris," she said around her fingertip. "But she wants me to talk to someone else."

"Who?" His smile broadened, adding more wrinkles to his face.

Bela's brows knit together. "Raina."

Mrs. Volaire sucked in a breath. "Mother."

Sanctus Bylan turned in place and approached the school board. He stopped a few feet from the semicircular desk and set Bela on the ground. They both held a hand out and I could've sworn I heard a distant bell toll as a wave of peace and love washed over the room. A bent-over wisp of a figure wrapped her hand around Bela's and straightened up. Like water soaking into a towel, the lady's transparent body filled out into an old woman with the same severe features as Mrs. Volaire, silvery hair pulled back in a tight bun, a proud posture, and chin held high, as if looking down at the world over her pronounced nose.

Mrs. Volaire stood, a hand over her heart. While the school board was positioned on a raised platform, she looked small as she gaped at her mother's ghost.

Bela closed her eyes and the ghost spoke.

"Raina Volaire." Her voice was thin, like she spoke through a hollow tube. "Love the child as your own. Love the child as you have forgotten to love yourself. You are loved. You have forgotten, as has the child."

Bela gasped and dropped to her hands and knees. The ghost faded like a setting sun and the room grew cold. No one moved. Mrs. Volaire's hands had moved to her mouth during the message and her eyes…what, no. Her? Someone like her was capable of crying? I squinted and took a step closer. Sure enough, Sanctus Bylan's glow reflected in the two growing lines of tears.

The Light priest picked Bela up and brought her over to Mom, who held Bela's limp body in a tight hug. "Oh, she's cold," Mom said.

"She's fine," Sanctus Bylan said softly. "She's drained from channeling a spirit. She'll be fine within a few hours."

Mom nodded and kissed Bela on the forehead.

Sanctus Bylan turned to the school board again. "So, what say you? Have we had a change of heart?"

I stared blankly, until the words registered in my mind. Sanctus Bylan was standing up for me and my family. A Light priest standing up for a Dark. Despite the help he'd given me with banishing Vergo as Allosyr, despite our trip to the Order of Leo, despite his grand entrance here, it couldn't overwrite years of hate and fear of me. Part of me was waiting for the trick, for the truth I was used to, but he stood proud and shining, a beacon of hope and justice in a sea of hate and prejudice.

"We—" Mrs. Volaire said. A hiccup interrupted the rest.

Everyone's attention turned to her and her gaze darted back and forth to the dozens of faces staring back. She dropped her hand and, arms clamped to her sides, hurried to a side door and slammed it behind her.

Chapter 6

Mrs. Volaire didn't return until everyone but my family and the other school board members left. Sanctus Bylan escorted Mrs. Volaire into the meeting room, said a few quiet words to her, and she told me to show up for classes on Monday. My mind blanked out. My parents gaped. We numbly exited the building as Sanctus Bylan spoke with Mrs. Volaire in private.

Returning to school was a new level of awkward. Instead of classmates avoiding me nonstop, like they had at the other schools once my secret was out, they stayed far away from me and stared. Stares bore into the side of my face during the ride in. Whispers filled the bus over the hum of the Fire engine. Occasionally, I locked eyes with the driver in the overhead mirror. One time, she swerved back to the center of the lane, making the whole busload of children cry out in unison. A student sitting a couple of rows behind me made a remark about how "the Dark" must be messing with the bus driver and was trying to kill everyone.

I sank lower into my chair and tried to focus on the blurry letters in my Yuna book. She had made it past the Earth elementals blocking her from reaching the satyr village, but not without taking a few good blows. The pain from her broken leg made it nearly impossible to concentrate on using any magic. Now, she was being dragged behind her horse in a litter while the satyr nervously guided them along.

"You need to stand up to them, you know," Vergo said. He sat with me on the wide seat, front paws spread to maintain balance.

I sniffed. "Why?"

"They won't stop until they learn they can't get away with it."

"They'll hate me even more for standing up to them."

Vergo considered me a moment with his blue eyes. "That's not the point, Little One. Let them hate you. That's their choice, not yours. Hate them back, if you feel like it."

I want people to like me. I wanted to blurt the words, but they couldn't make it past my aching heart. It was like my heart had a pair of arms and trapped the words in a bear hug.

"The point is to get them to respect you enough to keep their mouths shut around you. Let them think what they want, but so long as they know to keep their thoughts to themselves, that there are consequences for their harsh words, then you can go about your business in peace."

An endless tortilla of land dotted with bushes and

cacti spread outside my window. "How does that work if they hate me?" I turned when he let out a slow sigh.

He shook his head. "It's not perfect, but..." He scooted closer, raised a paw, and stopped. He set it back on the brown leather charmed to repel liquid spills of any kind. "When you stand up for yourself, good things happen."

"Like what?"

He nodded towards the back of the bus. "Why don't you stand up to those brats and find out?"

In the mirror, a sea of slabs of brown leather and the tops of heads in between filled up the entire pane around the driver's fearful face. Our gazes locked again. Closing my book, I hugged it to my chest and squeezed myself into the crux of the chair and window. "I'll try tomorrow." Maybe it'd would be a quieter ride and I wouldn't have to say anything to them.

Normal-volume voices disguised as whispers hissed away over the engine's hum for the duration of the commute, and then they turned into a mix of cheers and regular conversation when we pulled up to the drop-off point.

One boy said, "Yay, we made it alive."

I raced off the bus and hurried down the sidewalk, book pressed to my chest and face hidden behind my curtain of hair. I reluctantly accepted Vergo's company as he trotted alongside me up to the glass doors. My heart pounded even though I knew none of them could see him. He was so solid and real for me that it was hard to accept that he didn't exist for anyone else.

The two receptionists' eyes widened. "Mia," Desi exclaimed, her face brightening. "Welcome back."

Vergo hopped up on the desk. "Yes, yes, the hero

and her reluctant sidekick have returned," he said.

I walked over and gripped the edge level with my chin.

"We all heard what happened. You're so brave."

I blinked. "What did you hear?"

"You and a Light priest banished a demon to the Light. That's amazing."

"Oh, um, thanks."

Desi retrieved a stack of papers and notebooks from a shelf and set them on the counter. "By the way, here's all your graded work." She absently fingered a bouncy curl, then stopped when she noticed my confused expression. "What?"

Where was her fear and hate? Desi wasn't like Miss Wren or Nurse Kor. They'd been open and honest about their reservations with having a Dark student about before coming to like me. Desi just... "Don't you...?" I couldn't bring myself to finish the question. "I'm a..."

Desi gave me a dismissive wave. "Oh, honey, I don't care. You're a brave sweetheart." Her smile seemed genuine, or was it too big to be real? Heck, why was I questioning it if she was being nice? The blonde receptionist, whatever her name was, merely gave me an empty smile and polite wave.

"Miss Evers," a voice said from the hallway. It was Mr. Redd. "Welcome back. Come into my office a moment." He waved me over and disappeared into his office.

Desi beamed at me and bid me farewell.

I trudged into the principal's office, my heart pounding away. Vergo followed us inside and took a seat in the leather chair next to me. I hid my face behind my hair.

"Relax, you're not in trouble," Mr. Redd said. "I want to talk with you about a couple of things." He pulled a leather-bound folder over to him. My transcripts. He opened up to the notes about my alignment in the back, and picked up a pen. "Your recent actions deserve some positive attention. First, it's good to see that you're alive and well, so welcome back."

"Thank you." His businesslike expression didn't match the pleasant tone in his voice. Was this rehearsed or was he so used to being angry with misbehaving students that he forgot how to smile when saying nice things?

On second thought, why was I questioning this, too? He was saying nice things.

"Sanctus Bylan said many great things about you. Coming from a Light priest, his words are not to be taken lightly. It sounded like you've helped take my progressive ideals with Darks a step in the right direction."

Not according to the people on the school bus, but whatever.

"Thank you very much. This is more than I'd hoped for. So your actions deserve a positive note in your records." He scribbled away, and then read the words aloud. "Displays unmatched bravery when facing evil entities, understands right from wrong, and can successfully banish demons to the Light." He pushed the folder over.

Sure enough, his large cursive repeated his words right under all the negative notes.

"Congratulations, Little One," Vergo said. "You're

changing the world for the better, one person at a time."

I couldn't tell if he was sincere or mocking. I studied him.

His blue eyes widened. "What?" And then they rolled, a very un-catlike action.

A laugh rose in my throat. I clamped my mouth closed.

"Okay, so I have to work on my sincerity when giving compliments. Stop looking at me like that."

I pushed the transcripts back to Mr. Redd. "Thank you very much. This means a lot to me." I didn't know what to think or how to react at the moment. I was in shock over the kindness. That and the principal was staring in Vergo's direction.

"Something with you right now?" he said cautiously.

"Yeah. I can't help it. At least this one's harmless."

"Harmless?" Vergo gave me an indignant snarl. "I would very well think not. I..." He nervously licked a paw before hopping down. "I have claws, thank you very much." He took a seat under the chair.

"Well, that's good to hear," Mr. Redd said. "While I understand you can't help what's drawn to your alignment, I do expect you to study hard and keep everything in check. The school board has honored Sanctus Bylan's words, but not happily, despite what happened at the meeting. They very much want to justify their view of Darks, so you need to continue to stay on your best behavior and to prove them wrong. Understand?"

"Yes, sir."

He tapped my transcripts. "This is one step in the right direction. And if you ever end up moving again, at least you have this to help you."

I thanked him and he instructed me to head to class. Sliding off the chair, I followed Vergo into the hallway and headed deeper into the main office. He trotted past the nurse's office. I veered inside, memory of that shadow replaying in my mind.

Nurse Kor lifted her gaze from the pages of an ancient-looking medical book and brightened. "Mia. Welcome back. And congratulations on your sister's alignment." She looked perfectly healthy and happy, no shadows passing over her.

"Thanks."

"Yes, let's have a grand ole feast and celebration," Vergo said dryly. He parked himself at my feet.

"What's wrong? You don't look happy." She closed the massive book.

I walked up to her desk, vines following my every step. Her office was covered in vines and creepers like a wall of a garden maze. Nurse Kor was a Florakin, her specialty being able to heal people with plants and herbs. The first time I'd set foot in here, the vines had creeped me out. Now they were familiar, an extension of my favorite nurse. "How are you feeling?" I said. The vines formed a perfect circle a hand's breadth from my feet, a couple leaves stretching out to brush my shoes. They passed through Vergo as if he wasn't there, but a leaf fluttered when he swatted at it.

"Fine. Why do you ask?"

I swallowed, not sure I wanted an answer. If the Demon King had marked her… "What happened after Sanctus Bylan joined me in the classroom? I don't remember it very well." Please be okay. Please tell me that Ms. Weever and I are worrying over nothing.

Nurse Kor's gaze grew unfocused as she sorted through memories. "A lot of weird things. The building shook a few times and it sounded like a thunderstorm inside. I tried to get in, but the door wouldn't budge. And then it got really dark, like nighttime dark, before everything went back to normal." She held out an arm like she wanted to shake my hand, and a vine crept out of her sleeve. It was a deep green with heart-shaped leaves colored in bands of green, yellow and pink, with a splotch of white in the middle. "This little guy nearly squeezed the life out of my arm, but then Sanctus Bylan came out with you in his arms. The both of you were so pale and cold, and a huge wave of cold emptied out of Miss Wren's room. We took you straight to the hospital."

I nodded as the vine disappeared back into her white sleeve. I took a deep breath, bracing for the scrap of information that would reveal the truth. "Nothing happened to you?"

Nurse Kor wore an embarrassed smile. "I nearly peed myself when the door opened, but no."

"You don't feel any different after that day?"

"Should I?"

I fumbled for words. "No." Ms. Weever and I didn't want her to feel any different.

"I've been extra tired lately, but I think that's from being stressed out for so long, and then finally being able to relax. Our bodies aren't meant to be stressed for months on end." She let out a deep yawn. "That whole demon ordeal took a lot out of me. I'm exhausted now that my body has a chance to relax. I'll be fine." She sipped from a steaming ceramic mug and a whiff of herbs drifted my way.

If that shadow and falling sensation hadn't been there as well, I would've dropped the subject. "Ms. Weever and I were worried after we saw you at the first board meeting."

Nurse Kor waved a dismissive hand. "I was tired from my body finally getting to detox. On top of that, Mrs. Volaire didn't give me a chance to stick up for you. That really got my blood boiling. I was concentrating on keeping my mouth shut. People like her don't belong on a school board."

"Then why doesn't the school get someone else?"

"The District," she correctly absently, then shook her head. "Toolena Mesa is a remote town with a small population. Even if anyone wanted to challenge her for her spot, they wouldn't. The Volaires control everything this side of Marohu. It's the way things are here. To challenge them would be social suicide."

"That's not fair," I blurted before I could stop myself.

"It's not," Nurse Kor said.

"Oh, Little One," Vergo said in a tired voice, "you already know life isn't fair. Things like this need to stop surprising you."

"It's not the end of the world, though," Nurse Kor said. "The upside is the district gets a bunch of funding from the mines, so the Volaires take good care of the schools, students and staff. We have the best of the best out here." She swept a hand to the empty sick beds and everything beyond. "Heck, I couldn't ask for a better office and everything they let me stock."

Vergo's gaze followed the nurse's gesture. "Ah, so they're *those* type of people. Vain lot, they are. Their generosity only feeds their ego. They're bragging to their wealthy peers about how much money they can throw around. Don't trust people like them. They like you only so long as you do what they want. You saw how quickly that red-lipped beast wanted you gone as soon as you disrupted her little happy bubble."

Nurse Kor got up and rounded her desk. "Anyway, thank you for your concern. I'm relieved and happy to have you back." She wrapped me in a hug. I stiffened before forcing myself to return it. "Head to class before you're late."

Instead of a happy reunion, it felt like the same old routine when I left Nurse Kor's office and made my way to the playground.

Vergo padded alongside me. "I highly doubt your beloved nurse is fine."

I will let you have this one in exchange for another.

"I know. I just…"

"The Demon King is the master of subtle. I'm sure he only let you know he was trading my soul for another because he wants to teach you a lesson. Otherwise, he would've withheld that scrap of information."

"What does he want?"

Vergo looked out over the playground bustling with students ranging from kindergarten to eighth grade. "Chaos. You're going to have to keep an eye on her."

That was the plan. Sending Allosyr to the Light was supposed to feel like a victory, an accomplishment. Instead, we'd all traded one problem for another. I shuffled out of the way as classmates chased after a boy running with a ball tucked under an arm. The four chasers stopped and stared openmouthed at me. One taller boy said, "It's Mia. She's back." Whatever his name was, he sounded quite awed and delighted.

The boy with curly ginger hair gasped. "It is. Hi, Mia."

Blinking, I took another step back. Since when were classmates happy to see me? The other two who'd stopped ran away, terror on their faces. Okay, typical reactions mixed in with the new. "Hi."

"Our parents told us about how that Light priest yelled at the school board and everyone there. That had to be epic. No one ever stands up to the Volaires. Did she really cry?"

I remembered her eyes glistening, but I'd heard no sobs. "I don't know. She left the room real fast."

"I'm going to throw the ball over the fence if you don't catch up," yelled the boy with the ball. He stood at the edge of the playground, ball over his head, arm cocked to make good on his promise. The two nicer boys waved and ran off. And with their absence, I had a clear view of the swing set. On the nearest swing sat Deren, who smiled so wide it made his ears stick out even more. He ran over.

"We visited you at the hospital while you were asleep. Let's go play." He gestured for me to follow.

I couldn't help but smile. Nothing had changed between us. We were still friends after all I'd done. I started walking after him, but Miss Wren's voice stopped me.

"Welcome back, Mia." She pulled me into a hug, which I gently returned. "You gave us quite the scare, but you did it. You're okay. The Light priest said so many wonderful things about you." She waved me off. "But we can talk about it later. Go play." Giving me a nudge, I took off after Deren and met up with him at the swings. He handed me the chain to the swing next to his. I set my bag on the sand and hopped on, a smile stuck on my face.

"Did you really banish a demon?"

Okay, my smile wasn't as stuck as I thought. "Yeah."

"Was it scary?"

"Yeah."

"What was it like?" He appeared genuinely curious as he kicked his legs so fast he wobbled from side to side.

"Scary and confusing," I admitted.

A group of classmates walked up to us. Gwen and her friends. She didn't look happy. She stopped outside of kicking range. Deren stopped wiggling.

"Hey," Gwen said.

"Hey," I said back, unsure of whether to tell her to go away or let her talk.

"Oh, look, it's the royal brat," Vergo said. "Let me bite this one on your behalf."

I gave him a warning look. As much as I didn't like Gwen, I wouldn't go out of my way to be mean.

"I'm sorry," she said impatiently. She kicked at some sand. "I heard everything you said in the nurse's office, and my mom told me what happened at the board meeting. Sanctus Bylan also gave me a long lecture and told me I better apologize to you. So there. I apologized." With that, she turned around and marched off to the jungle gym. Everyone but Chibya followed her, who smiled and waved to me before heading off.

Deren and I stared after them, until he started kicking his legs like a swimmer again. "That was weird," he said.

"Yeah. At least we can be friends without her bothering us." He voiced his agreement and we began competing to see who could swing the highest.

Chapter 7

Mom and Dad acted all weird even for them on the first day of the new school year. Bela was starting Kindergarten and I was finally starting seventh grade. They ran back and forth across the house, looking for this thing or that, double and triple checking to make sure Bela had everything she needed in her new little blue backpack with cats drawn all over it. She and I sat on the couch as our parents paced around the house, trying to make sure everything was in order, as if some king and queen from a distant country were about to pay us a visit. Mom wore a yellow summer dress with white leggings underneath and matching cowgirl boots. Dad wore a pastel blue dress shirt, dark blue tie, and stuck to jeans, much to Mom's dismay. They'd argued over it before deciding they didn't want to argue on this special day.

"Why are Mommy and Daddy acting so weird?"

Bela said, holding Vergo in her lap. I'd removed his charm upon my sister's request and our parents' permission. He'd complained at first, but he kept purring on and off, stopping every time he realized he was enjoying being petted.

"I dunno." Bela and I wore matching white summer dresses and shoes. I remembered snippets of being her age, the rest gone to wherever childhood memories disappear. What lingered strongest was a mix of happiness and confusion. "Maybe they want your first day of school to be great." Whether or not our parents had made such a fuss over me on my first day, I couldn't remember. School went from something everyone did to something I had to do, whether I liked it or not. At least Bela's alignment would make school a more positive experience.

"What's school like?"

Part of me internally laughed at the question, while part of me wanted to go back to my room and cry. She was asking the wrong person.

Vergo said, "It's different for everyone, but we all go to learn things, to become smarter and stronger, and figure out our place in the world."

"I'm right here." Bela scrunched her brows.

Vergo opened his mouth to speak again, but paused, the tip of his tail flicking. "Yes. Yes, you are. You will learn things then."

"What kinds of things?"

Vergo gave me a suffering look. Bela was an endless string of questions, one he seemed to never be able to stop no matter how hard he tried. "You'll see when you get there."

By the Light, please stop asking questions, I

thought as I held in a scream. Why did little sisters have to be so annoying?

"All right, hide the cat and let's go," Mom said, grabbing Bela's backpack off the dining table. She could see Vergo only because Bela was holding on to him, but that would stop the moment Bela and Vergo broke contact. Our parents couldn't hear him, though, ever since whatever Sanctus Bylan had sprinkled on Vergo had worn off months ago. Now, the collar more served the purpose of stopping my sister from getting distracted by Vergo's presence.

Dad noisily chugged the last of his coffee and led us all to the car.

***

The parking lot was loaded with cars and buses, so loaded that a brightly dressed teacher who was aligned with Earth was funneling dust out of the parking lot and off campus. She held down her sun hat with one hand while rotating her other hand over and over, creating a tan funnel that arced over the cars and campus fence and into the desert on the other side of the main road.

Every teacher from nursery school to eighth grade had come out to the parking lot to greet us students. Bela climbed out and slung her backpack over a shoulder. Dad picked her up and planted a kiss on both cheeks. "You be a good girl and listen to your teachers. Have lots of fun. Can't wait to hear about your day." Bela giggled and Dad planted a kiss on her forehead before setting her on the sidewalk. Mom, eyes glistening, kneeled and smothered my sister in a hug. "I can't believe you're starting school already. You're growing up so fast."

"Why are there so many people here, Mommy?"

Mom carefully wiping her face in order to preserve her eye liner. "They're going to school, too, just like you and your sister."

Before Bela could ask her billionth question of the day, a massive shiny black car entered the parking lot with a deep purr, veering towards cones that blocked off a section of sidewalk. Mr. Redd, who wore a brown dress suit and dark shoes polished to mirror finish, removed the cones. The car was emblazoned with the Volaire family crest: a squiggly outline of a mountain range with a three-pronged lick of flame in the middle. The rumbling idled to a hum as the car came to a stop.

An impeccably dressed elderly man slid out of the driver's seat and gestured for Mr. Redd to open the rear passenger door. The principal gave a slight bow and obliged as the butler opened the trunk. Gwen gracefully stepped out and tossed a mane of tawny hair behind smooth shoulders. As always, she looked enviously pretty with her tanned skin, fair hair, and clothes only lots of money could buy. Her rosy pink dress had embroidered lace trim.

Our eyes met and hers narrowed a moment before she held her chin high and wore her subtle, smug smile. A burning hate lit in my chest. Despite her forced apology and mostly leaving me alone for the rest of sixth grade, she couldn't seem to resist getting in an insult here and there. Something about her filled me with the desire to punch things, preferably her.

Still, punching people even if they deserved it was not a smart idea.

Vergo brushed up against my leg. "Don't give them the satisfaction of seeing how much you hate them. It only gives them more power over you."

Closing my eyes, I took a deep breath. He was right. As much as I hated it, he was right. On top of that, I needed to stay in control of my emotions. Ms. Weever had made it perfectly clear that dark things would be lured by my strong negative emotions. Vergo as Allosyr had weaved his way into Ms. Weever's life while she'd mourned the loss of her son. Hate would open me up as much as grief.

"That's better," Vergo said.

The front passenger door swung open, a ribbon of gleaming light reflecting off it before a man a full head taller than Gwen stepped out. Mr. Volaire. He had the same tawny hair and striking blue eyes as his daughter, but his face looked like it was stuck in a slight frown and he'd start yelling at any moment. Even Gwen stiffened. He wore a black suit with lines of red that showed up when light hit it at the right angle.

"Sir?" the butler said, his brows furrowed together.

Mr. Volaire held up a finger wearing a large gold ring and strode over to Dad. He held out a hand. "Mr. Evers. A pleasure to meet you and your family." His piercing stare found Bela, who hid behind Dad's legs. Mr. Volaire openly studied her in fascination, and then sized up Dad. "You have the build of a strong man. Have you ever considered working in a mine? The pay is the best of any in the nation and so are the benefits."

"I've never worked in a mine before."

"We have entry-level positions you can fill. What's your current profession?"

Dad gave Mom a look of terror and panic before turning back to Mr. Volaire. "I transport goods around the state," he said offhandedly.

"Well, what do you say to less travel and better

pay? It's hard work, yes, but I believe you'll find it most gratifying."

Dad rubbed the back of his neck. "I'm flattered, sir, but why me?"

Mr. Volaire glanced at Bela. "Consider it an apology for how your family was treated." He held out a hand and Dad looked at it.

"I'm…honored. I'd have to talk with my current employer."

Mr. Volaire turned his hand palm up and gave a slight shrug. "I understand your hesitation. Your first impression of this area wasn't exactly positive. We're slow to trust outsiders here, but once we see their merit, we take good care of them."

"And what is our merit?" Dad said, an edge to his voice.

"Your family has shown it can stand strong in the face of hardship and great challenges," Mr. Volaire said with a hint of admiration.

"Someone's rehearsed this," Vergo said.

"Your eldest showed bravery and selflessness Sanctus Bylan spoke highly of, and now your youngest is a Light. Only good people can raise good children, and we like to keep quality people around no matter where they're from. I would personally like to offer you a job that will allow you to take good care of your family."

Dad stood there, his brow crinkled with concern.

"I wouldn't trust this man," Vergo said to me. "He's only interested in what he wants."

I didn't trust Mr. Volaire any more than I trusted his daughter.

Mom leaned closer to Dad. "Take it, Jay. It's better

than what you have now."

I had no clue what Dad did while he was out. By both parents' unwillingness to talk about it, I was growing suspicious of how he made money and bought us things, but it was one of those things that, while I thought I knew, I dared not look straight at the truth. I always wanted there to be doubt, always there to be the possibility that it wasn't what I thought it was.

Mr. Volaire held out his hand again.

Dad's shoulders rose and fell with a deep breath. He shook the hand. "When do I start?"

Something about Mr. Volaire's smile made me inwardly wince. There was no warmth in it. It looked like he was happy he got what he wanted. He beckoned Dad over to the shiny car as my least favorite classmate headed right for us.

Gwen's gaze shifted from her father to me, to finally on Bela. Gwen's too-pretty face lit up and she hurried over. "Good morning, Mrs. Evers," she said and crouched so she was eye-to-eye with my sister. "Hi, Bela. Welcome to your first day of school. Love your dress. You look very pretty."

Bela's brows knotted together and she sucked on a finger, her telltale sign that she was seeing or sensing something none of us could.

Mom placed a hand on Bela's shoulder. "Bela, what do we say to people who say something nice to us?"

"Thank you. You're Gwen."

Gwen's eyes widened. "How'd you know that?"

"Grandma told me." Bela let go of Dad's leg and hugged Gwen.

Eyes wide, Gwen hugged my sister back, backpack

and all. She looked up. "Mrs. Evers, I love your daughter."

Mom laughed. "She does have that effect on people."

Gwen's smile shifted to a triumphant sneer. She gave my sister one more squeeze, flattening the front of her expensive white summer dress before straightening up.

Vergo pawed my leg. "What did I say about not letting others see how they make you feel?"

I pointedly stared out into the desert and let out a huff. He was right. It was really annoying how often he was right.

Gwen waved at Bela and disappeared into the throng of students and teachers.

"She's sad a lot," Bela said, her face serious.

Mom and I exchanged surprised looks before turning to my sister. "Why?" Mom said.

"With parents like that, I'm not surprised," Vergo said.

"Grandma didn't say." As if suddenly remembering something, she turned around and hugged Mom's legs. "I'm off to school, now. I love you, Mommy."

Mom barely got a chance to pat Bela's head before my sister took my hand and led us into the throng of excited middle school and elementary students. Mom yelled something about me taking good care of my sister. This was going to be an interesting school year.

Chapter 8

Bela left me for the Kindergarten teacher without so much as a goodbye. It stung. She'd shown Gwen, someone she'd met for the first time, more affection than she did toward her own big sister.

I did my best to stuff down my pain with one deep, controlled breath after another as Vergo trotted along beside me. Shoes, legs, and clothes passed through him as if he wasn't there, reminding me he was a spirit animal and not the real thing. It was so easy to forget despite not having to feed him or clean a litter box every day. He felt real and solid, interacted with the physical world by using doorways and whatnot. I'd even given him a good beating with my pillow the first time we met on this side of his existence. The sight of people walking through him made me clench my teeth. It wasn't right.

I distracted myself by focusing on the main office

building, breaking away from the masses and veering down the sidewalk that led straight to the nurse's office. Nurse Kor never improved over the rest of the school year. She'd always appeared tired, but smiled every time she saw me, so I made it a routine to greet her every morning before heading off to homeroom. It seemed to give her an energy boost every time.

I pulled open the metal door and stopped. At first, I thought all the lights were off, but then the darkness sped off along the walls and ceiling, like someone had pulled back a black sheet to reveal the lights and wood-paneled walls. The darkness turned the corner and disappeared.

Vergo studied the ceiling. "Well, that shouldn't be here."

"What was that?"

"I'd say another demon, but my ability to identify them ended when I crossed over. What did you feel?"

I'd felt nothing until I'd spotted it, and then I'd been hit by a wave of terror that passed as quickly as the shadow disappeared. It'd happened so fast. I shook my head.

Gagging from inside the nurse's office galvanized me into motion. We darted inside and the vines and creepers blanketing the walls shivered in greeting. I ran past her desk, something most students weren't allowed to do, but Nurse Kor had made an exception for me. I stopped outside the bathroom. A woman in white scrubs clung to the porcelain sink and hunched over it as another bout of gagging hit her. Her light brown hair was swept back in a bun that trembled with every gag.

A large man stood next to her with a wrinkled hand on her back. I inhaled sharply. "Sanctus Bylan." His aged, grandfatherly face turned. His brows rose with recognition, but he held up a finger and turned back to Nurse Kor, who spit out some phlegm and turned on the faucet. Nausea hit me as I listened to her clear her throat several times, but at last she sighed and straightened up.

Sanctus Bylan said, "Amity, how long has this been going on?"

Nurse Kor filled a paper cup with water. "Not long," she said with a shake of her head. "I think it's allergies. Everything's starting to bloom now that monsoon season is almost over."

Vergo said, "She hasn't been the same since the day of my crossing. Something isn't right."

Sanctus Bylan placed a hand on the nurse's shoulder. "Have you been to the doctor at all this year?"

She nearly choked on her water with a stifled laugh. "I'm a nurse. Why would I?"

"You and I both know better than to self-diagnose."

Nurse Kor narrowed her eyes at her reflection in the mirror. It looked shadowed, but the bathroom light was off and only modest sunlight came in through a small window. She jerked her head back as she downed a paper cup of water. "I'm fine. It's just allergies." She turned around and came to an abrupt halt when she noticed me. Her eyes widened. "Mia. Hello. Welcome to a new school year." She wrapped me in a hug. I braced for an unnatural aura to needle at my senses, but it was her and the smell of flowers. "Who's your new homeroom teacher?"

"Mr. Gauss." I'd already memorized my bell schedule and, during summer break, visited all my classes so I wouldn't get lost. The event had been led by the Youth Luxion Society, a bunch of really smart high schoolers who did a bunch of clubs and sports, along with volunteer work.

Nurse Kor inhaled and clamped her hands together under her chin. "Oh, my gosh. You're so lucky. Just about every female teacher has a crush on him. He's new and we all got to meet and greet the new staff over the summer. He's so charming and dreamy, and I hear he's a good math teacher, too. I don't know how he's still single." Another coughing fit struck and she rushed back to the bathroom, Sanctus Bylan barely getting out of the doorway in time.

He and I exchanged worried looks. Vergo hopped onto one of the sick beds and curled his tail around his paws. "There was a shadow outside this room a moment ago. It fled when we opened the door."

Sanctus Bylan furrowed his brows, making his face even more wrinkly. "I didn't sense anything." He groped around the sick bed until he found Vergo. He removed the collar. "Ah, there you are."

Vergo shook his head, catlike and making a sound like a person rapidly shuffling cards. "Neither did we. I would've dismissed it as a shadow had it not taken a ninety-degree turn at the end of the hallway."

The gagging stopped long enough for the nurse to ask. "Who's that?" Her voice was tense with alarm.

Sanctus Bylan said, "A spirit cat. He's harmless."

"Harmless?" Vergo said indignantly, stamping a paw, but then he remembered himself. "Anyway, either we have a very weak demon lurking among us or a very powerful one who's adept at concealment."

"I'm more inclined to believe the former," Sanctus Bylan said, bringing his hands together, which disappeared inside his voluminous sleeves. "Would you agree that an adept demon wouldn't have been sloppy enough to allow you to catch a glimpse?"

"Unless that was on purpose," Vergo said, inclining his head. "I made similar moves in my days. It's a great intimidation tactic, and it often unbalances your target."

The priest considered Vergo's words and the hacking stopped. "You're certain of what you saw?"

"Yes."

The priest looked at me and I nodded, saying, "The whole hallway was black, until I opened the door wide enough." Sure, there was that momentary blindness when transitioning from bright sunlight to an indoor place lit up by magical means, but Vergo was right about the shadow moving like it had a mind of its own. Where had it run off to?

"There's no proof that it's connected to me," Nurse Kor said loudly, her voice echoing in the bathroom.

"That appears to be true," the priest said. "But I'd rather we figure out if it's related to Amity's supposed allergies, or if the Demon King has sent a replacement to haunt this property." He turned to Vergo. "He would do such a thing, yes?"

"We demons...I mean, demons can't enter the mortal plane without an invitation. It can be deliberate, like a summoning, or it can be accidental."

I said, "Darks have to be in control of their emotions at all times. We attract dark things if we're not careful. Maybe it's my fault."

"And maybe it's not," Vergo said. "So can non-Darks. They're weaker anchors, but a soul that remains troubled long enough opens themselves to the same entities."

"Is illness a form of trouble?" Sanctus Bylan said.

"No. It's all negative emotions." Vergo tilted his head. "So if you didn't know about the shadow thing, then may I ask what brings you to this school? I thought you worked at Buckeye Hospital."

Sanctus Bylan clenched his jaw. "My duties have changed."

Nurse Kor reappeared, redoing her twisted bob, securing it with two wooden sticks. She stopped at the sight of Vergo, her hands over her head. "Oh, my. A cat."

"Greetings, madame," Vergo said politely.

Her eyes widened. "It talks."

I quickly explained Vergo to the nurse. She cringed when I revealed that this was Allosyr, but relaxed when Sanctus Bylan assured her that Vergo couldn't harm anyone.

"You make me sound as useful as a dust bunny," Vergo said in a deadpan voice.

Nurse Kor snorted. "I like him like this. He's so cute." She reached out to pet him and her hand passed through. She recoiled, gasping.

"That's better." Vergo sat up straighter and faced the Light priest. "So what happened after we left the Order of Leo? That old crone was most unpleasant."

Nurse Kor leaned closer and lowered her voice. "This conversation is best left for another time. We don't think the school knows the whole truth."

Sanctus Bylan said, "I think Mia deserves to know the whole truth." He headed for the door. "Come with me."

"I'll catch you later, Mia," Nurse Kor said louder. "Enjoy seventh grade."

We waved to each other and Vergo and I followed the Light priest into his office, which sat across from the nurse's office. It was a miniature version of what he'd had back in Marohu, minus the giant window. He had fewer plants and books, but he'd stuffed his herb cabinet in the other half of the room somehow.

He took a seat in the chair wedged between the wall and desk, squeezing his barrel shape into the small space that somehow fit him comfortably. I shut the door and took a seat in one of the two old wood chairs in front of his desk.

Sanctus Bylan rang a bell that sounded far louder and deeper than its lemon-sized frame should've been able to produce. An energy rippled through the air, making it feel heavier. This reminded me of the time Ms. Weever had rung a small gong in her office after she'd pulled me out of the demon realm. It removed the risk of eavesdroppers.

Placing his elbows on the desk, he interlaced his fingers and fixed me with a serious gaze. "They say no good deed goes unpunished. Your deed with the demon certainly was not met with the proper praise."

"I don't want their praise," I said automatically, looking away. The words rang both false and true. I wanted people to like me, but at the same time, I wished they'd all leave me alone, except Deren, Nurse Kor, Sanctus Bylan and such, but people like Gwen and her friends. I wished that, if they were never going to like me, then they should at least leave me alone.

"They should learn to praise you," he said calmly. "You deserve kindness as much as everyone else. Society clearly has forgotten that."

"They've forgotten for a long, long time," Vergo

said. "The Necromancers War was not sparked out of boredom."

"Those people crossed a very bad line they shouldn't have."

Vergo puffed up his little chest. "And who forced us to cross it?"

"Those Darks crossed it themselves."

"Because Lights were on a crusade to eliminate every last Dark."

Sanctus Bylan opened his mouth to retort, but stopped.

Vergo said, "Sir, whatever your history books say, they likely report a very different unfolding of events."

"And you were there?"

"Yes, I'm that old." He hopped onto the desk. "And yes, Darks did despicable things that justify society's sentiment towards them, but both sides need to fix this imbalance."

"Agreed. We'll have to save this discussion for another time, though. Mia has only so long before the bell rings."

Vergo inclined his head.

Sanctus Bylan glanced at his wrist. "I thought it was supposed to ring a couple of minutes ago. Maybe that starts tomorrow." He fixed his aged gaze on me. "Anyway. Mia, you're wise beyond your years, and I believe you have a right to know what happened to me and why." He pursed his lips. "The Order of Leo expelled me a few months after Bela's alignment manifested. And then, over the summer, this school district offered me a post here. When one door closes, another opens. It's a pay cut, but us Light Priests are overpaid, self-absorbed fools anyway." He let out a weary sigh as he toyed with a stack of papers. "They severely disapproved of my decision to dance with demons. If I had left it at that, I would've received no more than a demotion, but the Order leader and I had a big argument in front of the rest of the committee. They concluded that the Light had left me. Instead of trying to save my soul, they deemed it prudent to get rid of me. I'm Bylan now. Alexander Bylan."

Vergo tilted his head. "The Light Order turning their back on one of their own? That's unusual, even for them."

"Things aren't like they used to be. The world has become a terribly unbalanced placed, despite our concerted efforts. I've been blind to it until now. I believe my expulsion is a blessing in disguise."

"Any Dark could've pointed this out to you long ago. The Light Order is full of themselves. They eliminate anyone who says otherwise."

Sanct…Bylan. Mr. Bylan? Nah, that sounds weird. Bylan narrowed his eyes, but then he closed them as his body rose and fell with a resigned sigh. "I don't think I would've been capable of believing you had this not happened to me. Light schools do a very thorough job of brainwashing you over the years."

"Then how did you break free of the brainwashing? You wouldn't have helped our Little One here if they'd done a thorough job on you."

"I've always been a curious fellow. I grew up with scraped knees and one question or another on the tip of my tongue. Teachers got impatient with me sometimes, so I turned to books for answers. The older ones are written far differently than others. I asked about that, too, but was told that times had changed. While I found that logic sound, the old ways in those books stuck with me, but they eventually got buried in my studies on healing arts. Meeting Mia here rekindled that curiosity. Our working together to send you to the Light confirmed their validity."

"Are you saying that Lights and Dark are supposed to work together?" Vergo sounded incredulous.

"Yes," Bylan said calmly. "I…I'm getting used to the idea as well. But the crossover ritual specifically stated the need for both a Light and a Dark to be successful."

"You were barely successful," Vergo said bluntly.

Bylan glanced at me before returning his attention to the cat. "What matters is we succeeded."

"Don't mind me if I don't shower you with praise and gratitude."

"You may in time. Perhaps not in my lifetime, but one day."

"Right," Vergo said sarcastically.

There were a firm trio of knocks on the door. Sanctus Bylan—I mean Bylan—touched the bell he'd rung and the concern on his face softened to curiosity. Hand wrapped around the metal, he rang it, but it made a muted clacking. The heaviness lifted.

"Come in," Bylan said.

The door swung inward and Ms. Weever stuck her head inside, and then fully stepped in when her icy blue eyes found me. She raised an eyebrow. "Welcome back, Miss Evers. Shouldn't you be in class by now?"

I gave a noncommittal shrug. "The bell hasn't rung yet."

My tutor thought a moment and shrugged. She closed the door behind her. "What's the nature of the conversation I interrupted?"

Bylan sat up straight. "I'm sharing the nature of my new position, among a few tangents. You look concerned. What is it?"

She held up a white piece of cloth with a trio of protective runes painted on it. "Something's here. Its presence activated only this ward. I don't know how. It should've activated others."

"Is that a motion ward?" Vergo said, a hint of derision in his otherwise polite voice.

"Yes," Ms. Weever said flatly.

"Those things are utterly useless. Any demon would set off a dozen other wards before that one."

"And yet our guest in question did the exact opposite." She stuffed the cloth away in a pouch.

"What does this mean?" Bylan said. "Another demon? We're worried about Amity."

"As we all should be. She was right outside the classroom during your crossover ritual when the worst of the worst showed up. I know he did something to her, but I dare not guess what."

"Can we even do anything to reverse what the Demon King did?"

Vergo snorted. "Good luck with that."

Ms. Weever approached the desk, her high heels clunking on the wood with every slow step. She put her fists on her hips. "You know more about him than any of us, than any book or tale. Clearly you can be more helpful than sarcasm."

Vergo looked up at her with his blue eyes. "There have been demons before my time that have tried to take the Demon King's place. Considering the nature of all the people that end up in his grasp, I think it's crossed all of our minds at one point. Wouldn't it be nice to be the ruler of such a realm?" He shook his head. "The Demon King isn't an entity so much as he is a force. You don't stop him any more than you stop the sun from rising. Your beloved nurse friend is his plaything now. I'm sorry. Fight it if you must. Mitigate the damage, but this battle is already lost." He hopped back onto the chair beside me.

"Spoken like a true coward," Ms. Weever said.

"By all means, prove me wrong. I'd love to see someone take his ego down a notch. But I ask you this: how do you stop there being a shadow where there is no light?"

The bell preceding the intercom emitted from the sound stone positioned above the office door. "Attention students and staff," sounded the stiff voice of Mr. Redd. "Please have all students report to their homeroom now. The bell didn't go off when it should have. We're looking into the issue. We will verbally cue transitions in the interim. Thank you."

Ms. Weever fixed Vergo with her icy stare and reached for the doorknob. "See you in a few hours, Miss Evers." She left, leaving the door open.

I slid off my chair and slipped the collar back on Vergo.

"We'll figure something out," Bylan said, standing as well. "Have a good day."

I said a farewell and slipped out the door, slowing to get a good look inside the nurse's office. It was quiet. The vines and creepers didn't react to my distant presence. I desperately wanted to pop in real quick to make sure she was okay, but my feet carried me off to homeroom.

Chapter 9

The hallways went from crammed to empty as we all filed into our respective homerooms. I kept my head down and my face behind my hair. Deren was in another homeroom as we'd learned during the summer, much to our disappointment. I'd have to find him later. We'd hung out a few times when Mom found the willpower to drive me there. She and Dad had been too engrossed in my little sister. They weren't on the list of people I preferred to leave me alone.

I found the desk with my name on it. This teacher had laid them out in the standard grid formation. Some teachers preferred a semicircle, others two rows facing the middle, but most like to organize us in neat rows with enough room to walk down each aisle. I sat near the front on the window side, catching a glimpse of the sunny desert before hugging the backpack I set on my desk. Vergo climbed onto the countertop running the length of the room.

"Everyone back out in the hallway," said a stern male voice over the dozens of voices loudly chatting away. That had to be Mr. Gauss if he was yelling at us. "Let's try this again."

My classmates let out a collective groan and chatter picked back up as we all trudged out into the hallway. Vergo hopped off the countertop.

"Quietly."

I snuck a glance in the teacher's direction. He wore khaki pants, a belt, and sneakers, along with a white shirt. I kept my head low as I filed out into the hallway, backpack in my arms. Other teachers had made their students line up in the hallway, too.

"I could've gone without experiencing middle school again," Vergo said dryly.

My classmates quietly lined up along the wall. Mr. Gauss's towering frame filled the doorway, but the sunlight spilling in from the classroom and the four glass doors at the end of the hallway turned him into a dark silhouette. He took a deep breath and his voice effortlessly carried down the hallway. "When entering my classroom, you will do so quietly." He gestured to the front of the line and we filed inside. However, the first students started talking and laughing, and we shuffled backwards to make room for the front of the line. It took us two more tries as a group to quietly find our seats. The only sounds were our shuffling feet and creaking desks. Once the classroom door closed with all of us finally in it, including the teacher, I looked up.

I couldn't breathe.

Mr. Gauss was handsome—no, gorgeous. He was tall and muscly like my dad, but probably taller. His polo shirt stretched across his massive arms and broad chest and hung loosely around a narrow waist. He had short black hair swept to the side, handsome blue eyes, and…

Mr. Gauss smiled, revealing bright white teeth.

I inhaled as my heart pounded away, franticly beating as I tried to decide whether to run into his arms or out of the room. By the Light.

"Steady, Little One," Vergo said.

"I'm Mr. Gauss. Welcome to seventh grade and to your homeroom. This is my first year teaching at Toolena Mesa, but I spent several years in Marohu before finally getting to move out here. This is my hometown and I'm relieved to see it hasn't changed much over the years. My goal is to teach you some core math skills that lay the foundation for various careers in adulthood, along with helping you manage money well. Math is the art of problem solving, and it can teach you that there's always a solution if you're willing to work out a problem."

Well, my problem was the inability to breathe, along with this sudden rapid thumping in my awfully warm ears. I hugged my backpack harder, until something black filled my vision. It had four furry legs. Vergo. He blocked my view of Mr. Guass, allowing me to grab a lungful of air.

"Did I really just witness you develop a crush on your math teacher?"

"No!" Even I could hear the denial in my voice.

The rest of the room fell silent, including Mr. Gauss, who scrunched his brows together.

"No, what, Miss…?" He eyed my name card. "Miss Evers."

Oh, dear gods. I'd said that out loud. Like, really loud. I hunched lower in my chair, until I could barely see over my backpack. Everyone was looking at me, trying to figure out if I was a jerk or crazy. I clamped my mouth shut. There was nothing I could say to the teacher that sounded good.

A girl in the back of the room laughed, which was cut short by a snort. Everyone's attention shifted to the snort. Gwen sat in the back row with a hand over her mouth and nose, and her face a deep shade of red.

Vergo burst out laughing. "Serves her right."

"Okay," Mr. Gauss said calmly, "just so everyone's on the same page…if you have something you need to say or ask, raise your hand first. No one likes being interrupted. I expect everyone to behave respectfully towards everyone else in this room. I won't tolerate disrespect towards me or a classmate, understood?"

My classmates murmured their consent.

"When I ask a question like that, I expect a 'Yes, Mr. Gauss.' Now, let's try that again. Do we all understand to be respectful towards one another?" He held his hands out to us.

"Yes, Mr. Gauss," we said in unison.

He nodded. "Very good. Thank you."

Mr. Redd came on over the sound stones and began morning announcements with a stiff welcome that sounded anything but welcoming. He led us through the morning devotional prayer to the Light and the pledge to our country, and then worked through a list of announcements about upcoming events and fall sports.

Mr. Gauss handed out several sheets of paper. I stowed them all in my backpack without so much as looking at them. With the last of the papers noisily making their way from one side of the room to the other, our teacher leaned against his desk. His elbow bumped a wooden box standing with its back pressed against a stack of four paper trays, each labeled by class period. He slid the box back. One of its little doors popped ajar. He hastily latched it closed, propped himself back up, and scanned the room. "This school has a lot of programs to offer and I would love it if every last one of you got involved. I know this is only homeroom and not math class yet, but I want to say this now. As an incentive, you can earn extra credit for playing sports, participating in clubs, and even doing volunteer work. Math isn't always easy for everyone, and it's got a reputation for being everyone's least favorite subject, but I hope encouraging you to get active outside the classroom helps you look forward to being in my class."

Part of me would've loved to take a stab at sports, but it was another opportunity for things to go wrong for a Dark. Besides, with the secret of my alignment out, it's not like anyone would put me on their team.

Mr. Gauss looked in my direction and dazzled me with his amazing smile. I inhaled as I daydreamed of me kicking a ball around a field with him watching, cheering me to score a goal. He stood on a sunny sideline with a bouquet of flowers. After I weaved through a few defenders and sent the ball flying, I scored the goal, cheers filled my head, and Mr. Gauss walked onto the field and wrapped me in a hug.

A paw pressed against my forehead.

"You're getting that look again—you and the rest of the girls in the room," Vergo said, amusement in his voice. "He is quite the tall, strong, and handsome type, isn't he?"

I clenched my jaw, biting back a retort. Vergo was being as annoying as my sister.

The cat flashed a fang, his way of smiling. "Ah, young love. Middle school might not be so dull after all." He turned to the front of the room. "I wonder how many hearts he'll break before the year is over."

The bell rang and I joined my classmates in heading for the door, sending Vergo tumbling with a rough yank of my backpack. He did a midair cartwheel, tried to catch himself on the counter, but slipped and plopped on the floor. He shook out his head.

"Ah, yes, teenage hormones. Now I remember how incurably grumpy children your age are."

Mr. Gauss stood outside the doorway, wishing everyone a good day as my classmates filed past. I stood near the back of the pack when Gwen and Sussi stopped next to me. Gwen looked cool and collected again as Sussi stood over us both with a nasty smile on her face.

"Don't think for one second that Mr. Gauss likes you," Gwen said in a low voice. "He already knows what you are. He's being nice because he has to. Do all the sports and clubs you want. It won't make a difference." She tossed her hair back and stood proudly. "Sussi and I are going to play bandyll. We're going to be every teacher's favorite."

"I don't care," I said flatly, which only garnered laughs.

"You just watch," Gwen said. "He's going to forget all about you. You're nobody. I'm a Volaire, daughter in the most powerful family west of Marohu."

Vergo crept over to Gwen's feet. "Please let me bite

her on your behalf. If you're not going to stand up for yourself, then allow me."

I turned away from the three of them and filed out into the hallway, losing myself in the noise of chatting students, footsteps on thin carpet, and glare of bright lights overhead. The world was a blur of clothes and shoes as I headed to my history class.

Part of me wanted to try out for bandyll to spite Gwen. I'd heard of the sport. Dad liked listening to it on the sound stone when we lived in Marohu, but I'd never seen it played. If I made it on the team and Gwen didn't, then I could rub it in her face, show her that she wasn't the best at everything, and maybe even Mr. Gauss would have a reason to like me for real.

But if I tried and failed? I'd never hear the end of it, never stop getting picked on for it. Everyone would laugh at me for trying to fit in and act normal.

No. It'd be better to let Gwen have her glory. I needed to get through the school year without getting in trouble or expelled.

I parked myself in the back of the line to my history class and kept my gaze on my shoes as the hallways slowly quieted. One student broke from the line and stood beside me.

"Hey, Mia," Deren said.

I looked up. There he was, wide ears, big smile and all. I couldn't help but smile back as the tightness in my chest relaxed, allowing me to breathe. "Hey, Deren. It's great to see you again." Was it ever.

His face went from happy to serious. He studied me with his dark eyes and my heart beat faster. A hand reached for my face and I froze, unable to process what was happening. He tucked a lock of hair behind my ear, his touch gentle, tentative, but determination filled his rounded face. "You look sad again." Before I knew what was happening, he had his arms around me. He gave me a good squeeze and let go quickly, taking the scent of mesquite with him.

I stood there, stunned, my brain not quite sure what to make of the gesture. We'd only shook hands and playfully shoved each other around a little before. I'd never had a friend hug me. It was…it was nice.

Deren's smile grew awkward. He rubbed the back of his neck and his cheeks grew pink. "Er, uh, you looked like you needed a hug."

I fumbled for words. "Thanks. Yeah." The silence stretched between us. "Thanks." I thought of hugging him back, but our history teacher, Mrs. Livy, ushered us inside under her heavily eye-shadowed scrutiny. Her eyelids were painted a deep purple and she wore matching lipstick. She was a stout lady with black hair pulled back in a thick braid, but she held herself in a way that subdued all of us to silence. This was not a teacher to make angry.

When the classroom door closed behind us, thoughts of Gwen's nasty comments slowly got drowned out by the memory of Deren's hug playing over and over in my mind.

***

Despite all the time I'd spent with Ms. Weever so far, I still got nervous every time I entered her office. Despite all we'd been through and even me being angry with her for a while last year, she still intimidated me. She held me to higher standards than any teacher ever had, and I couldn't help but try to meet them. Her rare smiles and spare compliments were two of the most rewarding things in the world.

Air sprites danced in my stomach as I opened the heavy wooden door to Ms. Weever's office. The smell of pine and mint greeted me as Ms. Weever made notes in a leather-bound notebook. She glanced at the small clock on her desk.

"Right on time. Very good." She finished writing a thought needed recording and dropped the pen in the center fold. "You'll find that last year was easy compared to what you need to learn this year. We'll revisit some basics, but Bylan and I agree you're going to have to constantly push the limits of your skills. Whatever the Demon King's done to Miss Kor, and whoever he's planted here, you and I both have our work cut out for us." She wore her typical black leather getup, a gorgeous corset, and knee-length boots, and fixed me with her icy, blue-eyed gaze. "Your inexperience puts you at great risk of becoming possessed, which makes you a danger to yourself and everyone around you."

My stomach dropped to my feet. Just when I thought I was getting strong and able to take care of myself, Ms. Weever's words shredded my confidence into tiny pieces. I could almost see it flutter to the ground like bits of paper.

"Chin up," Ms. Weever said firmly. "Face the challenge head-on. You've shown an aptitude for harnessing your alignment and you possess courage. Focus on your need to protect yourself and others. Respect the fact that this is dangerous, but don't let it discourage you. You can't afford to fail. Do I make myself clear?"

"Yes, ma'am," I said more confidently than I felt. I

met her stern gaze as her praise sank in. She thought I was a good, courageous Dark. I couldn't let her down. I had to make her proud. "I'm ready to start learning."

A hint of a smile touched the corner of her mouth, her lips crisply lined with red lipstick. She crossed to the piano nestled in the far side of her office and picked up the violin resting atop it. "We'll be skipping straight to violin. You're going to need it. Bells and pipes aren't powerful enough, and you can't lug around a piano."

I accepted the instrument and bow. It was so light, almost weightless. A pair of protection runes decorated the face, one on either side of the hollow center. They glowed when I touched a string.

"I've placed runes on your violin to make sure you don't accidentally do anything wrong," Ms. Weever brushed a second violin sitting atop the piano with her fingertips and faced me. "The strings are also made of simple steel, the wood has been blessed by Bylan, and the sound post is made of red alder for extra protection. Right now, it's just an instrument. You either make music, or you make ears bleed."

"There'll be a lot of the latter," Vergo said plainly. "I shall be outside today." He trotted through the door like the spirit he was, fur melding with wood as if he were walking into a shadow.

I shivered. I needed to open and close the door to satisfy my need to complete what should've happened.

"Yes, there'll be a lot of the latter at first. This isn't an easy instrument to learn, and it's even harder to master, but you need this tool."

"I understand."

"I've gotten it approved to have your one of your electives changed so you're in orchestra class."

I gave her a blank look.

"We can't waste lessons on the basics of violin. You'll get that from your new music teacher. Instead, we'll be focusing on what a Dark can do *with* a violin." She waved for me to back up. I parked myself by the door, leaving the width of the office between us. She stood in the center of the room. "The most powerful Darks can conjure a circle with a mere thought and wave of a hand." She held out a hand level with her face, concentrating on it, and then spread her fingers with a sudden jerk. White light shot out and lined the floor in a perfect circle. It glowed and hummed. It was a basic circle with four runes, yet it had power. Ms. Weever swung her hand downwards and the circle vanished with a sigh, taking its pressure with it. My ears strained to hear the hum that was no longer there.

"That's the best I can do. You'll be well into adulthood before you can do the same. It requires intense concentration and visualization, but I'm sure you can imagine the advantages of being able to act so quickly."

I nodded and then remembered my manners. "Yes, ma'am."

"However, before that day comes." Ms. Weever retrieved the violin and nestled it under her chin. "Every circle has a song—not exactly one you would perform before an audience, but a song nonetheless. Each rune has been translated into a note or series of notes." She played an ascending chord, and then reset her bow over the strings. She played the same three notes three times in a row. I pictured the gait of a galloping horse to match the notes. She followed with a descending series of notes in a higher octave before returning to the trio of notes.

On the second run through, her circle formed around her, lines and curves forming in time with her music. White and purple light shined all around her feet, and the hum returned with an intensity that made me back up a step. The circle complete, Ms. Weever stopped playing, holding her bow at the ready. The circle's breeze lifted her golden curls off her shoulders.

The power circle had a ring of runes lining the inside, all protection ones I recognized. The more triangular-shaped ones made me think of the trio of galloping notes. The more curved ones that followed paralleled the series of descending notes. The protection incantation was repeated four times, the same number of times she'd played the musical phrase. Whoever had first figured out how to translate runes into music was a genius.

My tutor looked at me, the circle's light casting shadows on her face that made her look otherworldly, an angel standing in light and shadow. "You need to be able to do this. And soon. Very soon."

Chapter 10

By the end of the first week of school, I had a violin in addition to a cat and backpack to bring home every day. My orchestra teacher, Mrs. Sterling, was nice enough. She'd been nervous around me at first, but got over my alignment as her need to teach the dozen of us students how to not make ears bleed took over. We sounded like a bunch of hoarse crows, but every now and then we hit a few notes that sounded whole and pleasing. My fingers hurt from not being used to playing a string instrument, my arms were sore from holding the violin and bow up, and my back was sore from trying to maintain a rigid posture. The only upside to all this was that I already knew how to read sheet music thanks to learning to play an mbira.

Also by the end of the week, Bela was accustomed to riding the bus to and from school with me. She babbled away about school and Bylan to me or bugged the students sitting across the aisle, allowing me to sneak in a few pages of my Yuna book.

Yuna was learning how to dual wield axes now that her leg was healed enough to move around. Recovering from the injury slowed her down, but she had a bigger problem ahead of her. In order to defeat the crystal serpents, she needed the help of a sorcerer who lived on top of a mountain. He didn't like visitors, so he'd magicked the air to repel anyone who tried to reach him by air. Yuna whad to climb the mountain, and that meant learning how to wield weapons that could also be used as climbing tools.

Yuna had made up her mind to climb the mountain despite the satyrs' protests when my sister and I hopped off the bus and headed down the dirt road leading to our house. Yuna wasn't fully healed, but after the serpent attacked a nearby village, she decided she couldn't wait any longer.

A few houses lay between the bus stop and our house. Most of our neighbors had farm animals, including goats, dogs, cows, and desert chickens, which were my favorite. The chickens had crested tails that rose above them to provide the rest of their bodies shade, and they came in a variety of colors. One neighbor had half a dozen desert chickens, each one with a different color tail. Today, they ignored us as we walked by their fence. I wanted to coax them over with a piece of tortilla I'd saved from lunch, but Bela plowed forward on her little legs, leaving me with no choice but to follow. Neighbors let their dogs roam the neighborhood and Bela was afraid of most of them.

The smell of herbs and flowers greeted us as we reached the front door flanked on both sides by a colorful garden. We'd spent the summer as a family coaxing all the herbs from the soil and the flowers bloomed and gave off wonderful scents that kept most pests at bay while attracting bees and the rare desert sprite.

One such sprite flew off on transparent wings. I caught only a glimpse of its humanoid beetle form before I lost it in the matching brown of the desert.

Vergo followed its movements, ears pricked forward. "Well, there's a rare sight. When I was alive, we considered sprites a sign of good fortune."

"Are they?" My hopes rose. I needed all the good fortune I could get.

Vergo watched the desert a moment longer before turning his attention to the flowers. "Just an old wives tale. The reality is that sprites in general are hard to spot. You make your own luck." He looked up at me. "Don't wait for outside forces to magically fix your life. That's not how life works, Little One."

Outside forces sure did a good job of making life harder, but I kept the sour comment to myself, not wanting my parents to overhear me talking to Vergo. They accepted his existence because of Bela, but they rarely stayed in the same room as him despite how much Bela liked him.

The front door popped open as Bela reached for the knob. Mom and Dad stood framed in the doorway, all smiles at my sister. Dad scooped her up and Bela giggled.

"Daddy."

Mom took off Bela's backpack and hugged them both. "Welcome home, Bela. How was school?" The three of them disappeared deeper inside the house. The door slowly swung to almost closed.

I stood on the porch, a sheet of wood propped several inches off the ground, and stared at the sliver of shadow that separated door from frame.

Vergo stood beside me. "Um, hello? You have two daughters."

As if someone heard him, the door swung wide. Mom pulled me into a hug. "Welcome home, too, Mia." The light cheerfulness sounded forced, tight, like she realized she'd forgotten me and was trying to cover up embarrassment. "Why are you still out here. It's hot." She led me inside by the hand.

Okay, she willingly held my hand. And she'd come back for me. All was forgiven. I eagerly followed her into the living room, where Dad stood, Bela in his arms. He wore a bunch of clothes I'd never seen before: a long sleeve shirt with reflective bands around the wrists, an orange vest with more reflective bands, thick boots, jeans without holes, and a hardhat with the Volaire crest on it. Bela removed his safety glasses and put them on herself, making her look like a bug with big round, clear eyes.

"Look, I'm you, Daddy. Now, I can go to work, too."

"Not without a hardhat." He placed his hat on Bela's head and it swallowed her down to her shoulders. Muffled giggles came out of the hat as her two little hands reached for it.

"It's too big."

"Well, you'll have to grow into it." He set his hat on the coffee table and sat on the couch with her on his lap.

I took a few steps closer, unsure of how close to

get. "Hi, Dad. Those your new work clothes?"

He transferred his happy gaze from Bela to me. I checked for any signs of anger or fear, but no new lines formed on his face. "Hi, Mia. Yes, they are. I start Monday. I'll be gone before you get up for school, but I'll be home around this time every day. We'll get to be more of a family."

I smiled back. Dad was acting like the father I barely remembered before my alignment manifested. Maybe the sprite was a sign of good luck after all.

Vergo said, "Now, where has this version of your father been all this time?"

I didn't know or care. If we were going to be a real family again, that's all that mattered.

"Mia, come help me make dinner," Mom said while studying our fridge's contents.

I rushed to my bedroom and dropped all my things on my bed, and rushed back into the kitchen to help with dinner, a fresh smile loosening up my stiff cheeks.
***

I pecked at my enchiladas while Mom and Dad fussed over Bela as she talked about learning the alphabet and counting to ten. I listened in silence from my secluded end of the table. I sat opposite the head of the table, Dad across from me with Mom and Bela scooted as close to him as possible without getting tangled in the table legs.

Bela held up a fist, wore her squinty concentration face, and then held up one finger after another. "One, two, three, four, five...n-nine?"

"Nope, try again," Mom said with a smile.

"Ten?"

"Nope, now you're guessing," Dad said. "What

comes after five?"

She counted again, tapping a fingertip with each number, and then stuck out her other thumb and stared at it.

"Six," I said.

Bela's eyes welled with tears. "I knew what it was. Don't tell me what to say." She buried her face in Dad's arm. Mom and Dad glared.

Mom said, "Mia, you know better than that. Give your sister a chance to figure it out herself."

I was trying to help. The words caught in my throat. It was probably better that I didn't say anything else. I'd probably be told to stop helping, that I wasn't helping, that I was upsetting my sister and so on. I pecked at my food in silence as my sister successfully counted to ten over and over, much to our parents' delight. By her billionth repetition, I mumbled something about having homework to do. Either they didn't hear me or they chose to ignore me. I dragged my plate off the table, creating a wooden rumble like a marble rolling across the floor. Dad looked askance in my direction before encouraging Bela to recite as much of the alphabet as she could. Vergo followed me into my room.

"I would advise you to stop trying so hard to get their attention right now. Let them get used to having a child starting school. This is an age where your sister needs all the positive reinforcement she can get to develop a love of learning and a suffocating amount of encouragement to build confidence in herself. I'm sure they did the same to you before your alignment manifested."

I couldn't remember anymore. I could only recall

moments of pure joy and delight, snippets of smiles and hugs, my parents' voices full of pride and praise. "Probably, but I was the only child at the time. Now, it's Bela this, Bela that, Bela everything. They didn't even remember me when we came home."

"Your mother doubled back for you."

"And Dad did nothing."

Vergo tilted his head. "I do agree both of them could've handled the moment with more grace and compassion, but at least your father spoke in a perfectly contented voice after you said hi to him."

Why did Vergo have to keep poking holes in my logic? Everything felt like I'd been wronged. Their actions upset me. How was it not right for me to feel upset? "I wanted to be able to tell them about my day, too," I said in a small voice.

"You can tell me about your day."

"You were there." I sat on my bed, eyeing my backpack, which was stuffed with way too much homework. "Besides, I don't like you."

Vergo sat in front of my feet. I looked away. A paw touched my shin. "Little One, we're stuck together for only the Light knows how long. Perhaps it would be best if we learned how to better get along."

"Then stop saying so many mean things." I hugged myself, my stomach hurting and eyes burning. No, stupid tears. Go away.

"What things are you construing as mean?"

Hearing a big word I didn't know, I looked at him, but then looked away. I didn't want to look at him. I didn't want to talk to him either. It wasn't like I had much of a choice. He was right. We were stuck together indefinitely. "What's 'construing' mean?" I said in my best "I hate you, but I want to learn something" voice.

"Interpreting or understanding things in a certain way."

His furry figure scooted closer. I pointedly looked at the wall. "Just about everything you say."

"Like?"

Everything, you stupid cat. I kept the thought to myself. There was no point. I couldn't shoo him away like a mundane ghost. I filed through all of our more recent exchanges. "Like when we got home and you told me to stop waiting for the world to fix my life or whatever."

"Okay," he said.

"And when you said to let people hate me. And when you made fun of me in Mr. Gauss's class on the first day of school."

Vergo thought a moment. "Okay, perhaps that one wasn't called for." He mumbled something about something being amusing. "Little One, young one, with exception of the math teacher comment, the other things were truths, lessons I hope you learn sooner than later, so growing up isn't so rough for you."

"You can't make growing up easier by telling me what to say, do, or think. I'm a Dark. People hate me for what I am. There's nothing I can do to change that."

"You're right," Vergo said.

I'd expected him to say another sarcastic remark, but there was a patience in his blue-eyed gaze that reminded me of my teachers.

"But you're also wrong."

"How can I be right and wrong at the same time?"

"Simple. It's called a paradox. You're right that I can't make growing up any easier for you, and you're right that you can't change the fact that people hate you for being a Dark. But do these things mean you have to live in hate-filled misery for the rest of your life? Not at all."

"How, if I can't change them?"

"Simple: you change yourself."

"I can't change my alignment."

Vergo's chest rose and fell with a sigh. "Perhaps you are too young. You are most certainly wise beyond your years, but some forms of wisdom simply come with age and experience. I apologize for bringing it up." He hopped onto the foot of my bed. "I'll let you get to your homework unimpeded now."

He licked a paw and washed behind his ears. His eyes went wide as he realized he was behaving entirely like a cat. He swore at himself and curled into a ball.

"Curse the Light for making me act like a cat, too."

I wasn't ready to start my homework and a part of me wanted to know what wisdom he was talking about. Curiosity winning over the need to do homework, I inhaled, bracing for a potential berating. "What wisdom?"

Vergo looked over his back at me. "I'm honestly not sure if you're ready to understand such a lesson, helpful as it would be."

"Will it really make growing up easier?"

"It can, yes."

"Then what is it?"

"All right." He rolled so he sat like a sphinx, facing me. "As much as neither of us like the Light and its teachings, there is one thing that's true for everyone: one must embrace the strength to accept what we can change, have the courage to accept what we cannot change, and gain the wisdom to know the difference. No truer words have been spoken."

"I don't get it."

"It's a fancy way of saying that there are things in life you can change, things you can't, and you'll be a lot happier if you know what you can and can't change so you don't waste time and energy on things that won't bring you happiness."

"So it's stuff I have to do?" I turned so I sat facing him.

"Yes. It's an empowering bit of wisdom from the Light." He sat up. "You can't change the fact that you're a Dark. That will never change. But does this mean you're powerless to be happy? No. You can choose to accept this truth and even embrace it, or you can hate this truth and your hate will make you miserable."

"But I'm not happy being a Dark."

"Your alignment saved Deren's life several months ago."

"He only needed saving because of you."

He bared his fangs and squinted his eyes, grimacing. "Yes, I was quite the nasty piece of work. Anyway, you couldn't change the fact that my demon self enjoyed torturing and killing humans. What you were able to change was my ability to influence the living realm. Instead of standing there and yelling at me to stop being so mean, you found a way to cross my soul over to the Light. By taking control of what you could change, you saved a life and many others that would've followed."

"I had to do something. He was my only friend."

"Right. Without realizing what you were doing,

you focused on what you could change and you changed it."

"But I had help every step of the way."

"And what did you do that motivated people to help you?"

My mind drew a blank. I shrugged.

"You made decisions that motivated people to like you, to see past your alignment, and get to know you for who you are. Remember your beloved nurse. She was terrified of you after learning about your alignment, but your actions helped her see beyond that, helped her see what kind of person you really are."

He was right. The nurse hadn't decided to like me out of pity. She saw my genuine desire to help save Deren and even risked getting fired for it by driving me to the hospital without permission.

"If it helps to hear, your parents do love you. They have an odd way of showing it, but I think that's normal for any family. Parenting is no easier than growing up, but that's a topic for another day. Anyway, Little One, what do you want to change right now so you can be happier?"

I lowered my gaze, hiding behind my hair. "I want my parents to love me like they love Bela." The words came out before I could stop myself. As much as I'd been thinking about this lately, I hadn't said anything. What could I say?

"So what can *you* do to help your parents show that they love you just as much?"

I shrugged again. How was I supposed to know? I wasn't a parent or an adult.

"Think on it."

I parked myself at my desk. "I need a break from

thinking about this kind of stuff." I dumped the entire contents of my backpack on my desk, which finally had four real legs. Two textbooks, several workbooks, and a bunch of papers spilled out, fanning across the wood surface. Ugh, why did teachers have to give so much homework? I sorted through the giant pile, organizing everything by subject. When I found my math stuff, I came across the flyer for bandyll tryouts, complete with a drawing of a player in a fully padded uniform and two big claws designed for scooping tied to each arm. I picked up the paper, rereading the part about extra credit and Mr. Gauss's love of sports.

I turned to Vergo, holding up the paper. Maybe this was my answer to everything. I'd never played bandyll before, but what if…?

He smiled at me.

Chapter 11

I hadn't wanted to say anything unless I made the team, but since tryouts were after school, I kind of needed to let my parents know I'd be taking the late bus. Violin and stupid heavy backpack sitting next to one foot and a spirit cat next to the other, I stood by the front door as Mom fussed over Bela's hair. It being Dad's first day of work at the mine, he was already gone.

"Mom?"

"Yes, sweetie?" she said without looking away from my sister.

I took a deep breath and my heart drummed against my chest. "I'm going to be taking the late bus home. I'm trying out for bandyll."

Mom let go of Bela's hair and turned her head so fast that I cringed. Surprise and delight brightened her face. "Really?" she said in a breathy voice tight with glee. "That would be wonderful. Your dad and I love bandyll. What position are you trying out for?"

She might as well have asked me to calculate the square root of 5004. "I…don't know. I'll try them all."

Mom gave Bela's hair one last stroke and clipped a flower above and behind one ear. She came over and went wide-eyed as she picked up my backpack. "Goodness. How much homework are they giving you?"

"A lot." I shouldered my backpack, the textbooks digging into my shoulders and pressing my feet into the floor.

"Anyway, follow your gut on which position feels right to you. You'll know it when you find it."

"How?"

She thought for a moment. "You'll want to focus more on what to do, instead of how to do it. I'm not sure how else to explain it." She tucked one of my bangs behind my ear. "I think you'll love bandyll. Go out there, give it your all, and make us proud."

"I will." Well, that settled it. I had to make the team. My determination turned the world into a blur until I reached homeroom and noticed Mr. Gauss's muscly figure standing by the door. Ducking my head, I replied to his greeting and hurried to my desk, my fluttering heart trying to lift me onto my tiptoes. This happened every time I got near him. The added weight of my backpack made the desk's legs creak as I shrugged it off. I took a seat and hid behind my pack.

Giggling in the back of the room drew my attention. Gwen sat with her friends, Sussi, Chibya, and Nonaya crowding her. She wore a sports jersey, matching skorts, and high-top sneakers, making her legs look enviously long as she sat with her ankles crossed and heels propped up on Sussi's desk. Sussi wore a matching jersey but looked boyish with her pixie haircut.

Gwen caught me looking at them and broke into a smug smile. "I so can't wait for tryouts today. Sussi and I are going to dominate everyone. They're so going to make us captains of the A team, and we'll get them that division champion trophy this year."

Sussi said, "I heard Toolena Mesa hasn't won it in years."

"That's because they didn't have us. We've played together for how long now? Five years? Six?"

"Six," Sussi said with a nod.

Nonaya caught me staring and glared. "What are *you* looking at? Mind your own business." She was pretty like Gwen, but had a narrow build that made her look super tiny. Still, no one picked on her for her size, not with Gwen guarding her at all times.

I rested my chin on one bulging side of my backpack. One of the rock-hard textbooks held my chin up.

"Remember, Nonaya," Gwen said, her voice dripping with superiority, "Sanctus Bylan told us all to be nice to everyone, even Darks. She has every right to hope and dream about making the bandyll team. Let her. She won't make it. I bet you she's never played before."

I clenched my teeth, tears stinging my eyes.

Vergo hopped onto my desk. "May I bite her for you now?"

I huffed and looked away. Why did I want on the bandyll team so bad? How was I supposed to make it when I had classmates who'd already played for years? This was stupid. I was stupid to think this idea would work. I wasn't going to be able to make my parents proud.

The morning bell rang and Mr. Gauss playfully rapped the backpack of a boy darting inside the room.

"Get back out there and walk in."

The boy rolled his eyes, but did as he was told before sitting at his desk. Mr. Gauss stood by the chalkboard to take notes during morning announcements, Mr. Redd's drawling voice taunting me with tryout reminders for all fall sports. Cross Country didn't require tryouts, but I didn't feel like running a billion miles a day only to fall behind everyone else. No, that sport wouldn't work, either.

Something hit me in the back of the head. I reached for my hair. Gwen and her friends all giggled behind their hands. A balled-up piece of paper lay near my feet. I kicked it away.

Mr. Gauss turned around, looking as handsome and happy as ever, oblivious to Gwen's nastiness. His gaze swept across the room. I could've sworn he made brief eye contact with me, but I *was* hiding behind a mountain of a backpack. "I want to remind all of you to join a club or sports team to not only get out there and enjoy something new, but so that you'll earn extra credit in my class."

Great. Clubs. Something I didn't have to try out for. I'd thrown away the paper because none of them caught my interest. Big mistake. I curled my toes in my shoes.

"On top of that, if you make a team, I'll come watch your games and root you on. I love sports and fostering school spirit." He held up a fist. "So, go, Miners!" A few boys echoed his cheer. "We'll work on that. I expect all of you to proudly cheer for this school before midterms." He turned back to the chalkboard.

Vergo's head perked up. "Mia, watch out. The little beast is about to pelt you again."

I turned. Something white arced through the air. I threw a hand up and my fingers reflexively closed around another paper ball. Holy crap. I'd caught it. I looked at the ball, and then at Gwen and the others. They mirrored my surprise.

Vergo said, "That was some impressive reflexes. I didn't know you could do that."

"I didn't either." As soon as the words left my mouth, I went wide-eyed. Oh, no. I'd spoken to an invisible cat again. I chucked the ball of paper and it sailed right through him.

"Really? That's the thanks I get for complimenting you?"

Someone in the back of the room inhaled. Gwen yelled, "Mr. Gauss, Mia's talking to demons."

Vergo narrowed his eyes. "If only I could show this class who the real demon in the room is."

I looked helplessly at Mr. Gauss, who stared with open shock. I sank lower in my chair as I registered everyone staring at me in horror. Here we go again.

Mr. Gauss said, "Miss Evers, is this true?"

I shook my head and kept my mouth clamped shut. The bell rang, telling us to head to our first class of the day. I gratefully shouldered my backpack and headed for the door, but Mr. Gauss politely put an arm on my shoulder before I could make good on my escape.

"I'll write you a late pass."

I hid behind my hair as the rest of my classmates filed out, shying away from me. Gwen and her friends held their tongues with our teacher nearby. They gave me a wide berth as well.

Once only me and Mr. Gauss were left in the room, he looked around. "Please tell me what's going on."

"Nothing," I said to the floor.

"Sanctus Bylan met with all the teachers and staff about what happened last year. He also mentioned the spirit cat that's with you." He looked around again. "Is there any way I'd be able to see it?"

Vergo and I looked at each other. He shrugged. "Sounds like the cat's already out of the bag." He hopped onto Mr. Guass's desk. "You have to do the honors. Whatever enchantments the priest put on this collar also block me from removing it myself."

I reached out to him, but stopped. Mr. Gauss watched me with open curiosity, not a hint of fear or hesitation anywhere. I removed the collar and Vergo shook out his head.

"By the Light. It is true."

Vergo looked up at him. "Like a Light priest of his caliber would lie about such things."

"And it talks."

Vergo's little shoulders rose and fell with a sigh. "Yes, I talk. Talking animals aren't exactly a novel concept."

Mr. Gauss stood next to me. "No, but this isn't something you experience every day, much less something anyone ever experiences. This is amazing."

"Little One, would you be so kind as to put the collar back on? I don't enjoy this attention."

Mr. Gauss chuckled. "I won't keep you two for

long." He gave me a studious look before retrieving the two balls of paper from near my desk. He hefted one of them like a baseball. "The floor was spotless before morning announcements, and now we have these near your desk. Is it safe to assume these aren't cat toys?"

"They most certainly are not," Vergo said indignantly. "I'm not a pet. I've been forced into this form. I didn't choose it. I'm no more a cat than you are."

Mr. Gauss gave one of the balls an underhand toss. Vergo's eyes locked on and he pounced before it could roll under the teacher's desk. He jerked back as he realized what he was doing. He swatted the ball under the desk and jumped back up. "That was entirely uncalled for."

"Nurse Kor says you purr, too."

Vergo growled and then went wide-eyed. "By the Light, that was pathetic. All right, I've had enough of this. Little One, I demand you put the collar on right this instant." He stamped a paw on the desk.

I smirked.

"All right, all right. I promise to leave you alone, spirit." Mr. Gauss smirked as well, but his tone was sincere.

"You better."

"Anyway, would either of you care to tell me what happened during announcements?"

I looked away from both of them. By the Light. Did he really expect me to tell him how the daughter of the most powerful family on this side of Marohu loved to pick on me? That would make me a tattletale. That was kindergarten stuff.

"Do I need to tell him, or will you?" Vergo said. He

watched me, all the bitterness and resentment gone. "This is a moment where you can change the course of things." Mr. Gauss gave Vergo a curious glance, but turned his attention back to me, expectant.

The words sat on the tip of my tongue, wanting out, but wanting to stay in. I took one deep breath after another, gearing up the courage to speak. What would happen if I finally spoke the truth? Word would get back to Gwen's parents, they'd get mad at her, and then would she be even nastier for tattling on her? That was a possibility. But what would happen if I stayed quiet? Nothing would change. I'd keep getting picked on, anyway. I had to say something. I took another deep breath. "Gwen was making fun of me for wanting to try out for bandyll."

Mr. Gauss went wide-eyed. "That's very rude of her."

"Please don't say anything about it. It'll only make things worse."

"Worse how?"

"She'll get nastier. She hates me. I want her to leave me alone."

"I'll see what I can do to get her to stop."

"No. I'll handle it." Both cat and teacher looked at me in disbelief. "I have to."

Mr. Gauss nodded thoughtfully. "Please come to me if you want help figuring out what to do."

"Yes, sir," I said to the floor.

"By the way, I look forward to hearing how tryouts go for you. I absolutely love the sport."

"I don't want to try out anymore. I've never played. There's no way I can get on the team."

"Clearly, your classmate was trying to intimidate

you and control your actions. Most kids out here have never played before. Toolena Mesa has two teams, A and B. If you show the coaches you have the right stuff, they'll train you up nicely to prepare you for the A team and even high school level play. Try out. I'll be proud of you for doing at least that. Are you willing to do that much?"

I made myself look up and my chest fluttered anew, the invisible wings nearly lifting me off the floor. "Yes."

Chapter 12

Every last scrap of resolve and determination dissolved at the sight of the sheer number of girls trying out for bandyll. I'd grabbed a book on bandyll and read up a bit during lunch. It was a seven-on-seven team sport that was super intense. Way more than fourteen girls were trying out. This was such a stupid idea.

We stood shoulder to shoulder to run the width of the soccer pitch. Two teachers watched over us as two more adults and a handful of students exited the school and walked towards us. Each student carried a large mesh bag stuffed with sports equipment over a shoulder. Great. More students trying out.

Still, I couldn't bring myself to leave the field. No one else had left. I so would not single myself out like that.

Even though the worst of the summer heat was past, the desert sun beat down on us all. Sweat coated me from head to toe, as it did everyone else. Not a single cloud decided to show up.

One coach turned out to be the curly-haired receptionist named Desi. Her ample curls bounced with every step as she moved with the grace of an athlete. Next to her walked Mrs. Viro, the sixth-grade PE teacher. Desi liked me, but Mrs. Viro treated everyone with the same permanent hard gaze on her face. She was there to teach us sports stuff, not to be everyone's buddy. She treated me no differently than she did Gwen. I liked her. My spirits rose enough to stop trembling.

Desi and Mrs. Viro stopped at the bottom of the center circle, and the eighth graders dumped the bags in a clump behind them before joining the rest of us. Mrs. Viro pushed up her sunglasses. "Ladies, welcome to bandyll tryouts. My name is Coach Viro. I'm head coach of the A team. This is Coach Khamai. She's head coach for the B team. We'll both watch all of you closely to compile two great teams. Now, we're not looking for the most talented players. I know there's a lot of talent here, but that means nothing if you don't understand the importance of teamwork. It takes the entire team to win and the entire team to lose. I need fourteen athletes, and Coach Khamai needs fourteen athletes willing to work together, eager to learn, and respond well to coaching. Raw talent alone won't get you on our teams if you have no work ethic. This includes keeping your grades up. You're useless to the team if we have to bench you for not passing all your classes. Do you understand?"

"Yes, Coach Viro," we all said in unison. Mr. Gauss would've been proud of our enthusiasm.

Her slight frown flattened into a straight line, the closest thing to a smile I'd ever seen on her face during all of my PE classes with her. However, the frown returned and she pointed down the line. "Very good. And you two, go change into your PE shirts. I don't care about what other teams you've been on. I won't tolerate this subtle intimidation tactic. Now, run."

Everyone, including me, leaned over to see that she was pointing at Gwen and Sussi. Gwen let out a theatrical sigh and the two of them jogged back to the building without protest.

Mrs. Viro—I mean Coach Viro watched them, fists on her hips, until they disappeared inside. She turned back to the rest of us. "There are a bunch of cones all over the field. We're going to start with endurance work."

Coach Viro directed us to take two laps around the pitch, followed by some exercises that left us huffing, puffing, and red-faced, even Gwen. She hadn't been kidding about the whole endurance thing. Throughout it all, Vergo stayed near me, encouraging me and giving me pointers on running form to help me move more efficiently. He was unaffected by climate or exercise, but his tone motivated me to keep moving when the ground seemed like such a great place to nap. I was slower than most girls, but I never quit.

Both coaches took notes and even looked at me a couple of times. I had half a mind to tell Vergo to go over and see what they were writing, but not only did I not want to be caught talking to him, I couldn't do anything besides breathe and follow Coach Viro's whistle cues.

We enjoyed a generous water break before moving

on to agility drills. Between the heat and the physical intensity, a few girls puked. All of them, plus a few more, walked off without returning. I felt sick, but the look of disappointment both coaches gave the quitters was all the motivation I needed to suck this up and deal with whatever came next.

After our second major water break, the returning eighth graders opened the equipment bags of helmets, padding, scoop-like paddles, and a bunch of balls the size of grapefruits.

The rest of us sat sprinkled on the sidelines or on the bleachers, me on the ground with Vergo. "I thought the balls were smaller."

Sussi, who sat nearby, lowered her water jug. "The boys use the smaller ones. Girls have larger regulation balls."

I stared. Did she just…? "Oh. Thanks."

Gwen hissed from up in the bleachers and spoke in a harsh whisper. "What are you doing? Don't help her."

Sussi let out a dramatic sigh and rolled her eyes.

Vergo swiveled an ear and then turned the rest of his head. "Hmm, looks like someone made note of the exchange."

Both coaches stood well within earshot. Coach Viro glanced at Gwen and finished jotting down a note. Viro nodded to the equipment. "Okay, everyone, suit up. Those who know how better, help the ones who don't. Both Coach Khamai and I expect our players to demonstrate teamwork on and off the field. We'll stay on the soccer pitch for this part of tryouts as well since not everyone has the right footwear for a bandyll court."

We jogged as a group over to the bags. Walking

was not allowed during practice, unless otherwise instructed. We haphazardly picked out helmets and such. An eighth grader helped me find a suit of padding and a helmet that fit. She also showed me how to adjust the length of the claw-like scoops so I could move without dragging the tips on the ground, which were scratched and scuffed by years of use. Many scoops were bent or warped. One of my scoops didn't want to stay on, and with my other hand already sheathed in a second scoop, I had no way of fixing the malfunctioning strap. Sussi, who was a head taller than me, huffed and grabbed my misbehaving scoop, fixing it so it stayed even with the other.

"There," she said in an annoyed tone and moved on to another struggling girl. She sounded like me when I got annoyed with Bela, but decided it was my duty to help with her hair and backpack and stuff. I knew the coaches were expecting us to show teamwork, but Sussi was the second-to-last person I expected to help me.

I felt like a knight in leather armor. I wondered if this was how Yuna felt fully suited up and ready for battle. She wore armor a lot and it often saved her life. Bandyll was a physical sport. The book said all the padding was there to protect players from getting pelted by the ball, smacked by scoops, and to help prevent injury when crashing into one another. I adjusted my helmet with my scoops and jogged into one of the four lines forming up at midfield.

Mrs. Viro stood at the base of the center circle and paced around as she spoke loudly. "Okay, time for everyone to become familiar with the basics of how to pass and catch a ball. I need lines one and three to all get a ball."

The girl standing ten feet away from me ran over to the pile and came back with a ball rolling back and forth in one scoop. Her face was mostly covered, but I could easily see her eyes staring back at me with an eagerness to get started. Like Yuna bracing for the climb up the mountain, I braced myself to learn something new.

We started with underhand tosses, which were easy enough, minus the occasional toss straight up, but I developed a feel for when to flick the ball away, and when to cradle it so it didn't bounce out when trying to catch it. My brown-haired partner spoke words of encouragement and gave me small corrections before Coach told us to switch to overhand. This resulted in many of us running around to catch an overthrown ball. My arms got tired and my throws left dents in the grass between us more often than not. My partner grew visibly annoyed to the point where her throws got worse, too.

"Slow down and give your arms a chance to rest," Vergo said as I retrieved an overthrown ball from the far end of the track circling the field. "Focus on getting it right, instead of lobbing it. You've been doing well so far. Don't get sloppy now."

Coach Viro blew her whistle and instructed us to get into three lines. Three eighth graders demonstrated a passing drill that had them moving in a weaving pattern as they passed the ball from side to side. I watched from near the back of the line as group after group weaved their way to the end of the field. The ball was dropped and overthrown a lot. Coach Viro gave constructive critique on every mistake, which resulted in immediate improvement for each girl.

My stomach nearly dropped to my feet when it was my turn to try the passing drill. I stood in the left line while Gwen stood in the right. She scowled, but when the middle girl started jogging, so did we. The girl passed to Gwen first, who expertly caught it as I veered towards the middle of the pitch. Gwen pelted it at me. I tried to catch it, but it bounced out of my scoop.

"Gwen, you threw too hard for such a short pass. Throw softer at that distance."

"Yes, Coach," Gwen said politely as she jogged behind me and headed for the opposite side, but not without whispering, "You suck" to me.

Scowling, I scooped the ball up, ran to the side Gwen had thrown from and threw to our eighth-grade teammate. My pass made an upside-down "u" through the air, but she was able to get under it in time.

"A little earlier on the release, Mia."

"Yes, Coach," I said loud enough to be heard, projecting eagerness to hide my nerves. I'd screwed up while Coach was watching, but so had Gwen. We worked our way down the rest of the field without incident, minus Gwen sneaking in a verbal dig every time we crossed paths. I tuned them out as best I could. They stung even though I could see it for the intimidation tactic it was. A or B team, I didn't care which one I made. I wanted the chance to make my parents and Mr. Gauss proud.

Passing drills turned into shooting drills. The bandyll goal was one-quarter the size of a soccer net, and no matter how hard I tried, I just couldn't find the back of the net. And a goalie would have easily stopped whatever shots did roll in. My heart sank and Vergo reminded me to keep trying.

Those who showed an aptitude for shooting stayed in the offense group while the rest of us were put on defense. Gwen stayed on offense and Sussi joined me on defense. Six eighth graders demonstrated a passing drill combined with a defensive drill that resulted in either the offense taking a shot on the open net, or the defense knocking or stealing the ball away.

Gwen was first in line, in the middle spot with the ball. She and her wingers jogged down the field, but instead of passing the ball, she juked the defender and kept running at the net. Coach Viro blew her whistle. Gwen shot at the net, sending the back of the mesh outwards.

"That was not the drill. All three of you get back to the line and do it right."

Gwen jutted her padded chin out. "That's how we do it on our Hornets team."

"I don't care. This isn't the Hornets. You can either do the drill I tell you, or you can escort yourself to the locker room."

Gwen stared our coaches down before roughly snatching the ball from inside the net and jogging back to the front line. She passed the ball on her second run-through, but the defensive line knocked the ball out of the air, ending the drill. Gwen let out a frustrated sigh and jogged to the back of the offensive lines.

"Run to the pass next time," Coach Viro told the girl. "Never wait for it to get to you. That's how the other team gets the ball before you. Next." She blew her whistle.

Sussi lined up with two other defenders and slowly closed the gap between them and the offense weaving their way closer. The ball was passed to Sussi's side.

The shorter, wider girl got her scoop out in front of Sussi's in time. Sussi spun as the girl tried to beat her down the sideline, and she used both scoops to block the pass attempt, ending the play.

"Very good, both of you," Coach Viro said. "Next."

I stepped onto the pitch, scoops up and ready, like I'd been told, hanging farther back than my fellow defenders. When the ball was passed to my side, I was too far back. I sprinted forward, but the offensive player slipped between me and my teammate to take the shot.

"Very good with taking advantage of the open, easy shot, Josie. Mia, always prioritize covering the middle of the field when on defense. Force your opponent to take the outside route to the net."

"Yes, Coach," I said loudly. I wasn't sure how I was supposed to do that. At the very least, I knew not to give up the middle. I returned to the back of the defensive line.

None of my other attempts went much better. I managed not to let another player squeeze between me and another defender again. I was proud of that much, but I wasn't feeling confident when we moved on to the last phase of tryouts: goaltending.

We all sat with our water jugs, backs to the sun, while our coaches let us rest in the 18-yard box. Coach Viro pushed up her sunglasses. "All right, ladies. We're in desperate need of goalies this year. All our goalies promoted to high school last year, leaving us with a defensive void. Now, before you all get excited at the prospect of an easy position to fill, let me tell you that goaltending is the hardest position in bandyll. When you're the goalie, you're the last line of defense. If you fail, then the whole team feels it and fails with you right then and there. On top of that, not everyone has the courage to handle fast, hard shots flying at their face. You need good reflexes for this position."

"Good reflexes, huh?" Vergo said mildly. "Sounds like we found your position."

I bit back a question about shots flying at my face, yet a part of me couldn't help but wonder if he was right. I'd somehow caught that paper ball and defense had felt more natural than offense. Even on defense, I had to fight the urge to hang behind everyone.

"Anyone interested in tryout for goalie, please stand up."

A few girls stood. None of them were Gwen or Sussi.

"Well, what are you waiting for?" Vergo said.

Before I knew what I was doing, I stood as well. Gwen snorted behind a hand. A sharp look from Coach Viro silenced her. Despite all the equipment, I felt weightless as I followed Coach Khamai to the last two mesh bags that had remained closed the whole time. Out poured what looked like giant baseball mitts and scoops twice as wide as the rest. The second bag contained leg padding. The handful of us brave enough to stand up swapped out our scoops for the new hand-wear and padding.

It felt heavy, but the mitt completely closed if I balled my hand into a fist. The wider scoop would make it easier to catch or block shots, and the leg padding made it possible to stand with my legs wider without letting a ball through, and gave me options to block without actually catching the ball. Hmm, I could work with this.

Coach Khamai put me in the net first, showing me

the crouching position to ready myself for a shot. Yes, like this, I could easily move in any direction to put myself between the ball and net.

"Ready, Mia?"

I nodded and held my arms wide, but not too wide, so as to create a gap by my sides. Coach Viro blew her whistle, and a trio of players rolled into motion from midfield. Middle, right, left the ball moved, players weaving and drawing closer. I shuffled with each pass, keeping myself between net and ball. The eighth grader fired a shot from the top of the 18-yard box. I took a snapshot of the ball's trajectory and threw out my mitt. My whole arm jolted and the ball made a leathery smack. I opened my mitt. The ball was there, nestled in the center. Both coaches looked at me, wide-eyed.

The shooter ran up to me and took the ball. "Nice catch," she said with genuine admiration and ran off.

Coach put me back in and the entire group took shots on me. Few shots got past me. Even Gwen failed to get one by. She'd tried to fool me, but something about the angle of her body told me to cover my near side. It bounced off of a leg pad and around the net.

"You got lucky."

"Aww, someone's feeling sore about getting bested in a one-on-one," Vergo said.

Coach Viro said, "I'd like to see you do better. You're more than welcome to gear up and show her how it's done."

A flash of embarrassment appeared on Gwen's helmet-covered face. "I only play offense," Gwen said, dishing me a death glare.

I smiled. My first save hadn't been a total fluke. I was sad when my turn was over. Something about defending the net and facing a shot thrilled me. My mind went blank. I acted and reacted to scoring attempts. All the other prospective goalies took turns as well. A few others made lots of good saves. Two girls cringed every time a shot came at them.

Coach Viro blew her whistle three times and a handful of eighth graders got us circled up and guided us through a stretching routine. Both coaches stood in the middle, whispering to each other and jotting some notes. Once we had bagged the equipment, we sat in a group on the bleachers. Coach Khamai passed out several bowls of chopped watermelon, oranges, and bananas. A ripple of delight spread through the bleachers.

"Make sure you eat up," Coach Viro said. "Your body needs all those electrolytes and nutrients to help your muscles recover. If you don't replenish, you won't be able to walk tomorrow, which is the first day of practice. If I put you on the team and you don't show up because you're hurting, you will be replaced with someone willing to push through the pain and take care of their body. We live in a harsh, unforgiving desert. Respect that and your body, and you will stay strong and healthy.

"Now, Coach Khamai and I will deliberate on everything we saw today. We will post the results tomorrow outside my office door, located in the girls locker room. For those of you who make it, you have 20 minutes from the dismissal bell to show up on this field, ready for practice, ready to work on becoming champion student-athletes. If you habitually show up late to practice, we'll replace you with someone who knows how to be punctual."

A girl raised her hand.

"Yes, ma'am."

"What's punctual mean?"

"It means showing up on time. Thank you for asking." She began pacing again. "Now, I want to thank all of you for trying out. It means a lot to me to see so many of you eager to play. If you don't make it this year, I want you to try out again next year, be it for middle or high school. We saw a lot of great effort today. Everyone rest up and get your homework done. We'll see twenty-eight of you tomorrow."

Chapter 13

I wasn't the only student who thought of seeing if tryout results were already posted in the girls' locker room first thing next morning. Other girls joined me, a mix of hope and fear on their faces, as I looked through the large glass window next to the door. Coach Viro sat at her desk with a bunch of papers fanned out and a pencil between her teeth. She looked up at the lot of us watching her. She reached for a fresh sheet of paper, scribbled something on it, and got up. We backed up. The door opened several inches. She slapped something on the middle of the door and slammed it closed. We moved to the paper.

"Come back after lunch for bandyll roster results."

"I like your coach," Vergo said. He sat near my feet. "Very succinct and direct."

Several girls sighed and walked away. I followed them out into the hallway and headed for homeroom.

Great. Now I had to wait even longer to find out. This day was going to take forever to pass.

I barely beat the bell into homeroom, bumping into some lady I didn't recognize. I mumbled an apology as she turned, startled.

"All good. I was in the way." She smiled, but it was forced, too tight to be real. She wrung her hands and looked away. Just great. My first substitute teacher of the year, and she'd been informed about my alignment. Keeping my head down, I took my seat.

Mr. Gauss said, "Good morning, everyone. We have a new student today."

I did a double-take. Mr. Gauss stood on the other side of some new boy who stood between our teacher and the new lady. Okay, so she wasn't a sub. I needed to stop looking at the ground so much when walking around. The boy was tall with a square build and a pronounced hunch. He shifted from foot to foot and locked his gaze on the floor. The lady beside him stood a couple of inches shorter, dressed like a teacher, and wore her straight hair down. She looked barely older than a high schooler.

"There's something strange about that boy," Vergo said.

Mr. Gauss smiled and put a hand on the boy's shoulder, who cringed and swatted the hand away. Mr. Gauss recoiled as if burned. "Sorry, didn't mean to frighten you there."

The lady held something wrapped in cloth in front of the boy's nose. His round face relaxed. "It's okay," she said and then whispered a few words to Mr. Gauss, who nodded in understanding. He turned back to the rest of the class.

"Everyone, please kindly welcome Garrett Antcil."

I kept my mouth shut as the rest of the class drawled a greeting in unison, sounding unenthused and disinterested. There was something about him that put me on guard. He didn't have the energy of a demon or ghost, but I felt compelled to summon my energy shield. I flicked a hand and the invisible bubble of energy enveloped me. The room shimmered as if I was looking through a sheet of water. The shield settled into place, big enough to envelop me, my desk, and everything on it, including Vergo. The world looked normal again.

Vergo looked up and around. "Hm. That didn't do anything. I don't think this boy has anything attached to him. Still, I'm in full support of such a precaution. I heard the lady tell our beloved teacher about his aversion to being touched. Possessed individuals share that trait."

I nodded slightly.

Mr. Gauss said, "And this is his aide, Miss Juvarra." My classmates greeted her as well. She smiled and waved, but unease settled back into her compact posture. She looked like she was trying to take up as little space as possible while keeping extra distance between her and Garrett.

Wait. Was she afraid of him and not me? I leaned closer to Vergo and whispered the question.

"That's the impression I have. I would very much like to know his alignment. Legalese aside, I don't see this school accepting another Dark. Keep an eye on him and keep your distance."

Garrett sat at the desk by the door Mr. Gauss indicated, and Miss Juvarra sat beside him, disappearing among the sea of heads.

"Oh goodie, freak number two," Gwen said. Only she and Nonaya laughed. Chibya and Sussi remained quiet, their faces creased with unease.

Homeroom took forever to pass—not so much because I was waiting for tryouts results, but because of that new kid. The only person who seemed unfazed by him was Mr. Gauss, who held out a hand to stop me from leaving.

"How'd tryouts go?"

Gwen gave me a smug smile before disappearing into the hallway. Sussi ignored me. I shrugged at my teacher.

"That well, huh? I hope you made it."

I slipped into the hallway in time to cross paths with Deren on his way to English class. He beamed and gave me one of his quick hugs. "Morning, Mia. See you at lunch."

"Morning, Deren." Why couldn't we have more than PE together? I returned the hug just as quickly, and we headed in opposite directions. I felt at ease in his presence and he was almost always smiling. It was like he didn't know how to be sad about anything. I enjoyed being around him.

I stopped in the doorway to History class, my stomach sinking to my feet. Garrett sat in the back, at the desk closest to the door. He was engrossed in some book Miss Juvarra told him to put away. Another classmate shoved his way past me, knocking me close enough to see the words on the page. Despite warnings from Ms. Weever to never read strange books without certain protections in place, my eyes picked out a sentence mentioning Yuna crossing a lake.

Yuna. He was reading the same books as me. That was the book I read during sixth grade.

Unease dissipating a little, I gave him a wide berth on my way to my desk, and got out my notebook and textbook, opening to the chapter on cursed objects throughout history. Mrs. Livy tossed her thick braid of black hair behind her and touched the board. Chalk lines shifted around, forming words and pictures. I scribbled notes.

"Last week, we finished our unit on the Necromancer's War and how that led to the Revival Age. And what age are we in now?"

Hands shot up. "The Light Age," Garret said, his gaze glued to his Yuna book. Hands half-lowered and everyone looked at him, including our teacher.

Mrs. Livy looked down her nose. "Mr. Antcil, you will raise your hand to speak in this class."

Gaze on his book, Garrett shot an arm up. "Light is all that is love and good. Dark is all that is hate and evil." He put his hand down, holding his book in both hands. A few classmates chuckled.

Mrs. Livy shook her head and gestured to six robed figures on the board. "The Necromancer's War left behind many scars, including cursed objects created by Darks to oppose the Light. The Order of Fyr is finding objects today, hundreds of years later. Unfortunately, most are found because of great misfortunes, deaths, plagues, and such cropping up around these objects."

Vergo lay propped up against my backpack. "I bet you her entire supply of eye shadow that she never mentions how the Lights laid curses of their own on huge swaths of land, making whole towns and villages uninhabitable." He looked up at me. "Yes, many Darks created cursed objects, but terrible choices were made on both sides."

I made note of what both he and my teacher said. Ms. Weever was a good cross-reference. However, Vergo had been alive during the war. He always had something to add to what Mrs. Livy said. Either our textbooks left out a ton of details, or Vergo was lying. Still, I couldn't understand why anyone would lie or omit such information in textbooks. This was all stuff we were supposed to learn.

"The main reason we're still finding cursed objects is due to the sheer number made. The other thing to note is that these objects could be anything, from a book or a box, to a rock or a desk." Mrs. Livy held up a fountain pen. "A Dark could even curse this pen to kill anyone who tried to write with it. How many people do you think would die with such a pen in their possession before anyone figured it out?"

She touched the board and the lines rearranged into a new selection of words and boxes of varying shapes and sizes, the words "Dabuk Boxes" hovering over them. "The most infamous of cursed objects are the dabuk boxes. Originally made to store family heirlooms, these boxes were meant to be passed down from one generation to the next, to be an heirloom as well. Their contents and the appearance of such boxes should tell your family's history.

"Legend has it that there are ten boxes in particular scattered around the world, each with a powerful demon bound to it."

"Ah, yes. Those monstrous things," Vergo said. "I stayed well away from those things and the rituals leading up to their creation."

"The Order of Fyr has found and destroyed six of them. As for the other four? One can only look for the signs of one of the ten plagues assigned to the missing boxes."

"Oh, what fun," Vergo said sarcastically. "Only four ways left to wipe out the continent."

I widened my eyes.

"Oh, yes. Embittered as I was at the time, destruction at that scale was against my moral code. May the rest of them stay hidden for all eternity."

Mrs. Livy described the six boxes and the plagues they brought before moving on to other objects capable of significantly less destruction.

***

Anxious to get answers, I tried to sneak a peek inside the girls locker room before lunch, but Coach Viro stood in the gymnasium, blocking off the only path to both locker rooms. Not wanting to get caught ignoring her handwritten sign, I backed out of the doorway and headed to Ms. Weever's office in the main office building. Vergo waited in the hallway while I closed the door behind me.

The scent of incense and herbs filled my nose, and a soft song played from a sound stone. Ms. Weever stood with her back to the door, musing over an open book.

"Get your violin out, please," Ms. Weever said in her typical firm but kind enough tone.

I obeyed, and when she heard me snap the latches closed, she gestured to a circle in the middle of the office. I stood in it. My tutor narrowed her eyes at a particular page and swore under her breath. "Must've been censored out of here, too." She tossed a white cloth on her desk. A proximity ward cloth, the one that'd been triggered the other week.

"Something still setting it off?"

"Every day." Ms. Weever retrieved her violin from atop the piano and stood facing me. She shouldered her instrument and played the middle two strings, filling the room with their rich, round sound. A wave of ease passed through me. "And it's avoided all my traps up to this point. It must have an anchor inside something or someone."

"How's Nurse Kor doing?"

"Atypically irritable. There's that regular moodiness all women must endure, but what she's exhibiting is not it. Bylan has confirmed that she's stopped shaking hands with people and has stopped exhibiting a bedside manner to all children who step into her office."

"Sounds like she has an attachment or is possessed."

"That is a very high possibility. Our only solace is that we can rule out the Demon King doing this himself. He rarely makes direct contact with the mortal realm. We are beneath his desire to meddle with us directly. He'd rather get other demons to do such work. He and Shinjan, the god of Light, both work subtly and have their loyal minions to boss around." She played an ascending chord. "Anyway, enough of that for now. I expect to be able to remove at least one of the protective runes on your violin today."

I blanched. That meant I could make costly mistakes if I played the wrong notes.

"Mrs. Sterling says it shows that you've played an instrument before. You merely have to learn the fingerings and proper bow technique, and you'll make a fine violinist. Let's warm up with some scales."

Taking a deep breath, I shouldered my violin. It looked like it should be heavy, but it was almost weightless. Ms. Weever tapped a song stone on the piano and it ticked a slow tempo. I set my bow on the first string, and we worked our way through the scales circle, me constantly reminding myself to steer the bow with my elbow and not my hand. That was the right way to do it. I tried to place my fingers right over the lines of tape marking where each note lay on the strings. Most of my notes sounded okay. I tripped up on switching from one string to the next, and constantly readjusted the bend in my elbow so the bow didn't slide off the edge of the strings. Muscle memory kicked in during the last few scales, allowing me to focus on the metronome ticks until we were done.

"Fair progress," Ms. Weever said. "You've been practicing hard."

"My sister likes sitting in my room with me when I practice. She insists she has to watch."

My tutor nodded. "A trait of young Lights. They're enchanted by music, even passable quality. She'll grow out of it." She played a string and adjusted the tuning knob. "Let's see how well you can play runes." She placed a music stand outside the circle. It held up a sheet marked with a few lines of music and a title that read "Basic Protection Circle." Above each line of notes sat the corresponding rune. Next to the rune was the translation, but I ignored those. Each series of notes shared a similar shape in ascending and descending order as the shape of the rune.

"The notes look like the rune."

Ms. Weever scrutinized the sheet music. "I guess. I don't see it. Anyway, this is the most basic protection circle you can conjure, either drawn or played."

"I remember it from last year." My heart sank. Maybe I imagined the similarities. I'd have to ask Vergo later.

"Good. You see it. Now you get to hear it." Ms. Weever played the same series of notes four times, and a protection circle came to life around her, glowing a swirl of purple and white. A breeze kicked up, protective energy riding on its currents, like feeling heat in the air. She then played the notes in reverse, and the circle evaporated. "Thankfully, the cost of messing up this circle's song is minimal. It simply doesn't activate, which is bad only if you're in immediate danger. More complicated and powerful circles will exert a backlash should you fail. You'll earn yourself a few cuts and bruises, or an upset stomach for the minor ones, but you can hospitalize or kill yourself for messing up on the most powerful ones. You can probably guess what I'd say about musically drawing power circle and confidence."

I needed confidence, and a lot of it. "Yes, ma'am."

"And let me warn you about two other things: one, you can play a circle's song somewhat incorrectly and still succeed. However, it'll be a weaker version of the perfect thing. It'll also drain you of energy far faster than a properly conjured power circle. Always dispel your circle before you pass out, or you risk going into a coma."

"Yes, ma'am. I'll immediately dispel it every time I mess up."

She nodded in approval. "And two: should you be

under attack while your circle is active, each attack will drain you a little or a lot, depending on the foe. With the right instrument enchantments, demons can also hurt themselves with every attack. However, protective circles serve best as a protection method. If you need to fight a demon, you'll need other tools and spells."

I nodded.

"Let's begin then."

Ms. Weever placed a few runes on her violin so she wouldn't conjure the circle. Using the song stone metronome as a guide, we played through the protection circle's song over and over, slowly at first, and then faster as my fingers grew progressively more comfortable with the sequence.

"Now try it with your eyes closed. Picture the runes."

I closed my eyes and pictured the runes with the notes overlapped. My first attempt started correctly, until I realized I'd completely let go of proper bow posture and movement. I opened my eyes at the sound of a screech.

"Slow down and try again." Ms. Weever stroked the song stone and the tempo slowed.

Closing my eyes, I felt out the tempo and pictured the runes in my head for several beats, then thought out the notes with each rune. I raised my arm and carefully played the notes. My tempo sped up and slowed, but I hit every note. Ms. Weever made me play the circle song over and over from memory, eyes closed, and eventually without the metronome. Soon, my arm and fingers moved with little thought. I pictured the circle and its runes in my head, and the notes followed.

"Excellent. I thought we'd spend all week getting

this far. Hand me your violin." Using a fingertip, Ms. Weever drew runes on my instrument. Each one lit up, and flakes of light lifted away from the wood, dissolving in the air.

My heart pounded as she handed it back. It was as light as before, but now it could do more than make ears bleed.

"Confidence."

Oh. Right. I took a calming breath. If I could feel super confident with all the protection runes in place, then I could feel the same without them there.

Ms. Weever stepped back and gestured for me to take her spot in the circle. "Again, the cost of messing up this circle is low. So keep trying until you get it."

I shouldered the violin and held my bow at the ready. Ms. Weever turned on the metronome. I felt out the steady beat and closed my eyes. Once more, the circle appeared in my mind. I played out the notes and an energy swirled around me, filling me up and making my feet feel stuck to the ground. I opened my eyes. A circle and four runes glowed around me, kicking up an otherworldly breeze. I was connected to the energy, like there were invisible lines between the circle and my feet. The energy was drawing on my life energy to maintain it. Amazing. I'd done it. I'd really done it.

Ms. Weever stared at me in open surprise. "One try." She cleared her throat. "Miss Evers, there is great hope for you yet. I hope the forces that shape this world let me teach you everything I can. The world desperately needs more Darks like you and me." She stepped closer and the circle's wind lifted her hair. She nodded for me to dispel it.

I played the notes in reverse and the air grew

colder. I felt isolated, exposed. I forced myself to lower both violin and bow, instead of bring the circle back. Still, it would've been so nice to always hide under such protection. My shielding spell was nothing compared to this.

"Now, I've already placed one outside Miss Kor's office. Bylan has already added his touches to it. With the Demon King's attention on her in one way or another, she needs all the protection she can get. I need you to add to it as well without getting caught."

Chapter 14

I took the indirect route to the cafeteria, trying one more time to peek at Coach Viro's office door, but one look through the glass windows revealed her leaving the basketball courts and heading into the girls locker room. Dang. Huffing a sigh, I went to the cafeteria and got in line for lunch. Today's menu featured burritos with a choice of toppings. The lunch ladies, a lively bunch complete with aprons and hairnets, worked an assembly line of edible perfection. I chose chicken, beans, rice, cheese, guacamole, and salsa.

The first lady laid out my tortilla with a wrist flick, perfectly placing it on a sheet of parchment paper with her Air magic. The second lady made a different hand gesture, and slices of steaming chicken rode more Air magic and piled up on the tortilla. The third lady added all the fixings, flourishing them through the air in a tasty tornado before guiding them on top of the chicken.

Mom tried to do that once and we had to clean the entire kitchen. The fixings lady had some crazy good control of her Air magic. The fourth lunch lady expertly wrapped up my burrito (with clean hands) and set it on a tray next to some fresh fruit and a colorful salad. Lunches this amazing didn't exist in city schools. This had to be one of the perks courtesy of the Volaires. I appreciated it, but I didn't like Gwen one bit.

I found my usual spot next to Deren among the rows of long tables that spanned almost the entire echoey room. The air was jammed with a hundred different conversations and several paper birds guided around by one student or another. Their wing movements were lifelike, but their paths were jagged as Air students guided the birds around out of arm's reach. Said birds were swiftly removed from the air and the guilty student reprimanded. Why couldn't teachers let us have fun while we were eating?

Deren looked up from his steaming tray of burrito and rice. "Hey, Mia. Do you know if you made the team yet?"

"No. Coach has been guarding the locker room all day."

"She yelled at Gwen for using a bathroom break to disguise her trip to the locker room."

"No." Gwen was the perfect student. Super polite. She never outwardly did anything to get in trouble and always got top grades.

Deren nodded. "Miss Viro caught her walking through the gymnasium while she was teaching one of the eighth-grade groups, asked Gwen what she was doing there and stuff, and then the vine in Mrs. Livy's room shivered. Mrs. Livy answered it, got super mad, and gave Gwen detention when she returned to class. I wish you could've seen how red Gwen's face got. A few of us got yelled at for laughing."

I laughed too. "I wish I'd been there."

"So how are classes going so far today?"

I happily told him about my protection circles lesson and how I'd done it in one try after the protection runes were removed. Deren was the only one besides Vergo that I talked with about my lessons. He was fascinated and unafraid, had been that way since the day we met.

"That's so cool. You must be really powerful or something. We're learning how to carve shapes and runes into stone, but it's real hard. Mr. Gines keeps getting annoyed with me and a few other people throwing rocks at each other."

"Then why do you keep doing that? You're going to get detention for it one day."

Deren shrugged. "It's fun."

I rolled my eyes. "Boys."

"What? You'd do it, too, if you were aligned with Earth."

Boys were always doing dumb things and getting into trouble more than girls, but I didn't feel like pointing that out to him. "What kind of enchantments are you trying to learn?"

"Protective ones, like what you're doing, but Earth style. We're supposed to make a doorway stone by the end of first quarter. Then next quarter, we take notes on how well our runes keep certain sprites away. Sounds boring." He munched on his burrito and swallowed. "What are your protection circles supposed to do? How does your tutor want to test if yours work?"

My heart dropped and my bite of burrito sank like a rock into my stomach. I slowly turned to Deren. "I never told you, did I? About Nurse Kor."

He gave me a blank look. "What about her? Is something wrong?"

"Oh, Deren." Somehow our lunch conversations had never gotten around to Nurse Kor's predicament. I explained the whole thing to him. His eyes got wider and wider.

"Is she going to get sick like I did?"

I shook my head. "No. This is a different demon," I said only loud enough for him to hear. "Ms. Weever wants me to place a protection circle around her office. I don't get to practice."

"Oh, man. Is there anything I can do to help?"

I opened my mouth to tell him no, but stopped. Maybe there was. "Maybe you can leave protection stones in her office?" Each alignment had its way of creating protective objects.

"I'll try harder in class. I like Nurse Kor. She's always nice." He leaned closer.

For an instant, I looked at his lips and imagined leaning in the rest of the way and kissing him. I wasn't sure what the big deal was supposed to be, but Mom and Dad kissed a lot and seemed to like it. Maybe if I—

"Do you have any clue where this demon is hiding?"

I blinked and sat up straighter. Who was I kidding about the kissing stuff? "No, and I need to find out."

"Where did Vergo hide when he was a demon?"

"He had a portal to the demon realm. I sensed it the moment I entered Miss Wren's room. I haven't felt anything like it since."

"Then it must be somewhere else."

"I'll have to look."

"You mean *we* will have to look," Deren said. He developed a slight pout, his eyes full of fierce determination. That was his stubborn look when he wanted his way.

"No, this is Dark stuff. It's dangerous."

"I can do more than throw pebbles around, Mia. I want to help."

I sighed in frustration.

My backpack wiggled and Vergo popped his head out. "Aw, the little lovebirds want to team up and save the day. How cute."

"Shut up, Vergo." I shoved his head back inside my bag and zipped it shut. I didn't know how he fit in there since the bag was full of books and notebooks, but I didn't care.

"What'd he say?" Deren said, who knew about my spirit cat shortly after I'd returned to sixth grade.

"Something stupid." I took a bite of my burrito, which was so tasty that I wolfed the rest of it down. Deren finished his lunch and still had that stupid, stubborn expression. I looked around the rest of the cafeteria, doing my best to try to ignore him.

That new kid, Garrett, sat a few tables away with his aide sitting opposite him. The tables were divided into sections big enough to seat six at a time. No one sat at the other spots. The students closest to them huddled over their lunches, talking and occasionally pointing or glancing in Garrett's direction. Garrett was engrossed in his Yuna book and appeared oblivious to the kind of attention he drew.

"Guess I'm not the only one weirded out by the

new kid," I said.

"Who, Garrett?" Deren followed my gaze. "Yeah, there's something off about him. He's in my math class. I didn't think he was paying attention to Mr. Gauss, but as soon as he finished writing an equation on the board, Garrett blurted out the correct answer. He didn't even do any work on paper. He looked up and solved it. It was crazy. Even Mr. Gauss was surprised. He's as smart as he is weird."

"Maybe we should sit with him and make him feel more welcome?" I hated the idea, but Deren had shown me kindness when no one else had. Maybe Garrett wouldn't be so bad if I gave him a chance.

Deren grimaced. "I dunno. He creeps me out. Let's give it a few days."

Garret closed his book and Miss Juvarra followed him out of the cafeteria.

I inwardly sighed with relief. "Okay."

"Oh, and I'm going with you when you go portal hunting. And that's final."

I gave him a sidelong glance. "You sound like your mom when she's bossing around you and your brothers."

Running a hand through his short hair, he gave me a dorky grin. "Yeah. Is it working?"

***

With a few minutes to spare before the lunch bell, Deren followed me into the courtyard separating the cafeteria from each school building. A handful of students played basketball on the cement court, sneakers squeaking and scuffing against the ground. Other middle schoolers, including sixth graders, enjoyed the playscape since the younger grades were in class at the moment. Only eighth graders thought it was uncool to use the playground.

I followed the stone pathway around the basketball court and stopped at the other end. Garrett stared into the desert through the link fence that wrapped around the entire campus. Miss Juvarra pawed at his shoulder. He swiped her hand away without taking his eyes off the desert. She wrung her hands.

I did a double-take and elbowed my backpack. "Vergo. Look at this. What are they?" A pair of dark shapes stood on all-fours on the other side of the fence, both facing Garrett. Mesquite bushes lined the fence, blocking a clear view of whatever those creatures were.

My backpack wiggled and Vergo propped himself up on my shoulder. "What on Aardra? The poor woman looks mighty distraught. Perhaps you two should rescue her if you want to practice playing hero."

"I don't wanna go over there. All my stuff is in the bottom of my backpack."

Deren said, "What does he want us to go over there for?"

I told him.

"Let's go. She does look really scared." He grabbed my hand. I yanked it away.

"Deren, no."

The lunch bell rang. Garrett stomped a foot and the two shadows ran off, disappearing beyond the 3-5 building.

Vergo switched to my other shoulder and studied where the shadows had disappeared. "I can't pick anything up. Do you sense anything about those creatures?"

Vergo's demon form had made me uneasy and

terrified, and sent chills up and down my spine by being near me. Ghosts had a similar effect. I could feel out where they hid, even if I couldn't see them. "No. They don't feel like anything." These shapes hadn't so much as given me a tingle. Sure, I felt uneasy, but that hadn't kicked in until I saw them. Ghosts and demons let their presence be known before I saw them. "Uh, does anyone know what his alignment is?"

Deren shook his head. "No offense, but I thought he was the same as you."

Despite not being tutored by Ms. Weever, I was beginning to wonder the same thing. This new demon was so subtle that neither I nor my tutor ever sensed it. Those two shadows had the same trait. Maybe Miss Juvarra was his tutor, or maybe he'd join me in lessons within the next few days. "I don't know, but we need to find out."

"I'll ask around. See you later, Mia." Deren gave me a quick hug and ran off.

Once again, my heart sped up due to his affectionate touch. He zigzagged among students until getting yelled at by Mrs. Livy to walk. He dropped into a stiff-armed walk and disappeared into the crowd.

Vergo tapped my shoulder with a paw. "Well, are you going to check the rosters or what? It's after lunch now, isn't it?"

I inhaled. I started to run, caught myself, and fast-walked to the gymnasium. Other girls hurried into the locker room and we crammed ourselves in front of the door. The place smelled of soap and metal. Coach Viro sat inside, eating a sandwich lunch.

Fingers skimmed their way down one list or another. Some girls squealed with delight and ran back into the gymnasium. I was several rows deep and too far back to see, despite all my squinting. The front girls filtered themselves out, and the papers' markings slowly grew into readable letters. A tall girl up front skimmed the A team list and gasped when she came across her name. The tall girl turned around. Sussi. She pumped a fist and ran off, wearing a huge smile.

"Out of my way," said a voice behind us. Gwen dropped her backpack and shoved her way to the door.

I moved sideways and finally reached the door. This was it. These two pieces of paper would determine how the rest of the fall quarter would play out. I wiped my palms and clamped them over my heart as I read through the B team roster.

They broke the list down into three groups: offense, defense, and goalies. Not that I wanted to be on offense, I read through the list. I wasn't there. That was okay. I read the defense list. I wasn't there either. The goalies were two other seventh graders. All the air left my lungs. My eyes stung. No. I'd tried so hard.

Gwen swore and slapped the metal door. Her eyes watered as she read the A team list again. I shifted my gaze to the second roster.

Her name was nowhere to be found on the offensive line. It was all eighth graders. So was the defensive line, minus Sussi. And the goalies…

I gasped. There was my name. "No way." I'd made the A team. This had to be a mistake.

Vergo tilted his head. "Will you look at that? Congratulations, Little One."

"There must be some mistake," Gwen said to herself. She shoved me aside to read the B team roster.

I was in too much shock to care. My name was in

bold ink at the bottom of the A team list, clear as all the other names.

"Why are you still here? Get out of here."

I pointed at the A team roster.

Her gaze worked from top to bottom. I half expected it to catch fire with how intensely she glared. She went wide-eyed when she reached my name. "What? Okay, that proves it. They totally messed up the rosters." She banged on the door. "Coach, may I have a word with you, please?"

Coach Viro looked up, eyes narrowing. She meticulously set her sandwich down, wiped her mouth, and took a sip from a glass before finally getting up. The door opened and Gwen took a step back. "Yes, Miss Volaire?"

"Coach, there must be a mistake. My name isn't anywhere on either roster."

"No, there are no mistakes. Good day, Miss Volaire." She tried to close the door. Gwen put both hands on it.

"I'm telling you, you made a mistake. I should be on the team. I'm better than everyone." Her chest heaved, and her breath grew wheezy.

"Little One, I advise we move out before she has a meltdown. You don't want to be in her path when that happens.

I heard the words. I agreed with him. Gwen was a monster when something upset her. Something as simple as someone bumping into her could send her into a fit. I took a step back. There was desperation in Gwen's watery eyes. She was in zero control of the situation and she knew it.

"Then why?" Gwen said in a tight voice.

Coach Viro's shoulders rose and fell with a sigh. "You displayed zero ability to embrace teamwork. One player does not win a team game. Ever. If you want to make the team next year, I strongly suggest you work on that with your club team."

Gwen stared and two lines of tears rolled down her cheeks. She swiped them away and glared. "You'll be hearing from my parents."

I and a dozen other girls stepped back as Gwen made to leave. She shoved me again, sending me pinwheeling into the wall.

"All right, that's it." Vergo hopped off my shoulder and stood in front of Gwen as she shoved a few more girls out of her way. Vergo stiffened and Gwen walked right into him. Instead of harmlessly passing through, she fell, landing on her arms. Vergo held his chin high and trotted back over to me. "There. Little One, I wish you'd stand up to her. It's painful to watch you take it."

Gwen whirled around and held out a hand, fingers curled like claws. Her palm glowed, but there was no flame. She had yet to master such a technique as conjuring fire. "Who did that?"

We all looked at each other, mirroring each other's shock.

"Fine. Don't answer me. You'll all be hearing from my parents."

"Miss Volaire, I watched you trip over your own two feet. Stop threatening everyone just because you're upset."

The rage drained from her face, replaced by heartbreak. She ran out of the locker room. Coach Viro didn't bother to tell her to walk.

Chapter 15

"Mommy, don't make me go to school." Bela sat on the edge of the couch, clutching a rag doll with yellow yarn for hair. She buried her face in the yarn, inadvertently yanking her hair out of Mom's fingers.

"But you love school." Mom regathered a lock of hair and placed a flower hair clip behind Bela's ear. She licked a thumb and flattened a few stray hairs.

"No, I don't." She looked off towards the curtained windows. Her gaze grew distant. That was the look of her sensing a spirit.

I scanned the house with my Dark senses and, to my surprise, something lurked outside the windows. I got up from the armchair and parted the curtains. Vergo hopped onto the windowsill.

"Grandma says I shouldn't go. I don't want to go. I'm scared."

A shadow of a man stood on the other side of the

glass. He had basic facial features and a human shape. Beyond that, he wasn't strong enough to fully manifest. He locked eyes with me.

Mom said, "Bela, I'm sure Grandma would want you to go to school, too. Now, grab your backpack and head to the bus stop with your sister."

Bela cried. They weren't tantrum tears. They were genuine tears.

I pulled the curtains closed and summoned my protective shield. I wasn't sure if Bela could sense it or if it would do anything for her, but it was worth a try. I sat beside her on the couch, enveloping us in my protective energies. Bela lifted her face and her eyes widened. The crying stopped. She looked around, until her watery gaze settled on me, full of open wonder.

I tucked some hair behind my ear and smiled. "I'll keep you safe. Let's go." A shadow person was no big deal. It was like having a fly in the house. They were annoying and that was it.

Bela accompanied me outside without further fuss, but she insisted on holding my hand, making it harder to juggle my backpack, bandyll sports bag, and violin all at once. Bela hesitated when we stepped off the porch and let out a whimper. She pointed to the ground and cowered behind me, clutching my bandyll bag and making the strap dig into the meat of my shoulder.

"Bela, stop. What's wrong?" I adjusted the bag and grabbed her hand again.

"It's dead."

Vergo searched around where Bela had pointed, sniffing the ground until he found it. A desert sprite lay there, unmoving. Vergo pawed at it and the humanoid beetle flopped face-first in the dirt. "It's dead. A bad omen."

The last time we'd spotted the sprite, it'd stayed in our herb garden long enough to be spotted before taking off. "I thought you said you didn't believe in these omen and luck things."

"I don't, but it's hard not to, especially with that spirit lurking around."

As if it heard Vergo, the shadow man lurched around the corner and headed straight for us. His movements were jerky, sometimes too fast for the human eye to follow. I held out a hand, expanding my protective shield as Bela put my summer dress in a death grip. "That's close enough. Leave us alone."

Help me. I'm scared.

"I don't have time to help you right now. We've got to get to school."

The shadow man reached for Bela. *I'm lost. Help me.* The shadow touched my shield, creating sparks. It shrunk away. *Please. I'm scared.*

"Mia, make it go away. I don't want to help it."

Please. There are so many horrors all around us. I want to be safe.

Don't we all? I thought to myself. I drew a line in the dirt and a trio of warding runes. I placed both hands on the ground. What I could make out of its face looked desperate. "In the name of the Light, you shall not pass." The line and runes flashed purple. My energy spread in opposite directions, creating a barrier between us and the spirit. I took a deep breath and stood, dusting off my hands.

The shadow man reached out. The air flashed a jagged patchwork of purple and white. He bowed his head and faded, alleviating the mild tingling in my spine his presence created. The air felt clear and empty, occupied just by living things.

Bela's grip on my dress relaxed. "Bye-bye, bad man."

"I don't think he was bad, just lost." I'd help him later if he showed up again. Ghosts like him usually left for good after a brief talk and being told to go with the Light.

Vergo rubbed up against Bela's legs. "You're going to have to learn how to be brave one day, Little—" He looked at her. "Tiny One."

"Kitty." Making contact with her made him perceptible to her, despite the collar.

"My name is Vergo, Tiny One."

"Your name is Kitty." She hefted him into her arms, causing his front arms to stick out straight and his hind legs to flex to maintain balance, toes spread.

Ears pricked back, Vergo gave me a withering look. I snorted.

"Now, don't you get any ideas about changing my name."

***

Instead of heading straight to homeroom, I slipped through a side door of the main office and peered inside the nurse's office as I kept walking. I caught a glimpse of a shoulder and arm behind the desk. Dang. She was there. I turned around and headed back outside, coming face-to-face with Deren. He was holding what looked like a giant potato etched with runes.

"Hey, Mia. Look what I brought." He held up the potato with some effort.

I blinked. "What is it?"

"A protection stone. My dad tested it. It works."

"What do the runes say?" Dark runes looked spidery, while Earth runes were blocky. The language of Earth was completely different from the language of Darkness.

"Protect this place and all who enter. Feel it. It's so nice and warm."

I tentatively placed a hand on the stone and opened my senses, but all I felt was a rock and Deren's eyes on me. "I'm not an Earth. I can't feel what you feel."

His smile waned. "Oh, that's right. I wish you could. It's so calming. Anyway, let's go give it to her." He started past me. I grabbed his arm.

"Wait. I have a feeling she shouldn't know it's there. I'll distract her."

His round face grew serious. He nodded.

I led him inside, trying to shield the stone as I entered. The vines lining the walls, floor, and ceiling shivered, announcing our arrival. Nurse Kor looked up. I inhaled. She looked pale. Her normally bright eyes looked dark, like someone other than her was looking at me. The energy in this room was off. I sent my awareness through my legs and feet, feeling the ground for Ms. Weever's power circle, but found nothing. I should've felt a tickle of energy that made me picture her in my mind. I sensed nothing until my awareness spread to her office deeper within the building. I inhaled, bringing my attention back to the room.

Nurse Kor's smile failed to reach her eyes, which I couldn't hold contact with. I focused on her forehead. "Good morning, Nurse Kor. How are you feeling?"

"Morning, Mia." Even her voice lacked warmth. "I wish everyone would stop asking me that. If I wasn't fine, I wouldn't show up for work." She measured out some pink herb powder and carefully poured it into a glass vial.

"I'm sorry. I won't ask again." That was the first time she'd ever been terse with me. It sucked all the air out of my lungs. I turned to leave, but Deren backed towards the corner. He gazed at me with brown eyes full of sympathy. He looked like he wanted to hug me, but he took another small step back.

"Thanks. What are you up to today? How goes bandyll practice?" She opened a leaf packet and poured some green powder on her scale.

"Good. Coach Viro is real tough, but I'm getting the hang of moving around on the bandyll court. I can skate backwards okay now."

"Good, good. I heard they let Gwen on the B team after her mom talked with the coaches."

I grimaced and glanced back at Deren. He looked around for a place to put the stone. Vines enveloped the spaces between chairs and cabinets. "Yeah. She's still complaining about not being on A team. I heard her talking to her friends about how even her mom wants her to learn teamwork and better leadership. She'll probably be made captain."

"Do you want to be captain?" Nurse Kor poured that powder into a second vial and grabbed a third leaf packet.

Me? Be a leader? Ha. "No. I just want to be goalie."

"Goalies are often the captains on professional teams."

I wanted to blurt that I wasn't a professional bandyll player, but something warned me not to argue with her. "Maybe I'll be ready for such a thing in high school." I had zero desire to be a captain. I needed to make my parents and Mr. Gauss proud, not tell a bunch of people what to do and show them how to do it.

Deren nestled the stone between a cabinet and a chair. Vines enveloped it as if hugging it and completely hid it from view.

"Deren, what did you place in my office?"

His shoulders rose to his too-wide ears, and he stiffened. "Nothing. I was looking at your vines."

Nurse Kor slowly stood and placed her hands flat on the desk. "I can sense a stone or something in the corner there. Remove it, please, or I'll give you both detention for trying to place unwanted objects in my office.

***

Like most days, I couldn't wait for Dark lessons. I felt safest, the most accepted in Ms. Weever's office, even though she intimidated me. However, today I was dying to talk to her about Nurse Kor. I rushed into her office, violin in hand, and shut the door. Vergo remained outside, as usual. My tutor refused to forgive him or tolerate his presence any more than she had to.

I set the violin case on a chair and reached for the latches.

Ms. Weever said, "Leave it. I've changed today's lesson. I think you noticed what happened in the nurse's office. I felt you probing the office, which motivated me to probe back."

"How did she get rid of it?"

Ms. Weever collected several brass bottles from her shelves packed with pouches, books, vials, boxes, bells, and other tools suited for our alignment. "*She* didn't, but whatever's attached to her did." She set the bottles in a row on her desk. There were seven in total. "Bylan and I weren't subtle about placing our protections. We didn't anticipate this creature being strong enough to break them."

"What do you think is attached to her?"

"That's the goal of today's lesson." She evenly spaced the vials and faced the runes etched on them towards me. The bottles were wrapped in metal wire, the brass caps melted to the bottles so they could never be opened. Each bottle had a paper tag tied to it with a white ribbon. Each tag had words written on them. I'd anticipated runes, but it was plain lettering. "The demon realm has a hierarchy much like human society. At the bottom are the poor, those living on the streets, addicted to all sorts of destructive substances, and so on. Then we have the lower class, middle, and upper, and then the pinnacle of society looking down on us all. Our hierarchy is a measure of wealth and status. Demon society is divided by the measure of power."

"There are seven divisions?" I took out my notebook and labeled the page "Types of Demons."

She nodded. "Eight if you feel like counting the Demon King himself. We can rule him out in our current predicament. He's sent someone in his place to milk the situation for all the chaos it can bring. As for which type of demon he'll send your way, I'm not sure. You're young and inexperienced, yet show great aptitude. It's hard to tell what his motives are. He's had thousands of lifetimes to perfect a cunning we mere mortals cannot match. We can only plan to combat his demonic minions."

I scribbled down some notes. "Why does he see it beneath him to mess with the mortal realm?"

Ms. Weever wore a rare smile and set some owl feathers on her desk. "Oh, how that question has become the obsession of philosophical minds throughout history. Many people will tell you that we mere mortals cannot comprehend the will and whims of Shinjan or the Demon King. We are too intellectually inferior and things like that."

"Are we?"

She shrugged. "In a way, certainly. But this reasoning explains nothing, helps you understand nothing. Claiming that the wills of the Light and the Dark are beyond our comprehension is a fancy way of telling people to stop asking questions and to blindly accept something as fact. If anyone tells you to stop questioning their facts, that's your warning to keep asking questions. Never ever be a blind follower or believer of anything."

I scribbled more notes.

"This has led me to believe that the Demon King's motives are simple: he's too prideful to meddle with us. The successful crossover ritual had probably been a blow to his pride. Still, he's also greedy. All demons are his. You stole something from him and he didn't like it. Yes, he could've killed you for it, but for some reason he found it in his best interest not to. Between his greed and pride, he devised another plan and brought Nurse Kor into the fold. As for what his new plan is, that is currently beyond my ability to understand."

"So he sent a demon specifically to deal with me?"

"That's my theory, yes."

My stomach dropped and my grip on my notebook and pencil went slack. The pencil rolled off my notebook and clattered on the floor, making me flinch. I snatched it back up. "I'm scared."

"As you should be. Remember to use it as a tool to sharpen your senses. Stay in control of your fear."

"Accept it and direct it."

"Correct, Miss Evers. Now, for the lesson at hand." She gestured to the bottles. "Each of these contains the energy signature of demons from each hierarchy. Weaker demons cannot hide their energy signatures while stronger ones can, ruling out these two levels." Ms. Weever picked up the two on the end, named Lesser and Nightmare respectively. She picked up the third one and set it near me. "I strongly suspect it could be a demon from the third level." That one was labeled Drude. She set aside the fourth one labeled Succubus/Incubus. "Based on your age alone, I seriously doubt it's this one." She set the fifth bottle closer. "It could very well be a Tempter or a Warmaker." She pushed the sixth bottle closer. "And we better hope and pray it's not an Archdemon." She set the seventh bottle opposite the others.

Sounded ominous. The name alone sounded terrifying. "Why's that?"

There was a look in her icy blue eyes, like she was remembering something. "You better hope to have several Darks in your company should you ever face one. That's a battle you cannot fight alone." Her gaze shifted, found mine. "I highly doubt we are dealing with this kind of foe. Few of them are known to exist, and few have been encountered throughout history."

I added that to my notes as well.

Removing the paper tag, Ms. Weever held out the Archdemon bottle. "Here. All you have to do is hold it and you'll feel what it's like to be in the presence of one."

I set down my pencil and eyed the wiring wrapped around the bottle. "Is there one trapped inside there?"

"No, but this object could create a portal or become an anchor, should anyone figure out how to break into it." She threw it at the ground with all her might. The bottle bounced several times, hitting the wall and floor with metallic pings before rolling to a rest near me.

I stared in abject horror, waiting for black smoke to burst out between the wires, but the bottle lay near my chair leg without so much as a crack.

"Go ahead and pick it up. No harm will come to you."

I set my notebook on the floor as I scrutinized the vial for broke parts and instinct warned me to stay away from it. Glass charmed to be that durable was meant to hold things in, something more dangerous than the materials to create a portal to the demon realm. It'd be best if I never touched the vial. Still, I was a Dark who had to be a master of her emotions. I made myself pick it up.

It slipped through my fingers on the first attempt. It was far heavier than it looked. I dug my fingers under it and stood up straight. Protection runes and one rune I hadn't learned yet flickered to life. "I don't feel—"

There it was. It was subtle, oh so subtle. This creeping fear in the back of my mind. The more I noticed it, the more it grew, enveloping me in terror. I couldn't move. My heartbeat filled my hearing. Red pounded in my vision in time with my heart. There was no hope. It was hopeless. It was best if I gave up and gave in to the darkness. It would win anyway. The world darkened and spun. I wanted to run and hide. I didn't know which way to go. The darkness was everywhere, everything. There was no light left.

Something grabbed my wrist. I screamed and tried to wrench away. A deep, menacing voice called my name. The touch seared into my skin. The air filled with rumbling. I clawed at it as something pried my fingers open.

Metal clanged on the ground. It sounded like the ring of a small bell. I blinked several times. The office enveloped me in its presence, incense filled my nose and Ms. Weever stood over me, holding my wrist in one hand and a bell in the other. She had red marks where I'd scratched her hand.

She gently let go and picked the bottle up. "And that was only a few seconds. Don't worry, I won't subject you to that again anytime soon. However, you'll have to handle the other six." She handed me my notebook and pencil.

The office door burst open and Desi stood there, eyes wild and breathing hard. She must've sprinted from the front desk. "What happened? I heard screaming. Are you okay?"

Ms. Weever let out a frustrated sigh. "How many times do I have to tell you that I'm teaching? Would you *please* put in an order for sound-canceling stones already?"

***

The rest of Dark lessons were tame compared to my experience with the Archdemon energy signature. Over and over, I blindly held bottles without knowing which signature lay trapped inside. The Lesser and Nightmare weren't so bad. Everything else nearly made me lose control of my bladder, which, at one point, I went to empty just in case. By the end of lessons, I could discern the Lesser and Nightmare from the other four. My senses weren't practiced enough to notice the subtleties to tell the rest apart. They were all equally terrifying and unsettling.

And since I needed a crash course in everything, Ms. Weever reluctantly sent me home with the Lesser and Nightmare energies to practice with. She handed me a small velvet pouch tied closed with a golden drawstring. "I swear, if you lose them, I will expel you myself."

"I'll take good care of them." I delicately held the pouch. This thing represented my ability to be responsible and not get myself expelled. Maybe it'd be better if I didn't take them home. Ever.

Ms. Weever studied me. "Better than my mbira, I hope."

I winced. I'd forgotten about that. It lay in pieces somewhere in the demon realm after my first attempt at banishing Allosyr. "Yes, ma'am."

No, I couldn't back away from this lesson. I had to learn who my enemies were.

The reluctance in her sharp features slowly shifted to acceptance. She slowly let out a sigh through her nose. "Good."

"Ms. Weever, should I bother placing a protection circle around Nurse Kor's office?" What was the point if it'd gotten rid of hers and Bylan's efforts?

She thought a moment. "Yes. Bylan and I will do something again. Best to try and make it more trouble to stick around than give in to its wants. We might be able to avoid a confrontation if we make it too troublesome to keep influencing her." She put a hand on my shoulder. "Do your part as soon as you can, and we will, too. There's hope to win this. Now, go eat lunch. You look ready for a nap."

I felt like it. Going through strong, adrenaline-pumping emotions over and over had taken a lot out of me. I thought of asking if I could nap in her office during lunch, but that meant missing out on seeing Deren. Grabbing my violin and backpack, I left the main office building, Vergo beside me.

"Lessons sounded intense today. Did you figure out which kind of demon I was?"

I thought back to all the torment I'd endured. "Something worse than a Nightmare."

He held his furry chin high. "You are correct. I was elevated to Drude. I—" He stopped and looked around. "Do you feel that? Do you *hear* that?"

I took a deep breath and sent my awareness out in all directions. There was a tiny tickle of something being out of place in the distance. On the air rode the sound of…pipes? Music? Yes, those were notes strung together to make a tune—one would expect to hear in a child's room at bedtime. "What is that?"

"I don't know. We better find out. Run."

I chased after him and ditched my backpack as the distance between us grew. He was a shock of black zooming across the campus. I held my violin tucked under an arm in case I needed it. He darted around the corner of the K-2 building. I followed, unlatching the case while keeping it clamped under my arm. I rounded the corner and was hit by a wall of terror. A massive black mass spun like a tornado, kicking up dust everywhere. It was as tall as a door and grew taller than the buildings. A girl screamed from within the darkness.

Vergo gasped. "She's in there." He leaned against the wind, and it pushed us both back.

I shielded my face with a forearm and took my violin and bow out. The wind blew the case along the ground and out of sight. The girl screamed again.

"We have to get in there."

I tried to step forward, but the wind held me back. I shielded my instrument in my arms and leaned into the wind.

"Hurry, Mia."

Vergo leaned into the wind and his fangs and claws grew more pronounced. His snout lengthened, his ears rounded, and his whole body swelled and grew. He grew to the size of a lion, Bylan's collar growing to accommodate a neck thicker than my body. His shoulder reached my chest, and his paws were as big as my face, his claws the size of fingers. He leaned forward and roared.

My eardrums vibrated, the sheer power of the roar stunning me.

Vergo leaned into my leg. "Grab on."

My fingers found his collar, now thick as a rope. The wind swept me off my feet. Vergo roared again and I landed on his back, sitting on him like a horse. I clamped myself and my violin to him, and he clawed his way into the black tornado. He roared several more times, creating a tunnel to get through.

Once we reached the center, the winds swirled around us. I slid off Vergo's back and groped through the pure black darkness, following the sound of crying. My toes bumped into something soft and the girl screamed again.

"Mommy. I'm scared."

By the Light. I dropped to my knees. "Bela."

"Mia?" Little hands found my feet, then pawed their way up my legs.

I dropped to my knees and pulled her into a hug. She was shivering. "It's me. I've got you. Are you okay?"

"Mia, I'm scared. I want Mommy."

Vergo's large, furry body brushed against us both. "We're here, Tiny One. We'll reunite you with your mother soon enough. Mia, we need a protection circle until help comes. I don't have the power to fight this demon off by myself."

"Bela, hold on to Kitty. I need to play my violin." I shook all over as I guided one small arm, and then the other to wrap around a foreleg thicker than my legs.

"Big kitty."

I stood and shouldered my violin. However, my whole body shook. I focused on my breathing, slowly in, slowly out. Yes, a demon was exerting its pressure on all of us and I couldn't see a thing, but I had to breathe. Slowly in, slowly out. I raised my bow. The protection circle I'd practiced a zillion times formed in my mind, the runes in their cardinal locations, and the notes overlapping. I took a deep breath and played the circle's song.

Purple and white light burst into existence all around us. The whirlwind leaped back and crackled against my circle, sucking the light into it. My circle dimmed.

"Keep playing," Vergo said over the roaring wind.

I played the circle's song again and my circle pulsed with new light. The whirlwind backed away again and bands of darkness lashed at my circle, devouring flashes of light. I played the song repeatedly until the circle hummed with light and power. I held my bow at the ready over the strings. "What do we do now?"

The whirlwind rumbled like thunder and something created sparks on the outside. Purple sparks enveloped it, tearing at it. The whirlwind let out a shriek.

I was promised this soul. Begone.

Like a chest rising and falling, the whirlwind rose and burst outward, pushing the sparks away. Something exploded outside and the sparks returned, followed by streaks of white. The whirlwind let out a pain-filled scream.

I will be back. The way is open.

The whirlwind thinned and its shrill roar rose in pitch. Streaks of the world outside shone through, revealing the campus. Bylan and Ms. Weever stood together, she pointing a wand at us and Bylan standing like a martial artist. He made some punching moves and a flash of white hit the whirlwind. There was a loud crack and one last gust. A shadow lowered into the ground. Ms. Weever sprinted at the shadow, wand aimed at it. The shadow seeped into the ground and disappeared.

"No, no, no. Get back here, you coward." She stomped a boot on the sidewalk.

Bylan rushed to the edge of my protection circle, his robes swishing. "By the Light, what happened here?"

Vergo lowered himself and Bela wrapped her arms around his neck. "We're not sure. We must've gotten here shortly before you."

Bylan blinked. "Vergo?"

"Yes, sir priest. The Light finally saw it fit to give me an upgrade, it appears."

I played the song in reverse, dismissing my circle. Once again, I felt exposed, less safe without it, but at least this time, I knew the feeling would pass.

Ms. Weever said, "Can your upgraded powers tell us why those three are here, too?" She pointed.

Nurse Kor, Mr. Gauss, and Garrett all sat up and rubbed their heads. Nurse Kor rolled to her hands and knees and threw up.

"What do we have here?" Vergo narrowed his eyes.

Footsteps surrounded us. Students and teachers spilled onto the sidewalks and formed a circle, everyone whispering and pointing. One group of students got pushed aside as someone forced their way through. Mr. Redd appeared, face flushed. He stopped, taking in the scene. Somehow, his face went redder. He pushed up his glasses. "Everyone get back to class. Now."

Teachers galvanized themselves and their students into motion. Slowly, they all filed back into their respective buildings and the campus was quiet, minus the sound of chirping birds and a gentle breeze.

"Tiny One, you're injured." Vergo's voice was full of concern. He nudged her with a head half as big as her, propping her up against a foreleg, and licked her arm.

Bela giggled. "That tickles."

"Good." He licked her one more time.

Bylan knelt by them and retrieved a vial from the depths of his robes. "I'll take over from here."

Vergo stood, backing out of the way.

I placed a hand on his flank. It was all fur and

muscle, a soft outer layer covering coiled power underneath. "How did you do this?"

"I don't know. I don't think it was me."

Nurse Kor wiped her mouth and crawled closer to Bylan and Bela. "Let me help."

Vergo bared his teeth and growled. "I think not. Your presence here is terribly suspicious."

Her pale face fell. "I don't even know how I got here. One moment, I was in my office. Next thing I know, I'm out here and throwing up."

"That's not good," Ms. Weever said, standing next to me as well. She leaned closer and whispered, "Excellent job on the protection circle. You bought us much-needed time."

I whispered a heartfelt thanks.

Vergo cursed. "No. I don't want to be small again. By the Light, please no." He looked skyward as he shrunk back to house cat size. He hung his head. "Guess I haven't suffered enough humiliation yet." His ears pricked forward. He lifted one paw and examined it, and then the other. The toes of both front paws were white. "Great," he said sarcastically, "now my paws match."

Mr. Redd stomped over, face red with fury, but his voice came out in forced calm. "All of you in my office. Right now."

Chapter 16

Ms. Weever and I stood behind Nurse Kor, Mr. Gauss, and Garret, all three seated at a small round table. Nurse Kor sat hunched, head lowered. Mr. Gauss sat with his arms folded, cheek muscles clenched. Garrett curled and uncurled his fingers and kicked his legs like a swimmer, hitting the table legs.

Mr. Gauss clenched Garrett's arm. "Calm down, Garrett. You're being distracting." Garrett yanked his arm free and kicked his legs harder.

Mr. Redd said, "Get him to calm down *now*." He stood behind his desk, fists on his hips. Though a short man, his rage filled the room, making me feel smaller.

Nurse Kor grabbed Garrett's other arm and he screamed. Mr. Gauss rummaged around in the boy's backpack and yanked something out. He looked at it before shoving it in Garrett's hands.

Garrett's attention locked onto the object, and he

stilled. He flicked the object with his other hand. A ring of stones spun on an axis, creating tiny sparkles and emitting a soft ring as if someone ran a fingertip along the rim of a glass. The spinning slowed and the ringing faded. Garrett flicked the stones and the pure sound filled the air again. A sensory spinner.

Mr. Redd studied Garrett a moment before nodding approval. "Now, while Bylan tends to Bela Evers, the five of you have got some major explaining to do. What in the hell was that thing doing on campus?"

Ms. Weever stepped forward, standing straight. "All I know is that we have a new demon to deal with. It fled before I could trap it."

"What class of demon?"

"Just a Nightmare variety, but still capable of great harm. Judging by the injuries only Bela sustained, it looks like it was after her and only her."

My chest tightened as rage bubbled inside me. No one was allowed to hurt my little sister. No one. My violin whined. I relaxed my grip on the neck and focused on slowing my breathing.

"Because she's a Light?"

Ms. Weever frowned with skepticism. "That would seem logical, but demons are usually attracted to Darks and generally stay away from Lights since their connection to Shinjan provides them natural protection. Maybe Bela's age had something to do with the atypical demonic behavior, but I doubt it. This feels like an orchestrated attack."

"Why would a demon want to hurt my sister?" I spoke with contained fury. I knew I had to get my emotions under control, but the way Bela had screamed inside that vortex tore at me.

"I'd very much like to know that as well," Mr. Redd said. "Can any of you give me a satisfactory explanation?"

Mr. Gauss said, "I would love one too. I was in the middle of escorting Mr. Antcil here to the front office. I thought that girl was with Trisha." He gestured to Nurse Kor with a thumb. "And then everything went black."

"And why were you bringing him to the office? I believe he should have been on his way to lunch."

"That's where I was told to take him."

"By whom?"

"His aide, Miss Juvarra, left it in the sub notes. She's out sick today. I offered to escort him here while Joli grabbed a breather in the teacher's lounge. Garrett's been a handful in every class today."

Garrett continued to flick his sensory spinner as if oblivious to the fact that he was the focus of the conversation.

Mr. Redd rounded his desk and stood before Garrett. The principal folded his arms. "Mr. Antcil, I have a few questions for you."

"I might have answers," the boy said casually, eyes on the spinning stones.

"What happened out there when everything went dark?"

"Funny sounds. Funny music. A confused little girl. Something came from below and swallowed us all."

"What's got you so agitated today?"

Garrett shook his head and held the spinner in both hands, hiding it. "They won't come. I call, but they won't come. They're too afraid."

Mr. Redd leaned closer. "Who?"

"My friends. I want them to come back."

"Mr. Antcil, your friends aren't allowed on school property. They need to leave you alone while you get an education."

He looked out the window, his fingers going white as he clenched the spinner. "They teach me things, too. I like what they teach me."

"Who are these friends of yours?" Mr. Gauss said.

Garrett's fingers grew red and white, and his face screwed up as if he were about to cry. He tilted his head back and howled like a wolf.

Both Mr. Gauss and Mr. Redd yelled at him to stop. Garrett howled on, eyes closed. Mr. Gauss pried at the boy's hands, while Garrett struggled to break free. Ms. Weever and I exchanged looks of shock. Garrett's hands came apart and Mr. Gauss held one of the boy's hands up so the sensory spinner was in front of his face. He spun the rocks and ringing filled the air. The howling stopped.

"Get him to the counselor," Mr. Redd said

Grabbing the backpack from the floor, Mr. Gauss stood. "Let's go, Garrett." He held open the office door and Garrett exited the room, eyes locked on the spinner again. The ringing ceased when the door closed. Mr. Redd faced the door, catching his breath. He shook his head.

"Something's not right with that boy," Vergo said. "I don't know if it's magical or otherwise, but he needs help."

Mr. Redd stood before Nurse Kor, his anger reddening his face again. "Miss Kor, you have some explaining to do.

The nurse hung her head. "I honestly don't know what's going on. I thought I was sick or something and had to power through it. I think it's more serious than that."

Mr. Redd considered her a moment. His eyes narrowed. "How serious?"

Nurse Kor shook her head. "I don't know."

Ms. Weever stepped forward and placed a hand on the nurse's shoulder, who flinched, but then placed a hand on top of Ms. Weever's. "Trisha was nearby when Miss Evers and Bylan performed the crossover ritual last year. I think we've finally seen the full consequences of that. There's no way any of us could've foreseen this."

"How were there consequences besides forcing the demon to cross over? This doesn't make any sense. What details are you hiding from me?"

Ms. Weever stiffened.

"Do I need to shut the school down? Is everyone in danger?"

"No. We're far from the first school that's had to deal with demons, Darks, or no Darks present. Half the schools across the country have lesser demons present due to so many raging hormones and roiling emotions concentrated in such locations. I can place protections all over campus to force the demon to go elsewhere."

"So we can get through this without having to notify the school board or the State?"

Ms. Weever tilted her head slightly. "That depends on the Evers parents." She and Mr. Redd looked at me.

As much as I wanted to cower against the wall, I stood up straighter and held my chin parallel to the floor.

There was a polite knock on the door, which then opened. Bylan entered carrying Bela in his arms, her head using his shoulder as a pillow, and her blonde-haired rag doll clutched in one hand. He pulled his robe out of the way and shut the door.

"Bela." I set my violin on the table and reached for her.

Bylan smiled softly. "She's asleep. I gave her some herbs and cast a spell to ensure she remembers nothing about the attack."

Ms. Weever said, "Did she tell you anything?"

He pursed his lips. "What type of demon uses music to lure children into their trap? She went on about trying to find someone playing music. I didn't hear any by the time we showed up."

"I heard it," I said. "And so did Vergo." I explained how he heard it first, how he knew something about it was wrong, and that we followed the music to the attack site.

Nurse Kor said, "How did she leave class without anyone noticing?"

"Easy," Ms. Weever said. "The same way you have no recollection of leaving your office around the same time. Unless you remember doing that?"

"I don't," she said unhappily. "What's wrong with me? How do I fix this?"

"Are you saying you're the one who attacked Bela?" Mr. Redd said.

Nurse Kor's eyes watered. "I hope not. I'm a healer. My heart and soul belong to medicine and healing."

Ms. Weever said, "I doubt you attacked her, but I have a hunch that whatever's attached to you is responsible."

Nurse Kor gaped. "Whatever's attached to me? Are

you kidding?"

Ms. Weever put her fists on her hips. "You yourself admitted that something serious is going on. I'm telling you that I have more than enough evidence to conclude that you have a demonic attachment. Mr. Redd, if we sever this attachment, then I'm positive the threat will disappear."

The principal nodded. "Get it done as soon as you can. We don't need the school board relieving us of our jobs."

Nurse Kor stood, hands clenched into fists. "How can you blame me so quickly? That boy was present, too, and he has some strange things going on with him. What's his alignment anyway?"

"Kindred," Mr. Redd said. "Strange as he is, he's innocent."

"You yourself told him he can't bring his friends on campus. Are you sure that's not what attacked Bela?"

Bylan said, "I've never heard of a Kindred being able to summon black whirlwinds. That thing was no plant or animal."

"It—" Thoughts buzzed behind Nurse Kor's eyes and she studied the priest with open disbelief.

"Trisha, it'll be all right. Once the attachment is removed, you'll return to your normal, loving, healing self."

Nurse Kor looked between the three adults. Her gaze found me and she glared. "This is ridiculous." She stormed for the door. "I don't have an attachment. Stop blaming me for something I didn't do." The door slammed behind her.

Chapter 17

I somehow made it through bandyll practice after all that had happened. Word had already spread throughout the school about me and everyone involved, and how something had tried to kill my sister. I heard one crazy version that involved me stabbing a giant cat with my violin bow. The truth only got muddier from there.

Hopefully, the myriad versions and their levels of total inaccuracy motivated the school board to ignore the whole thing. Other alignments caused magical chaos, from breaking floors, setting things on fire, flooded bathrooms, and stuff like that. The only thing that didn't really happen was dealing with demons. At least, if anyone asked to see the large cat I had with me, they would see only a normal-sized house cat. No one had to know that the size change was temporary. I could technically say classmates were exaggerating, which meant other details were also exaggerated.

No one learned anything for the rest of the day as teachers constantly barked at students to stop chatting and start paying attention. Even I couldn't remember a thing Mr. Gauss said, even though I loved listening to him talk. Everyone was talking about me, and I knew it.

Teammates tried to press me for details, until Coach Viro threatened to make us run laps until we threw up. We had our first match in two weeks, which we were reminded about every five minutes. Both she and Desi seemed entirely disinterested in what happened, which was strange. All my afternoon teachers had given me curious looks full of questions they didn't dare ask, unless they wanted to derail their lesson. Maybe our coaches were that focused on winning.

When the late bus dropped me off at home, Bela was playing with blocks and dolls on the floor while Mom read on the couch. A song stone under the window played a gentle tune that filled the air with calm. Mom looked up as I shut the door behind me.

"Mia. You're home," she said in a whisper. She slapped the book closed, giving me a glimpse of another shirtless man before she set it on a side table. Putting a finger over her lips, she waved me over with her other hand, her movements urgent.

I dumped all my stuff by the shoe pile and stood before her. She patted the couch. I hesitated before sitting.

"Your dad's napping. Had an extra strenuous day at work. Anyway, Sanctus Bylan told me what happened today. I'm so glad your sister is going to be okay. I wish those red marks would go away." Bela made her rag doll walk atop a block wall she'd built. "I'm trying to figure out what to say to your father. I don't want him to think we need to move again, especially not when he has a really good, steady job. Sanctus Bylan doesn't believe there's any reason to find another school, and I believe him. I don't know if your dad will."

"I hope he does. I believe Bylan, too."

"Sanctus Bylan," Mom said firmly. "Always use his title."

"Yes, ma'am." That's right. Mom and Dad didn't know Bylan had been kicked out of the Order of Leo.

Mom raised an eyebrow, a ghost of a smile on her face. "Did you call me ma'am? That's too sweet. You sound like you're in a military academy."

"Ms. Weever taught me to say that, instead of nodding or just saying yeah."

She broke into a full grin. "And here I thought I couldn't love your tutor any more than before." She hugged me.

I went wide-eyed, having not seen it coming, but I returned the hug. These last few months had seen their fair share of hugs and kisses. I breathed in her flowery scent until the vice-like grip around my torso released.

Hands on my shoulders, her gaze grew serious. "If your father notices the marks, tell him a classmate scratched her with a toy rake, okay?"

"I will." The words came automatically. Mom telling me to lie to Dad? This was crazy.

"Thanks, Mia. I know it's strange. I want your dad to be happy and keep his job. I want us all to be safe and happy. Now, come help me make dinner and tell me how you saved your sister."

I needed to start on my homework as soon as

possible, but I washed up and helped Mom with preparing pork tacos and cornbread while I told her about what happened with Vergo, the protection circle I summoned, and Ms. Weever and Bylan jumping in to help chase the thing off. I left out the stuff about Nurse Kor and the rest, and then I looked up, remembering.

I was promised this soul. The way is open.

How had I forgotten up until now? Who promised my little sister to a demon? What was open? In exactly how much danger was my sister in?

"What's wrong, Mia?" Mom paused in mashing avocado in a stone bowl.

Okay, I so couldn't tell Mom about this.

Vergo had been watching the whole time from atop a kitchen counter. "You look like you saw a demon."

Okay, what was equally as scary as this? I lowered my gaze to my pile of shredded pork. "I just remembered I have a math test tomorrow." My face heated with the blatant lie.

"Ah," Mom said. "I remember those days." She finished mashing the avocado for guacamole and spritzed some lime in. "I'm amazed you were able to pull off that protection circle."

"Honestly, I am, too," Vergo said. "You're way ahead of the curve. You didn't mess up a single note, and you centered yourself in seconds. I couldn't have done that at your age."

Vergo's tone and furry face were genuine.

"That cat talking to you again?"

"Yeah, he complimented me. I guess I don't understand how hard it was to do what I did." How had I pulled it off? I'd just acted. Breathed. Focused. Played. I couldn't remember moving the bow or the notes themselves. The protection circle came into existence. "I had to protect Bela. As annoying as she can be, she's my little sister. She was so scared. I had to be brave for her."

"Well, I'm glad you did. Very glad. And I'm so grateful for Ms. Weever. She's doing an excellent job of teaching you. I don't understand why all the other schools couldn't be bothered to do the same. They're doing a disservice to your alignment."

"It's okay, Mom." It wasn't, but I didn't know what else to say. I wished they treated me better, helped me more, but then I wouldn't be out here, enrolled at Toolena Mesa, and would've never met Deren or Ms. Weever. I'd probably be friendless and nearly powerless.

She added diced onion, tomato, and garlic to the avocado, giving it some color and extra flavor. "I guess. I still wish things had turned out differently."

"Me, too." I sprinkled a taco seasoning blend on the meat and stirred it with two forks.

Mom's movements slowed. "Mia, I was wondering." She set aside the guacamole and twisted off a chunk of dough from a larger ball. "Those protection circles... Can you place one around the whole house?"

"A more experienced Dark certainly could," Vergo said, hopping onto the last open spot on the island counter. He curled his tail around his forelegs and sat behind the guacamole bowl. "The general rule is the bigger the circle, the more people needed to create it. Still, this is a basic protection circle. Your prodigal skills might be able to pull it off." He shrugged and licked a paw.

"I could try," I said to Mom. Maybe I could pull it off.

"Great. Please do."

This gave me an idea. Since sneaking into the nurse's office to place a protection circle in there wasn't working because they locked the building before bandyll practice was over, then maybe I could stand outside the office and place one around the whole building.

Despite our height difference, mine and Ms. Weever's circles were the same size. She'd taught me to hand draw them in a certain diameter to draw enough power to do anything. What would happen if I made a bigger one? *How* did one conjure a bigger circle?

I listened to Vergo talk out the procedure and give me tips over dinner. We ate as a family of four, and Dad was in a good mood after a nap. Mom and I waited for him to say something about Bela's red marks, but he didn't notice. Either that or he didn't think anything of them. Maybe since Bela was back to her usual bubbly self, he didn't care. She moved around as if the marks didn't cause any pain or discomfort. Whatever it was, I was relieved I didn't have to lie to Dad.

The sun was almost down when Vergo accompanied me outside. I walked around the house, getting a feel for how big it was. The air was warm, with a breeze making way for cooler air blowing in. On it rode the smell of our neighbors' livestock and our herb garden. I tried not to breathe too deeply.

The sunset brought out the reds and oranges in the distant mountains, which were varying shades of brown during the day. I tore my gaze from the beautiful sight as I rounded the other side of the house. It was twice as long as it was wide, with an herb garden nestled against the front of the house and nothing but rugged desert everywhere else.

I stood at the north end of the house and traced a rune Vergo had taught me on my violin. "*Enthu*," I said to the lacquered wood. The rune lit up with a flash of green light before fading into the wood. The instrument vibrated with the power boost.

"Perfect," Vergo said and trotted off. "Now for the first rune in the circle."

I followed him to the north side of the house, measured out my steps from the wall, and turned around, facing the chipped paint. Despite having practiced the rune a zillion times, I played the notes in my head before placing the bow on a string. The notes flowed flawlessly, drifting out into the desert. The nor'gilda rune glowed with purple and white light at my feet, sending a layer of dust out in all directions. I moved to the east side, walking in as perfect an arc as possible, and played the es'gilda rune. It lit up and thrummed with energy as well. I moved and played the so'gilda and wu'gilda runes and headed inside. I had to be in the center of the house, the center of the runes for this to work.

Dad was already in bed since he had to get up so early for work. He sometimes nodded off during dinner and was asleep within the hour. Mom and Bela sat in the living room, Mom reading a book to my sister. Flip-flops kicked off, I stood at the opposite end of the living room and raised my bow. Vergo sat in front of me, watching.

"Moment of truth," he said.

I took a deep breath and felt out the runes'

locations outside. They pulsed with power waiting to be put to use, and glowed. They needed a complete circle to direct their energies. I closed my eyes and played. The first rune's notes came easy enough, but the second one came slower. I opened my eyes and gritted my teeth as I forced my arm to draw out the third rune's notes. My arm seized up, and I couldn't move it. Grunting, I tried to get the note out, but only managed a screech. An unseen force repelled the bow and my arm flung outwards. Somehow, I held onto the bow. My arm dangled at my side as I caught my breath.

"What happened?" Mom said.

All the energy that spread into the circle retreated into my body, making me flinch.

Vergo's shoulders drooped. "I was afraid of this. It was a grand effort, Little One. Another year or two, and you'll have the power to do this on your own."

"I'm not strong enough yet to make such a big circle on my own," I told Mom. "I got about halfway, and that was it."

She pursed her lips. "Thank you for trying."

Bela got that serious look on her face. "Okay, Grandma." She slid off the couch and marched over to me, eyeing my feet. Her own little feet made soft slaps against the wood floor. She dropped to her knees and placed her hands on my feet. Her fingers were cold, her palms warm. "Like this?" She nodded at Grandma, I guessed, and then looked up at me, her little face serious. "Grandma says to play again. I'm helping."

Doing a crossover ritual with a full-fledged Light was one thing. Laying a giant protection circle with a Light child?

"Can't hurt to try with this particular circle," Vergo

said.

"I'll try." I set my bow, rehearsed the circle's song in my head, and played. Energy flowed through both me and Bela, making the notes louder. The bow flowed back and forth over the strings with ease for the first two runes. The third took effort to complete. The fourth pushed back as I forced my arm to guide the bow. Bela grunted. The final notes came forth, and the house flashed with purple and white light. I gasped for air and barely avoided Bela as I dropped to my knees.

The circle was complete, humming with energy.

Vergo pawed my knee. "Quick. The final part before the circle sucks up all your energy."

My arms felt like they weighed a ton each as I shouldered my bow and played the new phrase Vergo had taught me. Seven notes later, the light sank back into the ground. The protection circle remained, hidden in the land.

This was so much better. I could move and breathe with ease again. I sat on my heels.

"All done," Bela said in a sleepy voice and passed out.

Chapter 18

Deren and I waited for my straggling teammates to head off to the middle school parking lot, where the late buses would eventually arrive. Thankfully, the 6-8 building blocked anyone's view of what we had planned next.

"Do you think this is going to work?"

"I don't know. You're not a Light, but I'm hoping all I need is some of your energy." We walked side-by-side around the main office, feeling out the size of the building like I had my house. The building was more square, and the sidewalk that looked like a tortoise shell wrapped around the whole thing. Outside the sidewalk lay manicured grass. Various prickly plants and pretty flowers grew between the path and the building. None of them paid attention to us like Nurse Kor's vines did.

She'd been out the past few days for unknown reasons. Bylan and Ms. Weever said the only explanation they heard was that she was out sick. We weren't sure whether or not it really had anything to do with her refusal to accept the truth and some help. Mr. Redd wasn't saying anything, and I dared not ask him myself.

"This is a big building."

"I know. Pay attention. We have enough time for only one try before the late bus comes."

"Oh. Right." Deren took something out of his backpack and slipped them on his hands and wrists. They were made of pieces of stone strung together, wrapped around his wrists, and looped around his middle fingers, placing a rounded stone in the palms of his hands.

"What are those?"

"Earth bracers." He held up his hands, showcasing the multicolored stones. "They help me concentrate and channel my alignment."

We finished our lap around the building, returning to the north side. I shouldered my violin and played the nor'gilda rune. Spidery lines lit up at my feet. Deren bent over, drew markings at all four nautical directions around the rune, and then placed his hands flat on the ground. His runes lit up gold and white. The energy of his power added to mine vibrated under my feet, making me feel more connected to the ground. "Whoa, I felt that."

"Yeah. This is cool. I can feel your runes, too. They feel cold, like I can feel cold water rolling down my arms, but it feels refreshing."

"Yours feel…earthy. I feel like my feet are stuck to the ground, and I feel taller." I wished I were taller. It would totally make me a better goalie.

Deren smiled at me and butterflies took flight in my stomach. I smiled back, torn between running and hiding or throwing my arms around him. Our alignments mingling made me feel like we were touching.

"Keep going, lovebirds," Vergo said impatiently.

I flinched. Looking away, Deren ran a hand through his hair. I said, "Let's go." We worked our way through the other three corners before I got us inside with a charm disc lent to me by Ms. Weever. I pressed the disc above the door handle. Something inside clicked. I led Deren inside the darkened office.

"How'd you do that?"

"You saw nothing. You know nothing. It's safer that way." Ms. Weever had told me to tell no one. She'd be fired if anyone found out I'd gotten it from her. I pocketed the lock charm. Together, we checked the building to make sure no teachers or staff were present anywhere, including the bathrooms. A couple of cars sat in the parking lot, but they were probably district vehicles reserved for school-related travel. We checked behind the front counter last and confirmed that everyone was gone, the counters immaculate, and every last stack of paper and pen in place.

I turned to head for the center of the building as Deren climbed onto the counter.

"Deren, what're you doing? Get down." Despite knowing we were alone, I looked around, anticipating getting caught.

Deren held up a finger and pointed at the doors. He deepened his voice and tried to sound authoritative. "This is Mr. Redd. I hereby decree that everyone will get churros with their lunch every day. Dessert is a part of a balanced lunch. Our students need their dessert."

I snorted and Vergo let out a withering sigh.

"Children."

A nice, warm, and cinnamon-y churro sounded great. I tugged Deren's jeans. "C'mon. Let's go."

"Did I sound anything like Mr. Redd?" He dropped down, landing on both feet with a thud.

"No."

"Dang. I tried."

Without further delay, we positioned ourselves in the center of the building and our runes. Deren stood behind me and placed his hands on my shoulders. His touch sent an electric thrill through me. I couldn't help but smile.

"Concentrate," Vergo said, his tail flicking in agitation. "You two are seriously nothing but trouble together."

Ignoring the comment, I concentrated on my breathing and the song I had to play. Deren breathed in time with me, and his energy grew calm and still. I closed my eyes and played. The notes filled the building as power spread out to the runes. The first one came easy, the second harder, and Deren and I grunted through the last two as my arm grew heavier with every note, but it worked. It actually worked. We both gasped and dropped to our knees, Deren knocking me over as the ground glowed with white, purple, and gold light. I cradled my instrument as I landed on a shoulder, and forced myself back up as the circle sucked energy from me. The runes pulled at my body from every direction. I hoisted the violin back to my shoulder, took a deep breath, and played the final phrase, completing the protection circle. The light seeped into the ground and winked out, but the circle's energy remained.

Our heavy breathing echoed down the hallway. We sat up against opposite walls. Deren laughed. "We did it. That was so cool."

"Yeah."

Vergo pawed my leg. "Little One, take my collar off for a moment so he can hear me as well."

I obliged and Deren started, letting out a small yelp before recognizing my personal spirit cat. "Vergo. Hi."

"Greetings, boy. You sure have taken an uncanny liking to me after trying to kill you not too long ago."

He shrugged. "You were a demon doing demon things. Now, you're not a demon, and you're helping us."

"I guess I am." His blue-eyed gaze drifted down the hall. "Anyway, the fact that forming the protection circle worked without him being a Light is rather interesting. Long before my human lifetime, there was this fabled group called the Order of Tula. Legend has it that all seven alignments were a part of it and worked together to perform miraculous feats, from building cities to reshaping the lands and even creating contraptions that flew through the air or dived to the ocean floor. The tales seemed so far-fetched, until now."

"All seven working together?" Deren said. "That sounds so unreal. Every alignment works separately. No one touches the other's territory."

"Right," I said, "but remember how Bylan and I worked together to get rid of Allosyr last year?" It made sense for Light and Dark, but... "Vergo, Light and Dark are really close, in a sense. We deal with similar things, so it makes sense that these two alignments work well together. How does bringing in the other five work? They all have opposites, except Kindred."

"Yeah, what's the balance to Kindred?"

"I don't know," Vergo said, "but you two demonstrated that any two alignments are magically compatible. Maybe the fact that they are opposites brings balance. Anyway, think on it and hurry up and catch the late bus."

I shoved the collar back on, and we scrambled to our feet. We ran out the door, and Deren turned around when he realized I wasn't following him. I took out Ms. Weever's charm and stopped with the disc hovering over the door. "Wait, I'm supposed to leave it unlocked." That was the coverup in case anyone found out about us getting inside. I placed my violin and the charm inside my violin case. We grabbed our bags. As soon as we stepped away from the building, something stopped us.

The energy in the ground felt jagged. It needled at my feet. The protection circle lit up and groaned like ice creaking before cracking. A pressure squeezed me. Deren clutched his head. The ground shook. The circle's light flickered. I clutched my head. It felt like it was being crushed. The screeching brought me to my knees and my eyes watered.

The circle's light shattered, sending fragments skyward before dissolving. My head spun, and the next thing I knew, I was looking at the sky. The pieces of the circle dissolved, lifting and dissipating like fog. Tendrils of shadow rose all around, gathering around the main office. The ground let out a rumble of thunder that sounded like a chuckle.

"Little One, get up." Vergo nudged me with his

head.

I wiped my eyes and sat up. The world spun. Deren lay beside me, sucking in air through his teeth and with tears rolling down his cheeks.

The shadows coalesced into a humanoid torso half as big as the office. What looked like a black tree without the trunk crowned its head, jagged leafless branches blocking out the sky. Clawed hands gripped the roof's edge, the fingers big enough to crush a car.

A trickle of terror crawled down the back of my neck, a subtle fear waiting to grow into a full-fledged scream. I scooted backwards and shook Deren. "Deren, get up. We need to get out of here." He whimpered. "Deren? Deren, c'mon."

Vergo, fur all puffed up, remained house cat size. "Mia, you've got to get him out of here. Neither of you are ready for such a foe."

The thunderous chuckle rose several octaves, smoothing into that of a woman's. Two round red eyes shone from the depth of the shadow. *Fear not, demon outcast. The Demon King wants this one alive. She's one of his instruments of chaos now. The longer she lives, the sweeter the victory.*

Deren whimpered and curled into a tighter ball. "Mia, make it go away." He sniffed.

The subtle terror spread to my limbs as I kneeled behind Deren. Tears welled in my eyes. I grit my teeth. "Deren, I need you to get up. I know this is scary, but you have to move." I lifted his shoulders and he wrenched away. "Vergo, help me. Get big again."

"I've been trying this whole time. I don't know what to do."

The demon chucked again. *Yes, run, little mortals.*

Run and hide if it makes you feel better, but it won't change a thing. Mia Evers, every choice you make, every action you take…it will all serve the Demon King in the end. Saving that boy's life will serve him. Stealing away Allosyr will serve him. All your efforts to protect your sister will serve him, too. Her life is already forfeit. It's only a matter of time before she falls from the Light and serves the Darkness. She's just one piece on the cosmic board that He controls.

"Stay away from my sister." I yanked Deren, but he didn't budge.

The demon propped its jagged head on a fist. Roots made of shadows spread from the elbow and crept down the side of the building.

Oh, Mia Evers, you have no idea what's going on here. There are more moves in play than you realize. You've already lost this chess match. Try all you want to prove to the mortal world that you're a good person and that Darks aren't all bad. Be brave. Be a hero. It doesn't matter. You're a child of the Darkness. You can't escape your nature. You can't defy the will of the Demon King. Every action you take is all part of the plan.

"Don't listen," Vergo said over the rumbling. "She's lying."

The demon straightened up, its round eyes giving off mirth. I felt a need to both laugh and scream.

Am I? Wouldn't that be so convenient? The giant head arched over the side of the office and plunged into the ground as if it were diving into water. Her voice emanated from the ground. *Until we meet again in due time, child of Darkness.*

The shadow spread like a storm rolling in. My eyes

rolled back and the last thing I heard was Vergo calling my name.

***

I woke slumped in a cushioned chair, my head tilted back with nothing but air and the corner of the chair under it. Neck stiff, I licked my dry lips. Vergo lay against my chest, front legs draped over my shoulder. He hopped onto a round table as I sat up.

I recognized the table from Mr. Redd's office. And the chairs my family and I had sat in almost a year ago. And the big, L-shaped desk. Mr. Redd sat behind it, elbows on the desk, chin propped up on interlaced fingers.

"Why do I keep finding you in places you shouldn't be?"

I froze. How did I get here? Deren sat next to me. He stirred at the sound of Mr. Redd's voice.

"And it looks like you've enlisted help in your troublemaking." He lowered his arms and sat up straight. "Miss Evers, what were you doing outside this building?"

"Careful, Little One. I don't think we're among friends." His blue eyes looked at me pleadingly.

"Mia?" Deren sat up, clutching his head.

I touched his arm. "Are you okay?"

"I think so." He opened his eyes and froze. "Where are we? Is this the principal's office?"

Mr. Redd said, "The both of you better have good reasons for missing the late bus."

I swallowed and sat up straight, trying to emulate Ms. Weever's proud posture. "I was trying to place a protection circle to help make the school safer. That's all."

"Did your tutor put you up to this?"

"Careful," Vergo said. "He's probing for information to use against you and others."

My gaze darted to the cat for a fraction of a second before I forced myself to hold Mr. Redd's glare. I didn't want him to know Vergo was talking to me. Information to use against us? It made sense. Something about the principal put me on edge like a demon's presence did. He was human, but I felt the same distrust Vergo warned me of. "No," I said, hoping he believed me. I'd be so lost if he ever fired Ms. Weever. "I'm worried about Nurse Kor. I want to help."

Mr. Redd let out an angry sigh. "You need to leave these things to your tutor and that Light priest, and stick to your schooling. Miss Evers, I put my job on the line for you last year and continue to this year. I can't keep you here if you keep misbehaving."

I opened my mouth, and he held up a finger.

"It doesn't matter whether or not you think you're helping. All I want you to do is go to class, do your homework, play sports, and learn to control your alignment. That's it. Do I make myself clear?"

I slumped, looking at my flip-flops. "Yes, sir."

"I hope so." He paused. "Now, Mr. Sevine, what were you doing here with Miss Evers?"

Deren inhaled, but I said, "He was keeping me company. He wasn't doing anything wrong."

I held Mr. Redd's suspicious gaze, ignoring whatever look Deren gave me. The principal's expression remained unchanged, offering me no clues. "Is that right?"

"Yes, sir," Deren said submissively. "I don't know how to make protection circles."

"Oh, thank goodness," Vergo said. "The boy has some sense."

"I hope that's true, Mr. Sevine," Mr. Redd said. "I understand both of your concern for Nurse Kor, but let the adults handle it. She'll be fine now that we're aware of the full extent of the problem. Stay out of trouble, both of you."

"Yes, sir," we said in unison.

"If I catch either of you in places you don't belong or doing things you shouldn't be doing, you'll both be kicked off your respective sports teams and suspended from school. Do I make myself very clear?"

Chapter 19

Deren probably listened, but I didn't. I didn't have that choice. I sat in Bylan's car with him and Ms. Weever in the front, all three of us on the lookout for Nurse Kor. Vergo stood on his hind legs, his front paws propped on the door. He watched out the window as he flicked the tip of his tail back and forth. This was so much crazier than Nurse Kor sneaking me off to the hospital.

"Are you sure I won't get expelled for this?" I said for the umpteenth time.

"Yes, already," Ms. Weever said, keeping her eyes on the parking lot. There were only a handful of cars left after practices had ended, school was out, and most of the staff gone for the day. "Besides, you need to learn how to do this. What better way to learn than a hands-on demonstration?" She'd penned a carefully-worded field trip form, mentioning something about going to the Order of Leo to watch a demonstration, and how we'd be there and back in a few hours.

My parents thought it was so wonderful an idea that they'd asked if Bela could go, too. Bylan said she needed to wait a few years. Mr. Redd had acted suspicious of why the trip had to take place after school hours. Bylan said something about it being best to wait until after the sun went down to perform such demonstrations. I had no clue if that was true. Apparently, Mr. Redd didn't either, and he approved the trip. Some magic was best performed during the day, while the opposite was true for other magic. Mr. Redd showed the utmost respect for the Light priest.

"Here she comes," Ms. Weever said, her voice tight with anticipation. She sat straighter in the passenger seat, making the black leather creak. Bylan still drove the big white car I'd snuck into last year, complete with its well-stocked apothecary cabinet. While the car was painted white, the interior was all black with silver details. It smelled like new leather with a hint of herbs and incense.

I lowered myself so my eyes were level with the bottom of the tinted glass window. No one could see in, unless we rolled windows down, but my ability to see the outside world insisted that, logically, the outside world could see in just fine. I clutched the neck of my violin case.

Nurse Kor glanced in our direction and headed towards her car without faltering. Her movements were slow, tired. She had bags under her eyes. I held my breath as she walked in front of Bylan's car. Her gaze remained downcast. She stopped by the driver's side of a gray car. At her touch, the floating charm activated and the car rose a foot off the ground. Her brows furrowed and she tilted her head.

"Go," Bylan said urgently. Donning a mask that covered her nose and mouth, and sticking in ear plugs, Ms. Weever exited the car. Bylan spoke some power words and a circle of white light enveloped Nurse Kor and her car. She backed up and an unseen force stopped her from leaving the circle. Ms. Weever held something up in one hand and entered the circle fist first. The light enveloped her and let her pass. She pocketed the object in a waist pouch and took out a vial and a bell.

Nurse Kor held up her arms, backing along the circle's edge. "What are you doing? Get away from me."

Ms. Weever held up her hand and shook the bell. I heard no sound from within the car, but Nurse Kor stood in place, swaying on her feet. Her head drooped and her arms groped the empty air. Ms. Weever rang the bell a second time and the nurse fell into my tutor's open arms. Ms. Weever plopped her in the passenger seat. Vines shot out of sleeves and wrapped around Ms. Weever's arms, who swatted and yanked at them before unstoppering the vial. Vines coiled around her neck and legs. She yelled a spell and the vines stilled.

Bylan let out a sigh of relief.

Ms. Weever stood still momentarily before uncoiling the vines and tossing them inside the car. She thrust the passenger door closed and sat in the driver's seat. Nurse Kor's car whirred to life with a gentle whine. Bylan turned on his car with the touch of a rune and we rose a foot into the air. I buckled up as we turned out of the parking lot.

"Tally ho," Vergo said lightly and hopped into the

front passenger seat.

We sped the whole way to the edge of Marohu, Bylan taking the lead once we hit the highway. He had exterior lights that flashed, signaling for other vehicles to move out of the way. At first, the extreme speed terrified me, but as we sailed mile after mile without slowing, Ms. Weever behind us, I wished we'd drive faster. Cars moved aside without question. I felt more important than I was. It would've been fun to drive around like this all the time.

The thrill died when we exited the highway and turned onto the road leading to the Order of Leo's basilica. Bylan turned off the lights. Pointy turrets loomed over endless blocks of city streets surrounding it. The building looked more like a castle than a church, all the surrounding buildings bowing to its superiority. A huge ring of landscaped property was dotted with bushes and mesquite trees surrounding the basilica. We turned onto the property near a pond shaded by palm trees.

I stiffened. "I thought you said we weren't going to the Order's basilica."

"Not the main building," he said, taking another turn. We navigated around the parking lot. It looked like half of Marohu could park here. Trees grew thicker as we approached a tiny mountain. The low canopy hid it from view and the world around us darkened. Rocks bigger than the car rose all around us, the trees dispersed, and we plunged into total darkness around the next turn.

The car veered downward. I inhaled sharply, and Bylan's eyes found mine in the rearview mirror. "You all right back there?"

"Yeah." I sat up straighter now that I understood we weren't driving off some underground cliff to our death.

The cave was aglow with small lights that reminded me of spots on a caterpillar. It was like we looked at the bug's back from the inside, each spot casting light on the rocky interior that was its body. The car's headlights illuminated a spiraling path that led us deeper underground. I felt sick to my stomach. The lefthand turns wouldn't end. I breathed deeper, trying to keep my stomach under control, but once I thought I was about to lose the battle, the path straightened out.

Two giant stone doors loomed in the headlights, the cave ceiling lost in darkness. The dotted pathway of lights lay along the ground. The headlights veered away from the doors as Bylan parked the car. Ms. Weever parked next to us.

"This is it," Bylan said.

"What is this place?" Vergo said. "This is very uncharacteristic of a Light Order."

"It's a catacomb that also hides an ancient chamber. It's maintained out of respect, but otherwise unused. Most Lights wish we'd bury the place." He exited the car and opened my door. Cold air smelling like water washed over me. I stepped out, violin in hand.

"Why?" Vergo said dryly, "Because this place contradicts modern Light doctrine?"

Ms. Weever walked over to us, scratching her neck. "Bylan, please tell me you have a remedy for those cursed vines. I think they're poison ivy." Her neck and arms were covered in red splotches. She grimaced as she scratched a wrist. "We better get this in one try. I don't ever want to go through that again."

The priest nodded and retrieved a spray from his car. He whispered a spell to the bottle and handed it over. Ms. Weever sprayed herself down. The redness turned pink and she let out a sigh of relief.

Bylan and my tutor strapped Nurse Kor to a wheelchair that looked more like a military tank on thin wheels. Ms. Weever strapped her wrists, chest, waist, ankles, and thighs to the chair while Bylan whispered power words and waved some vase on a chain over various parts of the nurse's body.

"Hmm, you Lights don't play around," Vergo said. "Is that silver?"

Bent over the sleeping nurse, Bylan nodded. "Silver runes, silver cuffs hiding in waiting should leather prove not strong enough. The leather is embroidered with satin thread blessed during a full moon. Whatever's attached to her has its work cut out for it."

"Impressive," Vergo said, a hint of admiration in his voice.

Bylan led the way to the giant doors. Carvings of the sun and a handful of Light priests were etched into one side, robed arms raised heavenward. The moon and more priests were etched into the other side, arms also raised. Between them and split evenly between the doors sprawled a contorted monster. A demon? Whatever it was, it didn't look happy.

Bylan placed a hand on either door and tilted his head back. "In the name of the Light, open this door." Runes lit up all along the doorframe and floor. The sun and moon blazed. The doors swung inward. Stone rumbled and a blast of stale air rushed out.

Vergo sneezed. "That was delightful. Oh, Light,

why did you grace me with these feline senses? I don't even need air to exist."

A lone pillar of sunlight shined down on the exact center of the huge space. The floor sloped towards the center like a giant dinner plate. Bylan gestured for Ms. Weever to take Nurse Kor to the middle of the room. My tutor marched onward, the steps of her knee-length boots echoing through the chamber. The ceiling reached all the way to ground level above us, the hole no bigger than a pencil eraser.

Bylan flipped a series of stone levers. The doors groaned, paused, and then slowly swung back closed. With a flip of another stone lever, water bubbled and flowed along the edge of the room. A third lever and something let out a short roar. Orange light flared to life. A hissing spread across the room. The orange followed the hissing and the entire room became wreathed in fire. A moat, narrow enough to step over, ringed the stone floor.

By the Light, this room was enormous.

Bylan yanked a fourth lever and runes under the flames flared to life. Small wall sections slid out and little fans spread their fins and spun. Air flowed, kicking up a few strands of my hair. I tucked them behind my ears.

"Air, Fire, Water, and I'm assuming the chamber itself counts as Earth," Vergo said to himself. "How very interesting."

Bylan wordlessly headed for the center of the room. I followed, violin case in hand and Vergo padding along beside me. The priest touched the back of the wheelchair. Four little legs dropped out of the bottom, the bottom half of the wheels folded to parallel to the floor, and the whole chair lowered to the ground.

"I could've used one of these on multiple occasions," Ms. Weever said. "You wouldn't happen to have a spare lying around, would you?"

One side of his mouth curled in a smile. "Afraid not. The Order doesn't exactly hand these out freely. They like to keep track of every last one of them." He draped a sash around his neck. "Shall we get started?"

Ms. Weever donned a silver necklace with an eye pendant. She put an identical necklace around my neck and placed her hands on my shoulders. "You'll do nothing but observe, unless I say otherwise. Don't say a word to me, Bylan, Kor, or the demon."

"Or me," Vergo said.

Since he wasn't wearing his necklace, Ms. Weever could hear him. She curled a lip. "Or that fool." She took a calming breath. "Remember, this isn't practice. This is the real thing. By the sound of what you described, this could very well be an archdemon. Trust Bylan and me to keep you safe. There's a lot of protective power in this place. It's the only reason I agreed to allow you here."

"I will, and I trust you." Even though that giant demon had said something about wanting me alive, Ms. Weever had explained that that could very well be a lie to trick me into complacency. Even if this demon didn't try to kill me, it could try to attach itself to any of us instead.

Ms. Weever squeezed my shoulder. "Good. Get your violin out."

I did as told and stood off to the side, Vergo beside me. "Pay close attention, Little One. Listen to what they do and don't say. Watch what they do and don't do. If this is anything like exorcisms of old, then you're in for a terrifying treat."

Bylan placed a hand over Nurse Kor's forehead and whispered, "Wake, child of the Kindred."

Nurse Kor startled awake, snapping upright. Her wild gaze found me. "Mia?" She tried to get up, straining against the straps. She looked at them. "What's this? Mia, get me out of this thing. What's going on?"

My heart reached out to her as I said nothing. Vergo placed a paw on my shoe and stayed quiet as well.

Bylan said, "Trisha, you have a demonic attachment. We brought you here to free you of it safely."

Her drawn face went from frantic to furious. "I already told you I don't have an attachment. Get me out of this thing before I go to the school board and have you fired." She strained against the arm and chest straps. "I'll get both of you fired and her expelled. This is all types of illegal."

"Trisha," Bylan said patiently. "Trisha Antyi Kor, the Light calls to you. Cast out the darkness and come back to the Light."

"I told you," Nurse Kor said angrily, but her voice lost some of its fervor, "I told you…let me…go."

He placed one end of his sash over her forehead and called to her again. She writhed under the sash's touch. Ms. Weever placed her hands on the meat of the nurse's shoulders, steadying her.

Nurse Kor snarled. "Let. Me. Go."

Bylan placed both ends of the sash on her forehead. The wheelchair rocked as Nurse Kor strained against the straps. "Leave this body. It's not yours."

"It is mine." Her voice sounded deeper, evil. I took a step back. Vergo sat in front of me. Nurse Kor growled like an animal, grunting and straining to break free. She screamed and an unseen force pushed both priest and tutor off her. They flung out their arms and caught their balance. A flash of surprise played across Ms. Weever's face before she regained steely focus.

Bylan took a bottle out of the depths of his sleeves and made slashing sweeps in Nurse Kor's direction. Two lines of red erupted on her skin. She screamed again, making my ears ring. Bylan said, "Leave this body."

"Never." She bared her teeth. Her eyes were all black, and she had long fangs.

I gasped and took another step back.

Those black eyes locked on me. Her mouth curled into an unnaturally long smile. "Mia, dear, release me. You know I don't deserve this." Her voice sounded like Nurse Kor's again.

Despite what I saw and heard, despite my fear, I took a step closer. Something compelled me to obey despite common sense knowing to stay put. Vergo arched and rubbed against my shin. He looked up at me, pleading in his blue eyes. His contact broke the compulsion. Horror sent a shiver up and down my body from head to toe. I took several steps back and focused on my breathing. I couldn't afford to feel horror at this moment.

Nurse Kor or the demon lost its smile. She tried to lunge at me and the whole chair jolted, thudding against the ground. Bylan sprayed more liquid on her, and Ms. Weever touched her necklace to the back of the nurse's head. Kor writhed and snarled. She drooled black ink. Something snapped and one of her arms popped free.

"Bylan." Ms. Weever grabbed the nurse's wrist and tried to force it down. Nurse Kor swung her arm and sent my tutor flying several feet.

Bylan slipped on a silver gauntlet and grabbed the nurse's wrist. She let out a sound that was both scream and roar. He forced her wrist back onto the wheelchair. He touched the back and the silver bands clanged into place. She stilled.

Ms. Weever slowly got up and brushed off her multiple layers of frilly skirts. She twisted her torso. Blood ran down her arm from the elbow. Marching back to the center of the room, she dipped two fingers in the blood and drew lines on Nurse Kor's forehead. "*Disper ent zwei.*"

Nurse Kor tossed her head back and screamed. Bylan draped his sash over her heart and dumped more liquid on her head. The scream turned into a growl, and then a gurgling.

"Here it comes," Bylan said. One hand over her chest, he and Ms. Weever tilted the wheelchair forward. The nurse growled and gurgled, then gagged. Her whole body shook. She vomited something black and tarry, choking and coughing. She vomited a second time and coughed some more.

Nurse Kor raised her head, gasping for breath. "Wha...what's happening? Where am I?" She sounded entirely like herself, and terrified. She vomited some more, creating a pile of black mud.

Bylan wiped her mouth and held a vial to her lips. "Drink, my child." Nurse Kor chugged until the whole thing was gone and threw up again. She gasped for breath as they set the chair back down. Bylan tossed what looked like sand on the vomit. It sizzled and turned to dust. Nurse Kor slumped in the chair, eyes closed and her body covered in sweat. "Trisha," Bylan said.

"I'm here," she said in a breathy voice. "What's going on?"

"You have an attachment. You need to cast it out."

"How? It won't leave."

Ms. Weever put her necklace on the nurse. "Yes, it will. Fight it. You're light. It's darkness. It cannot stand your touch. Fight it."

The nurse shook her head. "I can't."

Bylan said, "Yes, you can." He shoved something in each of her hands. She clutched them in a death grip, her knuckles white.

Ms. Weever took out her violin and played a slow song. The notes started low in octave, long and slow. Her fingertips danced across the strings as she played a rune's phrase. A section of the floor lit up as a rune activated. Her song rose half an octave and continued. Tears streamed down Nurse Kor's face. Her body rocked and jolted as she fought a battle we couldn't see. My tutor played the circle's entire song and the floor lit up along the edge, runes and all.

Ms. Weever waved me over. "Touch her shoulder and send positive, loving thoughts her way. You'll feel hers and the demon's emotions. Keep yourself separate from them." She placed her own hands on the nurse's shoulders.

Vergo touched his nose to one of Kor's legs and recoiled. "Goodness." He lay on one of her feet and closed his eyes.

Setting my bow back in the open case, I tentatively held a hand over her shoulder. Fear coursed through me, but I pushed it aside. Nurse Kor needed my help, not my fear. I took a deep breath and rested a hand on her shoulder. Rage, terror, hopelessness, and hope filled me, roiling around and battling for control of the nurse's body. It was like standing in the whirlwind with lightning flashing all around me. Each flash was a different emotion. The negative emotions came at me. I conjured my protective shield as I chased down hope with Ms. Weever, Bylan, and Vergo. Everything was so cold, but their presences added warmth. I latched onto hope and tried to hold it still. They latched on to me and warmth grew.

Something shoved me in the chest and sent me backpedaling. I slid to a stop, Bylan and Ms. Weever stopping with me. Nurse Kor slumped in the chair, unconscious and drenched in sweat.

Something dark shot out of her. It filled the vaulted space from top to bottom and morphed into the demon that'd appeared over the main office. Its crown of tree branches touched the ceiling and showered us with sparks.

I snatched up my violin. The demon barely fit in the space, looming over us like a storm rolling in, a black dragon considering which sheep to devour first. Claws big enough to crush a house clawed at the circle's edge. The two round red eyes faced us, two massive red lights glaring down.

You fools. Release me or I will kill you all.

Claws hit the ground on either end of the circle, making the room shake. Smoke tendrils and black roots spilled out around the claws, searching for a weakness in our defenses.

Bylan executed what looked like a martial arts form, waving his arms around him. The circle lit up, dousing the room in white light. The demon recoiled, shielding its face. A giant paw hovered over us, etched with roots and scales that constantly shifted around, as if trying to get away from the light. Ms. Weever held up her oak wand in one hand and a bundle of herbs in another. Stomping the ground, she threw her arms down and bent over, as if bowing. Purple light joined the white. The room hummed with power.

The circle's runes flared to life, a mix of spidery curves and angular lines. They were all protective in nature, and they each had a series of notes that followed the spidery shapes, completing the circle's song. The shape of the phrases was built right into the runes themselves, as if the circle's markings were the sheet music.

The demon dived at us and Bylan raised his hands. Bands of white light shot over us, creating a woven dome. Claw tips dug in between the strands and the dome bowed. The demon recoiled, dripping shadow drops like blood.

If you want this mortal so bad, you can have it. I'll find another.

The demon clawed at the circle, creating sparks with every strike. Fire flared up with each hit, the wind spun faster, and water splashed like a wave crashing against a cliff.

Ms. Weever held her wand and herb bundle overhead. "It's now or never, Bylan."

"I'm trying." His arms shook with effort.

My tutor shouted a spell. A band of purple

lightning erupted from the wand, hitting the demon square in the back. It didn't so much as flinch as it continued pounding on the circle's invisible barrier. She attacked again, only to get the same result. "Bylan."

Something was off with the dynamic of the situation. Even though the demon was trying to escape, they seemed unable to control it. I stepped closer to the edge of the woven light dome and studied the circle's runes, wind whirling around us.

Vergo said, "Mia, what are you doing?"

I ignored him, feeling out the runes' shapes. Yes, I could play this circle's song. The notes were laid out before me, plain as the ground itself. I shouldered my violin.

"Mia?"

I breathed deep and slow, slowing my heart rate and syncing my energy up with the circle's power. My body pulsed in time with the circle, flowing through me like waves breaking on the shore.

"Mia, no," Ms. Weever shouted.

I inhaled deeply, setting aside any concern about everything but the song. I set my bow over the strings and played. The song was steady, uplifting. The longer I played, the taller I felt.

The demon turned, fixing its round eyes on me. *You.*

I completed the song and the circle grew brighter. The demon recoiled as if burned, visibly shrinking. Ms. Weever blasted it with more purple lightning and Bylan threw the woven dome at it. It grew and wrapped around the demon's body, trapping it like a fish. The demon let out a screeching roar that shook the room. The ring of fire flared higher and water rose with it.

Cracks of light formed all over the demon's body.

You've won only this battle, but not the game itself. I'll see you all again. Chunks of darkness flaking off, the demon dived at the ground, face-first, like it had outside the main office. A black circle opened up as the head detached from the body. It plunged into the darkness and disappeared. The circle spun like a vortex and collapsed into its center, disappearing as well,

The ring of fire shrank back to a thin line of orange, the water sank back into its narrow moat, splashing water everywhere, and the little fans slowed, bringing the breeze to a trickle. The circle's light dimmed to a dull glow.

Vergo took a few steps closer to the edge of the circle. "You, my dear little one, are quite the prodigy."

Ms. Weever clawed at her blonde curls, her icy eyes livid. She stomped towards me.

Uh oh. I shrank inwards, bracing for a lecture, and held my ground. Running and hiding would only make it worse. I gripped my violin hard.

"You…I can't believe…You could've…" She clamped me in a hug. "By the Light, you stupid child. *Never* scare me like that again."

Okay, not exactly a lecture. I eased my grip on the violin. "You both looked like you needed help."

She fixed me with her icy glare, digging her fingers into my shoulders, then sighed and hugged me again. "How did you even figure that out? I didn't teach you this circle's song."

I opened my mouth to explain, and Nurse Kor coughed. Bylan removed all the leather and metal straps. She clutched her head. "That was horrible. Let's never do that again."

"How do you feel?" the priest said.

"Like I woke up from a six-month hibernation. I feel lighter." She pushed to her feet and her legs shook.

Bylan eased her back into the chair. "Take it slow. You're finally in full control of your body again."

She leaned back, then she shot upright, eyes wide. "Guys, I just remembered: there's a box in my office that doesn't belong. It's next to my supply cabinet. I think it's the demon's anchor."

"Well, that explains how it was able to escape this space," Ms. Weever said. "Who gave it to you?"

She thought a moment, rubbing her temple. "I don't know. No, wait." She mimed holding onto a box and setting it down. "Fabian. No... He couldn't have. That doesn't make sense. It was a present after our first date."

"Who's Fabian?" Ms. Weever said.

Bylan said, "Fabian Gauss, our new seventh-grade math teacher."

Chapter 20

The box was nowhere in her office by the time we got back. Our only clue that she hadn't been lying was a rectangle of dust outlining where the box had been. Nurse Kor ran a finger through the dust line. A wedge of dirty grey coated her fingertip. The rest of us stood behind her, near the trio of blue gurneys.

Ms. Weever said, "The demon was a step ahead of us."

She faced us, eyes glistening. "Do you think it's affecting Fabian, too? He's been such a sweetheart to me. I can't bring myself to believe he was using me to please a demon."

"Both scenarios are probable. We have to prepare for both."

"How?"

"Leave that to us. You, however, will take steps to protect yourself from another attachment."

***

For probably the first time in my life, it wasn't because of my alignment and all the trouble that came with it that I wasn't looking forward to going to school. Instead, I was afraid of facing Mr. Gauss after learning about his role in giving Nurse Kor a possessed box. I didn't want to believe he'd done it on purpose. He had to be a victim in all this. He wasn't a Dark. He wasn't an evil person, I told myself as I headed down the hallway.

For once, his mere presence didn't set off butterflies in my stomach as I headed for my desk, my head down.

"Morning, Mia," he said in his usual cheerful voice.

"Morning, Mr. Gauss," I said automatically, my face burning with knowing something he didn't know I knew. I weaved among the chair and desk legs.

"You all right, Mia? You seem out of it today."

I plunked down at my desk and rested my chin on my overstuffed backpack. This thing was going to break my back before midterms, if not before first quarter was over. "Just tired," I said to his desk. That much was true. I had hardly slept all weekend, anticipating Monday and having to suck up this moment.

He considered me before more students filed in. He greeted them with the same cheer.

Vergo hopped onto the counter space lining the windows. "He doesn't seem like he knows what happened last week."

I furrowed my brows.

"Either that or he's a very good actor, but I seriously doubt it."

I hid my face behind my backpack and whispered, "Why? He's the one who gave it to her."

"Box in his possession or not, he'd be affected by the demon within. He'd display rage or anxiety. He's too calm, unless he took certain precautions." Vergo looked at me. "Or he simply gave the box to Trisha not knowing what it was, making him an inadvertent accomplice. Still, I doubt it. It was no accident that your beloved nurse was given that box. There are no coincidences in any of this."

"So he could still be a bad guy?"

"Unfortunately, yes, but that's not the main problem. We need to figure out who moved that box and where it's hiding, or this will happen to someone else."

"Where do we even look? Couldn't it be anywhere?"

"Yes, but we won't find it if we don't look. One advantage we have is that cursed objects like the one in question have an unmistakable aura about them. You only have to get close, and you'll know it's near. As a Dark with the right tools and with a bit of training, you could sense it by being in the same building."

"What if they hid it somewhere outside?"

He tilted his furry head. "Magical objects of that nature tend to be hidden indoors. Trust me on this."
***

Something long and lumpy lay hidden under a silk cloth on Ms. Weever's desk. I shut the door behind me as my tutor placed several vials on the edge of her desk. Without looking up, she said, "Fair warning: today will be uncomfortable. Take this." She held out a bracelet.

I held out a hand, and she dropped it on my palm.

The bracelet was made of black string threaded through several types of stones, all earthy colors. There was a clear stone with a feather suspended inside. Attached to it hung a brassy loop with a few smaller discs, one inside the next, a little knob at the bottom of the loop.

"Put it on."

I did as told, tugging the two string ends in opposite directions to make the bracelet smaller.

"Get in the habit of wearing that at all times. The clear stone will heat and vibrate when you're near a cursed object. You can give the loops a spin whenever you feel yourself succumbing to an object's influence. In most cases, it'll neutralize the energy around you long enough to put up defenses. There are rare few instances where an object is so old and powerful that you'll be on your own." She held up a hand, pinching and un-pinching her thumb and forefinger together. "Give it a spin."

I studied the knob at the base of the loop, then held out my wrist so the rings dangled freely. I twisted the knob. The circles spun in opposite directions and whirred. A wave of energy passed through the air, making it feel neutral, calm. There was no energy there, nothing good or evil, just empty. As quickly as the air cleared, the subtle press of business, anxiety, eagerness, determination, and other emotions filled the space, creating a sense that something was just plain there. Depending on what I paid attention to is what I felt most. "That's neat. What is this?"

"A curse charm. It's not foolproof, but it's far better than nothing. I need your help finding this stupid box. I've scanned the entire campus and found nothing, but that doesn't mean it's not here. Whoever's after Trisha and your sister is most likely taking steps to avoid getting caught by me. So *you* are going to be the one who does the catching."

I reflexively wanted to say, *Me? Are you sure? Can I even do that?* I pushed aside the questions. They were stupid. I was being scared and uncertain. I could learn how to do this. I had to protect my sister and Nurse Kor. "I'll do my best."

Ms. Weever nodded. "That's all I can ask of you." She took a deep breath. "Now for the fun part." She touched the nearest lump under the cloth. "These are a variety of cursed objects I've collected over the years. If you're wondering why I have them, it's so no one else does. As you've already learned, stupid runs rampant around this world. I have yet to find a better way to manage cursed objects than by ensuring they don't fall into the hands of stupid people."

"Why not destroy them?" I took a cautious step closer to the desk.

"That's a lesson that's supposed to come before this." She thought a moment. "The essence of it is that destroying cursed objects is almost always a bad idea. Demons don't like it when you destroy their anchors. They tend to go find another object or person."

"So that's why we went to such extreme lengths to exorcise Nurse Kor?"

"Correct, Miss Evers. The other main reason it's best to leave the objects intact is that destroying a cursed object *properly* frees the associated demon. If you control the object, then you trap the demon, blocking it from influencing the mortal plane. Destroying the object, also properly, frees the demon back to the demon realm, allowing it to influence us again." She sighed and shook her head. "It's a delicate balance to walk: be the responsible bearer of cursed objects and hope they never fall into the wrong hands, or destroy them and hope the demon never causes that much chaos. It's truly being stuck between the proverbial rock and a hard place."

I looked at the lumps. So much potential for harm sat in this one office. So…either hang on to the objects, keep the demon trapped, and try to make sure no one else ever has the objects? Or destroy them, free the demon, and hope the demon's meddling in the mortal plane isn't that bad? Both scenarios had their problems. "Who makes these objects?"

Ms. Weever lifted one end of the cloth and draped the excess over the second object. A second cloth, a white square with embroidered runes, sat alone over the first object. "Stupid people and powerful demons." Pinching the middle, she lifted the embroidered cloth, revealing a square porcelain container painted in pastel colors. "In the human's defense, we can make them on accident. Prolonged periods of rage, fear, or sadness can build enough energy and get implanted in an object. Like a fish to a lure, the energy attracts a demon and latches on, and a cursed object is born." She touched the porcelain container with her fingertips, twisting it a few inches. "On the other hand, humans can purposely lure a demon and trap one inside an object. This gives a person some ability to control a demon and force it to do his or her bidding. You most often hear about such things, like djinns, spirits that supposedly grant wishes to the holder." She looked me squarely in the eye. "That's not how this world works. Djinns don't give anything without getting something in return."

"Like what Allosyr tried to do to me?" I rubbed my arm, remembering the tattoo that had once been there. That had been a close call for sure. For some reason, I needed to leave the room.

"Exactly. So what's the moral of this lesson?"

I gave her a wan smile. She'd made it perfectly clear. "Cursed objects are dangerous, and trapping demons is never a good idea." I shuffled a few inches closer to the door. "Maybe we should have lessons elsewhere today." Where'd this thought come from?

"Ah, so you feel it, do you?"

"Feel what?" I shuffled back a bit more and bumped into the door.

"That feeling like you need to leave is this container's aura. Spin your bracelet."

I badly wanted out of the room now that I realized it. I could spin the loops from the hallway, couldn't I?

No, that was the container's aura, as my tutor said. I forced myself to lift my wrist and give the loops a spin.

Calm washed over me. I twitched my hand, conjuring my protective bubble. The object's aura needled at my shield, weak as a fly bouncing against a window pane in a futile attempt to get inside a house.

"Good. Did you see how subtle that was?"

***

The rest of lessons consisted of subjecting me to various terrifying auras while I fought the urge to flee the office. One object filled me with rage and I swore at Ms. Weever. She wafted some dust in my direction with the help of an owl feather and I broke into tears apologizing. I had such a hard time calming down that she fixed me the same cocoa drink she'd given me after pulling me out of the demon realm last year.

The worst object was a creepy doll. Bela and I had our fair share of dolls, but I bolted out of the office building before Ms. Weever caught up to me. Those eyes had been far too lifelike, the blonde hair too real. The demon within the doll didn't want me anywhere near it. Of course, I was happy to oblige. Of course, Ms. Weever made me get back in the same room as it. I cried as I forced myself to put its cloth back over it while my tutor watched. And as soon as the cloth was on, the tears stopped, the fear disappeared, and foolishness made me hide my face behind my hair. Ms. Weever reassured me she'd done the same thing when she had this lesson in high school.

Ms. Weever had me keep the bracelet. If we were lucky, I'd stumble upon the box in question. If not, at least the 6-8 building would be under constant scrutiny. We were safe for so long before the demon gained the energy to strike again. As for how much time we had, even Ms. Weever could only guess. Still, we needed to find the demon before it could latch on to its next victim.

The school day ended up being a perfectly normal one. Even math class went on like no hidden magical objects were trying to possess and kill people.

My sleepless concerns carried over into practice, hampering my attention until Coach Viro threatened to bench me for our first game in two weeks. Well, I couldn't find the box or stop the demon during bandyll practice, so I might as well focus on something I enjoyed. I kept the bracelet on, just in case.

The bandyll court was shaped like a rectangle with curved corners and a wall that rose like a bowl, making it possible to skate parallel to the ground for short periods before gravity pulled me back down. We skated lap after lap around the court, arcing up to the rim at both sides of center court and behind the nets, which, unlike soccer nets, had a gap between them and the ends of the court. We could skate behind the net and keep playing.

Our skates rumbled along the curved and varnished wood court that looked like the basketball court. I skated in my goalie gear, as did the other goalie, some seventh grader shorter than me, but equally unafraid of the ball. Everyone else skated in their pads, helmets, and dual, claw-like scoops. We goalies brought up the rear, the defense ahead of us, and all the offense players in front. A whistle finally blew, releasing us from lap number one billion. We formed a circle and our captains led us through stretches.

Sussi was one of the three captains. The other two were eighth graders, two tall, pretty girls with super shapely legs I wish I had, and who yelled at us much like Coach Viro did, but they also pushed us. They were moving on to high school after this. They didn't want to go their entire middle school career without a championship trophy, so I understood the pressure they put on us. Sussi yelled, too, but only at us goalies and the defense. She was bossy, like Gwen. She didn't like me. I didn't like her either. We both made ourselves get along for the team's sake, but only during bandyll.

We ended up scrimmaging against the B team towards the end of practice. I skated to my spot in goal, Sussi to my left on defense, an eighth grader named Ansa on my right, and another eighth grader named Kentra took the middle, blocking my view of the center of the court, where the ball would be tossed straight up to start the scrimmage. Three more eighth graders filled out the front line for offense.

Gwen and two more seventh graders skated to center court for B team's offense, lining up face-to-face with girls anywhere between half or a full head taller than them. My center forward, Kelsi Roy, stood almost a head and a half taller than Gwen. Rumor had it that the high school coach couldn't wait for her to play for him next year. Kelsi was an excellent skater and our best shot on the team. I had a hard time stopping her when she shot on me during practice.

Coach Khamai skated with a ball in one hand and a whistle in the other, rolling to a stop between Kelsi and Gwen. "Remember to practice like you play, girls. Go one hundred percent." Helmets bobbed assent. A whistle blew, echoing off the floor and transparent walls fencing the court, and skates rumbled to life.

Kelsi passed the ball back to Kentra, who tossed it to a wing player. My defensive line advanced to behind center court as the front line invaded the opposite court, Kentra planting herself between them and the center line. A few zigzagging passes and Kelsi scored an easy goal from the top of the goal box. Coach Khamai blew her whistle and reset back at center court. Coach Viro subbed Kelsi out for Rachelle, a smaller eighth grader who couldn't move as fast, but could shoot almost as well.

Coach Viro bumped fist to glove with Kelsi. "That's my girl."

The whistle blew again. Gwen won the ball toss this time and dropped it back to her center defenseman. They moved in a formation similar to ours, passing the ball around like we did, but using the ramp-like walls to help them pass over the heads of our taller team. Gwen skated up the side wall, passed the ball to her center forward, and used her momentum to zoom behind the net and around the other side. Another pass and she caught it in her scoop at the peak of her ride up the other wall. She veered towards me on the way down and took a shot before Sussi crashed into her in an attempt to block. They spun and fell in a heap as I got a glove out to block the shot. It bounced out of my grip before I could hold on.

Gwen shoved Sussi off, kicking her with a skate for good measure. "Don't touch me."

Sussi kicked her back. "Then stay out of my way."

A whistle blew. Coach Khamai gestured to the face-off circle to my right. "Don't know what's gotten into you two, but knock it off."

Instead of Gwen looking superior and proud of herself, she glared at Sussi. Had I missed something? When had they stopped being friends? Maybe that was her game face. I could only see Sussi's profile. My other two defenders stationed themselves in a semicircle around the face-off zone and offense marked up man-to-man around the top of our half of the court. Coach Khamai blew her whistle and the ball went skyward.

Sussi being taller, won the face-off, scooping and tossing the ball to a teammate in one smooth motion. Players skated into motion and a B team player knocked the ball out of Kentra's scoop. Bandyll was a real physical sport. We could smack each other with our scoops all over the legs and torso, but not the head. If an opponent knocked the ball out of your scoop, that was on you for not protecting or passing it. A stocky girl from my science class skated down the left side of the court before passing it off to Gwen, who took another shot around Sussi.

I barely saw the ball in time and once again couldn't trap the ball in my glove. One thing I learned quickly was that keeping track of the ball's movements was hard. My team and the other team could block my view of the ball, and if it got passed around too much, I got caught out of position. I only got in front of Gwen's shot because I knew she liked to shoot. The ball bounced away from me and right back to Gwen. Sussi tried to beat her to the ball. Another shot sailed by my head and over the net. I was only a head taller than the net.

"C'mon, Mia," Sussi said as she skated past me. "Catch those." She and Ansa scrambled for the loose ball behind the net.

Something in her tone made my blood boil. There was hate in her voice, which usually wasn't there.

Two B team front linesmen tried pushing them out of the way and shoving their scoops away from the ball. It was something called a scrum, a moment where a few players bunched up in one spot and fought skate and scoop for the ball, using the wall to hold themselves up and try to gain an advantage. Sussi popped out with the ball and tossed it to Kentra, who advanced it to center and passed it on to our front line. A triangle of passes around the net, and one of the wings scored a goal feet from the net, getting it behind the goalie before she could skate to the other side.

We reset, Sussi skating back to her position, scowling.

"Why are you so grumpy?" I said.

"I'm not grumpy. Just play better." She spun in place and faced center court, scoops held at the ready at her sides.

I glared at her back.

"Mia, down and ready," Coach Viro yelled from the bench.

Huffing a sigh, I crouched and held my glove-like scoops out.

Coach Khamai blew her whistle and the scrimmage rolled into motion.

"Little One, don't make her anger your anger," Vergo said from his perch behind the clear walls.

I ignored him. Sussi didn't have to like me, but she was supposed to be my teammate. Her attitude was totally uncalled for, totally un-teammate-like.

The ball weaved back and forth, side to side, in the neutral zone in the middle of the court, not quite making it towards one net or another, until one of our front line players misjudged a throw and missed the ball with her scoop. It bounced and rolled to the side of center court, up the ramp, and back down, veering in my direction. Players scrambled for the ball. Sussi tipped the ball with her scoop and bobbled it. Kentra tried to catch it as Gwen swooped between them. She made to shoot with an overhand throw, but the ball sailed to the other side of the court. It was a feint. I slid to the other side of the net, scoops up around my torso. The B team player tossed the ball back to Gwen as I finished my transition and she took an easy shot on the empty side of the net. Coach Khamai's whistle blew.

Sussi skated up to me as I scooped the ball out of the net. She towered over me, fixing me with her glare.

"Mia, what are you doing? You need to stop those shots."

"What do you think I'm *trying* to do?" I shoved her when I said trying. Sussi pinwheeled her arms and caught her balance, rolling backwards. She gaped at me. I was just as surprised. I'd never pushed anyone in my life, much less into a fight. My exchange with Gwen on the playground last year had been the closest thing to it.

Sussi closed her mouth and body-checked me hard enough to make me fall into the net. I scrambled back to my skates and went at her, scoops swinging. She swung back, but I didn't feel it. We were both too heavily padded to do any damage. We bashed each other. The world became nothing more than smacking and thumping, until the world spun and I fell on top of Sussi.

A whistle blew in our ears and hands yanked us apart. "All right, that's enough," Coach Khamai said firmly. She hauled me, and then Sussi, to our feet.

Coach Viro rolled over to us, wearing her usual half-serious, half-angry face. She took her time crossing the court, giving me a chance to absorb what I'd done.

Oh, by Shinjan. I'd royally screwed up. She was about to kick me off the team. As soon as word got to Mr. Redd, I'd be kicked out of school. My parents would be so mad. This was it. I was so on my way to a boarding school.

Coach stopped mere inches from us, taking us in. Her eyes narrowed. "Go sit on the bench. You both have detention tomorrow."

Sussi and I both went pale and exchanged wide-eyed stares. The same horror and dread filled her face.

She removed her helmet and skated over to the bench. I removed my helmet and dropped onto the opposite side of the bench.

Chapter 21

The next day after school, Sussi and I sat outside Mr. Redd's office, Garrett sitting with us. Sussi looked anywhere but in my direction, arms folded over her chest. I sat with my hands in my lap, and Garrett sat with an ankle over his opposite knee, wiggling his foot and playing with his laces. Parents stopped in to pick up children or drop off stuff by the front desk, oblivious to my misery. I could see only half a glass door from this far down the narrow hallway.

"So what are you here for?" Garrett said, gazing at my sneakers.

We'd been told to wear our gym uniforms and sneakers, but not why. Even Garrett was in his gym uniform. I tried to make eye contact with him, but his gaze lowered to my shoes. "Detention," I said.

"Me, too. Whatcha do to get in trouble?"

Sussi wheeled around. "None of your business."

Garrett jiggled his foot faster. "I wasn't talking to you."

Sussi let out an angry "tck" and spun in her chair, giving her back to us. She folded her arms.

Garrett nodded and focused on my lap again. He pointed to my bracelet. "What's that?"

I turned my wrist. "It's a curse charm. It gives me a warning if there are any cursed objects nearby."

"What do you need something like that for?"

I glanced at Sussi, who'd turned her head slightly. "Something was hurting Nurse Kor and tried to hurt my sister last week."

"A demon," he said gravely.

"Y…yeah," I said unhappily.

"I like Nurse Kor." His foot bobbed rhythmically as if he were listening to music.

A door opened and Mr. Redd stepped into the hallway. We all looked up and Sussi sat properly in her chair. I sank lower in mine as his scrutiny lingered on me. "Miss Evers, I'm severely disappointed in you. I thought I made it clear that you needed to be a model student. You can't afford this in your unique situation."

I looked down, half hiding behind my hair.

"And you, Miss Ferus. I have never seen this behavior out of you. A captain should know better than to get into fights. I don't care if the other person starts it, but I never want to hear of this again."

"Yes, sir," she said submissively, hunching.

Mr. Redd shuffled so he stood before Garrett. "And you, Mr. Antcil, need to learn to reel in your temper. People are going to get the wrong idea about you. You don't want that, do you?"

"No, Mr. Redd," he said, avoiding eye contact. His

tone was automatic, as if he'd been through this a dozen times already.

"And Miss Evers, take off that bracelet. There will be no jewelry wearing during detention."

I looked up. No. He couldn't be serious. "But Ms. Weever…"

He took a step closer and held out a hand. "No jewelry."

My heart sinking, I loosened the drawstrings and handed him the bracelet.

He studied it a moment before closing his fist. "Now, all of you follow me." He pocketed my bracelet and we followed him out of the main office.

The last of the buses trundled onto the main road as we followed Mr. Redd to the high school. The staff parking lot was full, forcing us to use the sidewalks instead of cutting straight across. He led us through several gates that separated the elementary and middle school buildings from the high school campus. Since high school got out before middle and elementary, we cut a diagonal path across the high school parking lot and passed through the main entrance. The high school matched the middle school in appearance, but everything was bigger, roomier. A trio of high schoolers eyed us with raised brows as we headed deeper inside. Sussi and I drifted shoulder-to-shoulder. Man, they were so tall and mature and adult-like. I felt like a child as we tried hiding behind Mr. Redd. The high schoolers smirked and laughed into their hands before disappearing through a pair of wooden doors.

Great. I wasn't in high school, and I was already uncool.

Sussi and I bumped into each other. She nudged me

away. The principal led us to a bunch of display cases that spanned an entire wall. A table with a bucket and a pile of rags sat waiting for us. A bazillion trophies sat inside the cases, many draped in medals. Stone slabs of color team pictures sat at intervals. A hundred years of athletic greatness sat on display, buried under a thick layer of dust.

"Are you serious?" Sussi said. "I am *not* cleaning all those." She folded her arms and stuck out a hip.

Mr. Redd gave her an amused look as he fished out a wad of what looked like tiny wands from his pocket. They hung in a row on a metal loop. "By all means, if that's what you want to do," he said casually, sifting through his sticks. "However, your coach has yet to decide whether or not to keep you on the team. I'm sure you'll make her decision a whole lot easier if you stand there for the next hour."

A wave of horror paled her face, but she regained her scowl and snatched a rag from the bucket.

Mr. Redd touched one of the tiny wants to a lock on the case. It glowed, and something inside clicked. He removed the lock and slid a glass pane open. "Your coach said the two of you are to work together on every object you clean." Sussi's jaw dropped. The principal held up his hands. "Coach's orders. I suggest you do as she says if staying on the team is important to you."

"I can help," Garrett said.

The amusement left Mr. Redd's face. "No, you'll be working alone on the smaller plaques and trophies while those two teamwork the bigger ones."

Garrett's face fell. He picked out a rag and selected a small trophy.

"And you'll work alone on the middle school

trophies if you break any of these, Mr. Antcil. You've already spent quite enough time at the high school. I suggest you clean with care. Do you understand me?"

"Yes, Mr. Redd," he said in a defeated drawl and set to work on a one-foot-tall brass trophy.

On the bottom shelf sat a trophy big enough to stick my head in. It was attached to a thick wood base and an engraved brass sheet. Sussi grabbed the handles and tried to lift it. The trophy tipped towards her before she set it down with a thud. She tried again, straining. It slid out of the display, and the base thudded hard enough on the tiled floor vibrated under my sneakers. She huffed. "I need your help," she said grudgingly.

We each grabbed a handle and hefted it onto the table. Holy crap. This thing had to be heavier than Bela. What was it made of? We set to wiping down every last speck of dust, our fingertips often bumping into each other. Her face creased with annoyance every time that happened. I tried to make a point to stay away from her hand, but I couldn't read her mind.

"Just do your half of the trophy. I'll get the middle when you're done."

I nodded, not trusting her temper to say anything. Her expression relaxed when we finished bringing the trophy to a nice shine. Together, we returned it to the display case and grabbed the next brassy monster. At least it was encouraging that this school had a history of bringing home division titles.

Garrett worked alone in his corner while Sussi and I worked together on trophy after trophy, carefully wiping down medals and plaques. When one rag got too black to make much difference, we swapped it out for fresh ones. Mr. Redd inspected each one before we were allowed to put them back in the case. After we finished draping four medals over the arm of a brass male figure in bandyll gear, Mr. Redd said, "All right, you three, I'll be back with Coach Viro. You better be scrubbing when I return, or I'll add another day of detention." He pointed to where the ceiling and brick wall met. A line of vines ran the length of the wall, continuing onto the adjacent wall and out of sight. "These vines are listening. I better not hear you slacking off when I listen to the song stone later."

Sussi and I promised in monotone voices to behave. Garrett remained quiet. I'd learned from being in the same history class as him that that didn't mean he wasn't listening. It was like he could listen with only his ears and remember everything without looking. It was weird, but he was definitely smart.

As soon as the front door finished swinging closed, Garrett said, "Mia, do you really have a spirit cat that's with you at all times?"

Vergo lay in a sphinx pose atop the display cases.

His ears curled back. "Exactly how many people know about me?"

I met Garrett's hopeful face, his gaze not quite meeting mine. "Did you see him last week when the demon attacked you all?"

"No, but you and Sanctus Bylan talked to someone I couldn't see."

"I've heard the same thing," Sussi said. Her tone was irritated, but her scowl was gone. She wiped at her half of a giant brass cup.

"Can we see it? Please?" Garrett clasped his hands like he was praying. Sussi paused with her rag near the trophy.

Shrugging, Vergo sat up. "All the teachers know, and so do the students, it seems. There are no secrets in schools, are there?" He hopped onto the table and sat next to the rag pile. "Well, off with it. Let them have a look."

I removed his collar and he shook out his head. Both Garrett and Sussi gasped.

"No way," Garrett said in an excited whisper.

Sussi said, "I thought Gwen was lying. Is that a demon?"

"No, it's a Light spirit bound to this mortal here, against both our wills," Vergo said, making them both wide-eyed. The cat rolled his eyes. "By the Light, why is a talking animal so surprising to everyone?"

"So he's not a demon?" Garrett said, stepping closer.

"No," I said, explaining to them how Bylan and I sent the demon to the Light, and Vergo was sent back to me as a spirit that needed to atone for his sins. When I finished the story, Garrett crouched before Vergo so he was eye-to-eye with him. He stared, like creepy stared.

Vergo drew his furry brows together. "Boy, what *are* you doing?"

"You didn't hear me?" He straightened up.

"Considering the fact that your lips aren't moving, I daresay not. I lack the power to read minds."

Sussi snorted. "I like him."

Vergo said, "Oh, I'm full of quips and witticisms, but you, my dear, I do not much like, especially not while you call that beast of a spoiled girl your friend."

"You mean Gwen?" she said.

"I do. She's…"

"She's not my friend." Sussi turned back to the

trophy and roughly wiped it.

Whoa. I halfheartedly joined her. She ignored me while letting me have my half to work on. "What happened?"

Her eyes watered and she sniffed. She rubbed her face. "She's mad at me because I won't give up my spot and join her on B team."

"What a selfish, conceited brat," Vergo said, his voice dripping with venom. "No true friend would do such a thing to you, child. Consider it her loss and move on."

"We've been friends since we were four."

"And she threw your friendship away just like that."

Sussi's face screwed up. She gave her back to us as she sniffed and wiped her face repeatedly. Garrett went back to wiping his share of the trophies. I made my cloth move, but I couldn't stop focusing on Sussi.

"I'm sorry she did that to you," I said softly.

"Leave me alone," Sussi said in a thick voice. "It's not like I treated you any better."

I shrugged even though she couldn't see me. "You helped me during tryouts and after we both made the team. Yesterday was the first time you've been mean to me in a while, but now I understand why."

She sniffed. "I'm sorry."

"It's okay," I said automatically. It wasn't, but that she'd willingly apologized to me, despite my alignment, meant more than I was willing to admit. I resisted the urge to hug her, afraid to find out how it'd be received. It's what Mom did when I was upset, awkward as her hugs were sometimes, but I wasn't Sussi's mom. I'd never hugged anyone besides my family and Deren before, and she and I weren't friends.

Sussi took a deep breath and turned around. Her face was red, but she wasn't crying anymore. "Let's get back to work before we get in more trouble."

I nodded and moved to put Vergo's collar back on. He held up a paw. "Quick question first: Boy, why on Aardra did you stare at me so a moment ago? It was rather unnerving."

Without looking up, he said, "I was trying to see if you could hear me."

"Are you a Lionspeaker?"

"Wolfspeaker." He carefully set a runner-up trophy inside the case and took out another. "But some animals besides canines react when I try speaking to them."

Vergo opened his mouth, but stopped and turned to me. "Little One, do you remember the shadows we saw that day? The ones that had Juvarra all nervous."

I vaguely recalled the pair of shapes that'd run out of sight before getting a good look at them. I remembered Juvarra's obvious terror. "Garrett, what *were* those things you were looking at outside the fence during lunch?"

"My friends," he said sadly. "Snooter and Longears. They're coyotes. I thought I'd never see them again when we moved, but they somehow followed my scent all the way out here. That was the first time I'd seen them in days."

Not demons. Oh, thank goodness. He was a Kindred, and a wolfspeaker, too. Sussi and I returned the latest clean trophy and set a fresh one on the table, our arms shaking with the effort. They were getting heavier and heavier. "What were they doing at school? Your aide looked scared." I put Vergo's collar back on and returned to wiping away dust.

"They were trying to lick me through the fence. It kept lifting their lips and showing their fangs." He giggled. "They looked so silly. I was so happy to see them again. They wanted to make sure I was okay. I let them lick my fingers, but they weren't happy. They want me away from the school. They say there's something bad here. I believe them, but my parents make me come every day."

"Is that why you're anxious a lot?" I said.

"Yeah. These last few days have been better, but it feels worse again. It's like there's something wrong with this building."

Sussi glanced at Garrett. "Have you heard about the student who died here a few years ago? Bad stuff happened in this building." He admitted that he hadn't, so Sussi and I took it upon ourselves to fill him in. I even added that Orton Totes' soul finally found peace after Bylan and I had forced Allosyr to cross into the Light.

Sussi said, "I thought only Lights could talk to ghosts."

I shook my head. "Darks can sense and interact with ghosts that haven't returned to the Light."

"Isn't that, like, real scary?"

I shrugged. "Sometimes. I'll take a ghost over a demon any day." My heart pounded away as I wiped the plaque and wood. I'd never had this kind of conversation with a classmate before. To my great surprise, neither of them ran off screaming. Sussi and I finished another trophy and carefully set a dusty one on the table.

The high school's front doors swung open, and two

figures entered. With ample light pouring in from outside, they were only black shapes until enough overhead light shone down on them. Coach Viro and Mr. Redd headed toward us. I stiffened, and all three of us worked faster at our task.

Mr. Redd said, "All right, Mr. Antcil, finish that one you're on and come with me. That'll do for today." Garrett wiped off a trophy and held it out for the principal's inspection, who nodded approval. He quickly yet carefully returned the trophy to its case and followed Mr. Redd out of the high school, leaving Sussi and me in awkward silence with our coach. We returned the latest large trophy to the case and looked to her for what to do next.

She narrowed her eyes. "I didn't tell you to stop."

Sussi and I looked at each other. I felt my face go as pale as hers. We hefted another trophy onto the table, both of us huffing with the effort, and got back to work.

My arms were tired. How long had we been at this? Sussi breathed through her mouth as well. We cleaned on in silence. I wouldn't test Coach's patience by complaining. Trophy after trophy went in and out of the display case, each one getting harder to lift and taking longer to clean. It seemed like they were getting bigger and bigger, but each championship trophy was the same size as the previous, their now shiny rims having the same spare few inches of clearance under the shelf above them. We were halfway through the display case when we both tried to lift another trophy. We grunted and strained and nearly dropped it.

"Let's go already. You're only halfway through the case."

Sussi's eyes glistened. Mine stung. This was

horrible. There were way too many trophies, it was getting late, and my arms and hands burned from all the work. This was worse than conditioning practices. Sussi took a deep breath and grabbed the trophy. I joined her, bracing for the great weight, and somehow we got it onto the table without dropping it. Coach Viro folded her arms and watched us clean, her glare making me feel so small and worthless.

When we were done, she ran a finger along it and nodded. "Another."

We hefted the trophy back in the case, using our legs to help us lift it, and reached for the next. We tried to pick it up and barely caught it before it could fall. We set the base on the floor and paused to catch our breath.

Sussi said, "Coach Viro, may we finish this tomorrow?"

"No. I'm not convinced either of you have learned your lesson yet."

Despair lined Sussi's face. Tears fell. Two hot lines slid down my cheeks. Great, I was crying, too. Why couldn't Coach see that we'd learned our lesson? I know I had. I'd never fight anyone again. I wanted to tell her as much. Something told me to keep my mouth shut and keep going. The both of us struggled with the next trophy. We took turns sniffing and wiping our faces, but we finished that one, and then another, and then yet another. The late bus had to have come and gone by now. It felt like we'd been here for hours. I could barely move my fingers or lift the rag.

With the last speck of dust removed from our present trophy, we tried to lift it, first with our arms, and then with our legs. We let it go, huffing and sniffling.

"Let's go. You're not done."

Sussi looked at me, tears in her eyes. Something in that look told me she was done. She didn't have it in her to clean any more trophies. If she was done, so was I. We threw our rags down and sat on the ground. I laid my throbbing arms in my lap.

Coach Viro's shadow fell over us, and we looked up. A corner of her mouth…no, that couldn't be a smile. Was it? That's the look she gave any of us when she was happy with our performance.

Coach hefted the trophy and set it back in the case. "There's the teamwork I want to see. I'll see you both at practice tomorrow."

Chapter 22

I told Deren about our detention the next day over lunch and everything that happened, minus the fact that I'd cried. Nobody needed to know about that. We sat in our usual spot at the end of one long row of tables tucked in one corner of the cafeteria. Teachers stood at intervals, watching us all and making sure we behaved. The air filled with the sounds of hundreds of middle schooler voices and the aroma of today's lunch: macaroni and cheese loaded with chicken, bacon, and broccoli bits. The bacon and cheese masked the broccoli's bitter flavor, enabling me to eat my vegetables like I knew I should.

"So are you two friends now?" Deren said, helping himself to his loaded mac'n'cheese.

I thought a moment. Detention had left me feeling like she didn't hate me anymore, but she didn't offer friendship either. "I don't know."

A tray dropped on the table with a loud slap, making its steaming contents jiggle. Sussi shrugged off her backpack and dropped onto the chair opposite me. She stirred up her noodles with a spork and stopped, as if she realized she was being stared at. She looked up. "Is it okay if I sit with you?"

Whoa. Were we friends now? "Sure," I said, trying to sound casual.

"Yeah," Deren said. "Welcome to the group."

"Well, well," Vergo said from his spot in my backpack, "isn't this an interesting development? The girl has some sense, after all."

"Thanks," Sussi said, unaware of Vergo's words, and pecked at her food. She downed the rest after her first bite of cheesy, bacony goodness. "I'm so over Gwen. Vergo was right about her. I didn't realize how much she bossed me around."

"You've met Vergo?" Deren said, breaking out into an excited grin.

Sussi looked at him over the end of her water bottle. "For a little bit. He said stuff about Gwen that I hadn't seen, until she turned on me. She can rot on B team."

I snorted. I tried to hide a smile behind my fist. We both giggled. Sussi's smile switched to a frown.

Deren said, "I'm sorry she wasn't as good a friend as you thought."

Sussi slapped her spork down. "Why do you both keep apologizing for her?" Deren shrugged. She let out a frustrated sigh and poked at her fruit cup. "Forget about her." When we said nothing, she said, "What were you two talking about a moment ago?"

Deren and I exchanged glances, and he shrugged.

That was his way of saying he would go along with whatever I decided. I looked under the table at my backpack.

Vergo said, "She might prove useful in our hunt."

I put my elbows on the table and leaned closer. Deren and Sussi did the same. I had to resist the urge to smile. I suddenly had two friends at once. And we were all in on this together. "Did you notice how Nurse Kor has been acting strange all year?"

"I only saw her once, the day after tryouts. I thought she was grumpy."

I shook my head. "That was the demon influencing her. Bylan—I mean Sanctus Bylan, my tutor, and I took her to some underground place at the Order of Leo and exorcised her. She wasn't the original anchor, so it's still around, hiding somewhere until it feels better." Hopefully, they didn't think anything of my forgetting to use his former title. No one knew besides a few of us.

"Hiding where?" Sussi's eyes widened with horror.

"That's what we're trying to find out," Deren said. "We think it's somewhere on campus." Deren and I filled Sussi in on the box, how Mr. Gauss gave it to Nurse Kor, and how it went missing before we returned from our exorcism trip.

"Who the heck moved the box? The demon?"

I opened my mouth, but stopped. I didn't know.

Vergo pawed my leg. "No. Demons can't move their anchor. Whoever moved it was human."

I relayed the information to them.

Sussi said, "Then it's someone in this school. I wonder if it is Mr. Gauss. He almost seems too nice to be a good person."

"What do you mean?" I said.

Pushing aside her tray, she leaned closer. "You know how some people come off super nice and sweet only to find out they were fake the whole time?"

Deren nodded.

I said, "I've had people pretend to be nice, but it was obvious that they didn't want to be because of my alignment."

Sussi crinkled her nose. "Okay, so you're a special case. But yeah, people do that. They act super nice because they want something, and then blow you off as soon as they get it."

"Are you saying Mr. Gauss dated Nurse Kor to give her a cursed box?"

"It's possible. Are they still dating, or did they break up?"

"I don't know."

"We're trying to figure out if someone gave him the box without telling him what it was, and if he's being influenced, too."

Sussi let out a thoughtful hmm. "So he could be a good guy or a bad guy. Demons are really sneaky."

"Yup. And we need to find that box before it attaches to someone else." I touched my wrist. Instead of a bracelet under my fingers, there was skin. I inhaled. "I never got my bracelet back from Mr. Redd."

"He probably forgot," Sussi said. "We did leave at a different time than Garrett."

"Why did he take it?" Deren said.

"Probably so it wouldn't get dirty," I said. It would've gotten grimy. I'd washed my hands for a full minute before they stopped feeling dusty and gritty.

He nodded thoughtfully. "Okay, that makes sense. So then where have you been while wearing the bracelet?"

"All over the elementary and middle school campus." I'd been able to scan the K-2 and 3-5 buildings multiple times, using Bela as an excuse to be in there. Nothing had set off the bracelet.

"Hey, Mia," Sussi said thoughtfully, "remember what Garrett said yesterday about how something felt wrong about the high school. I think we need to look in there."

"When?"

"After practice. I'll have my parents pick us up. They won't suspect we're up to anything."

"I'll wait for both of you by the cafeteria. We'll all go together."

Sussi and I nodded. Great. Another crazy idea. We were so dead if we got caught.

***

I stopped by Mr. Redd's office after Dark tutoring, my heart pounding. I would've forgotten again if Ms. Weever hadn't asked me where my bracelet was. I knocked on his door and his muffled voice told me to come in. Mr. Redd sat at his massive desk, poring over papers. He looked up and closed a leather-bound folder.

"Miss Evers. How can I help you?" His serious face didn't match his polite tone.

"Mr. Redd, may I please have my bracelet back?" I stood with my gaze lowered to the papers on his desk as I paid attention to his face.

His jaws clenched and unclenched before popping a tight smile. "Certainly." He opened a desk drawer and plucked something out. He looked at it before tossing it onto his desk. "There you go. I apologize for not getting it back to you sooner. Slipped my mind, until I checked my pockets before heading home last night."

I tentatively approached his desk. He interlaced his fingers under his chin, and I snatched my bracelet. "Thank you, sir."

He nodded. "Again, I hope to never see you in detention ever again. I expect you to be on your best behavior for the rest of the year."

My face burned like I'd stuck it over an open flame as I mumbled something about promising to behave. It took all my self-control to walk instead of run out of his office.

I checked into orchestra class before the bell rang. I set my violin case on the table in the back, scrambling to hurry up. Everyone but me was seated in the semicircle of foldable chairs, sheet music propped up on music stands, and instruments resting on their laps. My fellow violinists all looked nerdy, most of them wearing glasses.

Mrs. Sterling, an orchestra teacher whose pixie haircut made me think of a fairy, looked up from her music stand. "Hurry up, Miss Evers. We'll start as soon as you're seated." She was a petite lady who was thorough and effective in our lessons, and could play all the string instruments beautifully. She'd given us a demonstration on the first day of school. Her orchestral perfection made me feel like I sucked, but it also set a bar for the sound quality we all aimed for.

"Coming, Mrs. Sterling. I apologize for running late." I unlatched my violin case and flipped it open, only to have my violin fall, strings down on the other half. I'd opened it upside down. Clenching my teeth, I picked up my instrument. Thankfully, it was in one piece and appeared no worse for wear. I drew a rune on the lacquered wood and activated it with a whisper. There, now I wouldn't cause any chaos.

I reached for my bow. Something round and metallic had fallen out of my case. I went wide-eyed. Ms. Weever's lock charm. I'd forgotten to return it to her. I snuck it into my backpack. She could wait one more day. We'd probably need it later.

Vergo looked at the semicircle of impatient students and padded towards the door. "I'll be outside, as usual." He passed through the closed door as if it weren't there. I rushed over to join my classmates.

***

Bandyll practice came and went too fast. Even Sussi walked stiffly as we snuck off, our coaches focused on making sure everyone else filed onto a late bus or into family vehicles. With dozens of other students around, we most likely would be overlooked. Tons of students stayed after for clubs, sports, and tutoring.

All the coaches and teachers had their backs to me and Sussi as we disappeared into the 6-8 building. We fast-walked down a hallway, waving to Mrs. Livy, our history teacher. Thankfully, she was too busy flipping through a packet to give our presence another thought. For all she knew, we'd forgotten something in the locker room.

We entered the gymnasium and broke into a run. Our footsteps thudded along the wood floor and echoed loud enough to fill the whole space. Our footfalls had the cadence of a clock ticking. We exited the gymnasium, spilling out onto the quad that connected all three elementary buildings, one on each side of the rectangle. We dumped bags and backpacks against the gymnasium wall. Sussi donned silvery bracelets that helped her focus her Water magic and shouldered a small water pouch. I pocketed the lock charm, double-checked for the bracelet on my wrist, and took Vergo's collar off. Since we only intended to find the box, I passed on grabbing my violin. Together, we ran over to the cafeteria building, Vergo bounding beside me, and caught up with Deren, who sat propped against the cinderblock walls. He popped to his feet, and together, the four of us snuck around the building and encountered the fence separating our campus from the high school's. It was made of vertical bars crisscrossed with chain link fencing. There was no way we were squeezing through or climbing over. The vertical bars ended in some very sharp-looking points several feet overhead.

Sussi slapped the fence. "Great. We forgot about the fence. Now what?"

Deren adjusted his Earth bracers and stuck out the tip of his tongue. That was his concentration face. "I've got this. Everyone stand real close to me."

"Um, what is your plan?" Sussi scrunched her brows.

"Throw us over."

"Do you have enough control over your alignment not to kill us all?"

"Yeah. My brothers and I do this all the time at home to jump in the pool."

"Okay," Sussi said, not sounding the least bit convinced. We bunched near him anyway, Vergo in my arms.

"No, absolutely nothing wrong with this plan at all," he said. "I'm so glad I don't have a physical body."

Deren said, "Hey, if we could use the gate without getting caught, I'd suggest that, but it's right by the entrance to the main office." He rolled his wrists and stretched his arms. Deren was right. There were only two gates in the fence, one by the elementary main office, and one by the staff lot, where the late buses were going in and out. At our section of fence, the cafeteria building blocked everyone's view of us.

Deren drew a rune on the ground, clapped his hands, and then slapped the ground. A ring of dust shot up around us. "Bend your knees and hold onto my shirt." Sussi and I gave each other nervous looks as we grabbed a chunk of shirt. "Yeh cho-kig meh." He reached for his neck.

We let go of his shirt, allowing him to breathe again.

"I said hold on, not kill me. Just grab my sleeves." We adjusted our grip and he dug his fingers in the ground. The hard dirt gave way to his touch. I'm sure I would've jammed my fingers if I tried to do the same. While it looked like pale dirt, it was hard clay. The ground was as tough as life in the desert.

The ground shook. I bent my knees a little more. One moment the fence was in front of us. We shot into the air, and the fence was below us. We arced over as if we'd leaped off a swing. Sussi and I cried out and flung out our arms. Without meaning to, I dropped Vergo. He flung his limbs out, his body pinwheeling. The four of us landed on the dirt disc, sinking up to our ankles, and then unceremoniously rolled to a stop.

I stood and my brain registered stinging pricks all over my body. Little brown clusters of thorns were lodged in my arms and legs. Goat heads. Ugh. I carefully removed them without stabbing my fingers. Sussi and Deren did the same, and we all dusted ourselves off.

"Deren, I hate you right now," Sussi said.

He gave her a dorky grin. "Sorry. Forgot about the landing. Used to splashing in water."

"Well, remember there's no water when we head back."

Vergo said, "How did I forget I could *walk* through the fence?" He growled at himself before trotting towards the high school.

We followed him, jogging to catch up. There were only a handful of cars, probably groundskeepers or something. High school sports were over, the stadium empty. Vergo headed for the front door, and Deren waved for us to follow. "This way." He led us to a metal door stenciled in black paint with the word "Auditorium." He yanked the metal handle. The door remained closed. "Dang. They locked it. Must be too late in the day."

"Wow, neither of you thought this through," Sussi said, arms folded and a hip stuck out.

Vergo said, "If I recall correctly, it was your idea to search the high school. Clearly, you put in as much thought as these two did."

Sussi narrowed her eyes and said nothing. I stood before the door and fished out my lock charm. "I've got it." I pressed the metal disc to the door, and something clicked inside, thudding hard enough to feel it. I opened the door.

"Whoa, what's that?" Sussi said.

"Nothing. It's not mine. I forgot to give it back."

"I think those things are illegal."

"Where did you get it?" Deren said.

My stomach dropped. Okay, I needed to return this charm after we were done here. "Don't worry about it. You saw nothing. You know nothing." I trusted Deren, but not Sussi, to keep their mouths shut about my tutor. "Let's go. Keep all your senses open for anything that doesn't feel right. Let me know if you start feeling really scared, angry, or anything else. That's a sign we're getting close. The box will most likely try to keep us away."

With the help of a Water charm spell, Sussi made a ball of water give off light. We covered the entire auditorium, sticking close to each other. She held the glowing water floating overhead. It created long shadows everywhere we went. Row upon row of folded chairs and an empty, quiet stage was somehow creepy. It felt like a performance should be going on instead of this eerie silence. My bracelet stayed cool and still. Nothing in the auditorium.

Vergo wandered in and out of sight, doubling back to us when we reached the other side. "I don't sense anything in here, but there's something off about this building, like that Garrett boy said. Deren, is there a floor below this one?"

"Yeah. Follow me." He led us out into the main hall. We ended up right near the main entrance and the trophy cases. We gave the cases a wide berth and headed deeper inside the school. A few turns down dim hallways, and I smelled chlorine and water. A pool? Deren tried a particular door next to a section of glass wall. Nothing but darkness lay beyond the glass.

The door was locked, so I used my illegal charm to gain entry. A strong wave of chlorine and water scent filled my nose, and the carpeted floor switched tiny tiles, the floor sloping towards the pool. Sussi sent her glowing water above us again, revealing an eight-lane pool, the water as smooth glass. The water reflected the light, brightening up the space even more. Opposite the pool sat several rows of cement bleacher seats, looking like stairs made for giants.

Deren led us down a short, narrow hallway to a door labeled "Boys Locker Room." He tried the handle. It was locked, of course.

I read the letters over and over. "Deren, that's the boys locker room."

"And?"

"We're girls," Sussi said, glaring.

"No one's here to care but you two. Do you want to find the box or not?"

Huffing, I pressed the lock charm to the door, and it did its thing. Sure, there was no one but us to care, but I couldn't entirely set aside the fact that this space was supposed to be for boys and boys alone. Under light of the glowing water, we followed Deren past showers, bathroom stalls, and urinals to a flight of stairs that led one way before doubling back and leading farther underground.

Somehow, this space felt darker, blacker. Even Sussi's light didn't spread as far. We all stopped at the bottom of the stairs.

"I'm feeling more spooked," Deren said, his voice echoing.

"Me too," Sussi said.

I didn't, and my bracelet was dormant, but a tickle ran up my spine. With a flick of a hand, I conjured my protective shield.

"Whatever you did, that feels better," Deren said, and Sussi voiced agreement. We took several steps and froze. The lights turned on. We looked behind us, and no one was there. Deren let out a sigh of relief. "Motion sensor lights."

Vergo laughed. "A little on edge, are we?"

"Shut up," Sussi said. "You would be, too, if you risked getting into major trouble if we get caught."

He gave a little kitty shrug. "Fair point. And in your defense, the energy is stronger down here. We're getting closer. Do you feel it, Little One?"

It was faint, but it was there. "Kinda, but my bracelet isn't going off."

"Might have to get closer."

We crossed the generously-lit room, Sussi's water stowed in her pouch. Weight-lifting equipment and the stink of sweat surrounded us. Boys were so gross. Did they forget about soap and deodorant even in high school? How did anyone ever get married if boys stank so much?

I set the thought aside as we crossed into another room lined top to bottom with metal lockers. They were wide enough to accommodate full bandyll and football gear for each player, the metal doors perforated to allow for generous airflow. Each aisle had a wooden bench in the middle, dinged up by cleats and years of use. Across the doorway that opened into this locker room sat another large metal door. Something drew me to it. I went over and touched the door. It was cold and felt perfectly normal. And, of course, it was locked. I pressed my lock charm to it and waited for the sound of metal thunking on metal, but the door remained perfectly silent, unmoving. I tried the knob. It wouldn't turn. I tried the charm again, and nothing happened. "My lock charm isn't working."

"That's odd," Vergo said.

Deren and Sussi stood halfway between the mystery door and the doorway, eyes wide and bodies stiff.

"What's wrong?" I said.

"You don't feel that?" Sussi said, wrapping her arms around her waist.

"Feel what?"

"I'm not getting anywhere near that door. Something doesn't want me near it."

"Or me," Deren said. "Can we go, now?"

Ms. Weever had subjected me to the torment of dealing with cursed objects for a few days. I'd felt every last one of them. If the box was behind this door, how was I unable to sense this one? "Stay there while I figure out how to unlock this door."

One of Vergo's ears pivoted. "Someone's coming. Hide."

The ground tilted, and bile rose in my throat. Oh, no. I jammed Vergo's collar back on and scanned the room. Deren climbed into a locker and wedged himself inside. Sussi climbed into a fifty-gallon garbage can and yanked the plastic lid over her. I tugged the edge so it looked more natural. Footsteps hit the stairs, echoing closer.

"Hurry," Vergo said in a hoarse whisper.

I barely heard him over, my heart pounding in my head. Where could I hide? With whoever that was so near, they'd hear the locker latch, and there was no way I could wedge myself next to Sussi. I ran to one end of the lockers and pressed my back to the painted metal.

The footsteps stopped at the bottom of the stairs. My stomach twisted. How had anyone figured out we were here?

A second set of footsteps scrambled down the stairs and stopped at the bottom. My eyes watered. This was it. I was getting expelled. It was my fault for real this time.

"Oh, Little One…"

"Damien. What are you doing here?" an unfamiliar voice said.

"Never mind that. Who's in here?" That was Mr. Redd's voice. What was he doing here?

There was a moment of silence before the unfamiliar male voice said, "I don't know, but they must be in here. The motion sensor lights are on, and all the doors leading to this place have been unlocked."

Oh, no. I'd left a trail.

Vergo said, "Mia, you need to get rid of that lock charm before they find it on you."

I looked around. I was too far from the garbage to toss it without getting caught, and the holes in the lockers were little squares big enough to stick fingers through, but not a piece of metal the size of a cookie.

"Give it to me." Vergo put his front paws on my knees and opened his mouth. I handed over the charm and he darted over to the garbage can. He slipped the charm between the bag and the side of the garbage can. To my relief, no thump followed. Vergo stuck his head through the can. A muffled yelp came from within.

"What was that?" the unknown man said.

Vergo looked over a shoulder. "Mia, get over here. We need to cover for her. Someone has to know where the box is hiding."

I felt sick and lightheaded as my feet guided me closer to the garbage can. Vergo darted off towards Deren's hiding place.

"You take that side, and I'll take this side," Mr. Redd said. Footsteps shuffled a few rows down, surrounding me.

Vergo said, "Deren, no matter what happens, stay hidden. You and Sussi need to get word to Bylan and Weever about the box's location. Remember the demon. Lives are at stake. I'll take care of Mia."

It felt like a giant had its hand clenched around my chest. I stepped into sight, standing by the garbage can and mystery door. Mr. Redd checked down one of the rows of lockers before moving to the next. He stopped and did a double-take. His face turned crimson. "Miss Evers, what in the nine circles of the underworld are you doing here?"

Chapter 23

Mr. Redd kept his hand clamped around my wrist the whole way back to his office, giving me no choice but to match his brisk pace. He was only a few inches taller than me, but I struggled to keep up. Deren and Sussi stayed hidden, as Vergo had instructed. Hopefully, they'd make it out of the high school without getting caught.

How could we have been so stupid? Of course, the schools had security wards in place to alert people of trespassers. Any of the doors could've been warded. Heck, even the fence could've set off a charm sitting in the high school principal's office.

Mr. Redd stormed into his office, yanking my arm hard enough to make me fall into one of the chairs sitting opposite his desk. I hugged my arm to my stomach and massaged my shoulder. I was too out of breath to cry.

Vergo hopped on the chair next to me. "Only answer the questions he asks, Little One. Do not give him detailed explanations. He's on the hunt. He's not our ally. Why else would the middle school principal show up at the high school at such a time?"

I inhaled. The principal was under the influence of the box, too. Oh, no. It'd never occurred to me that the demon might've attached itself to multiple people. Ms. Weever said it was usually one attachment per demon, but there were cases where demons got powerful enough to influence multiple souls at once. We'd all been so hyper-focused on Nurse Kor. I had to tell Bylan and Ms. Weever as soon as possible.

Mr. Redd stood with his fists on his hips, his face so red it looked purple. He breathed heavily through his nose. "Give me one good reason not to expel you right now."

My stomach roiled with nausea. How could any school excuse a student for trespassing and using illegal objects, even with demons in the mix?

"Steady," Vergo said. "Tell him the truth, but only enough."

The truth? Yes, I could do that, but what would he believe? Bela's scream of terror from that day replayed in my mind. My heart wrenched. "I was trying to protect my sister."

"From?" The word came out like a growl.

"There's a demon anchored somewhere on this campus."

"Impossible," he said with a shake of his head. "The campus was exorcised almost four years ago, after Orton Totes died and that Dark student was expelled. We haven't had any issues, until you showed up last year."

"This is a new one, sir," I said meekly. "And it's after my sister." I refrained from mentioning what the Demon King said last year and what he'd had a demon do to Nurse Kor. Things had escalated after Bela started school. Demons hated Lights. Whatever was here wanted my sister out of the picture so it could carry out the Demon King's will with less interference. It was probably too afraid of Bylan and his lifetime of experience to bother with him. The old man would have too many skills and techniques to ward a demon off. But a child who understood nothing about her alignment? What better way to stop there from being another powerful Light?

"Are you saying this demon showed up because we have a Light child on our campus?"

Considering the fact that demons usually influenced mortals slowly and subtly, instead of outright attacking a person in broad daylight. "Yes, sir."

Eyes narrowed, his jaw muscles clenched and unclenched. He ran his hands through his graying sideburns.

Vergo cocked his head. "How deeply influenced by the demon is this man? I can't tell if that rage is his or the demon's."

"Why didn't you tell Sanctus Bylan or even have your tutor take care of it? Did it never occur to you that maybe adults should take care of such things? You're young and inexperienced. You could've caused more harm than good if you'd found this demon. How can you expect to change people's opinions of Darks if you won't obey the rules, stay out of trouble, and let adults handle situations like this?"

I opened my mouth to apologize, and he raised a hand.

"If anything, I'd say you brought this demon about because you're jealous of your sister and her alignment."

My eyes stung and the world blurred. That was a low blow. I lowered my gaze.

"Steady, Little One. Remember, those are probably the demon's words. Don't let yourself be manipulated by lies."

I sniffed and tried to will my tears away.

Vergo lifted a paw. "Wait. Are you jealous?"

Mr. Redd said, "Saving her during the attack was a great way to cover up your intentions."

I snapped my head up, meeting Mr. Redd's glare. "I love my sister. I'd never hurt her."

A hint of smugness curled into his glare. "Is that so? Her alignment is the most loved and revered, while yours is the most feared and reviled. Your parents dote on her nonstop and forget you exist half the time. They clearly love your sister while you have to fight for so much as a smile. What better way to put an end to that than by becoming an only child?"

"Ignore his words, Mia. The demon is trying to manipulate you." Vergo shoved his head under my hand, forcing me to pet him. His touch broke the tension building between me and Mr. Redd. I gulped in a deep breath.

Calm. I had to be calm. The more emotional I got, the more power I handed over to the demon. I took one deep breath after another, focusing on even breaths in and out. Give the demon nothing to use against me. Protect my sister. Protect my friends. I petted Vergo and he purred. The sound was gentle, soothing. Oh, thank the Light for a cat's purr.

The office door slammed open and I flinched. Vergo puffed up, eyes wide.

Ms. Weever's layered skirts swished over her knee-length black boots. Her icy blue eyes scoured the room, spotting me, and then Mr. Redd. "What's the meaning of this?"

"By all means, come on in," Mr. Redd said dryly.

"Forgive my intrusion," she said, her tone flat. "I heard shouting."

Mr. Redd pointed at me. "Miss Evers here has developed a certain disregard for the rules as of late. The high school principal caught her sneaking around the boys' locker room."

"The high school boys' locker room?"

"Yes. She claims to be hunting for a demon. She insists our campus has a new one anchored here, and that it's after her sister."

Ms. Weever narrowed her eyes at the principal, and then they widened. She looked at me, a mix of horror and realization playing across her face. She slowly approached Mr. Redd, positioning herself between me and the principal. "I assure you Miss Evers has not lied to you. Ask Sanctus Bylan. He will report the same thing. As for her sneaking activities…I put her up to it."

Mr. Redd's eyes were about to pop out of his head. His face turned a new shade of crimson. "You *what*?"

My tutor clasped her hands behind her back, squared her shoulders, and stood tall. "There's a demon anchored somewhere here. I've put various wards and protections up, but it's been evading them all." Her hands moved slowly. A white cloth emerged from under her blouse as her fingers worked the fabric free. "The demon knows I'm hunting for it, so it has taken great pains to evade me. However, it hasn't given Miss Evers much thought." A white cloth dangled behind her like a short tail. She let it go and it fluttered onto my lap. A handkerchief?

"Hide it," Vergo said.

Moving as little as possible, I balled the cloth in my fist. Ms. Weever blocked my view of the principal with her waist and skirts, but how much of my arms and shoulders could he see? I slowly stuck my hand under my shirt, stuffed it in my sports bra, and straightened my shirt. It looked normal and flat. I barely had anything to flaunt to begin with.

"What are you saying?" Mr. Redd said.

"That I put Miss Evers up to the task. I'm the one who encouraged her to break the rules for the sake of locating this demon's anchor."

My mouth dropped open. What on Aardra?

Vergo hopped onto my lap. "Stay silent, Little One. She knows what she's doing, and she's protecting you. Let her do what she thinks is right." I shook my head. Vergo placed both paws on my mouth. "Stay. Silent. Go with her story."

"She's innocent in all this," Ms. Weever said. "If you need to punish her, then punish me instead. Don't blame her or hold her accountable for my actions."

A "no" lodged in my throat. She was the adult. She was the more powerful and knowledgeable one better equipped to handle this demon. She should've let me suffer the consequences. This wasn't right or fair. Vergo rubbed his head against my chin. I wrapped my arms around him, at a loss for how to right this situation.

"Ms. Weever, if this is true, then this is a most grievous oversight on your part."

"I know, sir," she said calmly.

"I don't think you do. You sent an inexperienced child in your place to deal with something she doesn't understand. You put her life in danger, along with everyone else's. That's unforgivable."

"I trust her to act wisely. I've been training her, after all."

"Perhaps you trust her too much and think too grandly of your prowess as a Dark. You clearly need a lesson in humility and prudence. You are hereby suspended with pay. The school board will hear about this and decide your ultimate fate. Get out of my sight."

"Yes, sir." Giving a slight bow, Ms. Weever did an about-face. Her calm gaze drew mine in. She hid her emotions behind a neutral expression. She squeezed my shoulder before heading out. I put my hand where hers had been. The heavy click of the door closing sounded like a gavel bang.

What just happened?

Mr. Redd rounded his desk to stand before me, fists on his hips. I couldn't bring myself to lift my gaze beyond his polished shoes and charcoal dress pants. I wanted to get as far from him as possible. He said, "Is what your tutor said true?"

No. It wasn't. Bring her back. I nodded, unable to speak around the lump in my throat.

His feet remained still a moment before giving me space. The air grew cold, heartless. I hugged Vergo tighter, pressing Ms. Weever's hidden cloth against my chest. I froze. What had she given me and why?

"Miss Evers, what's your ley line route?" Mr. Redd

brought the end of a ceiling vine to his ear, which curled around it, setting a leaf in front of his mouth. He was calling home. I gave him the latitudinal and longitudinal coordinates that would direct the vine's ley line connection to my house. He stroked the vines and they shivered. A moment later, he straightened up and took a breath. "Ah, yes, hello, Mrs. Evers. This is Mr. Redd, Toolena Mesa's elementary principal. I have your daughter with me. She missed the late bus. Are you available to come pick her up?" He listened to Mom's reply. "Great. See you in a bit." He removed the vine and it retreated.

Vergo said, "What's this man playing at?"

I shrugged. If I was going to get this one reprieve, I'd take it.

Mr. Redd stood by his office door, a hand on the knob. "Miss Evers, we will forget about today if you go back to being on your best behavior. I'm wholly confident you'll do that without your misguided tutor around. As for the demon, the district will look to the Order of Leo for guidance. The adults will handle it from here on out. Your sister will be perfectly safe." His tone was pragmatic, businesslike. I didn't believe a word of it.

Mr. Redd escorted me to outside the middle school gymnasium, where Sussi and I had left our stuff. Just my bags and violin remained. Thank goodness. They'd gotten out safely and without getting caught. I grabbed my things and was escorted to the pickup lot in front of the main office.

When Yuna set off to face the wizard atop the mountain, she did it without the allies she'd thought she had. Like me losing Ms. Weever, it'd been a heartbreaking moment. After all that work, we thought we wouldn't have to do this alone. Maybe Yuna could've left the satyrs after they decided they were too scared to help, but she didn't. At least losing Ms. Weever wasn't out of fear, and she'd given me a parting gift that I now had buried in my bandyll bag as hopefully a good hiding spot.

Yuna chose to face the wizard because he had a history of conquering and enslaving whole villages. He wouldn't stop with the satyrs. There would be more victims to follow. I'd face this demon too. He wouldn't stop with Bela, and no one was allowed to hurt my sister.

Waiting for Mom to show up felt like a week passed before our new car turned into the lot. Mr. Redd stood quietly the whole time, hands clasped in front of him, looking calm. The sudden shift in emotion furthered my unease. It wasn't the spine-tingling anxiety a demon triggered. It was the discomfort of being around someone who was unpredictable with what would set off their temper. He even waved and smiled while I buckled myself into the passenger seat. I forced myself to wave back, hoping that was the real principal and not the demon's influence putting up a pleasant front. There were plenty of stories about how demons posed as children and other innocent creatures to lure people into their traps.

"You all right?" Mom said. "You look upset."

"Tired," I said, which was true. Every bandyll practice tuckered me out, leaving me relying on dinner to perk me back up.

"I hope you have energy for Bela. She's been asking for you ever since she got home. She says that ghost is back and it won't leave her alone. Your father and I have tried to calm her, but nothing's working."

I sat up straighter. Thankfully, this was something I could handle. If only I could teach her my protection shield technique. It wouldn't go over any better than Sussi trying to teach me how to make her water ball glow. "I'll take care of it."

"Thanks. You're such a good big sister."

***

I'd barely kicked my flip-flops off before Bela tackled me with a hug. "Mia, make it go away. It won't listen to me."

I hugged her back, understanding her fear. Before figuring out my protection shield, I'd been at the mercy of lost souls drawn to me. It was confusing and terrifying when you didn't understand why they were there, much less what to do to keep them at bay. She was a beacon to ghosts, until she learned how to harness her powers and put protections in place. "I will. What have you done so far?"

She clutched my hand and led me to the window, her little fingers digging into my palm. Her grip was surprisingly strong for such a small kid. And sure enough, the tingle down my spine alerted me to a ghost's presence. The same shadow man from before stood on the other side of the glass. He must've died not too far from this house to be hanging around. Bela's alignment manifesting must've stirred his lost soul, drawing him over as soon as he had enough energy. Bela pointed to the glass. "That." She touched the pane, and a crooked "t" flashed white. A protection rune. Not bad. She probably wasn't strong enough yet for it to do much good.

"Good job, Bela. That's the right one."

"Then why isn't it working?"

"It is. The shadow man isn't in the house, is he?"

Her cute face grew serious. "No. I did it?"

Honestly, no. I'd placed protections galore around the house to stop ghosts from getting in, but she didn't need to know that. She needed confidence in herself and her abilities. "You did. I'll take over from here."

Shadowy hands touched the glass. It sparked as my ward activated. The ghost backed away, its shadow of a face locked on Bela. *Help me, please. I'm so lost.*

Bela whined and hid behind me. I gently shushed her, giving her a reassuring pat on her head. I raised my bracelet wrist. I didn't want to summon my protection bubble to have her cling to me until she fell asleep. I twisted the knob and the little discs spun. Instead of emitting a whir, I heard nothing. Instead of spreading a wave of calm, my spine tingled. I grabbed the discs and studied my bracelet. It looked the same as before Mr. Redd had confiscated it. I gave it another spin, just in case. Nothing. Bela remained glued to my legs.

Vergo looked at me. "Is it just me, or is your bracelet not working?"

"It's not. I don't know what happened."

"Your principal is what happened, and that demon is meddling with him. No wonder it didn't go off in the locker room. We're navigating the school blind."

Chapter 24

"Mia, you're okay." Deren wrapped me in his arms in the hallway. For a moment, everything was right in the world. He was okay. School went on as usual. He liked me despite the close call yesterday. He held me by the shoulders before any teachers could snap at us for PDA. "What happened? I thought he'd at least suspend you."

I looked around, worried that referring to the principal would summon him. Students veered around us as teachers monitored the hallway while stationed by their doors. No principal in sight, but I put a finger to my lips. "I'll tell you and Sussi at lunch. It's bad. Mr. Redd is being affected by the demon, too."

Deren's eyes widened. "Are you serious?"

"I wish I wasn't."

Once again, I related to Yuna. After nearly dying on her climb up the mountain, the very wizard she hoped to find help from turned out to be in league with the crystal serpents. The wizard and the serpents very much wanted to see the satyrs gone. The number of available allies was shrinking. Both for Yuna and for me.

***

Lunch was a beautiful presentation of bean and cheese tostadas topped with shredded lettuce, diced tomatoes, and a dollop of sour cream. I loved tostadas, but I couldn't eat. For some reason, Mr. Redd patrolled the cafeteria, the side Deren, Sussi, and I sat on. She was as relieved to see me as Deren had been. That was all she could say before Vergo warned us of Mr. Redd's alarmingly close proximity. He walked with his hands clasped behind his back, surveying the rows of tables, his gaze frequently circling back to me.

"Talk about class or something," Vergo said. "You all look guilty."

I stabbed my tostada with a fork. "Sussi, what did you think of Mrs. Livy's class today?"

She raised an eyebrow at me. "Boring, as always. I hate history." She took a bit of tostada, the grilled tortilla crunching.

Mr. Redd meandered past us, taking forever to move out of earshot. When he was a few tables down, he turned around and slowly headed back. I busied myself with my lunch, taking one bite after another despite not feeling hungry. I'd hate myself come bandyll practice if I didn't eat. I ate my fruit cup, too, to avoid cramps and stiff muscles.

Sussi nodded to us, indicating he was far away enough to chat. "Maybe we should talk at my house. I think the enemy is keeping an extra close eye on Mia.

When can you get permission to visit?"

"Whenever," Deren said, and so did I. If anything, my mom would be overwhelmed with joy knowing there was yet another person fine with having me over. Two friends in two years? Crazy. But crazy good.

Sussi's idea proved necessary as Mr. Redd never stayed away long enough for more than a sentence or two at a time. Either he was making sure I behaved, or the demon wanted him to keep me close whenever he could. I'd sat outside his office when I normally had tutoring lessons and got all my homework done. It was boring. At least I wouldn't have so much homework to worry about later. It was also a painful reminder that Ms. Weever was gone. Would they ever let her come back?

Deren and I were walking back across the campus after lunch when Nurse Kor hurried over to us. She waved for us to stop and leaned over, speaking in my ear. "Check your sister's backpack when you get home." I furrowed my brows at her. "That's all I can safely say. I'm sorry."

She headed back for the main office.

Deren said, "What on Aardra is going on at this school?"

***

As much as I wanted to go straight to Bela's backpack when I got home, I couldn't think of a polite way to stave off eating dinner with my family. I wolfed everything down and bounced a leg while everyone else finished their meal. Bela chatted about sweet nothings, as usual, and our parents ignored me, also as usual. Maybe I'd get more attention as she got older. Maybe not. Or maybe bandyll would be my ticket to earning their smiles and praises. Our first game couldn't come fast enough.

After dinner, I showered and changed into a loose t-shirt and shorts, my version of pajamas. Years ago, I'd gotten in the habit of sleeping in clothes. Dead things had a habit of bugging me at night. I made a point to be able to get rid of them while dressed.

Vergo led the way to my sister's room and guided me to her backpack resting on a child's desk. Among several papers, toys, and a tin lunchbox sat a bulging manila envelope with my name on it. I took it out and set the backpack back the way I found it.

Mom and Dad paid me little mind as I exited my sister's room. Dad lay on the couch, already dozing off, while the song stone emitted voices narrating the evening news. Mom sat reading a book, Dad's head propped on a pillow in her lap. Bela practiced drawing protection runes and speaking their names every time she finished one. At this rate, she'd know her runes before she could write the alphabet. Like me, she was going to need it. I retreated to my room, closed the door, and tore open the envelope as I sat on my bed.

Vergo hopped onto the foot of my bed and curled his tail around his paws. "Finally. This day couldn't have dragged by any slower."

I peered inside before upending the contents onto my comforter. A bracelet and wand fell out. The bracelet was a replica of the first one Ms. Weever had given me. I spun the discs. They emitted a whir and a calming sensation. Good. It worked. I slipped it on and withdrew the pages of a handwritten letter from inside the envelope. The wand could wait.

I took one look at the pages and gasped. It was Ms.

Weever's small, elegant handwriting.

Vergo said, "What is it?" I pointed to the letter and he hurried over, perching on my shoulder so he could read.

Mia-

I apologize for any confusion my actions may have caused. Whatever happens, keep yourself and your sister safe. I've informed Bylan of the real reasons for my removal and the events surrounding it. We've all overlooked Mr. Redd as a potential enemy. I'd thought he was simply an unpleasant man. I was wrong and now we're all paying for it. Stay away from him as much as you can, protect yourself from demonic influence whenever you can't, and don't let him know you know about the demon meddling with him. This feigned obliviousness will afford you and your sister some protection. Sometimes, to defeat the enemy, you must play their game.

I know your Dark tutoring lessons will either be abysmal or nonexistent. I'll send you regular work through Bylan, so check your sister's backpack daily. It will be up to you and whatever help you can recruit to find this demon's anchor and cast it out. I guarantee I won't be allowed back so long as the demon remains. I'll give you what help I can. Please write back with any questions, and leave your letters in your sister's backpack. Bylan will get them to me. Don't go directly to him. He's being watched as well. Redd likely knows about Bylan's expulsion from the Order of Leo.

Unless the demon starts making any moves, stop your hunt for the box for now. Let the enemy think it won. Let it grow complacent. If the demon makes its next move, your sister will likely know before anyone else. Pay close attention to what she says and does. Keep an eye out for anything unusual.

Keep that white cloth I gave you on you at all times. You don't have to wear it, but check it often. It'll change color if the demon is near. If that happens, go straight to Bylan so he can contact me. That may also be our first clue that the demon is back on the prowl.

Should you find yourself face-to-face with the box, do NOT touch it under any circumstances. The demon will be able to attach itself to you. The wand I gave you is for an emergency. It's a one-time use, but it packs a lot of power. The activation incantation is engraved on the handle. Aim, hold on tight, speak the words, and it'll fire.

You can do this, Mia. Trust in yourself.

-Lyra Weever

I read the letter a second time before setting it down. "How am I supposed to sit here and do nothing until the demon makes its next move? That doesn't make any sense."

Vergo said, "It makes perfect sense. She's buying as much time as she can to teach you as much as she can."

***

Sussi's mom picked us up after bandyll practice the next evening. She drove an impressive car like Gwen's mom's. Big, shiny, and quiet. The hover charm kicked up minimal dust. Sussi held the back passenger door open, and we filed in. She parked herself in the front passenger seat and buckled up.

"Hi, Mom." Sussi's tone was automatic. There was practiced politeness to it. She looked out the window as she said it.

Her mom shifted the car into drive and didn't so much as grace her daughter with a glance. "Hello, dear." Her voice was rich, her tone formal. Her long hair was a work of art, complete with a small, glittering band of jewels pulling her bangs back. She had manicured nails that looked more like claws that delicately gripped the steering wheel. She glanced in the rearview mirror, taking in Deren and me with pale eyes heavily lined with eye shadow. "Please introduce your new friends to me."

Sussi leaned towards the middle of the car and held out a hand. "Guys, this is my mom, Mrs. Ferus. Mom, this is Mia, our goalie, and that's her boyfriend, Deren."

Wait, what? I said, "He's not my boyfriend!" at the same time Deren said, "She's not my girlfriend!"

Mrs. Ferus smirked and Sussi rolled her eyes. "Geeze, sorry. I thought you were."

"Good. You're all too young for that sort of thing. You need to enjoy being children for as long as it lasts, which is never long enough."

Sussi let out an annoyed "tck." "Easy for you to say. I'm ready to be an adult."

Mrs. Ferus's smile broadened as she pulled out onto the main road. "By all means, let's trade places. I'll do your homework for a week, and you stay on top of paying all the bills." The Fire engine purred loudly as she sped up.

Folding her arms, Sussi sat with her elbows propped on her knees.

"Don't slouch, dear. It's unattractive and bad for your spine." Her daughter straightened up and looked out the window.

"Ah, such a prim and proper family," Vergo said

lightly.

All five of us, including Vergo, were quiet for the rest of the ride. We turned onto what I thought was a long dirt road that was the Ferus family's driveway. A broad, two-story house with stucco walls and a red clay tile roof sat inside a semicircle of palm and mesquite trees. It was like an oasis complete with an inviting house.

Sussi led us to a living room decorated in bandyll team colors of forest green, cream, burnt red, and black. Marohu had a professional bandyll team called the Thunderbirds. Players in full uniform and in the middle of play hung inside burnished gold frames at intervals along the walls. Each of them had handwritten signatures. The three couches had a Thunderbirds throw blanket, the coffee table was bigger than my bed and sat on four bandyll balls.

Sussi tossed her bags on one of the couches and kept walking. "Make yourselves comfortable. The bathroom is down the hall if you need it. I'll be right back." She pointed to a modestly lit hallway and disappeared down another.

Deren and I took in the vaulted space. He plunked onto one of the couches, and then sank into it. "Oh, man, this is so comfy."

Each couch was deep enough to stretch out my legs and only have my feet hang off the edge. They were all bigger than my bed, too. I set my bandyll bag and violin next to Sussi's stuff and laid some books and notebooks on the coffee table. I'd come prepared for more than catching them up on Mr. Redd and Ms. Weever.

Sussi returned carrying a tray of snacks and a pitcher of sparkling water. Kneeling, she slid the whole thing onto the coffee table. There were several bowls of grapes, orange slices, honeydew melon, cheese, crackers, and mixed nuts. "Dinner's in an hour, so remember to save room."

"Oh, wow. Thanks." Deren reached for the grapes.

"Don't mention it," Sussi said to notes spread over the table. "What's all that?"

I took off Vergo's collar and waved Sussi over. "We've got a box to find. Ms. Weever gave us some information to work with, but we've got our work cut out for us. All we know is that it's the one Mr. Gauss had in his class for a while."

"The one with two doors and a tiny latch?" Sussi said.

"Oh, that box," Deren said. "Yeah, I remember it. I didn't even notice it was gone."

"I thought your tutor told you not to look for it," Vergo said, annoyed.

"I know, but it doesn't feel right to sit around and do nothing."

"You need to focus on her lessons."

"We need to find the box."

"And do what with it? We need to think this through more than last time."

"I have an idea." I opened one of the books to a specific page and flipped to a fresh sheet of paper in my notebook. "I got to see my first exorcism not too long ago. It gave me an idea. I'm going to need both of your help."

I described the exorcism chamber to them, how the four main alignments had been a part of it, and how Ms. Weever and Bylan had worked together to draw the demon out and get rid of it. Each alignment had its way of protecting itself from negativity. Deren told Sussi what he'd done with his engraved rock that Nurse Kor had forbade him from leaving in her office, and the runes he'd added to my protection circle around the main office.

Sussi's face brightened. "Waters create little ponds or build moats to protect locations. We can also infuse water with runes drawn on containers. As far as adding Water runes to a protection circle, that's something I'd have to learn. We haven't gotten to that section yet in elemental training class.

If only we had an Air and a Fire in our group, I'd feel so much better about this plan.

***

We spent days trying to figure out the parts of the full exorcism circle, then weeks practicing combining our runes over and over. Sussi's parents never bothered us when we came over, never asked us questions over dinner. It was strange and so unlike Deren's open and welcoming family. Neither of us were in a hurry to invite Sussi over to our houses. Hers was so much bigger and nicer. She never asked us to take turns. Mom started sending me to school with food to share since the Ferus family fed me so often. Deren occasionally tried eating his modest burrito, but Mrs. Ferus wouldn't let him. She was happy to feed us and see her daughter enjoying our company so much.

By the end of first quarter, we had our combined protection circle down pat, but I didn't know how to feel confident about it without Air and Fire being a part of it. The three of us stood in the middle of our latest creation, where the coffee table normally was. My runes glowed purple, Deren's golden orange, and

Sussi's sky blue. The circle kicked up a breeze and wrapped us in its energy. As wonderful as it was, we were missing Air and Fire. There were plenty of Airs in the school, but not many Fires, besides Gwen.

"We still need an Air and Fire," I said over the circle's hum. Mrs. Ferus had come to investigate the hum when we'd first started practicing before Sussi said it was something we were practicing for school. Mrs. Ferus had raised her wine glass to us and disappeared deeper into the house.

"Yeah, but who?" Sussi said. "Gwen and Nonaya have threatened everyone harm if anyone tries being friends with us, and most students would freak out if we told them about the demon."

"And there are people who still hate Mia for being a Dark," Deren said unhappily.

"Well, they're stupid and they can rot, too," Sussi said. "Mia, you're nothing like I thought a Dark would be. You're normal like the rest of us."

"Thanks," I said. "You both make it easier for me to be me." I wanted to say something about being thankful that we'd become friends, but we'd never said anything about actually being friends. She'd sat with us at lunch that day, and that was how things had been ever since. She was so much nicer while not around Gwen. I wouldn't point that out to her. What I did need to say, though… "We have to find an Air and Fire to help us, or we'll be in trouble. That exorcism circle barely contained the demon."

"Yeah, but you said a bunch of stuff placed elemental wards around the room instead of actual people. Maybe we can do the same thing."

"We need an Air and Fire to make them," Deren

287

said.

"Both my parents are Air," I said. "I bet at least my mom would help."

"So then that leaves us with Fire," Deren said.

"Both my parents are Water, like me," Sussi said.

"My family's a mix of Earth and Air," Deren said.

I studied Sussi, trying to muster the courage to suggest something I knew she wouldn't like.

Sussi noticed my gaze. Her eyes narrowed. "Why are you looking at me like that?"

Pretending I was in the presence of a demon, I took a calming breath, leveling my emotions. Bela had an annoying habit of hugging Gwen every time we got off the bus and Gwen left her car. Gwen gloated every time, but a moment of pure joy played over her too-pretty face when my sister showed her affection. Since it made my sister happy and she liked to spend time with me and Vergo, I didn't tell her to stop. It was what it was at this point. "She adores my sister. Maybe she'd help us for Bela's sake."

Horror played across Sussi's face. "You don't mean…her? Of all people?"

"Who else?"

She flung out an arm. "No. She can rot. I hate her. She doesn't care about anyone but herself."

"What if she says yes?"

"Then you can find another Water. I want nothing to do with her ever again." She folded her arms, signaling she was beyond persuasion.

Deren said, "Even if she did agree, what would she tell her parents? Her mom might expel you and think the problem will go away."

"He has a fair point," Vergo said.

My shoulders sagged. "Okay, not her." Well, there went my grand plan.

"Sorry, Mia," Deren said. "We'll figure it out. There has to be a Fire willing to help us somewhere."
***

The schooldays ticked by, and none of us came up with an alternative to Gwen. First quarter wrapped up, and Sussi's and my focuses shifted to bandyll. We'd progressed through the regular season, having won all our games except one. With it being playoffs, practices grew more intense, and Deren and Garrett volunteered to be ball boys during games. Garrett's coyotes often hung out beyond the fence during our home games, hoping for a stray ball to go flying. Every so often, one would fly and bounce its way out of the court and off campus, and the coyotes would take turns chasing each other around until Garrett called them over and made them cough up the ball. At some point, Coach saved a rag towel for those balls.

Thoughts of bandyll vanished when Mr. Redd waved me into his office when I was supposed to have Dark tutoring. Until today, I'd sat at a desk parked in the hallway for me and used the time as a study hall to get my homework done and secretly practice Ms. Weever's lessons that didn't require a song stone secreted home with my sister.

Confused, I followed him inside. He waved for me to sit at round table as he shut the door. I did as told and settled my backpack on my lap. Vergo took the chair next to me, his blue eyes scrutinizing.

Mr. Redd slid a stack of papers closer to the edge of his desk. "The school board is working on acquiring a new tutor. Ms. Weever will not be returning. This individual will be better and more…obedient."

My throat tightened. "But I like her."

"I understand, but you need someone who'll be a better influence on you."

Vergo said, "I know you hold Lyra in high regard, but you need to let her go. Besides, you haven't even met this new person. He or she might not be so bad after all."

I swallowed, but the lump in my throat remained. I didn't want a new tutor. I wanted Ms. Weever.

"We're in the process of finding you the perfect tutor." He picked up a booklet and handed it to me. "In the meantime, the board has asked me to give you lessons. You must learn to control your alignment as a Dark, lest you turn out like that Dark from a few years ago."

"I understand, sir." I opened a notebook and took out a pencil.

"Since I'm not a Dark, my ability to teach you anything will be limited. The board has asked me to make sure you keep your powers in line and prove to them you aren't a threat. We all believe the best way is to teach you how to suppress your alignment."

Vergo hissed. "He wouldn't dare."

Suppressing a person's alignment was something I'd heard done only to Wilds who'd murdered people. "Suppress my alignment?"

"Little One, don't do anything he or this demon says. They're trying to disarm you."

Mr. Redd nodded. "I've been speaking on your behalf at board meetings. They're on the hunt for a reason to expel you. I've been pleading your case, despite your poor choices during first quarter. Your exemplary behavior as a student and exceptional performance on the A bandyll team is making them come around. Now, they want proof that you aren't attracting more creatures to this campus."

"Translation: they want to tie your hands behind your back. Little One, you need to write to Lyra immediately. The demon is preparing to make its next move."

Chapter 25

The next evening, I took out the letter from Ms. Weever and unfolded the paper. Her familiar handwriting covered the page.

Dear Mia,

Consider it a good thing that the demon is going to such extremes to remove you as a threat. You unsettled it with your stunt during the exorcism. However, this means you have to walk a fine line between playing the demon's game and protecting yourself. I've enclosed a meditation technique that will keep your third eye open and heighten your senses over time.

Bylan is keeping a close eye on your sister. He's placed a ward on her and is hunting for the box to the best of his ability. Lights don't have the connection with demons that Darks have, so this is challenging. On top of that, he can only do so much without revealing that he's no longer with the Order of Leo. The school board may deem it prudent to relieve him of his position if they discover he's marked as anathema to all Light Orders. Depending on what happens, we all may be forced to show our hands.

-Lyra Weever

I sighed through my nose. I'd been hoping for some good news. I set the main letter aside and skimmed through the meditation instructions. Proper posture, eyes closed, thumbs and forefingers pinched together, protection words, a breathing technique, and a chant to keep my third eye open. All straightforward and simple enough.

I sat in what was now a proper desk chair and got myself comfortable, resting my hands in my lap and adopting the described pose. Vergo read the instructions to me, and I repeated the chant at the end. My body grew heavy. My feet felt like they were glued to the floor. My awareness expanded, startling my eyes open. Instead of being able to feel out the energy of the space of an average room, I could sense the whole house and much of the land around us. "Whoa."

"What is it?" Vergo said.

"How much I can sense all at once." There were a few benign ghosts on the property, and now I could tell they were completely harmless, even the shadow man that kept spooking Bela. All three ghosts turned as my awareness brushed over them, and they sank back into the ground. Even though I could've gotten rid of them by now, I wanted Bela to get rid of them once Bylan taught her how.

I meditated again the following morning. The awareness was distracting until I got used to it, tuning out unimportant feedback. The campus had some ghosts, too, including one looming around the elementary pool. They were all benevolent. The one near the pool liked to keep kids away to make sure no one drowned.

Mr. Redd invited me into his office again for tutoring. The last few days, he had me read a booklet about Darks and where they fit in with the rest of the alignments. Whoever had written it didn't like Darks. The booklet told me repeatedly that Darks existed to keep to the shadows and let the Light shine down on the rest of humanity.

Mr. Redd must've noticed my frown. "I know the information is rather outdated and doesn't match my progressive views. The school board chose this content. Go with it and make them happy. You don't want to have to make friends all over again at another school, do you?"

"No, sir," I said meekly. Despite this school's flaws, I didn't want to be torn away from Deren and Sussi, and a bunch of teachers who treated me like everyone else. Granted, things had calmed after word got out that Bylan and I had worked together to get rid of a demon. This was the best my family and I had been treated ever since my alignment manifested. If I had to pretend to be a brainwashed Dark to avoid getting expelled, then I would do that.

"Very good. Now, let's practice that suppression meditation. Sit comfortably with your feet flat on the floor and your hands in your lap."

I looked askance at Vergo. He hopped onto my lap, curling up between my hands. "Pretend to go with it, but don't meditate." I got comfortable, taking the upright posture Mr. Redd described.

"Good. Now close your eyes and take three deep, slow breaths."

The thought of closing my eyes in the presence of someone with an attachment got my heart pounding. I took three deep breaths.

"Slower and deeper," he said, sounding annoyed.

I tried again, the breaths tight in my chest with every inhale and my heart pounding away in my chest and neck. This was the exact opposite of relaxing into a meditative state. Mr. Redd and the demon didn't seem to notice. He guided me through a visualization sequence as I clung to Vergo. He purred, his furry sides vibrating. I focused on the purring and my breathing slowed. Tension eased out of my limbs. Mr. Redd's voice drawled on in the background as the purring provided a buffer between me and the demon's instructions.

I had no idea how much time had passed by the time the purring subsided. Mr. Redd said, "Now, slowly open your eyes and notice the world around you. Feel the chair holding you up, the air on your skin, and every breath you take."

Mr. Redd stood before me, arms folded. I sat relaxed in my chair, as if I'd woken from a nice nap. My breath was slow and even, the air cool and pleasant. Vergo arched his back, stretching as if he'd napped. I checked my awareness, which spread over the entire office to the road on one side, the parking lot outside the front entrance, and the pathways connecting to the K-2 and 3-5 buildings. My senses were intact. Good.

Mr. Redd's eyes darkened and narrowed. His face reddened. "What did you do?"

I stiffened. Was the demon able to sense my

probing like the ghosts could? "Meditated, like you told me to."

"Did you follow all the steps exactly like I told you to?" He leaned closer.

"Y-yes?"

"You're lying." He lunged forward, bringing his face level with mine and clutching the arms of my chair. "*What did you do?*" A female voice overlapped his and both bellowed at me. The chair groaned and the air grew chill. Through Mr. Redd's eyes, I saw a pair of round red ones framed inside a crown of tree branches.

I shrank into my chair, my chin pressed to my chest. "Mr. Redd, you're scaring me."

Vergo hissed. He stood with his claws dug into the arm of his chair, ears back and eyes narrowed. His body was puffed up. Mr. Redd looked right at the spirit cat, who growled. The principal straightened up and adjusted his tie. The air warmed and lifted its pressure, letting me breathe.

The bell rang, signaling it was time to move on to the next class. Mr. Redd opened the office door. "We'll try again tomorrow. Clearly, you need practice for this technique to stick."

I hesitated before grabbing my things and hurrying out of the office, Vergo bounding alongside me.

"He saw me," he said in disbelief. "He looked right at me."

I barreled through the door leading outside without breaking stride. The sun momentarily blinded me as my feet carried me down the sidewalk. One wave of middle school students left the cafeteria while the next headed for it. A few students tossed a football around. The air was full of happy, excited voices. If only I could live in their blissful ignorance instead of constantly facing demons. "I saw the demon through his eyes," I said unhappily.

Vergo stopped. "You what?"

"She stared at me through him."

"Wow, she must hate you. Normally, a demon wouldn't be so reckless as to reveal themselves to a human, unless they already feel in full control of the situation."

"Maybe it was an accident."

Vergo trotted towards the cafeteria. "It could very well be. Demons are known to make mistakes, too, a trait carried over from being human."

The lunch ladies were cheerful as they served us lunch with a flourish, making meatballs fly through the air and form animal shapes before settling on a hoagie roll. Marinara spiraled through the air before settling on top of the meatballs, it snowed shredded cheese, and the final lunch lady used a charm to spit fire like a dragon and melt the cheese. They smiled as I numbly took my tray and added some fruit and vegetables from the buffet.

Maybe that pamphlet was right on one thing. Darks lived in the shadows of demons while everyone else lived happily removed from such dangers.

Sussi, Deren, and I ate lunch together. I meant to stay quiet, but Deren frowned. "What happened?" he said.

I looked around. For once, Mr. Redd wasn't patrolling the cafeteria. Maybe the demon had messed up and was taking a moment to collect itself. Whatever the reason, some tension eased out of my chest and back. I leaned closer and told them about seeing the demon and it wanting me to suppress my alignment. Both of them inhaled sharply.

Deren said, "Mr. Redd can't control himself anymore. He has to know that's highly illegal, even with Darks."

"Maybe it's the school board making him do it," Sussi said.

"Maybe it's all of them," I said unhappily. Maybe Mrs. Volaire didn't care. She'd seemed content to expel me last year, until Bylan stepped in.

My heart wrenched at the thought of my former tutor. I hadn't seen her in almost two months.

Sussi said, "Whoever it is doesn't matter. We clearly can't go to any of the adults with this."

Deren voiced agreement.

"We need to hurry and find an Air and Fire to help us before the demon suppresses my alignment." I studied my meatball sandwich, inhaling the sauce's sweet, tangy aroma. "Are you sure there's no way you two could get along for this? We're running out of time."

Instead of a verbal outburst, Sussi glared at her lunch. Her frown softened. "We're running out of time, aren't we?"

***

All three of us chickened out over asking Gwen for help. Even though I was mad at Sussi for not having approached her over the last few days, I kept my anger to myself. It's not like I'd sucked it up and done it. I hadn't asked my mom either.

All that was pushed aside come bandyll championship day. We'd rolled all but the semifinal team. I was so mad that they'd scored on me. Coach

Viro only shrugged and told me that it happened now and then. And on top of that, we'd technically scored for the other team. An attempt to block the shot turned into a redirection. I'd stood in the ball's original trajectory only to have it deflect off Sussi's shoulder and sneak under my arm. She was mad, too, but at herself and not at me. We promised each other to make sure that didn't happen in the finals. We beat our semifinals opponent 3-1.

On the day of championships, I wore my best autumn dress to school. Mom did up my hair extra nice and had Bela wear a flower clip in her hair that sported our school colors of dark red, white, and dark gray. Even Mom wore our fundraiser bandyll t-shirt and had Dad's draped over his dining chair, ready for when he got home.

"Your dad'll be getting out early today so he can watch the whole game."

"Really?" The word left my mouth before I could stop myself. Dad had shown up to all of my home games and cheered us on, but he always left early or showed up late. The fact that he wanted to watch the whole thing made me want to cry. He loved me. He was proud and wanted to support me. Playing bandyll was working.

The bus driver smiled broadly when she swung the doors open for me and my sister to board. We climbed the steep steps and students cheered.

"Go, Miners," Bela said and plunked in our usual seat in the front. Everyone was wearing school colors. Even the bus driver wore the Miners bandyll shirt.

Trying not to faint, I waved to everyone and buried myself under my bags and violin. What had gotten into everyone? Since when did classmates cheer at the sight of me?

Vergo climbed his way atop my bags. He opened his mouth to speak as the bus lurched into motion. His claws harmlessly slid across my hard violin case. I caught him and set him back on top of my things. "Thank you," he said unhappily. "Now, why are you sulking? Did you not see how happy everyone is to see you?"

The students sitting across from us smiled and waved. One wore school colors and the other wore a Thunderbirds jersey replica, the angular wing tips shaped like bandyll scoops. The thunderbird wore a helmet and a glare.

A small smile formed on my face and I waved back.

The school was as decorated as the students. The fences had charm bubbles sporting school colors bobbing around in the breeze, elementary students had covered the sidewalks in crude chalk drawings and barely legible words of encouragement, signs hung in almost every window, and all the teachers were dressed in school colors as well, some of them wearing our fundraiser t-shirts.

Bylan wore his usual white robes with a red and gray sash draped over his shoulders. He smiled and held out a hand as I walked by. I shook his hand, feeling the warmth and love radiating from him. Part of me didn't want to let go. It was such good energy to be around, but...

My brows furrowed. There was something pressed against my palm. I let go, hiding the piece of paper in my fist. Students moved with me as I headed past Mr.

Redd, who wore all gray. He gave me a smug smile. "Good luck today, Miss Evers." His tone was anything but kind. I thanked him anyway and walked to homeroom, finally unfolding the paper. There were two words in Ms. Weever's unmistakable handwriting: *Good luck!*

My eyes watered. She remembered.

Mr. Redd reminded everyone of the championship game over morning announcements, even though the entire school already knew. This garnered the "Go, Miners!" Cheer Mr. Gauss had been hoping for all year. He beamed at everyone. He'd behaved no differently than before the box had been moved.

Every class sported its bandyll-themed lesson. Mrs. Livy taught us this history of bandyll, its origins in our country's culture, and how we'd arrived at our modern equipment. Our English teacher taught us about some of the most famous bandyll players throughout history and had us write short biographies for one of our choosing. Mr. Gauss had us calculate ball speed and how fast we skated, and our science teacher got into something called physics, demonstrating how hard a ball hit a player or a goalie's glove. I'd had no idea, but I felt stronger and braver knowing I'd taken such a beating all season. Mrs. Sterling had us learn the school fight song in orchestra class, which was quite peppy and enjoyable. Vergo hid in the hallway.

The only part that wasn't fun was Mr. Redd forcing me to undergo suppression meditation. Vergo and I both agreed to go with it so I could focus on the game later. I didn't need a demon fraying my nerves any more than my anticipation already was. Each class that passed brought us one step closer to game time.

Our bandyll team was released early from the last class of the day, which happened to be PE with Mrs. Viro for me. Mr. Redd made the announcement over the sound stone system. I stopped walking laps around the basketball court and disappeared into the girls locker room. I put my bracelet back on, which hadn't gone off so far, slipped Ms. Weever's wand and lock charm in my violin case, and wedged my violin case inside my bandyll bag. It barely fit with my uniform, helmet, and skates, but I wanted it on me, even though Bela hadn't given any outward sign of the demon meddling with her. Ms. Weever had taught me I would rather have it and not need it instead of need it and not have it.

There was also the cloth my tutor had snuck into my possession. It had stayed pure white all this time. Well, she'd given it to me for a very good reason. I transferred it to my bandyll bag as well.

Sussi entered the locker room and stopped, her autumn dress swishing around her ankles. Her short hair had streaks of our red and gray school colors above one ear, and she wore bandyll earrings. She sagged with relief at the sight of me, then bunched up her skirt, revealing shorts underneath. "I need to get out of this thing." Vergo and I gave her privacy, until she told us she was done. She transferred her Water bracers and a full pouch to her equipment bag. I gave her an appreciative nod and she nodded back.

The rest of the team trickled in. Our voices echoed off the abundance of metal and cement as we changed into our uniforms, minus our skates, helmets, and goalie pads. Our regular padding made us look like stone golems, our jerseys, and shorts stretched to contain them all. Our knee-length socks bulged with shin and calf guards.

A short whistle echoed over our voices, bringing us to silence. Coaches Viro and Khamai stood in the hallway leading out into the gymnasium, both dressed in blazers and dress pants. Coach Viro wore sneakers while Coach Khamai wore heels. She gave us a look, a nod, and we donned our skates. The offensive lines led us onto the court and I brought up the rear. We skated to our bench as students put the finishing touches on the bleachers and wrapped ribbon through the chain link fence so it read "Go Miners! Beat the Knights!" in blocky red, white, and gray letters.

We loosened up with a few casual laps around the court, riding up and down the curved walls at the ends and half court, our wheels making a satisfying rumble. A noise in the distance rose over our skates. The deep rumble of a bus's Fire engine reached our ears, bringing us to a stop. Above the hum, a chorus of female voices chanted the Knights' fight song.

They were here. The one team we'd lost against had returned for what they hoped was a repeat performance, and what we were eager to prove wouldn't happen again.

The bus stopped and fourteen girls spilled out, jogging straight over to the away team bench, which sat separated from ours by a few feet. Their faces were painted, hair tied back with black and white bows, their school colors. As a team, they removed the bows from their heads and clipped them to their equipment bags, neatly lined up under their bench. Coach had taught us to place our bags with care. Many teams our age didn't pay attention to this detail. The Knights cast a few smug glances our way. They were a rural school like us and had good funding like us. They were all like Gwen in attitude and, most annoyingly, they were good at bandyll.

Our captains called us into motion, and we worked through our warmup routine, taking shots, making saves, passing, riding the walls, and stretching. The Knights did the same, their actions a mirror to ours. It was the standard bandyll warmup routine that covered all aspects of the game. Coach blew her whistle and we returned to the locker room fully dressed for the game. We sat in two rows and faced our coaches.

Coach Viro studied us all for a moment before taking a breath. "This is it, ladies. You've all put forth an incredible effort to get here. I'm proud of every last one of you. This was a team effort all around. Everyone has contributed to making it this far. Now, we have one more game to focus on. Today's. Yes, this is the one team that beat us, but we will use that to our advantage to surprise them. They're expecting a repeat of what they saw at the beginning of the season. They don't know what you've learned or how much you've grown. They're expecting an easy win." She paused, taking us in again. "This isn't going to be a win for them. It's going to be a win for us. We know where they like to shoot from and how they like to play defense. We're going to deny them their usual strategies and play our game. We're going to stick to our plan all the way to the final whistle. This is our day and our game. Who's with me?" She held out a hand, palm facing down.

Yes, we would show them how much we'd learned and grown. This wouldn't be an easy win, but I wholeheartedly believed Coach's faith in us. I was so with her. Every last one of us scrambled onto our skates and piled our scoops on top of Coach's hand. A few girls lost their balance, and the rest of us held them up. Giggles rippled through the team. I smiled.

Coach's face was serious, but the muscles relaxed and one corner of her mouth curled up in what was a big smile for her. "All right, ladies. Go, Miners."

"Go, Miners." As one, we threw our scoops skyward and filed out of the locker room.

The bleachers, which lined the court from end to end behind the team benches, were packed with students and parents from both teams. More fans and fold-up chairs lined the bandyll court, their waists level with the peak of the curved walls. The court itself was dug into the ground. Among the fans stood my parents, Bela in Dad's arms. Mom waved and Dad smiled. He was here. And he was happy.

I skated to my spot in net as the rest of the starting lineup rolled into position. Mr. Redd was here, too, as was Mr. Gauss. No Nurse Kor or Bylan. Nurse Kor wasn't a sports person, and Bylan never stayed after school for anything.

We had three referees in striped shirts, dress pants, and skates. They had repel charms on their upper arms, protecting them from getting pelted by the game ball. They didn't stop players from bowling them over, though. That'd happened a few times this season. The middle referee skated up to center court and blew her whistle. As one, my team and I crouched into down and ready, scoops at our sides. Kelsi, our big star scorer, faced off against an equally large girl. The ball launched into the air. So did Kelsi and the Knights' center forward. Kelsi reached her scoops higher and deflected it to Lynn, a wing player. Skates rumbled to life, and the first of four periods began.

Bandyll was a very physical sport to the point that it was normal and legal to knock people over when scrambling for a loose ball. Arms suffered lots of bruising as players attempted to knock the ball out of an opponent's scoop. This wasn't a sport for wimps.

A Knights wingman slapped Lynn with both scoops. She veered up the curved wall, catching some air, spun, and threw the ball back to Kelsi, who caught it and rumbled towards the net. Two defenders blocked her path. Kelsi tried to roll around them. She and one defender tumbled to the ground. The ball went rolling. Rissa, our other wing player, switched sides with Lynn, skating behind the net, bent low to scoop up the bouncing ball. She and a pair of defenders swatted at each other. She elbowed one girl and came up with the ball, skating up and down the wall to break free. She passed back to Sussi, who stood on the center-court line. She advanced it to my right-side defender, Ansa, who tossed it underhand to our sweeper, Kentra. Kentra charged the net, feinted a shot, and instead passed the ball back to Kelsi. Kentra spun, facing the middle of the court, and blocked their goalie's view. Kelsi skated down the center, leaped into the air, and took a shot. Arms and scoops rose, trying to block the shot, and one Knights player dived at the ball. It sailed past everyone and everything, sneaking between the goalie's shoulder and the top bar of the net. The crystal charm attached to the net glowed green. The lead referee blew her whistle, and my teammates raised their scoops skyward. The stands erupted in cheers. Everyone on the court but me rushed Kelsi in a group hug. I whooped from my spot in net and took a swig from my water bottle resting on top of the net.

Vergo lay on his side next to my bottle. "Excellent start. They weren't expecting that out of your team."

The Knights players skated in annoyed circles before returning to their starting positions. Their coach stood with her arms folded as she barked instructions and criticism. Coach Viro shouted over her. "That's it, girls. Keep it up. Don't give them a chance to recover."

Whatever the Knights coach said to her players, they recovered and kept at least one player on Kelsi the whole time. Everywhere she skated, so did one opponent or another. The rest of the first period saw almost nothing but back-and-forth as both teams pushed for each other's net. Both teams chased after the ball and players, bobbing and weaving up and down the court, occasionally flying up the sides. We got in a few more shots on goal, but so did they. I stopped all of them, as did their goalie. We finished the first period up 1-0. Both teams left the court and crowded their benches for a three-minute intermission.

The stands cheered and booed on both sides. It didn't look like anyone was sitting. Signs and ribbons shook and waved among the sea of arms and faces, my parents and sister among them in the front row. Deren, Garrett, and two other students stood around the court on ball duty, Garrett's coyotes resting in the shade of a mesquite tree.

Coach Viro waved everyone closer and held up a stone sheet for all of us to see. It had permanent lines etched in for the center court, offsides lines, and both goalie nets. Using a stylus, she drew lines on the stone. White lines sparked into life like pencil on paper. "All right, they've gotten over their surprise and are focusing on trying to win. We knew not to expect them to make winning easy. Yes, we have the lead, but we need more goals. Their morale isn't broken yet. They think they can still win. So here're the adjustments we're going to make." Coach walked us through an attack plan and assigned girls to cover certain players.

The lead referee blew his whistle. We piled our scoops together and cheered "Pass, shoot, score" before rolling into position. The Knights stood waiting for us, down and ready, scoops at their sides. As one, we got down and ready as well. The whistle blew and second quarter began with another toss-up.

The Knights came at us fast and hard, forcing us on defense. They used the ramps and brute strength to push us out of the way as they peppered me with shots. I stopped all of them, but most of their shots bounced out of my glove before I could catch them, putting us all in a scramble to win possession of the ball. They spent a lot of time behind my net, trying for short passes right in front of me. I blocked off sharp-angle shots and pushed opponents out of my goal box. They were allowed to block my view, but not invade my box.

One large girl kept sneaking into my box, getting shoulder-to-shoulder with me, which was against the rules. I shoved her away with my shoulder. She came right back, bumping into me. I shoved her again as the ball moved around the court in a triangle of passes. The player shoved me one more time as I got my glove up. My arm jolted as a shot buried itself in the back of my glove.

Sussi darted over and barreled into the Knights player, knocking the girl onto the ground. A whistle blew. Half the stands erupted in anger. "Get out of our box and stay out." She loomed over the Knights player, who swung a scoop at her. It bounced off Sussi's shin guard, and she shoved the girl a second time, laying her flat. The other half of the stands booed and voiced anger while our side cheered.

The whistle blew a second time. A referee, arm raised to signal that a penalty had been called, inserted himself between Sussi and the fallen player, and told Sussi to stop. Kentra and Ansa, our other two defenders, guided Sussi away, who continued glaring at the girl. The Knights player laboriously got up, and her teammates escorted her away. The referee skated to center court, stopping before the bench officials who sat between the team benches. He lowered his arm. "Miners, number twenty-two, two minutes for roughing." He pantomimed a push.

Our side of the bleachers erupted in outrage while the Knights side cheered. Our bench yelled, and even Coach Viro got a verbal warning to mind her sportsmanship. Shoulders slumped, Sussi skated to center court. One of the seated officials pointed a freezing charm at her. A thin box of ice formed, trapping her inside. Penalties eliminated a player from play for either the penalty duration or until the other team scored, whichever came first. The penalized player became an obstacle on the court, creating a new level of strategy and challenge.

The referee skated over to our side of the court, and both teams set up for a face-off to my right. The referee blew his whistle and tossed the ball skyward. A Knights player beat Ansa to the toss-up and tipped it to her back line. Players, both teammates and opponents crowded me, blocking my view of a large section of the court. I veered to one side, didn't see the ball, and veered to the other. Ansa dropped into a split, raising her arms into a "T" and blocked the initial shot. The crowd cheered. The ball bounced around and a Knights player scooped it up. Rissa and Kelsi chased her down. She passed the ball back. I veered back to the other side of my screen, pushing the Knights player for good measure, and caught sight of the ball as it darted back across the court again. I shifted back, glove up and ready. A Knights player rumbled past the net's near side, passing the ball over my head and to her teammate. The girl fired as I lunged to get back over. The ball flew between my padded arm and leg. The crystal attached to my net glowed green.

The far side of the stands erupted in cheers. The ice box evaporated, releasing Sussi from her penalty. My benched teammates lowered their heads. Coach Viro clapped her hands vigorously and urged us to keep our heads up and in the game. It was only a tie, and we had over half a game left. My teammates crowded me, Sussi joining us last. She said, "They needed the man advantage to score on us. Don't let it get you down. We've got this."

Hope rose in my chest. Other girls voiced their agreement. We piled our scoops in the center of our circle and cheered our team name to get ourselves synced back up. My teammates rolled back into starting position and played our hearts out, ending 1-1 at halftime.

Coach Viro gave us another pep talk in the locker room while we snacked on orange slices and water. We returned to the court with determination, fully aware we would have to work for this win.

The game grew more physical in the second half. Players skated into each other, beat each other with their scoops, and the number of shots on net both ways increased. I made save after save, pushing harder to protect my goal box and preserve my view of the ball. Kelsi snuck in another goal right before third quarter ended, pumping the crowd back up. Even my mom and dad cheered.

Fourth quarter saw a new level of fierce. It was like the Knights were trying to kill us. The refs called three separate penalties on them, but we were unable to build our lead. Their defensive unit was big and fast, and created a human wall while on penalty kill. The game clock wouldn't wind down fast enough.

During the last sixty seconds of the game, the Knights pulled their goalie, swapping her out for an extra attacker. We found ourselves stuck on defense, seven versus eight, counting me in the net. The Knights skated in dizzying patterns, trying to mask where they handed off the ball. Sussi helped me keep the goal box clear as players tried to screen my vision.

The clock ticked down. Thirty seconds and we'd win it. The Knights circled tighter. The stands were one intense roar. My focus shrank to the court, to the ball's movements, and to where the net was behind me. I moved with the ball.

Twenty seconds.

A ball zinged over my head. We scrambled. The Knights regained possession. They set up near the top of our half of the court and looked for an open shot.

Ten seconds.

The ball moved. I lost track of it, but I kept moving to where I had a feeling it would show up next. I caught a glimpse. Yes, there it was. The same pattern. A Knight skated past my near side. I darted to the opposite end of the net, veering forward to cut off the angle as the ball sailed over my head. Her teammate caught the ball and fired.

My mind blanked out as my body moved. My glove came up and my arm jolted. My fingers clutched the softball-sized orange ball. The final horn blared.

I sat propped up on my padded knees and opened my glove. There was the ball for real, nestled in grubby gray padding, safely outside my net. Something bowled me over and screamed in my ear. Sussi. More teammates piled on top of us, all screaming and cheering. We'd done it. We'd ended Toolena Mesa's losing streak and earned the championship trophy. And I'd helped. And people liked me for it. Tears welled in my eyes. I undid my glove and scoop and hugged my team back.

It all felt surreal as we lined up to clap hands with the Knights. Almost every last one of them was crying. Their head coach gave me a pat on the back and complimented my goaltending. If I said anything back, I couldn't recall. One moment I was looking up into the opposing coach's disappointed face, and the next thing I knew, we were receiving a big and shiny trophy from the officials. Kelsi and the other eighth graders crowded together and hoisted it up for our fans to see as the Knights fans trickled out into the parking lot.

The surrealness of the moment shattered to the sound of frantic barking. I blinked, taking a step back from cheers and congratulating each other. Garrett ran to the fence and tried to calm his coyotes. They wagged their tails as they kept barking and whining, one of

312

them trying to jump the fence.

I turned to Vergo, who sat near me on the court. He said, "They sound distressed."

I pulled my sleeve and arm guard back, revealing my bracelet. It wasn't vibrating, but I was so hot and sweaty that it could've warmed up, and I'd have no idea. I searched the stands. My mom and dad stood clapping and cheering and smiling. Bela was neither in Dad's arms or by either of their legs. I scanned the parting crowd. I didn't see her anywhere.

I skated over to my equipment bag and dug out the cloth Ms. Weever had given me. It was black. I looked up again. "Bela."

Chapter 26

I skated up the edge of the court and clung to the wall's rim. "Mom. Dad. Where's Bela?" They both wore smiles and a faraway look, like they were about to nod off. I pounded on the magical barrier meant to keep bandyll balls in play. Pink rings rippled away from my fist and I called to my parents again.

Mom shook her head and her brows furrowed. She looked around before her eyes fell on me.

I pounded the barrier again. "Where's Bela?"

Mom looked at Dad's arms. Her eyes widened. She checked both sides of his legs. My sister wasn't there. I wanted to scream as I gave my parents a chance to shake off whatever spell had affected them. Mom shook Dad's arms and he shook his head.

"Where's Bela?" she asked, her fingers digging into his biceps.

Dad checked around his feet before looking

around. He paled.

Oh, no.

I skated to the bench as my parents called out for my sister. This was it. The demon had finally made its move while we were all distracted. I threw off my goalie gear and helmet before digging my violin case out of my bag. My hands shook. There was something terrifying about knowing I would face the demon again. It was terrifying knowing I was the only one to stop it. Ms. Weever wasn't here to bail me out if I found myself trapped in the demon realm again.

Sussi skated up to me. "What's wrong?"

"Bela's missing. I've gotta find her."

She inhaled, hopped over the wall, and grabbed her bracers and water pouch. We skated off the court together, ignoring our coaches and the rest of the team.

The coyotes howled and barked, their voices mingling with the crowd's cheers and celebratory talk. Deren ran up to us, putting on his bracers. His mouth was drawn in a line. "Where are we going?"

"The high school," I said. It was the only logical place to go. Sussi and I skated ahead, veering towards the parking lot clogged with cars and a bus.

Mr. Redd blocked our path, putting his fists on his hips. "And where do you two think you're going?" A red sheen flashed over his eyes. Sussi and I slid to a halt.

A roar reverberated behind us. Deren mounted Vergo's back and the panther bounded for us. If I hadn't known he was on our side, I could've passed out from sheer fright. A large black cat bearing down on me sent a primal fear darting up and down my spine.

"Let's go," Vergo said as he ran past, knocking the

principal aside.

I grabbed Sussi's arm and skated into motion, chasing Vergo down as we followed the sidewalk connecting the elementary campus to the high school. We weaved among the half-full parking lot and skidded to a stop by the main entrance. My whole body shook. Even knowing the principal had an attachment, I couldn't wrap my head around outright defying him. I pushed the thought aside as best I could. Calm. I needed calm. Anything but would give the demon power over me.

"Which way?" Vergo said.

Sussi stared at the panther, her eyes wild. "Is that…?"

"Yes," Deren and I said.

"How?"

"Later," Vergo said.

I held one corner of the black cloth so the rest hung down. The opposite tip rotated to the left, lifting the rest of the cloth. I skated left and everyone followed. The cloth led us to the auditorium door. My bracelet vibrated. "Here." I tossed aside the cloth and retrieved the lock charm from my violin case. I slapped it to the door and yanked. The door remained shut, the metal stinging my hand. I recoiled.

Growling, Vergo reared and swiped at the door. The handle sheared off, leaving a gaping hole in its place. I yanked on the door, but it remained closed. Vergo reared a second time and buried his claws in the metal. Corded muscles bulged under black fur. He let out another roar and tore the door off. It flew overhead, clanging and bouncing on the broad sidewalk.

I grabbed my violin and pocketed the wand in my

shorts before detaching my skates from my sneakers. Sussi did the same and shouldered her water pouch.

Ribbons of fog streaked past the entrance. Shielding my head with my forearms, I leaned into it, forcing my way forward. The demon's ward pushed back like I was trying to force my way through a mattress. Sussi and Deren pushed on my back, but the ward held. Vergo roared and the three of us stumbled through, plunging into darkness.

The bracelet vibrated and seared into my wrist. I wrenched it off, tossing it aside. Wind roared in my ears as my vision adjusted to the lack of sunlight. House lights flickered overhead like lightning. Fear filled me from head to toe. I recognized the spine-tingling sensation of a demon's presence and focused on my breathing to bring calm.

More flickering light poured onto the stage, where a small body lay. "Bela."

She lay at Mr. Gauss's feet, unconscious. My math teacher had black markings all over his arms and face, and his mouth stretched unnaturally wide with arms raised to shoulder height. He stood in the middle of a power circle creating the whirlwind. At his feet sat the box, its two little doors open, nothing but blackness inside. The demon's anchor. Mr. Gauss chanted and a black tendril reached from inside the box for my sister.

"Guys." I shouldered my violin and then lowered it. Deren and Sussi sat huddled in the crux of the last row of chairs and the floor, their heads buried in their arms. "Guys? Get up." They whimpered and shrank lower. I tugged at Deren's shirt and he shied away.

"Get away from me."

A roar emanated from outside. Vergo muscled his

way through the ward. It sparked against his side as he took one laborious step after another, digging his claws into the thin carpet. With another roar, he pushed his way through, and the swirling slowed, flickering. He licked his flank and padded over to Sussi and Deren. "What's wrong with them?"

"They're too scared to move."

Vergo nudged Sussi's arm with his nose. She screamed and backed away, tears streaming down her face.

I searched the floor for my bracelet and spotted it by Deren's sneakers. I snatched it up and gave the discs a spin. Its hum washed over us, calming them enough to remove their hands from their faces. I shouldered my violin and played a basic protection circle song. I should've expected this. Deren had become a hysterical heap that day outside the main office. My fingertips danced across the strings and soothing notes flowed. I breathed with the music and the circle's runes enveloped the four of us in their purple light.

Their faces softened and hands lowered. Mr. Gauss continued chanting in the background.

"Can you get up now? I need your help." How had Ms. Weever trained me to face fear? She'd done so well that I hardly noticed anything beyond her patience, determination, and dedication. Sussi's face creased with anxiety. I said, "I know you're scared. It's okay. Don't fight your fear and instead accept it. I need you to stand up. Can you do that?"

Sussi took a calming breath. Terror remained plastered on her face as she used the chair back to hoist herself up. Deren stood on shaky feet as well.

"The demon is making you feel scared so you leave

it alone. It's trying to win by avoiding a confrontation. You're both stronger than that."

Vergo stood between them, nudging them with shoulders that reached their hips. They both dug their fingers into his fur and held on tight.

"You can do this, little ones. We are four and he is one."

Deren nodded and wiped his face with a forearm.

Sussi said, "I didn't come all this way to chicken out now."

Vergo tilted his head to look up at me. He was a powerful sight to behold. "We need to get closer."

I felt out the size of the auditorium. It could probably house a thousand people, half on each side of a wide, sloped pathway leading to an orchestra pit. I stood in the center of the path and closed my eyes, visualizing a circle that wrapped around the whole space, minus the stage. I took a deep breath and played the circle's song. A light wind that wasn't the demon's flowed counter to its ward.

The whirlwind sparked against my circle, a little at first, and then more and more. What was a flash here and there turned into a shower of angry red sparks. Each spark clawed at my mind, like someone punching me in the chest. I grit my teeth and played a more powerful protection circle's song. Notes spilled forth, rising and falling, filling the room with their power. A second circle flared to life, a swirl of purple and white light. Sparks screeched all around us. The chanting stopped, replaced by an ear-piercing shriek too large and bestial for any human to make. I clenched my teeth, resisting the urge to drop to my knees. A curtain of sparks spilled all around us. The air creaked with what sounded like cracks forming in glass.

The whirlwind exploded, knocking me down. I scrambled back to my feet, violin in hand, and patted the wand sticking out of my pocket. It didn't feel right to use it yet, but I had a feeling I'd need it soon. I wasn't sure what exactly for. The sparks faded like the last embers of New Year's fireworks, allowing my circles' glow to fill the auditorium.

The shriek coalesced over the stage. Mr. Gauss collapsed and a shadow burst from the box, engulfing the stage from floor to the curtain. The shadow coalesced into a giant monster of nightmare. The demon had a huge, triangular jaw, a curved emaciated body, mossy-looking hair that hung off its head, and two horns. Claws big enough to shred an adult in two settled on either side of Bela and Mr. Gauss. Boils erupted all over the black body, dripping tar-like tendrils of shadow.

Eyes as big as my head narrowed. *Again, you meddle. I'll kill you myself.* Triangular claws rose and bounced off my protection circle's energy field, creating purple sparks. I clenched my teeth as each blow squeezed my head.

Vergo roared, making my eardrums vibrate, but it filled me with the will to face the demon. Sussi and Deren stood on either side of me, bracers on and ready for a fight. I nodded to both of them and shouldered my violin.

The demon struck again and my knees buckled. Vergo roared and the demon raised both paws. Sussi muttered a spell under her breath and flung out an arm. Icicles buried themselves in the demon's ribs. It shrieked and staggered back.

Foolish child.

It lunged forward, maw wide enough to swallow all four of us. Deren drew some runes in the air and slapped the ground. A shard of rock surged forth, sucker-punching the demon in the jaw. Arms going slack, it rocked backwards, dropping onto its haunches. Vergo bounded forward as Sussi shot more icicle spikes at it. He leaped into the air and latched onto one of the demon's horns. Even though he was a kitten compared to the demon's sheer size, one yank, and he drove the demon's head to the ground. "Now, you three." He dug his fangs into the demon's hide and growled.

I entered the orchestra pit and stood on a chair to see the power circle the demon used Mr. Gauss to make. The demon growled. Deren shouted something and two more rock spikes burst out of the ground, forming a triangle over its body and pinning it down. Sussi spoke another spell. Water formed on every surface, even my skin, as the air dried. Another word and the water droplets flew to her outstretched arms, forming a huge water globe. She made some swirling hand gestures and the water split into two large blobs and lengthened into icicles. She threw her arms forward and the icicles buried themselves in the demon's clawed hands. It let out an injured roar that made the ground shake. It sounded so pathetic that I almost felt sorry for it.

The demon's power circle glowed a deep purple. Its spidery runes looked different from mine, but I could read them. This was a power transfer circle. He'd intended to transfer their life force to him to gain a power boost. I forced myself to take a deep, slow breath. Both Mr. Gauss and Bela were deathly pale.

Their chests rose and fell with shallow breaths. I had a chance to save them.

I read and reread the demon's power circle runes. My fingers played out the string fingerings against my thigh, and my body swayed with the song's tempo as I felt out the notes. Yes, that was the song. Now, to play it in reverse. I shouldered my bow.

The demon struggled a moment before collapsing back on the stage. Vergo let out a warning growl, fangs buried in the creature's body. Tar-like tendrils of shadow oozed all over the lacquered wood.

Taking a deep breath, my body swayed to mark the time. I played the circle's reverse song. It grated on my ears, requiring notes a half-step apart to be played together, making me sound out of tune. The song was like the stroke of a needle and thread sewing something back together. I played the final discordant notes and the circle faded, the last shreds lifting away like ash flakes rising above a fire.

The demon shrieked, making me flinch. It tossed its horned head and Vergo crashed into the orchestra pit. One claw broke free of an icicle spear and shattered the other with a swipe. It lurched to its hands and knees, breaking Deren's rock shards. It opened its great mouth and the sound that blasted from its throat was a mix of roar and scream. The sheer force of it blew me, Bela, and Mr. Gauss off the stage and into the orchestra pit. Violin in one arm and sister in the other, I pinned her to me so my back took the brunt of the landing. Music stands and folding chairs broke my fall. I gasped for breath as pain exploded all over my back.

Claws dug into the edge of the stage. Wood groaned and cracked. *Give the morsel back. She was promised to me.*

"Who promised her to you?"

Give her back. A paw big enough to crush me reached for Bela, pressing against my protection circle. I fumbled for the wand as Vergo launched at the claw, pushing it away.

"Mia, the exorcism circle. Do it now. Remove his attachment."

I released my grip on the wand as if it had burned me. Right. I needed to remove the attachment before anything else, or the demon would have easy access back to the mortal realm, anchor or not. Sussi and Deren joined me once again, hands up and ready. I closed my eyes and pictured the exorcism circle inside that stone chamber. I played the north rune, the east, the south, and the west. A shockwave pulsed from my violin with each rune. Sussi and Deren chanted their runes, adding gold and blue runes to my purple ones.

Vergo pressed his forehead to Mr. Gauss's. Kneeling, I placed a hand on his chest. "In the name of the Light, I command thee to leave this body."

The demon flinched as if I had physically struck it, turning its head. It faced me and bared way too many fangs.

"In the name of the Light, I command thee to leave this body."

It flinched again and stalked me like a tiger preparing to pounce on its prey.

As I'd feared, three alignments in one exorcism circle weren't enough, but I couldn't stop. I had to finish what I'd started. "Leave."

No. Give her back.

"Mia, what do we do?" Deren said, fear making his

voice shake.

"I feel my runes slipping," Sussi said.

"I don't know," I admitted, despair creeping into the back of my mind. Cracks formed in our circle as the demon's will pressed down on us. The air grew heavier and it was getting harder to breathe. It felt like we were trying to hold up the ceiling, lights, scaffolding and all. Between trying to push the demon out and maintain the exorcism circle, my head throbbed, and my breath came in ragged gasps. The demon slashed at the protection circle. Vergo swiped at it and missed.

I tilted my head back, trying to get enough air.

Something howled in the back of the auditorium, followed by another creature. Two coyotes bounded over to the east corner as Garrett ran over to us, out of breath. He held his hands out to the east and said something that sounded like snarling. The coyotes howled, heads tilted back. An earthy brown rune flared to life, sending a fresh wave of energy over us. Garrett and his coyotes repeated the process at the south side, and another wave of energy burst forth.

Stop that. The demon reared up and came crashing down on my protection circle. I clenched my teeth as the impact rattled in my skull. Vergo tried to attack. The demon darted out of the way and kicked with a back paw as Garrett added the west rune. I sat up straighter, breathing hard. Almost done. I gripped the neck of my violin as Sussi and Deren placed their hands on my shoulders. A fourth ripple of power passed through me. I took a deep breath and met the demon's glare. My voice came out deep and resonant, powerful and commanding. *"In the name of the Light, I command thee to leave."*

The demon stiffened, its jaw going slack.

Mr. Gauss rolled over and vomited black tar. He heaved so violently that I felt sick. Sussi gagged and covered her mouth with the back of her hand. Vergo backed inside the protection circle. Our math teacher wiped his mouth and sat on his heels, his face covered in sweat. His eyes were wide and wild, going wider when he spotted the demon. He cried out. "What is that thing? What on Aardra?"

The demon let out its roaring shriek and turned for the box sitting alone on the stage. Somehow, it stayed put and unharmed during all this. I drew the onetime-use wand Ms. Weever had given me.

Demons couldn't be destroyed any more than a soul could. Blasting it with the wand wouldn't stop it from returning to meddle with the mortal plane one day. I stood and aimed at the box. Ms. Weever had warned me about the consequences of destroying a demon's anchor, but what other choice did I have? The world seemed to drop into slow motion as the demon lunged for the box, its body morphing and stretching to fit through the small doors. Power words formed on my lips. The wand warmed and a huge blast erupted from the tip, throwing me backwards. Purple lightning struck the box, sending a blast wave through the air. Sussi and Deren caught me in their arms. The demon dived into the epicenter of the explosion. Instead of disappearing, it unceremoniously bounced and slid to a halt upstage. Curtains billowed to make room. The demon's body coalesced into a bubbling blob before shifting and reforming into the horned, emaciated monster it was.

Footsteps stomped in from the back of the auditorium. Sunlight poured in behind Bylan and Mr.

Redd. The Light priest took one look at the scene and ran over to us, his voluminous robes flowing behind him. He patted my shoulder and squared off with the demon.

The demon looked in Mr. Redd's direction. *Treachery.* It drew something in the air and a black portal opened.

Bylan circled his arms in martial arts movements and closed his hands into fists. Chains of pure white light wrapped around the demon's torso and mouth, trapping and silencing it. The portal evaporated. Vergo paced around it, hackles raised. Bylan turned to me. "Mia, do you remember the Crossing Ritual?"

How could I forget? I'd practiced it a zillion times. I nodded.

Bylan raised his arms and jerked his fists to his sides. The demon's trapped body slid off the stage and crashed into the orchestra pit, crushing every chair and stand. "All of you stay very close. You, too, Vergo." The panther hopped off the stage and crouched by Bela, nudging her with his nose. She remained out cold.

With a snap of his fingers, Bylan summoned the Crossing Ritual circle. It blazed pure white light. The demon struggled and tried to speak around the chains. I shouldered my violin and added my power to the circle. Bylan placed a hand on my shoulder and took a deep breath. His voice came out deeper, forceful, as if the power of a god fueled his words. "In the name of the Light, I command thee to tell me thy true name."

The chains around its mouth broke away. The demon grimaced. "Payton Arian Sorenson."

Bylan furrowed his brows, then shook his head and puffed up his chest. "Payton Arian Sorenson, I hereby break the chains enslaving you to Molech's will and free your soul." The demon twitched and writhed.

I said, "I call forth the Light to pass judgment on all your deeds and protect your soul from the darkness." Please don't give me another spirit pet. Please. The demon twitched again and struggled against the chains.

We both said, "In the name of the Light, we banish the Darkness from thy soul and deliver thee to the Light."

White light shot up from below, blinding me. The energy made my head spin and the room tilt. I reached out for Bylan. All went cold and black.

Chapter 27

I sat up, gasping for breath. Cold washed over me. It felt like I kneeled on ice. I braced for an attack as I stood. There was nothing but black all around me. Pure black wrapped in more black. I groped the air in front of my face. Nothing but black. I wasn't afraid of the dark. I knew what was there and if it was there. But this?

Look who's come knocking on my door again. And so soon.

That voice. Deep, gravelly, powerful. It had the weight of thunder, sending chills up and down my spine like no other demon could. I summoned my protective shield, but the Demon King's presence was so overwhelming that he might as well have me wrapped in his coils, whatever he looked like.

Breathe. Breathe. Just breathe. Remain calm. I tried to breathe deep and slow. It must've been twenty heartbeats in and twenty heartbeats out that felt like a mere second per breath. How did one stay calm in the presence of the Demon King?

"Why am I here?"

Why? Because you stole another one of my demons, of course. You think I'd do nothing?

I turned in place, trying to see anything other than black. "But my circle was strong. How were you able to pull me in?"

Oh, Miss Mia Evers, a Crossing Ritual connects my realm to Shinjan's. It is only for a moment, as mortals perceive it, but a moment is all we need.

"Then why isn't Bylan here, too?"

I see no need to meddle with such a mortal. Only you interest me. I very much enjoyed this little game. You've only removed a pawn. My queen is still in play, as are more pawns.

Game? Last year, he'd said something about letting me have Vergo. "You let me take this one, too?"

I had nothing to do with your success or failure with that weakling. His booming voice was casual, haughty. *He failed to kill the child of Light and failed to defeat you in the process. That was all his fault. He proved himself unworthy of my gifts.*

"Then why bother me if you don't care about him?"

The Demon King chuckled. It was like thunder rumbling with the cadence of a laugh. *I have plans for you, Mia Evers. Grand plans.*

"I won't play into them. I'll find a way to beat you." The words left my mouth before I realized what I'd said. Why did I say that? Out of fear? Sure, it was a stupid thing to say in this moment. At least the first part was true. As far as beating the Demon King?

Beat me?

Rumbling shook the blackness I stood on, making the chill air vibrate and my skin tingle. The Demon King laughed harder.

I'm not a thing to be beaten. I am a force. You don't stop a force such as me any more than you stop the sun from rising and setting each day, and no more than you can stop the world from turning.

Although his voice came from somewhere above me, his presence surrounded me.

Ah, you wonder what I look like. Does it really matter? What do you fear most, Mia Evers?

A hint of light appeared in the darkness, reflecting off a writhing mass surrounding me. It looked like a garbage heap plagued with worms.

Maybe something like this?

The worms morphed into something spidery, legs everywhere. Each leg was taller than a house and covered in hair. Skittering surrounded me like the tap of claws on walls.

Or this?

The legs swelled and morphed into the scaled body of a serpentine dragon. Wings thudded all around. A flash of fangs appeared outside arm's reach to my right. One fang was as big as my entire body. Acrid breath stung my nose.

Or this.

The fang morphed into a girl with long hair and a face like mine. I gasped. She looked out into the black nothingness and hugged her torso tight. No one to like her, no one to love or hug her. No one to show her kindness or compassion or help her when life got hard.

Loneliness wrapped its icy grip around my heart. A lump formed in my throat. Tears blurred the world into splotches of color. Two hot lines rolled down my cheeks.

Something flicked my chin. A flash of a forked tongue. I flinched and reached for my cheek.

Ah...

The Demon King sounded like he'd laid down in a nice hot bath.

Delicious despair. We'll have such fun, you and I, Miss Evers. Just you wait and see. Do try and stop me. Try to thwart me all you want. I'll savor every last failure and vain effort.

Just like that, he was feeding off of my emotions. I closed my eyes and focused on my breathing. Nothing. I had to give him nothing. He wanted all my hate, my fear, my despair, every last negative emotion. I breathed in, picturing my body filling with white light, and exhaled blackness, releasing the negative, pushing away the tears. Calm seeped into my stomach and spread to my limbs. The chill surrounded me. I accepted it. It was beyond my control, but my breathing wasn't.

Warmth touched my feet and spread. My eyelids turned red. A light shone around me, emanating from the ground. Love, warmth, and life enveloped me like a blanket fresh out of the clothes dryer. I smiled.

Ah, our moment together has finally come to an end. Farewell for now, Mia Evers.

The Demon King didn't sound remotely upset. I didn't care. I submitted myself to the warmth and light. My body filled with a falling sensation, coming to rest on a familiar leathery and squishy surface. I opened my eyes in the physical world, coming face-to-face with a house-cat-sized Vergo curled up on my chest. He opened his blue eyes.

"There she is. It's about time. I was starting to get worried."

The familiar leathery surface was one of the sick beds in Nurse Kor's office. Shifting my legs over the side, I sat up and Vergo shifted to the foot of the bed. I barely had enough time to recognize Mom's frantic face before she wrapped me in a fierce hug.

"Mia, you're okay. What on Aardra happened?"

I had no intention of telling anyone about my exchange with the Demon King, not even Vergo or Ms. Weever. No one needed to know. Now that I was out of the demon realm, I could understand that he was trying to scare and intimidate me. Still, I couldn't help but feel a hint of dread after how lonely he'd made me feel. "How did I get here?" I said, meaning my transfer from the auditorium to this bed.

"Vergo carried you over," Bylan said from behind Mom. He stood with his hands hidden in his sleeves, his aged face full of relief. "How are you feeling?"

Never mind that. "Where's Bela? Is she okay?"

Bylan stepped aside, revealing Dad with Bela in his arms. She was out cold, but she had her color back and looked peaceful with her head resting on Dad's shoulder. He held on tight. Bylan said, "She'll be fine, thanks to the five of you. I was already home when the ward I'd placed on Bela got set off. You bought me enough time to reach you. Whatever you did, I'm wholly impressed."

Deren and Sussi stood at the foot of the sick bed, Sussi with her arms folded and a hip sticking out. "Let's never do that again. That sucked."

Deren, who looked ready to burst, wrapped me in a hug. "I'm so glad you're okay. You scared me when you fainted."

"Are you sure you two aren't boyfriend, girlfriend?" Sussi said.

Deren and I both rolled our eyes. I said, "He's not my boyfriend!" at the same time he said, "She's not my girlfriend!" The adults laughed. I didn't see what was so funny. I folded my arms in my best imitation of Sussi.

"Anyway," Sussi said, "the team is wondering what happened to us. We better get back."

Bylan said, "You four go enjoy the party. We'll catch up with you later." He nodded to my parents and held the office door open for everyone. Deren, Vergo, and I followed Sussi out, both of us carrying our skates. Garrett was nowhere to be seen. He'd come and gone like a spirit wolf.

Vergo trotted alongside me, and I finally noticed the new patch of white on his chest, between his forelegs. I gestured with my skates. "That's new."

He glanced at his chest. "Yes, it is. Another good deed in the books. I appear to be well on my way to atonement, so this humiliating form won't be for so long after all, especially if we keep facing danger on a regular basis."

My smile died as quickly as it formed on my face. I was happy for him, but what would happen the day the Light finally deemed him fully atoned for his sins? Would he be allowed to cross over and rest in peace?

A pang of sadness gripped my chest. I was getting used to having him around.

No. He used to be a demon, one who'd tried to

trick me into striking a bargain with him. I was still mad at him for that. Yes, very mad. "I'm happy for you," I said.

Vergo studied me for a moment as we walked up to the gymnasium entrance. "Me, too." He sounded like he meant it as much as I did.

Voices spilled out the moment the door opened. Overhead, the air was full of enchanted bubbles, ribbons, paper Miners mascots, confetti, and miniature bandyll jerseys, one for each member of the A and B teams. In the middle of the basketball court sat several tables of food, including a huge cake that'd already been cut into. A few teammates looked up at the sight of us entering. Kelsi led a small group of players charging right at us, arms raised and huge smiles on their faces. They wrapped Sussi and me in hugs.

"There you are. Why on Aardra did you run off like that?" Kelsi said.

Ansa appeared with a slice of cake on a paper plate. "Mia, we saved this slice for you." A black frosting goalie net had been drawn atop a red and gray bandyll court.

I accepted the slice, getting a strong whiff of vanilla and buttercream. My mouth watered. "Thanks." I needed a break from thinking about demons. Taking a moment to absorb and enjoy the fact that we were league champions was a great way to do that.
***
I accepted the slice, getting a strong whiff of vanilla and buttercream. My mouth watered. "Thanks." I needed a break from thinking about demons. Taking a moment to absorb and enjoy the fact that we were league champions was a great way to do that. I stuffed a

forkful of cake in my mouth.

"So where did you go?" Kelsi said. "Mr. Redd was so mad."

Cheeks puffed, I projected an apology. She and the rest of our teammates giggled as I finished chewing and swallowed a perfect balance of cake and frosting. "The high school. What did Mr. Redd do?"

"He ran after you guys, but Sanctus Bylan showed up all scared-like and spoke with Mr. Redd, who turned around to congratulate us and stuff. He was red-faced the whole time."

That sounded like our weird principal. He was up to something, but I'd worry about it later. I took another bite of cake.

Ansa said, "He squeezed my hand too hard."

"I'm not the only one," someone in the back said. Others voiced agreement.

The bandyll court and the high school gymnasium were only a few minutes' walk apart. I had no clue how long it took to get there and save Bela. The whole thing was turning into a scary blur of a memory. Bylan arrived after we had the situation mostly handled. "What did B—Sanctus Bylan do?"

Kelsi said, "He threw a bunch of wards down all over the place. It got so bright. The Knights team was so confused until Sanctus Bylan told them to get on the bus."

"And that's when he ran," Ansa said. "I didn't know someone that old could move that fast."

"Mia, where's that panther?" Kentra said. "That was epic watching him ride Vergo and nearly bowl over the principal." Her hazel eyes were bright with excitement, the freckles on her cheeks standing out.

Other girls voiced their eagerness to see my spirit cat.

Vergo looked up at me with a suffering expression. His ears drooped, looking like little bird wings. "Go ahead and satisfy their curiosity."

"You sure?"

"No, but the cat's out of the bag, as they say."

Clamping my fork to my plate, I removed Vergo's collar. He shook out his head. My teammates gasped.

Ansa let out a gushing aww. "He's so cute." She picked the cat up. "What's his name? Where'd you get him?" Vergo gazed heavenward. "And why's he with you?"

"Where'd the panther go?" Kelsi said.

"Right here, in the arms of one of your beloved teammates," Vergo said.

Everyone but Sussi froze and went wide-eyed, who said. "Yes, he talks."

Ansa turned, clutching Vergo to her chest. "Wait, you knew? Why didn't you tell us about him?"

Sussi shrugged and pet Vergo under the chin. He closed his eyes and filled the air with the tiny rumbling of a purr. "He's really smart."

"Finally, a more accurate assessment of me." He closed his eyes and tilted his head so Sussi scratched his cheek.

Ansa petted his head. "And he's so soft and soothing to hold." She squeezed him in a hug.

Girls crowded closer, everyone asking for a turn to hold the cat. Ansa handed Vergo off to Kentra, who held him like a baby. His tail flicked in irritation.

"Light, exactly how many people must I tell that I'm not a pet before you relieve me of this suffering?"

"He's funny," Kelsi said. "What's his name?"

I had half a mind to tell my teammates that I'd named Vergo Ser Purrs-a-Lot, but he ruined the chance and explained his limbo status to them as he was passed from one pair of arms to another. Everyone hugged him and scratched his head. He purred on and off as their chin scritches triggered his instinct or punishment to act like a real cat.

"Yes, yes, I'm an adorable and heroic little fluff ball. Would any of you care to put me down, now?" My teammates giggled and kept passing him around, asking Vergo questions about what it was like to be a spirit cat.

"Torturous, as you can see." He flashed a fang as another teammate squeezed him in a tight hug. "And humiliating. How would you like the Light to transform you into some diminutive beast and force you to stay near another soul?"

"Then turn back into the panther," Kelsi said.

"Would that I could, but the Light seems to be in charge of that. I can transform into a panther only during a time of need."

"That sure is handy," Sussi said. "It helped us beat that demon trying to kill Mia's sister."

"Say what now?" Coach Viro said. She and Coach Khamai had watched on with open interest. She held a plate with half of a slice of cake. "Is that where you two ran off to?"

Sussi turned to me, her expression unsure.

"Yeah. Sorry, didn't mean to worry anyone. We didn't have time to explain."

Kentra said, "We saw Garrett's coyotes climb the fence and take off after you with Garrett. Mr. Redd went scarlet yelling at them. It was so funny."

I could imagine the furious look on Mr. Redd's

face. Garrett had gotten in trouble so many times already for letting his coyotes run crazy around campus, and leave, uh, certain brown presents all over the place. I explained to them how Deren and Garrett had worked together with Sussi and me to save my sister, beat the demon, and everything that happened after that. I refrained from telling them about Payton and him being the Dark from four years ago who'd gotten another student, Orton Totes, killed. I didn't need anyone thinking I'd turn out like him."

"So what happened to Mr. Gauss?" Kelsi said.

"I dunno. I passed out." And then had a terrible conversation with the Demon King.

Sussi said, "I'm not sure either. Mr. Redd stayed behind while Sanctus Bylan and the rest of us carried you the nurse's office."

"He should probably go to prison, by the sound of it," Coach Viro said. She polished off the last bite of her cake.

"No, not Mr. Gauss," someone said in the back. "He's so dreamy." I felt my face heat as other teammates voiced agreement and gushed over his muscles.

"He might be innocent," I said, clutching my empty plate. By the Light, why did I still feel this way about him? I took a deep breath. "There was a demon involved." I looked around, checking for terror-filled faces. Everyone looked at me with open interest, even our coaches. It was so good knowing I could use that word and none of my teammates would run off. They were still here despite learning about the awful things I had to deal with. I focused on my plate so I wouldn't cry. "When dealing with demons, it can be hard to tell when it's the demon's influence, or when it's the person who willingly did bad things. Demons are real sneaky. They can turn people into someone they're not." Allosyr had managed to trick Ms. Weever into striking a bargain with him despite everything she knew about demons and bargains.

Kelsi said, "Oh, come on. He totally has to be the bad guy. He's a math teacher, for Light's sake." Girls laughed. One joked about how math had to be the work of the Darkness, and that's why everyone hated math.

Sussi said, "But why would he want Mia's sister dead? It doesn't make any sense."

"No, it doesn't," I said. He was an Earth. He erased the chalkboard with his magic all the time, and he liked to play rock catch with Earth students during lunch break. He hardly ever saw Bela, and this was his first year at Toolena Mesa.

"So then it was the demon," Kentra said and several girls agreed.

I shrugged. It made sense. Hopefully, we'd see Mr. Gauss tomorrow and he could explain what the heck happened. Maybe he'd thank me for removing the demon from him. Maybe he'd give me flowers and wrap me in those strong arms of his. A paw touched my leg.

Vergo said, "You're all getting that faraway look again."

Almost all of my teammates wore smiles and dreamy expressions. By the Light, was that how I looked? I so needed to stop. "That's what I'm hoping it was."

"That's scary if it's true," Ansa said. "That means demons can affect any of us, can't they?"

"Yeah, but that's what I'm here for. It's my job as a Dark to protect all of you."

Kentra said, "Wait, you don't attract demons just for being a Dark?"

"Duh, no," Sussi said, folding her arms. "It totally would've gone after her instead of her sister if that were true."

My teammates and coaches looked at me in open wonder. I didn't feel like giving them a lesson on how humans attracted demons to us—at least not right now. The cake was delicious. "Sussi's right. The demon specifically targeted my sister because she's a Light, but she's safe now." I wasn't sure how safe, but they didn't need to know that.

Ansa took a step closer. "So then you're, like, our protector?"

More or less, I thought. "Yeah."

Vergo said, "And with her mighty spirit panther present to aid her in every battle."

Ansa said, "Dude, you two are so awesome. We're so lucky to have you as a teammate." The rest of the team voiced agreement and piled onto me in a group hug. Coaches Viro and Khamai smiled at us.

Tears of gratitude stung my eyes. "Thanks, guys. You're the best teammates I could ask for."

***

When Yuna faced the wizard atop the mountain, she'd started the fight alone against the wizard, their clashing magics creating a brilliant display of power and scarring the surrounding land. No matter how hard she tried or what she tried, she couldn't gain the advantage. However, the satyrs appeared when she thought she was about to die. Like when Garrett had appeared at the last moment, the satyrs leaped into the fray, overwhelming the wizard.

With the unexpected help, Yuna was able to fight her way to within swinging range of their foe. The crystal serpents flew in, their roars leading the way. She tried to cut the wizard down using her axes, missed his chest, and broke his staff in two. A shockwave burst from the broken staff, releasing them from the wizard's control. The wizard teleported away before Yuna or the satyrs could enjoy their victory.

The day after winning the bandyll championship, Bylan led me to his office before I could head to homeroom. With the demon gone, my parents and Bela agreed that returning to our normal routine was safe. Considering the problem of the demonic attachment to Mr. Redd, I wasn't in a hurry to agree, but I was in less of a hurry to give them anything to worry about. The calmer and happier my family was, the easier it was for me to focus on whatever came next.

Bylan's office looked like a smaller version of what he'd had with the Order of Leo. Books lined one wall end to end, top to bottom. An apothecary cabinet sat on the opposite end, and a large mahogany desk sat between everything with enough space for practicing circles by the books. He gestured for me to sit opposite him in one of the two chairs.

Vergo took the chair beside me and curled his tail around his paws. "Not a bad setup you have here. I see the Order let you keep all your possessions."

Ignoring the comment, Bylan straightened out his robes and sat up straight. His aged face was all business, his aura subdued. "I hope the championship party was enjoyable."

"It was," I said, recalling how amazing the group hug felt. I wore my champions t-shirt. We'd agreed as a team to wear them today.

He nodded. "Good. Sadly, it's time to get back to work. That demon we sent to the Light wasn't the same one from the exorcism. That has me deeply worried."

"That one's attached to Mr. Redd. I saw the demon looking at me through his eyes once, when he got really mad."

"Hmm, so it's still recovering."

"What do we do?"

"I'm not sure yet. We need to tread very carefully from here on out. Mr. Gauss was a pawn in all this and has been removed from play."

My stomach fluttered at the echoing of the Demon King's words. "What happened to him?"

The Light priest shrugged. "I don't know. He's absent today and Mr. Redd walked off with him yesterday while we carried you to the nurse's office. They were both gone before you woke up. Anyway, I did a bit of digging and Ms. Weever did some snooping. Mia, have you ever seen your principal use his alignment?"

I filed through my memories, from the day I was accepted to Toolena Mesa to yesterday. All our teachers and even the staff blended their alignment with everyday activities, from writing on chalkboards to handing out homework. Even Coach Viro used her Earth alignment to recover loose bandyll balls. But Mr. Redd? Nothing. I shook my head.

"I thought as much. And I highly doubt he has an attachment. He's aligned with Dark.

Acknowledgments

I have so much to be thankful for. So many people have cheered me on over the years. Every last one of you helped me see this through to publication. A big thanks to my mother, cousins Jessie, Jennie, Jon, and my late grandmother for being my biggest fans of even the first chapters I dared call writing. You gave me the gumption to keep learning and growing.

Thank you to the WANA Tribe for all your support as well, for being my sounding board when I needed it, for all the help with the dreaded blurb, for helping me get unstuck on the rare occasion, and for just being there day after day, especially through the pandemic. We were not alone.

And, of course, thank you to my husband, who keeps me grounded and, for some reason, is willing to put up with my crazy. Well, I do put up with his stupid, so that makes us even.

About the Author

Angela Guajardo is an award-winning author, blogger, sports journalist, and editor whose heart lies with young adult fantasy. She currently lives in the Phoenix metro with her husband and fur babies. You might spot her walking her dog, ice skating, or catching an Arizona Coyotes game. When not writing or editing, she nerds it out on various video games and binges on various paranormal programs.

Join the Mailing List

Get informed on the next book release without worrying about spam or filler. Keep an eye out for updates and chances to become a beta reader.

Go to AngelaGuajardo.com today.